family
Values

A Novel

Peter Hassebroek

Upbound Solutions

Also by Peter Hassebroek

Upbound

Melange and Other I. T. Stories

The Dancer's Spell

Greenplays

Thylacine

The Journal Keepers

The Condo

family
Values

A Novel

Peter Hassebroek

Upbound Solutions

family Values

Copyright © 2022 Peter Hassebroek

Published by
Upbound Solutions
Courtice, Ontario, Canada

This is a work of fiction. Names, characters, businesses, places, events, locales, and incidents are either the products of the author's imagination or used in a fictitious manner. Any resemblance to actual persons, living or dead, or actual events is purely coincidental.

Cover photograph by Chong Wei on Unsplash

ISBN: 978-1-9991815-3-6
E-Book: 978-1-9991815-4-3

www.peterhassebroek.com

family
Values

Ontario

Grade 5 Report by Otto Neilson

Ontario is a young country in North America and it was created just seven years ago in 2034. Before then, for almost 170 years, it was the second largest province in Canada, which was once the second largest country in the world. To become its own country it let the Ottawa capital area join Quebec and a large northwest section join Nova Canada. Also Niagara and Windsor belong to the United States so they can protect our borders. Ontario is still large and these sacrifices ensure it stays safe from global threats despite the US civil wars, because we are their largest trading partner and each side there agreed to protect that.

Ontario's wealth comes from natural resources that are mined by machines using few humans. So what do the millions living in this country do? Many work in jobs that fix things that break down. Many more clean or serve food or drive buses or perform other services. However, the fastest growing careers for which many migrate here are for government administration. Eighty-eight percent of these live and work in NewTor.

NewTor is the capital of Ontario, it used to be called Toronto. Its population is over ten million and nearly all its citizens live and work in gigantic buildings of concrete, glass and steel. The birth rate is low but when people leave or die they are generally replaced by others escaping the conflicts in the United States. NewTor sits on Lake Ontario, across from the US mainland. Its harbour is safeguarded by the United States Coast Guard.

NewTor changed names after the family Values government got in power. It is a new type of government, it has no Premier or Prime Minister or President. It does not create or change laws like before. Instead there is *arbiter*, with built-in algorithms that manage laws, programs, budgets that are equal for everyone. It, and not humans who may be prejudiced, selects the homes and jobs people get, for example. All NewTor citizens are linked to *arbiter* and each other by tokens they wear on or even in their bodies. This only exists in NewTor at the moment because it is the only city at Stage Four of family Values. Other Ontario cities like Barrie and London are planning to achieve this before long.

It would be interesting to visit NewTor, but it doesn't sound like a place where I'd want to live.

Teacher's Remarks

Otto's essay demonstrates advancement in both his reading and writing skills; however, there is room for improvement in terms of his analytical abilities and scope. For instance there is nothing in his report about the recently announced program to eliminate racism. As a youth of dark-skin, raised by a white guardian, it would be interesting to hear how it affects him. There's also no mention of the impact of family Values on indigenous peoples, especially the opportunities provided by this new government for us to recoup our heritage. Nevertheless, a promising effort by a pupil who started school as late as he did, and who clearly prefers applying his energies to the outdoors over academic pursuits.

Mr. Allen Montcalm

Ken and Otto

Seven years since Otto wrote that essay, seven years since Ken last read it. He didn't recall its content as much as his reaction to it. In his raw isolated primitive existence at that time it plagued him with a gut feeling his old world was about to infiltrate the peaceful one he'd built for them at that camp. It got so bad Ken decided to move farther north to make this home their last and best and most inaccessible.

Thankfully this time the paper only incited curiosity, with no inclination to move again. But why didn't the boy leave it back at the other camp along with his school books? More intriguing: why leave it on the table where Ken couldn't possibly miss it? It wasn't in Otto's nature to exhibit guile. Though he'd be eighteen now, at least, more susceptible to adult ways.

Above, beyond nature's pristine network of pine, a murder of crows flew by. Ken never learned the omen's meaning, only that it was always bad, so as a child he'd watch them until they were out of sight, avoiding counting, knowing the number also had significance. Superstitious silliness, but on no occasion he did so had any of the truly bad things in his life ensued. They occurred on their own, without warning. He found himself counting this time, but only summed a few before his vision was blocked by a large, lanky, erect presence across the campfire.

Otto's face was eerily reshaped by a plume of smoke from the flames. A brief glimpse of the man he'd become. The air cleared to reveal his familiar unworldly youthfulness. Firelight blended with the moon and countless stars, casting a heavy tan tint over the boy's shirtless torso. The tremor in Otto's voice belied his adolescent anxiety, mixing gravely with a forced determination in how he gripped his prized hardcover of *The Odyssey*. From inside its pages Otto extracted a document, and began speaking as if resuming an earlier discussion.

"This might help us find our way."

Otto daintily spread out a map that covered the wooden table. It was dirty, torn in folds. He brushed it flat with his fingers, turned on the portable light, then beckoned Ken to come over. Ken stemmed an urge to grin at Otto's clumsy attempt to assert himself as he rose to look on what he recognized as his obsolete highway map of Ontario, before its separation from Canada.

"Find our way? Where?"

Otto nodded at his school report.

"To NewTor. To where you're from. You said as soon as I was eighteen we'd go."

"I said that?"

Ken couldn't remember this and for the life of him could not conceive having said it. Any inkling to return had expired years before. The primary reason to take Otto out of school and move farther north was to add distance; promising to shrink it didn't make sense. Yet it was also inconceivable Otto would lie. Was it old age? Was he losing his memory?

"If you try to talk me out of it . . . I'll go on my own."

"You realize the map's almost thirty years old."

"There wouldn't be any new roads, at least not at the start."

"It's not the roads, it's . . . we're talking about a major trek, just to satisfy idle curiosity."

"It's not idle curiosity. I want to find out about my parents. To find out who they were. Why they left me here."

Ken was stunned. This was Otto's first allusion to his origins since he was a small child. Did the boy really mean it, or did he think this extra motive would help persuade Ken to go?

"What makes you think you'll find your parents?"

"What makes you think I won't?"

Ken said nothing. Then, as if aware of disrespectfulness in his sulky tone, Otto took a deep breath.

"At least I need to try. If you don't want to, I'll go on my own."

This, of course, would be impossible to Ken. Otto was capable of functionally surviving such a trip, but he was naive, a prime target in urban areas. Otto had never been to a large city. While Ken had no desire to go, he had no option but to accompany the boy and look out for him.

"Okay, yes, I'll do it."

"You mean it?"

"Yes. Now how about you catch us some dinner?"

The joy on Otto's face was a just reward, enough to hold back the reservations and doubts building up within Ken.

"When would we go?"

"At dawn."

Now it was Otto's turn to be caught off guard, which amused Ken until the boy was out of sight and he was alone to tend the last fire for some time at this fine camp. A true home. The others built for expediency, with the expectation they'd be temporary. This was a place of which he could say his attempts to escape had ceased at last. Paraphrasing a quote from some Arab writer named Mahfouz, one of many she'd shared, one of the few he'd retained. A challenging trip physically, but also spiritually, for having to temporarily abandon this Eve-less Garden of Eden.

A camp ideally situated by a lively stream well stocked with walleye. A kilometre away was the big river and the secluded cove to harbour the canoe for the now rare supply trips to town. All they needed came from around them, the sky, the water, the woods. All Ken needed to live, all Otto needed, but could the boy grasp that? His imagination and curiosity had been stoked by the damn books Alan had given him, which Otto read over and over. Books of unrealistic settings and characters that could not be possible in the real world.

That made it somewhat disappointing to see Otto, with whom Ken had bonded so much while building this camp, exhibit no qualms leaving it. The product of his efforts as much as Ken's. Their long hours building the pieces, the arduous, often tricky, always slow canoe trips getting them here to be assembled. Just the two of them for months and months since that summer after the boy wrote his school report. The result: Ken's proudest off-the-grid build, and his remotest, which he'd only share with the boy; no one else knew its location, not even George or Heather.

The fire was dwindling. Ken lifted himself up, causing a new ache—was it hesitation?—that worsened with the weight of two logs, but thankfully lessened once he added them to the fire to triple the height of the flames and provide an instant warmth to relax his muscles enough to make the preparations.

Ken could never shake his doubts each time he camouflaged a camp: they never felt concealed enough. Any wanderer seeking a shelter with enough desperation could spot it, he felt. He had to make a greater effort this time because it was not an Eden, he wasn't an Adam: he'd return. His certainty about this provided the momentum to keep his muscles going until the task was done to his liking. However, unlike the well-fuelled fire, his energy fizzled once he finished.

Now Ken was filled with regret for not resisting, for holding back the information that would inevitably come out, that could delay or even prevent the trip. For he feared the journey less than the outcome of the revelation. Not so much the truth itself as the explaining. Ken always exuded fierce confidence with the boy but that would be tested because of the likelihood all he'd told him to this point was a lie. About Otto's arrival being a coincidence, indirectly denying Ken was Otto's grandfather and

Otto wasn't the son of—then again nothing was proven beyond doubt. The only recourse was to find the truth once and for all, then come back and put it behind him his remaining years.

2

His large hands fumbled with the slippery bait. It didn't help that his heart still beat rapidly from Ken's saying they would go at dawn. As if there was some urgency to Otto's wish to find his parents, magnifying the mystery surrounding how they'd come to be together. Ken's finding Otto in a basket by his door was so farfetched. How could anyone have found such a remote place without having been there before? Ken called it a coincidence, squatters seeking an empty and uninhabited cabin, happening on that one, seeing it in use, then deciding to leave their child. Each time Ken gave that explanation, Otto got more nonchalant about the truth.

Otto cast his line into the stream and leaned back against his favourite tree stump. His parentage was not the primary reason behind his desire to go, but made an excellent cover. He wasn't ready to share his recurring dream. In which he's gazing at the northern lights, shimmering, shaking, billowing into ribbons, solidifying into colourful vertical bands to form a city skyline. From below the horizon a domineering yet also angelic woman rises. Her skin is shiny, smooth, purely black. She is dressed in majestic, flamboyant robes that flow behind her, blending into a moving sky. She beckons him hypnotically with green eyes that frighten him at first, but then calm him. He tries to reach out to her but she's inaccessible. It isn't frustrating, more of a game, as with each attempt he gets closer. He never succeeds and wakes, occasionally disturbed, but usually fascinated, anticipating the next occurrence.

This spot by the stream was ideal to conjure up such visions, few trees blocking the aurora borealis, a mental model for these dream images. On rare occasions it got so intense he'd swear the lights emitted sound. The thin humid air felt as if this would be one of those nights. Alas, he couldn't indulge now, there was a journey to pack for after eating, and then rest.

Otto jerked up the reel and pulled in a small walleye, barely big enough to feed Ken, never mind himself. He deftly removed the hook from the fish's mouth while walking to the edge of the stream. He cupped handfuls of water on the fish before letting it free. A minute later he snagged a walleye large enough to feed them both. Perhaps the small one's parent? He chuckled at that, though unsure why.

As Otto cleaned the fish, it came to him this could be the final meal they shared here. It gave him a brief pause, counteracted by the vista before him, an ever deeper blue sky, each emergent star representing a stranger he was to meet. The universe telling him his future was awaiting to engulf him. Perhaps the woman from his dream would be his guide, his Athena.

Other than his time at the reservation school and brief visits to town for supplies, Otto had had little exposure to people. Some kids he'd liked at school but they were memories now. Anyone he saw in town was like Ken, kind but stoic. Matter-of-fact. No Candide or Odysseus or Telemachus or Sancho Panza or . . .

Some clouds shifted to reveal an orange streak on the horizon, indicating he should go back. Ken had a good fire going. Otto saw a pile of tools—including the pistols on top—a second pile of clothes, a third with supplies.

"Nice catch."

"Thanks."

Ken paused to take the fish from Otto and placed it carefully in the pan over the fire, generating a loud sizzle that settled into a constant simmer. Ken gathered a few more clothes and added them to the pile, then tended to their dinner.

"See my clothes? Put together a similar amount, no more. We need to travel as lightly as possible."

"How many books can I take?"

"No books."

"Not even *The Odyssey*?"

"It'll be safer here. No chance of it falling in a river."

Otto wanted to argue but didn't want to agitate Ken in case it gave the old man a reason to back out, or test Otto's resolve to go alone. Otto needed Ken to take him as far as he could while still up to it. For Ken was clearly slowing down. He struggled chopping wood, more at lugging it, doing two-thirds loads of what he did just last year. At best. Lately their meals consisted of only the protein Otto found. The garden, Ken's responsibility, produced little. Ken's hunching was more pronounced at the fire, due to his restlessness and lack of sleep no doubt.

Most of the cabin was already camouflaged making for a tight entry for Otto. He assembled his cleanest clothes—two pairs of khaki pants, a fleece, a quick dry sweater, three t-shirts, socks, swim trunks, his windbreaker, and his best underwear.

When Otto came upon his fancy hardcover of *The Odyssey* he hesitated. He wanted to bring it but it might make Ken mad to go against his wishes. Not mad, disappointed. Ken never really got mad. Not with Otto. Had he gotten angry when young? The question sparked fresh excitement in Otto by reminding him of the letter he'd found while moving to this camp. There it was, marking the chapter when Odysseus returns to Ithaca. Another reason to go, a mission: to find this Esmeralda and deliver the letter on Ken's behalf.

Taking the book with the letter would keep the document safe and dry, but if Ken found the book, he might open it. He might get angry at Otto for possessing the letter. So taking the book wasn't worth the risk, the letter was more important. Otto put the sheet in a plastic bag he rolled up into the long underwear he was unlikely to need but decided to take along.

Ken was attending to the fish. The fantastic smell triggered Otto's appetite. A pike would have been nice but he never tired of walleye the way Ken cooked it, even without vegetables. Still, he was looking forward to trying new foods. Ken cut the fish in thirds, two of which he placed on Otto's dish, one on his own. Otto doubted Ken would even finish that.

"Excited about going?"

"Not trying to change your mind, are you?"

Otto was joking but as he said it the notion of going alone that had struck him with fear earlier now brought exhilaration, but then relief when Ken emphatically shook his head.

"We'll take the river into town as usual. In town we'll ditch the canoe and hike the highway. Unless we find transportation. I have to admit I'm not sure what we'll find so it's not much of a plan."

"How long will it take?"

"Hard to say. A month? It's upstream to the highway. From there it depends if we find transportation or encounter trouble."

"You think people will attack us?"

"Not that kind of trouble."

"Then what? We can handle any river. We have the guns."

"Physical dangers aren't the only kind. Eat up and let's finish packing so we can get an early start."

3

Surprisingly, the upstream paddling wasn't as strenuous as he'd expected, once Ken got past the initial pain surges. Perhaps his constant aches came from inertia since the more they paddled the more it felt like a routine trek into town. Except the sturdy canvas bags stashed between he and Otto added weight to an upstream journey, instead of acting as ballast for the trip home.

Otto made it easier, carrying most of the load on portages, along with his powerful strokes. The boy had grown in girth the past year, put on muscle; he'd make a great tight end. Was football still played anywhere in the world?

One area in which Otto didn't outshine Ken: navigation. Thus Ken's contribution was finding efficient portage routes. A great, albeit silent team. Their mutually calm competence brought a notion to mind he'd once heard a friend say: that greatness only becomes apparent in silence. That words cheapened greatness, diluted it. They reached an opening to the navigable stream Ken knew well. He steered them that way.

"Where are we going?"

"I didn't want to say anything earlier but I injured myself with a slip back there. The pain is intense."

Otto gazed at Ken, then sighed resignedly. Impossible to read that reaction. Did Otto suspect Ken of faking it? He had twisted it slipping while getting into the canoe at the last portage. He'd almost forgotten about it but knew that if he didn't rest it, it'd be a problem later.

"Think we'll find a spot in there?"

"You don't recognize where we are?"

"No. Should I?"

Ken shrugged but kept quiet. They paddled a hundred meters when Otto suddenly became alert, possibly even sentimental.

"Is this our old camp?"

"I thought it'd be a good place for a break."

Otto pointed upstream to the other side.

"Wait, that's where you taught me to fish. Up on the hill there, that's where I shot a deer."

"That's right."

"Was it my first?"

"No. Your first was beyond that rock outcropping over there, the one with the lone pine."

"Right. Say, this wasn't the camp where you found me, is it?"

"No. Let's keep paddling."

"We're not stopping here, then?"

"Never did figure out an easy way to enter from upstream. So we'll shoot past about fifty metres and turn around."

"Hey, that's where you taught me to swim."

"So you know to keep paddling, there's a current."

Otto wrested his gaze away from the shore to obey. He had to paddle harder because Ken's steering took all his effort. Finally they reached a calm point to pause for a brief rest before lining up to enter at the right angle. To his relief, Ken was still up to it, but if his injury forced them to camp here too long, Otto might run out of patience.

"Ready?"

The boy didn't answer. He was staring at the pebbly beach on which they often picnicked. About thirty metres ahead, in the water, a human head was bobbing up and down. They paddled silently until within ten meters. The person was still submerged, unaware. She glided towards the shore, keeping her head out of the water, then stood to walk the rest of the way. She was nude, her long wet hair behind her. Otto's whisper, lowered to ensure no carry over the water, startled Ken.

"Who's that?"

"I don't know. Let's find out."

Otto started paddling and Ken steered them to keep them out of her view. Ken was perplexed: this was likely the first woman Otto had seen without clothes, yet she was no more interesting to the adolescent than a new landscape, or a rodent.

Ken's steering took them too far and they lost sight of her. He brought them back but only got partway before they saw the woman standing, knee deep in the water, unashamedly naked, a rifle pointing at them. A good-sized girl, sensual with a lovely symmetrically rounded, yet powerful body, evidenced by how she held the rifle, as if no heavier than a toy. She spoke first.

"Who are you? How did you find this place?"

"Who are you? How did you find this place?"

"Don't be smart. Keep paddling. Move on. I swear I'll shoot."

A quick glance at Otto showed the boy unafraid, repelled by the girl even. She was plainly pretty, in a girl-next-door way. A scar on her abdomen, a recent young mother. Otto nudged his back to signal the boy recognized the rifle and knew to follow Ken's lead to remain still. Their fearless inaction clearly agitated the girl, who brought the rifle sight to her eye, raised her elbow, slowly panned the barrel at them. The trigger hand muffled her voice, what she said was inaudible.

They paddled forward but stopped when she let out a shriek, dropped the rifle, and ran onto the beach. She slowed to whistle before grabbing a towel to wrap around herself. The brownish terrycloth accentuated the whiteness of her skin. She stayed put as Ken and Otto reached shore, got out of the canoe, and tugged it between the pair of dying but sturdy birch trees where they'd always tied up. This had an oddly calming effect on the woman whose gaze transformed from fear to curiosity. Then, if Ken was not mistaken, one of lust as her eyes fixed on Otto.

A rustling from the trees diverted her gaze. She ran over to a dark, shirtless, bearded man in red jeans whose eyes took in the intruders. They seemed to act like a couple but didn't strike Ken as being together that way. A disturbing thought: could they be brother and sister? Fraternal twins?

4

The woman is insane, Otto thought. He didn't see the man she leaned against as a threat, more a relief. The way she'd stared at Otto before he came out was how women would stare at Ken in town, before his face started aging. Ken used to like it a lot, and that would amuse Otto those times; now he felt mild disgust.

The thought passed as Otto realized he had to deem the male a threat, even without a visible weapon. He carried himself with the arrogance of having fought before, his hands below his ribs, in a pose similar to that of a boxer. Such experience could trump Otto's raw strength. He also doubted Ken was strong enough to take on the girl, less so if she was truly crazy. But this was their property and he wanted Ken to command them to vacate.

The man said something to calm the woman. She pointed at the water, perhaps telling him about the useless rifle. Suddenly the man smiled, before he pulled the woman's ear to his lips, whispered something to get her to retreat into the trees. To get another weapon perhaps, but that was doubtful; if they'd had a good weapon it'd be out already. The man smiled warmly as he approached Ken. Wrinkles were more apparent the closer he got, more likely they were father and daughter. Ken relaxed but Otto tensed and that slowed the man's pace to a stop. Then Ken stepped forward.

"Do you two live here?"

"This is our cabin. Yes."

"How did you find it? It's so remote."

"Find it? I built it. Me and her built it. She's not only beautiful, she's strong capable. Very capable."

Otto took a few slow steps, until a glance from Ken halted his movement. Up close, the guy looked almost as old as Ken.

"My name is Ken, and this is Otto. What is your name, sir?"

"Wesley."

"A fine place, Wesley. How long have you and . . ."

"Monica."

"How long have you and Monica been here?"

"Like I said, since we built it . . . maybe a year."

Wesley's tone was casual but reserved. A born liar. Otto was close enough to tug Ken's arm, but Ken shook it off, a signal for Otto to keep quiet. That was too infuriating to obey.

"Ken, tell him they're tres—"

"Otto, not now."

This time Otto obliged and became rigid. The two men closed the gap, put out hands as if they were business partners, only to be interrupted by a short shriek. The woman was back, wearing a pair of loose jeans and a snug t-shirt that in Otto's opinion was too small, emphasizing her breasts and flat belly in a cartoonish way. She clutched a thin flat object she handed to Wesley.

"You were right. It is him."

Wesley studied the object, glancing between it and Ken, then handed it to Ken who took it but didn't look at it.

"Licence expired twenty-five years ago. So you've been gone since—why, that would be around the time of . . .?"

"The pandemic."

"The original pandemic made you go away?"

"There were other factors."

"Of course. Say, why don't we all . . .?"

He didn't finish, instead motioning Ken and Otto to follow as he walked up the hill to the flat clearing on which stood the log structure Otto knew well. It looked smaller than he recalled but otherwise had changed little beyond wear-and-tear.

The natural bond developing between the older men eased Otto's anxiety. So much he failed to notice Monica shift close to him until he sensed her body heat and the subtle fruity smell of shampoo. Both were pleasant and softened his initial opinion of her. She put a warm hand around his bicep to pull him aside. He hesitated, but relented when Ken nodded at him.

Monica led Otto into the single room inside the tiny house he used to call home. The two beds low to the floor were as he and Ken had left them, two bear furs covering greyed cotton sheets. Nearly all the wooden furniture was gone, the dining table, the chairs, stools, bench; perhaps all used for firewood. Appliances, utensils, tools, dinnerware of course also gone, taken with them to the new camp. Their absence had an oddly melancholic effect on Otto. The old stove, too heavy to take, seemed to be working.

The room had acquired new items, including what looked to be a makeshift crib, and a thick duvet covering a lump of clothing or supplies. The cabin was clean, had been swept recently, the only dirt on the floor what they'd brought in. The sole window was also free of dirt and brought in sunlight with a clear view of the dense forest beyond.

The room felt less spacious than before, less enchanting. One bed was half covered with clothing but with enough room for Monica. She chose the larger on which to sit and beckoned Otto to sit beside her. He hesitated but then relented. Her physical warmth felt good, until cold drips from her wet hair fell on his shoulder and made him shift to the edge.

"You and your father are trespassing."

"He's not my father. He's my uncle. My aunt's ex-husband."

Otto fidgeted. He wanted to move to the other bed, but feared she'd follow him. He asked how old she was.

"Twenty-two. And you?"

"Younger."

"You look and seem more mature. I mean, you saw me naked and didn't, you know, react like boys usually do. Or is it you've never been with a girl before?"

Despite his inexperience, Otto knew what she meant but had no wish to share that with this stranger. Also, he was still irked by her presumption this was their home.

"When did you and your uncle find this place?"

"I don't know. A year ago or so?"

"Long enough to burn the furniture that was here?"

"We made do as best we could. If you don't know our story, don't judge."

"How did you find it?"

Monica shrugged and it seemed pointless to press the matter. She began to stroke his arm between his shoulder and bicep.

"You really are unusual looking. Your skin is so . . ."

"What?"

"Your features are so, so, how should I put it? Unique. On first glance you seem fragile, young, but it's an illusion because you are obviously strong."

She tightened her grip on his arm as if to demonstrate, then drew her fingers down his chest. He was about to swat at her hand but she pulled it back first, rested her knuckles against her lips a moment before putting her arm next to his. The contrast wasn't as obvious as expected, as if their skin tones had blended to make them a chameleonic pair.

"Your skin. It's dark, but not dark like Wesley's. I see why Ken is on the run but you shouldn't have any fear."

"We're not on the run. We're certainly not scared of anything."

"Oh? Where are you headed?"

"NewTor."

"You're kidding. You, I can see. But him?"

"Why not? It used to be his home."

"Twenty-five years ago. Back when NewTor was still Toronto. Long before family Values."

Behind her wide mouth and huge eyes, Otto detected a mix of concern and admiration. He remembered writing about family Values in his report, but little else, especially not how it related to what she'd said. He figured asking her to explain could only lead to confusion. After a soft sigh she spoke again.

"When do you plan to move on?"

"As soon as we can."

"So why do you care if we're here?"

Otto kept silent.

"Well, good luck."

She abruptly rose to go outside. Otto waited a moment before he did the same. She was already out of sight. He saw Ken and Wesley at the canoe, sharing a flask of rum Ken had stashed in a hole up in the woods with others. Was Ken giving everything away? It bothered Otto too much to talk to Ken now. He went to the canoe to get a fishing pole, glad to have a chore.

When he reached his favourite fishing spot, he cast a line and leaned back against a tree. The effort of the trip hit him, he felt sleepy, with a desire to summon his dream of the black woman. Only each time he came close his dream was interrupted by the chop of an axe on wood or the amiable laughter from the men.

5

The rest and Otto's lack of impatience to get going helped Ken regain his strength, as did the flask of rum he was sharing with Wesley. He liked the man and could tell Wesley liked him. If it wasn't mutual before, it was after Ken had revealed the cache of booze he'd left behind. The liquor tasted just as good as before, enhanced by adult company and enough cloud cover to prevent sunburn as he'd taken off his sweaty shirt.

They were mutually coy sharing personal details beyond their ages at first, with Ken surprised to learn Wesley was barely six years younger. Ken had little to reveal, his current life constant, his past one distant. When Wesley pointed out the disparity in skin colour between Otto and Ken, Ken did share the boy was an orphan and that their goal was to seek information about his parents, which they hoped to find in Toronto.

"But you and Monica. You're also different."

"It's why I took notice. I'm particularly sensitive to that issue."

"How's that?"

"Because you see, we're refugees. From Cochrane."

"Refugees? What for?"

Ken offered more rum but Wesley declined.

"Cochrane's committed to transitioning to Stage Four without delay, and hence agreed to adopt racial blending immediately."

"Stage Four?"

"Of family Values."

Ken nodded though not grasping, recalling the words "family Values" from Otto's essay, words he'd disregarded. He hoped to not appear ignorant so didn't ask. A halt to the wood chopping, made him think to start a fire or get lures for Otto. A glance at the canoe showed Otto's fishing gear gone. Wesley held a hand out for the rum and while taking it his unreadable eyes scanned Ken's, as if expecting a prompt or question. Then the chopping resumed and with it came a realization this might be important, that Ken ought to overcome his pride.

"family Values. Some government thing, right?"

"You have been away a long time."

"Yes. So anything you can tell me . . ."

Wesley smiled understandingly.

"I'll admit I'm not well versed in it beyond the weird spelling, in that the word 'family' is un-capitalized, but the word 'Values' is capitalized. It's important, don't ask why. Maybe a trademark thing. You get in trouble not doing it properly, or mocking it."

"Even if it's an honest mistake?"

"Hey, even back in 2020 it didn't take much to get punished or cancelled for the tiniest, inadvertent mistakes. So it'd be wise to also remember to not say Toronto, but NewTor."

"You're kidding."

"Before that it was famTor, un-capitalized as well."

Ken shook his head as Wesley explained that a city adopting family Values went through stages. Initially it kept its name, but once past the first stage would change it to append "fam" at the front and abbreviate the rest. It would keep that name until the city achieved the final stage, at which point it would replace the "fam" with "New," which only Toronto had achieved to date.

"We left a year ago. Who knows what Cochrane is today. Is it famCoch or did it achieve NewCoch? Or maybe it's famRane to avoid juvenile mockery."

"What specifically got you to leave?"

Wesley waved for the flask and took a long swig.

"Racial blending. Monica was pregnant."

"Oh."

"It's not that. The issue is she's white and so was the father. As I said, Cochrane is all-in making a transition to family Values as quickly as possible. To achieve this, city council agreed to adopt short cuts, including the controversial component called racial blending for beta testing before Stage Four."

"Racial blending? That sounds . . .what the hell is it?"

"Its purpose is to biologically eliminate racism by eliminating pure races. In other words, by forcing mixed childbearing. Our town was seen as ideal due to the high volume of refugees from the US civil wars who are mostly black. We were nowhere near balancing out the racial makeup to make this viable yet it went ahead. For family Values administrators our remoteness kept the program discreet so they could refine it."

"So the US civil wars are still going on?"

"Bigger and nastier than ever, particularly every other year in election season. And it's the black population that's caught in the middle usually. They come to see Ontario and family Values as a haven, which for some it is, for others not. Unfortunately, as you know, once they're in, they're unable to leave."

"Actually, I don't know. Why can't they go back?"

"Because Ontario is now a one-way closed society. People can emigrate here, but not leave. Considering all the global turmoil, that makes us one of the safest places on the planet, perhaps the safest urbanized one. The US defends our borders and its desire to do so is bipartisan, supported by whichever side is in power. It cost us our borders at Niagara, Windsor, Sarnia, etc., the price enough were willing to pay to deter imminent threats, globally, and from Quebec and Nova Canada."

An image of the map of Ontario on the picnic table flashed in Ken's mind. Still a giant in geographic terms, but shrinking, and closing in. He wanted to know more but Wesley returned to the original racial blending topic.

"Grandfathering clauses were established for married people, but not unwed Caucasians like my niece. If caught the child is taken, put in a special school, the parent or parents arrested and sent to camps of all white females or all black males, depending on sex. Or they can get sterilized. Its pejorative nickname is off-whiting, but never let an official hear you call it that because, in theory, it applies to all races."

"Did you say sterilized?"

"To them any sign of non-compliance is a sign she'd repeat the offence, with the same man, or with another white male."

Wesley added Cochrane had volunteered to enable the racial blending feature of family Values without notice. Monica was in the hospital having her baby when the deadline was announced for unwed mothers. Wesley, a cop, used his badge to get her out along with the baby. He ditched his uniform and they used his skin colour to convince people he was the father.

"Now we're outlaws."

"Where's the baby?"

"She was weak to begin with, always suffering colds or fevers. I'm afraid she got pneumonia during the winter. We got to the hospital in Hearst too late."

"They couldn't save her?"

"She was already dead, we didn't bother. We bribed someone to have her cremated."

"Does she miss her?"

"Terribly. I don't dare bring it up."

"What about the father?"

"Monica won't talk about him, just says he's lost in the wind. I suspect the father is the son of one of the councillors leading the charge for family Values, and implementing off-whiting. Would look bad to have his own white son father a white kid, which a simple DNA test would prove. I suspect him too since it always seemed too easy for us to get away, and to stay away. He'd have the resources to help. Though I had friends too."

"And her family?"

"They wanted Monica to surrender, to get an abortion, then to be sterilized. They support what the Cochrane leaders are up to, but I really think they wanted her to comply more so she could stay and be safe. Like so many their belief is driven by fear, and blind trust, not principle and thinking for oneself."

"And they call this family Values?"

"family Values itself is much broader. It's more of an ideology governed by a technological infrastructure. It affects everything in life, more than I can explain. You'll see for yourself—when or if you get to NewTor."

"Why, has it become dangerous?"

"Not physically. In fact, people have never been so safe."

"I'm not following. What would make me not go?"

"Well, for Monica and I and everyone else, it kind of crept up. For you it could be a shock."

Ken's mind was suddenly fraught with apprehension of what lay ahead. Wesley might be telling the truth, but he might not. How many like Wesley and Monica might they encounter? Who could they believe?

"You look as if you doubt me, Ken."

"It's just hard to . . . so people just let this thing take over?"

"Most did, some didn't. Those who didn't left as soon as they saw what it was, leaving the less self-reliant people to adapt. It's a pattern of mass migrations, population shifts. You'll likely see the same in Kapuskasing or Hearst if you stop in those places. You probably should, just to acclimate before NewTor. I have to admit there are appealing aspects to it. At least some someone like you might find positive."

"Oh?"

"The social media companies, tech giants, large corporations? All absorbed into family Values. And while a general decline in technical skills is a negative, it also means there's no one skilled or smart enough to even accidentally set off nuclear weapons."

"Interesting."

"There's more. In NewTor, and eventually in all family Values cities, there's no law enforcement or government overreach, not even vagrancy. Gone are violent protests, all civil misbehaviour. Bureaucracies are fused into an entity called *arbiter*—also lower case—that via algorithms ensures fairness in law and order in a way to deter corruptions inherent in democracy, communism, or any political system."

Ken shook his head, affecting disapproval, but in actuality to cover his bewilderment. As if sensing his needing a moment to process, Wesley walked off to the bushes. It wasn't enough. Ken couldn't reconcile it with what he remembered. In his youth, if he'd been Otto's age, it might be exciting. Now, old and cynical, it only brought apprehension bordering on indifference.

Wesley returned but refused more rum. Something was on his mind and he seemed to be working out how to share it.

"I was thinking. Monica could go with you, part way, at least, if there's room. It'd be good for her to see her family. Or at least find out information about them."

"What about you?"

"Me? I'd stay. I have no desire to go back."

In that moment Ken knew he was with a man of his own kind. The joy that came with the realization was diluted by envy for a man in a place Ken wished to remain, while Ken was returning to what both had put behind them.

"But isn't she a refugee? Won't she get arrested?"

"It's a risk but less likely if I'm not with her. She's a bright girl, careful, she'd know to give up if there was trouble. She's a good worker. She built that."

Wesley pointed at a neatly stacked pile of wood underneath a roughly built but functional wood and brush covered tent next to the cabin.

"Who's a good worker?"

"You, honey."

"Oh. Where'd Otto go?"

"Probably gone to fish to get us some dinner."

"I'll go find—"

"No, no, sit with us a minute. Something we need to discuss."

As Wesley shared the talk the two men had, Ken saw value in bringing along someone familiar with family Values. She could prove beneficial, even essential. Wesley's idea she and Otto act as a couple was one Ken suspected the boy might not take well.

Only when Wesley shared the idea with her, her face betrayed an eagerness that worried Ken. Maybe a desire for motherhood made her see Otto as a potential surrogate. Then again, would it be so bad? Otto never exhibited interest in sex, had never been enticed by attractive girls in town. At that age, Ken was all over the girls, and women. Maybe Monica could help draw this out. He smiled at the girl, said she'd be welcome, as long as she was ready to go shortly.

"Thanks. I promise not to be a burden."

6

It didn't matter to Otto that Monica was with them. She wasn't light but did paddle beyond her weight and they moved faster than they had with just he and Ken. Twice as fast on portages. It helped that Ken's ankle had healed fully too. But there was one thing that annoyed Otto about her: she talked too much. Worse, Ken encouraged it. Since she joined them, his recurring dreams about the black woman in the large city had stopped. He missed them. Not because he enjoyed them but for how they motivated him to keep going. The initial appeal was wearing off.

It would be different if he had any interest in what Ken and Monica talked about. This family Values thing had no meaning for Otto. Ken was all the family he knew, that and the little he gleaned from books that were about individuals. Their families played little or no part in the plots. Except Odysseus, of course, with Penelope and Telemachus. He liked to imagine himself as Telemachus, with Ken as Odysseus, the woman in his dreams as Penelope. Who could Monica be? Nausicaa? Certainly not an Athena. Might she turn out to be a Circe?

Ken pointed to a secluded tiny beach and suggested they stop for lunch. After getting agreement he described how to navigate the several short but tricky bursts of rapids they'd face before making a sharp turn requiring hard paddling into a small cove where the water was calm. It tired Otto more than expected. He saw Monica out of breath too but surprisingly Ken showed little fatigue and after landing immediately set to preparing a fire to cook the extra fish they'd caught last night. Otto took the basket and declared he'd explore the woods for something to augment the protein. Monica seemed unsure what to do until Ken waved to say he had everything under control with the fire.

"You two go together."

Otto would have preferred to go alone and let them talk their hearts out and exhaust all they had to say, but he didn't protest. Monica followed Otto, trusting he'd know where he was going. He didn't tell her it was his first time this way and he tried to conceal his difficulty distinguishing loose mud from trail. They came upon a tiny bountiful grove where they filled the bag with blueberries and blackberries. Monica found black morel, which she pocketed. That would delight Ken. Otto was satisfied.

"We eat well now, we may make some distance today."

"Oh, so you're speaking to me now?"

"What?"

"You dislike me, don't you, Otto?"

"What are you talking about?"

"That's why you ignore me."

"I don't—I'm just not used to someone being with us. And the stuff you and Ken talk about . . ."

"Really? Those conversations might be useful to you."

"Well, they bore me. Especially this family Values business."

"You should listen. Talking to him, it's obvious it'll be a shock. You two have been gone so long."

"Not to me, I haven't been anywhere else."

"I suppose . . . but didn't you go to school?"

"When I was little, on a reservation. I didn't learn much."

"Yet you're not, you're not . . . dumb."

"I've read books. Old books."

"So they didn't teach you about family Values at school?"

"They glossed over it."

Otto didn't care to pursue this and moved on, pausing to let her extract three more mushrooms. She had a wistful look now, not sad, but pondering. She strolled past Otto then halted, as if waiting for him to lead. A strange impulse made him squeeze her shoulder tenderly.

"I'm really sorry about your baby."

"Thank you, Otto."

Then she grabbed him, hugged him, with surprising strength, making him almost drop the berries. He set them down and put his arms around her. The first time he could recall reciprocating an embrace. Her soft flesh felt pleasant until her salty tears ran onto his neck down his spine. He broke it off. They exchanged glances, nothing more.

"What was his name? The baby's."

"Her name. I didn't have a chance to give her one."

"I'm sorry."

"I would have named her Miranda. Miranda Annabelle."

"We should get back to help Ken."

"Can we just sit for a minute?"

He found a side trail that took them to a clearing overlooking the river. From here they could see Ken. He looked up, as if he knew they'd be there. They waved, he waved back.

"He doesn't look like he's waiting for us."

"No."

"Where's he going now?"

"I suspect he'll want to stay the night and is hoping to find a good shelter. One someone else left behind."

"Kind of like Wesley and me finding your camp?"

"I suppose."

"You and Ken seem close. But I take it you're not related?"

"I've lived with him all my life."

"Does Ken have children of his own?"

The question disturbed Otto but he wasn't sure why. Ken had had twins, according to the letter, but never talked about them. Since discovering the letter Otto had grown apprehensive about prying into his past. What troubled him was how her questions exposed his naïveté, ignorance, and lack of curiosity.

Several dark clouds shifted and now blocked the sun, creating a sudden coolness. Otto shared the story of Ken finding a baby in a basket with a sheet of paper bearing his name. And how, after a failed search for the parents, Ken raised Otto himself. It amused Monica to learn the basket was the same one they were using to collect the berries.

"A modern Moses."

Otto smiled but had no clue who Moses was.

"Ken is impressive with all he can do. Resourceful."

"Yes."

"He seems to have a rare competence that makes me think of that Greek, Odysseus. But a good version."

Her words took a moment to register.

"What do you mean 'good version'?"

"You know Odysseus? *The Odyssey*?"

"I know it. I have it. I've read it. Many times."

Her expression transformed into one of admiration. Then she revealed she'd only studied the one chapter, which was enough to point out the evil in the main character.

"Odysseus was not evil. He was good. A hero."

Monica's maternal smile only aggravated a growing irritation within Otto.

"To you, because you never learned to read it in a critical way that reveals the real truth. Look at how he treated Polyphemus, the poor Cyclops minding his business on his own island. Who could be more marginalized than a being with one eye. Only a conniving hating type would resort to such trickery to subdue a creature who'd captured him fair and square. Then stab him in his only eye."

"But the Cyclops had eaten Odysseus's men."

"Because they were trespassing. He was a simple soul and his reaction was natural for him, being threatened and all. Your so-called hero exploited it, rather than fighting as a man."

Monica's face bore an odd confidence, as if she was sure she'd made a convincing argument but still needed the other person to agree. Otto didn't agree. Nor did he consider it a convincing argument. She was twisting the story. Yet the way she did so, it was impossible to respond. Not impossible but pointless. As if he had to untangle her silly logic first before he could state his view, and that by the time he'd done so it'd be beside the point, and his point, his perspective, would have little meaning, if any. He doubted she'd done this on purpose but instead had learned how to talk like this.

"Don't feel bad. People used to feel the same way as you, and were fooled for the longest time."

There she went again. However her self-assurance cast doubt within Otto. He hadn't had schooling from teachers who could show the correct way to interpret it, and could show he'd read it wrong. It bothered him all the way down the trail to the beach. A robust fire awaited them and Ken told them his plan that they sleep there for the night and leave first thing in the morning.

What Monica had said about Odysseus spoiled Otto's appetite with a sense he needed to tolerate the tedium to pay attention to what she and Ken discussed. Thankfully, they were too tired for conversation for once and also wanted to get to the cave shelter before dark, before the rain. Lying next to Monica helped as it made for a warm and cosy sleep. She didn't smell as bad as Ken.

The night was eerily quiet, ideal to conjure up his recurring dream. With partial success. The woman was a blur, the skyline obscured by a dark haze of varying but smudged deep colours. A persistent, pelting rain sounded on the leaves and his dream was lost to a flash of lightning followed by crashing thunder.

7

The cave provided shelter but wasn't immune to the increasing humidity. Then again, if they'd left earlier they'd have missed a good omen: the brilliant rainbow arcing northwest. For that and an extra bit of sleep, Ken could endure a little discomfort. Otto was off to catch fish, leaving Ken with the girl who again was bathing herself, fully naked, less than ten metres in front of him. Her brash lack of modesty might be common nowadays; he'd be wise getting used to it rather than comment. He hoped once off the water, on the road, it would be different.

While Monica was attractive physically she was far too young for Ken. Her usefulness was her most appealing feature to him. She'd proven herself on land and water. Nonetheless, her habits did test his libido occasionally, but that was easily managed by looking away to tend to the fire or perform a mundane essential task. It might not work if Monica actively tried to seduce Ken, if she was spurned by Otto's obliviousness to her sexuality.

Monica emerged from the river and unselfconsciously strolled past Ken to a lonely patch of grass where they had laid out their clothes to dry. She touched each, then turned them over, before joining Ken at the fire. He was about to ask her to cover up, but with what? She'd dry faster by the fire, in the sun.

"Where's Otto?"

"Catching fish. Maybe we can go without stopping today."

"Sounds good. These ought to be dry after you two get a swim in. The water's warm."

Otto arrived then with a large splake and half a bag of berries. The boy paid no notice to Monica's nudity while he looked for a spot to clean the fish. She watched him scrape the fish, admiring his efficiency with an occasional nod.

"Hand me your catch when done, Otto. The fire's ready."

"When do you think we'll get going, Ken?"

"Right after we eat."

Monica grunted but neither responded.

"Before we eat, you two are taking a swim."

She grabbed the fish from Otto and took them to the fire.

"I'll cook. You two get as much dirt and sweat off as possible. I can't sleep another night around you otherwise."

No room for argument. The water felt invigorating and by the time they'd dried and put on fresh clothes, the fish was ready. It tasted better than expected. They ate alone as Monica had eaten and dressed and was packing the canoe, reorganizing it in an efficient way Ken hadn't tried before. Otto was watching her do so intensely but relaxed when she set his bag aside. She pulled out one of the Glocks, held it up to study in the sunlight.

"What are you doing? Put the gun down."

Just as Ken yelled, Otto rushed at her. Monica dropped it. Her embarrassment indicated she hadn't recognized what it was at first. She took an apologetic step back before retreating to check the cave for anything they'd forgotten.

They got in the canoe and pushed off in a silence that lasted a few kilometres, except for occasional expressions of admiration for scenic vistas of hills and forests emerging as the river grew wider. A sea of majestically calm water lay in front, about to be sliced by their oars, so broad between the tall walls of trees on both sides, as if funnelling them to their destiny. The ambience was aided by their hypnotically percussive paddle strokes with a synchronism that steadily became indistinct as the faint roar of rapids grew louder, perceptible again once through the white water. Ken almost felt he could guide by sound variations.

But there were larger, less predictable rapids to contend with. The next series compelled a slowing to strategize. A lighter load and younger body would have given Ken no pause to ride them out, but a voice told him to portage. He hoped to hear Otto say this but the boy insisted on the faster option. So they lined up a route that looked clear. It wasn't. The canoe scraped rock a few times. Luckily, when they pulled it ashore they saw the damage was minimal. A quick patch with an hour to dry and they were off again. They agreed to portage until they'd cleared all stages of these rapids, despite two steep climbs and narrow trails. The slow haul gave Ken time to think and vow to never again yield his navigational instinct to youth or pride.

A long rest to the middle of the afternoon helped Ken and he felt great once they got moving, an aiding wind making up for lost time, almost neutralizing the resistance from the upstream current. Their revitalized spirit was tempered by Monica's sigh.

"Why do you have a gun? Don't you know they're outlawed?"

"Actually, we have two."

"You'll have to get rid of them at some point."

"We'll deal with that then. We're still a ways away."

"I've never seen one like that before."

"I'll let you shoot it, for the experience."

Monica stopped paddling and tapped Otto, then Ken, before pointing to an inlet where a pair of bright yellow kayaks leaned flimsily on a rock on a pebbly beach. Two large unshaven men wearing baseball caps, in khakis and light beige jackets, paced the beach, as if searching. The first people Ken and Otto had seen other than Wesley and Monica.

"Do we stop for them, Ken? Or move on?"

"Let's paddle closer, maybe I know them."

It took only a few strokes to confirm they were strangers. Ken glanced at Monica but she remained still as he reached for the Glocks, one of which he handed to Otto. They kept the guns at their sides and paddled towards the kayaks, slowing to a glide at a shallow point twenty metres off shore. Ken noticed Monica shift closer to Otto who then shifted as if to avoid her, until she whispered in his ear. He sighed, then let her grab his hand.

"Hello there."

Ken's call startled the men who came to the water's edge, then waved. Their beards helped conceal their expressions, but their manner seemed friendly. One kept back while the other took off his jacket and shirt and, perhaps to indicate he had no weapon, waded into the water to them as they came closer, halting once they were within speaking distance. He was heavily tanned.

"We're lost. I think we're on the Kenogami but the area isn't at all what we expected."

"That's because you're actually on the Kabinakagami. Just go downstream, you'll hit it by end of day, sooner if you're lucky and the winds shifts around."

"Thanks."

"Where are you headed?"

The man shrugged. Ken sensed Otto fidgeting and didn't ask a second time. A relief seeing them paddle away in the opposite direction for Monica, who was trembling.

"What's wrong?"

"Maybe they're looking for Wesley and me."

"But you've been away a year."

"Yes, but we passed through here. Maybe they found a clue to keep the search going."

Ken said nothing, not wanting to encourage a paranoia that to him seemed unwarranted.

"If you're scared of being found, why go back?"

Otto had a good point, Ken thought, though the way he asked it and then let go her hand could have been more diplomatic.

"It's worse not knowing what's happening at home. This just means I'll have to be more careful."

They developed a smooth pace and agreed to forge ahead and subsist on the remaining berries until dark. They did encounter others on kayaks and canoes, mostly Indians, no one Ken knew.

The reservation near where he'd built his second camp, the one at which he'd found Otto, was close. Usually he and Otto bypassed it on trips to town; now it was worth a detour. For advice, to freshen up, even acclimate to people, before finishing the water portion of the journey and undertaking the highway.

8

Ken's desire to rest a day or two at the reservation made sense, for Ken. And Monica. If not for her, Otto would have pushed to press on. She was thrilled to bathe in a real bathtub, to wash her hair with real shampoo, while their clothes were laundered.

They were at the home of George Montcalm, Ken's long-time friend from childhood. George was an elder of the reservation, and Otto had attended its school once. George's son, Allen, had been his teacher until Otto stopped attending after Ken built the camp Wesley was at now. Thereafter Otto stayed at George's on trips that lasted more than a day or even weeks if Ken was on a major construction project. Otto enjoyed those visits, chances to learn from Allen, who in turn used Otto to rehearse and refine class lessons.

Otto barely recognized the living room's open space, the walls separating the foyer, kitchen, and dining room gone. The carpet, along with its tobacco odour, had been ripped up and replaced by artificial flooring with sporadic area rugs of native symbols. A new giant L-shaped sofa could seat at least a dozen people. It was so comfortable Otto found it hard to not nod off. The old wood burning fireplace had been replaced by a gas one, yet still retained its cosiness. Everything else fresh and new. The kitchen had sparkling stone countertops and ornate gleaming overhead lights shining over sleek barstools lined against a long island. It contrasted but didn't clash with the living room where the large flat television had been replaced by a three-dimensional wood carving of a bear and two cubs. The small screens in each room were more like computer monitors than televisions and seemed meant for other purposes. All as blank as Ken's expression. Otto asked if he was okay, assuming he'd been anticipating watching a little television and now couldn't.

"Just wondering how George paid for all this."

"Monica's sure taking a long time in that bath."

"I just hope she puts a towel on when she comes out."

Ken's whispered remark made Otto chuckle, just as their host came in carrying a tray of drinks and two bowls of potato chips. George set down the drinks on square metallic coasters bearing a strange design: a heart-shaped logo with two facing letters "f," one pink, one blue, nestled inside a "V" in deep blood red.

"What's funny, Otto?"

Monica was behind George, in a terrycloth bathrobe, carrying a pile of clothes. She ambled past Otto to sit at the dining table and begin folding. A fresh scent hit him in her wake, emanating from her hair, which cascaded in lush curls down her back."

"Nothing. Why?"

"Looked like you were amused about something."

"Are those our clothes? Are they clean already?"

"Yeah. It's a really old washer but it works fast."

"The last one I got didn't last me three months. The one before it, not even that. So glad I kept the old set."

"You're a wise man, Mr. Montcalm."

George smiled, clearly charmed by Monica. With deference he brought her a glass of lemonade and a coaster. Otto noticed he'd put on weight yet looked haler. Probably stopped smoking.

"Thank you, Mister—"

"George. Please call me George."

Monica smiled, then lifted her glass and drank it in one gulp. She set it down but then lifted it up again to stare at the table. She picked up the coaster and studied it.

"Everything all right, young lady?"

"No . . . I mean, yes, George. I'm fine."

"Otto, maybe you can take Monica to the lake. Wawastew can be excellent there. Would you like that, Monica?"

George's tone didn't invite a negative response and she took a pair of jeans and a shirt and went to change.

"Be sure to drop in on Allen. He'll still be at the school."

It was a warm, humid night but Monica acted chilled. Instead of going back for a jacket she opted to walk next to Otto, arms locked. He didn't mind, barely noticed in fact, his attention on the surroundings. Not much had changed in terms of the layout but the roads were improved, as were the houses and buildings. Freshly paved and painted, roofs redone. Except for the cars, all of which looked no newer than the ones he remembered. It was dark, he could be imagining this. Yet the feeling persisted. As if the auto industry had stopped building cars, or had cut off the reservation's inhabitants from purchasing new ones.

Monica seemed distracted, content to let him lead her around. The buildings were dark so when they reached the schoolhouse it was unnerving to see lights from two windows.

"That's the library of my old school. That must be Allen."

Otto peered in a window and almost didn't recognize his old teacher whose hair was cropped and contrasted starkly with his thick beard. Otto tapped the glass and waved.

"I'd rather just go to the lake."

"He's seen us, he's waving us in. Come on."

She relented when she saw Allen holding the door for them.

The school had changed little except for new banks of lockers lining the halls. Allen directed them to the library, where he'd been researching for a lesson. He wasn't surprised by Monica's presence—his father had talked to him earlier—but did appear impressed by her. It amused Otto until he saw Allen slip what looked to be a wedding band in his pants pocket. An awkward silence was broken when Otto brought up how Monica believed Odysseus was a villain.

"An interesting idea."

"What? Her opinion is based on one chapter, the one with the Cyclops. Nothing more."

"Otto, interpretations of books, especially old ones, change as times change."

Allen stepped into a shelf aisle to retrieve a paperback copy of *The Odyssey*. He handed it to Monica.

"Keep it. Otto is right, you should read the entire book. It'd be my pleasure if you came back to discuss it some time."

"Thank you."

Their hands touched longer than needed during the exchange. It bothered Otto, made him anxious to leave. He'd gotten used to having Monica with them, liked her company, and feared she would be tempted to remain. Then again, if she were to stay, would it be so bad? Yes, if Allen was married. His old teacher then excused himself to take a call from a screen.

"I see. Yes, I'll tell them."

He returned, smiling.

"My father. He'd like you two to return right away."

"Now? I was going to show Monica the northern lights."

"It's not a good night for it."

"Thanks for the book."

"Have a good journey. Stay safe."

The strange vibe Otto felt from this exchange continued inside George's house where they found George and Ken sipping beer quietly, a subtle but noticeable tension in the air. It was different from past arguments between Ken and George they'd resolve with a few beers. Otto could tell Ken's smile was forced.

"Everything all right?"

"Yes, Otto, everything's fine. Only our plan's changed. We're leaving before dawn. Not to the highway, but another camp."

"The one where . . .?"

"Yes, that one."

"Is it because of me?"

"I'll explain tomorrow, Monica, after we're gone."

George said goodnight and left, but came back to wish them a pleasant journey. His manner was more standoffish, especially with Monica who took her book to Allen's old room. Otto got a glass of water and sat with Ken.

"So how's Allen?"

"I think he liked Monica."

"Did he?"

"Why do you say it that way? Is he married?"

"No, not yet. But he is engaged."

"A lot has changed, hasn't it?"

"That's just it, Otto. It isn't so much that things have changed, but that I feel it's in the middle of changing."

He felt a need to ask Ken what that meant. Only the image of Monica clutching the paperback lodged itself in his mind. Otto imagined her reading it in Allen's bed. It upset his notion of this trip as an odyssey, made it impossible to distinguish which hero was which.

9

The tasks involved packing and setting off effectively disrupted sorting and processing a stream of thoughts from the long talk with George, particularly determining what he wanted to share with Otto and Monica. Her asking if the sudden departure had to do with her had been perceptive. George was uneasy about her presence on the reservation, elliptically hinting her presence would be a risk the longer she was with them. Then shutting up when Ken pressed him to be specific.

The old camp they were going to was less than an hour away, likely not as far as George would have preferred, but it seemed necessary to recalibrate their plans before venturing away from a familiar environment. Still, Ken hadn't come this way in over seven years and found it hard to locate, taking nearly as long to pinpoint as it had taken to paddle this far. Luckily neither Otto or Monica complained. She was reading a book Allen had given her and Otto enjoyed talking to her about it, though it tended to result in arguments that echoed those of the twins.

There it was at last, the stone marker covered in brush in front of the pine tree stump, a remnant of an ancient beaver dam.

"Hey you two, we're here. I need your help."

Monica put the book down as they halted their discussion to get out and drag the canoe ashore. Otto left to clear the old path with a machete while Ken and Monica unloaded items to a spot sheltered by deciduous trees in full bloom, before pulling in the vessel far enough to tie to one of the trees. Otto's progress was slow. The brush was thick with clots of leaves hampering their movement. A good sign the cabin, the second Ken had built, the one at which he'd lived longest, hadn't been found by squatters. The brush had preserved the structure too. There were only two cots, though, complicating sleeping arrangements.

"Is this where you found me, Ken?"

"This camp? Yes, it is."

"No, I know that. I mean this particular spot."

Otto was pointing at a bush next to the step-up into the cabin. It was the only logical place but Ken for the life of him couldn't remember. He'd been fishing for a couple of days and had come back exhausted, thinking only of getting indoors, making a fire, and having a Scotch or two once he'd put the equipment away and taken care of his catch. It must have been an hour before he saw the basket amongst everything else. It was heavy because of a sleeping child curled up inside. He recalled being suddenly disoriented. This could have been the spot, so he nodded.

"You raised Otto on your own?"

"I did."

"You never knew who dropped him off? No suspicions?"

Ken hesitated. He couldn't prove it but there was little doubt in his mind. He'd long ago decided that until there was proof he wouldn't share that with anyone unless he had to. Well, now he had to, though not necessarily this instant.

He shook his head and asked Otto to retrieve the sandwiches George had graciously left in the fridge for them. He started a fire and asked Monica to clear debris from the picnic table. Tea poured, food apportioned, they now sat like a family might at a dinner table. Otto waited only a bite before speaking.

"So why are we here, Ken? It's out of the way."

"George and I were talking—"

"It is me, isn't it? I saw the family Values coaster at George's."

Monica's interruption threw Ken off, until he realized it gave him a viable opening.

"The what?"

"His coasters. They had the logo of family Values."

"Why would that spook you? Wesley told me you left because of the racial blending, not this family Values thing."

Monica became silent. He let her be, figuring she'd open up eventually. When she did, her voice was increasingly mournful.

"That's what got us to leave. But family Values is at the centre of it all. My family, except Wesley, was for family Values. They even pushed me to have an abortion because all the turmoil in Ontario was putting people out of work. It threatened to isolate us in the north if we didn't go along. If not for my baby, I might have. Only Wesley was openly on my side. It led to him and his wife, my mother's sister, separating. While he may blame racial blending, I blame family Values."

41

"So why do you want to see them again?"

Otto was merely repeating his earlier question but it sounded different because now his tone was empathetic. Monica took a moment to compose herself.

"Not everyone in my family privately felt the way they acted in public. Some sympathized, but couldn't say it. Like my Mom. She gave me money as if she knew what would happen. I want to see her, to at least tell her I'm okay. My little sister too."

Otto nodded and this relaxed Monica.

"Sorry for giving you that kiss earlier in front of those men, Otto. When Wesley and I left with the baby we had to act like a couple to fool people. It worked then."

"It's all right."

It amused Ken to see Otto blush slightly, and it pleased him to see them friendly. It made it easier to share what he and George had talked about. How Indigenous peoples across Ontario were negotiating with family Values to assume authority over rural zones—George was adamant about calling them arrangements, not treaties—establishing native autonomy and also exempting natives from family Values policies, such as racial blending, so long as they exited and stayed out of family Values cities. Since there was no limit set to the expansion of family Values it could theoretically wipe out all native lands if populations grew and required more cities. Unlikely, given Ontario's size. George and his fellow elders saw this as their opportunity to re-grow native communities and restore traditional ways.

"Having two white people like you and me around, Monica, could complicate his life if he'd gotten a sudden visit from those family Values administrators."

"So us leaving wasn't about me specifically?"

"I didn't say anything about you or Wesley, he never brought it up either. So I think it's coincidental."

"But that doesn't mean . . . what about those men we saw the other day on the river?"

"I asked about them. George has no idea who they might be."

"Then they could still be—oh God, what if they find Wesley?"

"He strikes me as a survivor who's cleverer than those men."

"Maybe I should go back. I don't want to be a risk for you."

Ken shook his head but kept silent, suddenly feeling confused and lacking confidence, with a growing sense this trip would be far more complicated than he'd originally thought.

"Are we in danger, if we we're spotted there?"

"I don't believe so."

"You're sure no one would be following us?"

"Just in case we'll hole up here tonight. If anyone is behind us, we'll let them get ahead and keep in front of us. There's only the one road so we'll be taking the same route for some time."

They finished eating and had a second cup of tea. For once no chores, it became a pleasantly lazy day. Monica read her book, after asking Otto to let her finish before they discussed it again. Otto left to fish while Ken, as he had last night, took advantage to indulge in nostalgia.

Despite the seriousness, it had been wonderful to talk with his old friend. Lots of shared memories of his stepmother to whom he owed so much. He particularly liked hearing George say he saw Vanessa's traits in Otto, though of course there couldn't be a biological link. It reflected the depth of her inside Ken, George clarified, when Ken pointed that out.

Daylight lasted long enough for Monica to finish her book and Otto to catch a feast of fish. The wind picked up as they ate, bringing a rapid coolness and lower humidity. Amid the stars far above the trees waves of blue, green, purple danced. Aurora Borealis. An auspicious sign for Ken, an indicator he was where he belonged. Only soon he'd be travelling away from it, this one possibly the last he'd enjoy for a long time. It seemed his travel companions felt the same, putting off their book discussion.

10

Otto blamed his overworking imagination for the resistance he felt at each stroke, but couldn't help wanting to blame Ken for slowing them down. He avoided verifying this, kept pressing forward. Too many delays, it had taken too long in his opinion to get off water and onto land. If it was up to him to provide the extra effort he was willing to do so. He had to admit, all the talk of family Values stoked his curiosity to see it firsthand.

"I finished the book yesterday. Want to talk about it?"

"Let's keep paddling, Monica. You can tell me later."

"We can paddle and talk. I thought you'd be glad I finished."

"I am. You read it fast."

"That's it?"

Otto looked back at her, then at Ken. Both paddling normally; it had to be the current causing the plodding pace after all. Now he felt bad for his terseness with Monica.

"So you've read it. Isn't it obvious Odysseus was a hero?"

"I wouldn't say obvious. Heroic, maybe. At times."

"How can you not see he's a hero?"

"He's extremely selfish. He's cruel. And violent."

"Only when he needs to be."

"He's no Ken, that's for sure."

"What?"

Ken's bewilderment made her laugh, which irked Otto.

"You two still going on about that damn book?"

"I was just telling Otto I finished it this morning."

"Discuss it later. One more tough portage, after which we'll be hiking. You'll have plenty of time to talk about anything then."

They were efficiently silent through this last portage. It wasn't that bad. Not as tricky as figuring out how to conceal the canoe, then stash the bulkier, heavier items—cooking gear, utensils, tools, extra bags, heavier clothing—and keep them findable for later. The digging and dirt moving left them exhausted but also liberated at a lighter load. It was another blessing to find a trail leading to the highway.

A tidy expanse of tar cutting through a barren, flat landscape, a pair of yellow stripes, one solid, one broken, down the middle turning into single white and broken lines farther down. The shoulders were gravel with solid white line lines separating them from the road and metal railings and wilderness on each side. Otto was drawn to its utilitarian yet appealing symmetry.

Thick grey clouds eerily obscured an unknown world to Otto in both directions. A truck drove past, its rumbling belying the road's rough condition. Ken pointed after it.

"Hearst is that way."

"How far?"

"Just over thirty kilometres."

"Maybe we can catch a ride."

"I doubt that'd be wise."

"Ken's right, we must be careful with rides. Besides, there isn't a lot of traffic. At least none that will stop for us."

Otto frowned, wary of a possible switch in expertise from Ken to Monica as she was proven right. All the vehicles that passed were commercial. According to her, it was illegal for drivers to stop to pick up passengers.

"If in fact they have a driver. Most are driverless. Those with a driver are monitored by a central office that can lock its doors if it makes an unscheduled stop and keep it locked until the cause of the stop is determined."

"We certainly can't trust private vehicles."

"They wouldn't trust us either."

Monica chuckled.

"Unless they're stupid."

"Those'd be the ones we'd have to be most cautious with."

A new weariness overcame them as they walked due to the exertion on their legs instead of their arms, notably on the long, gentle inclines. Still, they maintained a decent pace and luckily the weather cooperated. The clouds behind blocked the sun to keep them cool. Their water would be sufficient until they got to Hearst, meaning not having to figure out how to operate the purifier contraption George had given them, supporting Otto's argument to have left it behind. He held on to a hope there'd be a store or some place to get a snack with flavour.

Tedium soon became the greatest danger. Unlike being on the river where variety in action and countryside helped pass time, their conversations grew as sparse as the traffic. The flat road, supposedly easier to walk on, seemed to be less efficient than a dirt trail. And the sameness of it sparked doubts in his desire to reach a destination that started to feel increasingly unreachable. An occasional distance sign provided relief for perhaps a half hour. Ken wasn't talking at all, possibly in the tracking mode he perfected living with Indians when he was young. Frequent pauses to identify moose or deer, as much as they impressed or even enthralled Monica, were of no interest to Otto. Not even a wolf pausing in the road to inspect the remains of a dead crow forty metres off, before sauntering on. The structures they saw had been abandoned, including the rusted remains of what Ken believed were once cell phone towers.

Monica's silence was surprising, considering her anxiousness to talk about the novel earlier. Maybe she was waiting for Otto to bring it up, or maybe Ken's reaction had made her hesitant. Talking about the novel could pass the time nicely, unless she persisted in thinking her way, frustrating in itself, unbearable here. Maybe this was an opportunity to strategize about ways to convince her Odysseus was a hero. But when he tried he had to face the futile pointlessness of proving what was self-evident.

Ken paused to drink some water. Monica and Otto did so too. It tasted better than usual, rejuvenating. A few trucks passed in both directions. Their combined sound lifted Otto's spirit. An indication they were approaching a milestone. One even slowed

46

but sped off when Ken turned to look at it. Monica asked how much farther to go.

"Maybe another hour."

"That's it? That's not bad."

"We're not going all the way into town. I have a friend on this side of Hearst we'll stop to see."

"Do I know him?"

"Her. And no."

"Is she one of the women you used to—?"

"She's an old friend of my stepmother's, Otto."

"Are you sure she'll still be there?"

"According to George she is, Monica."

"At least it's a destination."

"That's the spirit."

Before they resumed, Ken told them that at his friend's house he'd go ahead on his own first while Otto and Monica waited. She pulled off her pack to sit on a guardrail, then zipped it open to fish out the novel. She leafed through it before looking up at Otto and flashing a coy smile.

"It's a great book. If you like propaganda."

"If you like what?"

Ken returned to motion for them to follow him on a dirt road, to a brownish brick house with a black roof and a long gravel driveway, willow trees on each side splaying broad shadows as the clouds dissipated. A large German shepherd barked at Otto and Monica, who jumped and clutched his arm.

"Heel, Packer."

The dog stopped barking instantly but kept its eyes on them. The command had come from an old but sturdy woman leaning on her elbows looking over a porch rail, silver hair tied back in a ponytail. She wore overalls and a blue and green flannel shirt. From Otto's vantage she seemed hardened but up close she had a smile he found warmly inviting. The dog led them, huffing. An old beast, no threat. Still, Monica clutched Otto's bicep.

Ken introduced them to Heather, George Monctalm's cousin, who had expected them. Strange Ken hadn't shared that earlier. Unless he hadn't known. Heather beckoned them in for iced tea.

Her house was the same size as George's and looked the way George's used to look, with old cloth furniture, wood panelling, and large rugs. The sofa and love seat in front of the fireplace in fact may have been the ones that used to be in George's living room. Same with the television above the mantle. The room had a cozy mustiness Otto liked but Monica apparently didn't as she seemed sad all of a sudden. He didn't know whether to ask her about it. It was a relief when Ken asked Otto and Monica to give the "older folks" time to talk in the backyard. Heather suggested they take a nap. The promise of a soft mattress filled him with joy. Monica wasn't interested in resting, though.

"Mind if I try your television?"

"Go ahead. If you like family Values stations."

"Oh."

"There is a pirate station out of Timmins but its signal is often distorted. The old DVD player works. You can look through the drawers for old movies."

"I'll find something."

"Sure you don't want a nap with your husband?"

A guilty grin from Ken revealed Heather believed the story of Otto and Monica as a couple. He was too tired to make a fuss or protest sharing a bedroom with her. At least it was a large room and had a large bed. If she took a nap she wouldn't disturb him. Even better, an en-suite bathroom. He took a quick hot shower before laying down.

Sleep came instantly, dreamless and deep, until broken by a noise he couldn't identify. Rain tapping a roof? He knew where he was, not how much time had elapsed. Dark curtains made it impossible to tell if it was still daytime. No clock. His ears grew accustomed to the sound and he fell back asleep.

And dreamed his dream.

The woman's face was sharper, blacker, lovelier than ever, her powerful presence dominating the city behind her lush flowing robes, so vibrant. He became startled when she abruptly turned to him wearing a grim expression that abruptly turned kind and motherly. Her lips parted.

"Otto. Otto."

His eyes opened to see Monica by the en-suite door, a towel wrapped around her, another to dry her hair.

"Were you having a nightmare? You sounded scared."

"At least you're not naked for once."

She laughed, stopped drying her hair to motion as if she was taking off the other towel, laughed harder as he turned away.

"Why do you and Ken insist on wearing clothes if it's warm and you're alone?"

"You're not alone."

She smirked before readjusting the towel and going back into the bathroom, closing the door. She emerged moments later in her yellow shorts, which looked gold in the light. She had on a black t-shirt he hadn't seen her wear before, saying Eagles and Hotel California Tour 2021. He pointed at it.

"Where'd you get that?"

"Like the shirt? Heather let me have it. Said it now makes her ironically sad."

Monica's expression implied she didn't understand what that meant either, then added that this happened when Monica gave her Allen's book to return to him.

"No use carrying it around now that I've read it, right?"

"What's propa—that word you used before?"

"Propaganda. It's what people use to convince others of what they want them to think by manipulating words or pictures."

"Reading the whole book didn't change your mind?"

"What's written isn't the issue, it's how it's written. No one can say Odysseus was a hero precisely because he was portrayed as one by an author intent on portraying him that way. Killing any chance for objective assessment from the start. With centuries of interpreters and critics doing the same it ensured your hero and his son could only be seen as heroes. Until finally someone saw it for what it was and had a chance to show the discrepancies."

What she said troubled him. It was wrong but seemed to hold a truth he couldn't grasp. A truth that could lead to looking at things in ways he'd never thought of before, that Ken couldn't ever teach him. Never would teach him either.

"If you don't mind, I want to get some rest now."

Otto went downstairs. The house was quiet, highlighting the appetizing odour of meat cooking. It told him Ken and Heather hadn't gone far. He was starving, anxious to know when they'd eat. Otto checked the rooms, all unoccupied. Then through the master bedroom window he heard soft voices. Ken and Heather talking outside. In the rain and dark. He moved to join them, then decided to stay inside and listen.

"Sure you can't stay longer? We have lots to catch up on. It's lonely here, I'd love the company. Otto and Monica seem nice."

"You're a great hostess Heather. I would love to stay, if only to reminisce about Vanessa. But it's best that we keep moving. For a number of reasons."

"I understand, I suppose."

11

The patio umbrella did a fine job protecting them from the rain. It was great to be with Heather again. Her calm demeanour, her sage advice, her humour, all valuable aids after his father killed himself and Ken returned to Kapuskasing to live with Vanessa, his stepmother. Without Heather's support in those adolescent days, Ken's standing with the Cree, even with childhood friends such as George, might not be as stable as it was nowadays.

His life's turmoil began after Ken's mom left with his younger sister for Halifax, just before Ken's ninth birthday. Even then he knew his birthmother, city girl at heart, was unhappy in remote Hearst. What he didn't discover until later was the depth of her hatred for his father, his drinking and gambling. The separation shattered Ken who twice attempted to escape home himself, but was found the first time and returned on his own the second.

Then his father met Vanessa, a Cree girl fifteen years younger. She fell for his charms, as had Ken's birthmother, but had other motivations to be with him, resenting pressure to marry a Cree boy she didn't much care for, let alone love. Not only that, her extended family, including George, despised Ken's father for his poor reputation. They were polite to him because of friends like Heather who defended Vanessa. Yet it was always tense for Ken with everyone except Vanessa. He cherished her and the feeling was mutual. She tamed his wild nature. She soothed the pain of losing his mother and sister and taught him to respect others' perspectives by adopting her belief no one has the right to judge someone else.

Things turned sour when his father, feeling oppressed by her family, decided to move them to Kapuskasing. The larger town did offer better work opportunities, but also vices, to which he added affairs with three women, one of whom was the sister of a prominent elder. Vanessa's family confronted him about it in front of his friends at his favourite tavern, embarrassing him so much he took it out on Vanessa the next day, then more often, while Ken was at school. That led to another intervention that made staying there impossible for his father. For a second time in his brief existence Ken's family life was shattered, as he was obliged to join his father in Toronto. Until the old man's suicide forced Ken, a minor, to return to his legal guardian just as he was settling into his Grade Eight class.

While happy to be back with Vanessa, despite being innocent of all their issues with his father, Ken faced resentment from her family, except George and Heather. This was compounded with the suspicion of Vanessa's uncle killing Ken's father when doubt was raised about its being a suicide. It again came out about his father's abuse, with people speculating how the apple didn't fall far from the tree anytime Ken got into a fight or mixed up with a girl. All that might have been forgotten over time if not for the sudden unforeseen foreclosure on Vanessa's house. Apparently his father had re-mortgaged it years before and squandered the funds before his death. It was easy for their family to blame the culprit's teenage son.

Ken dropped out of high school at sixteen and went to work. He was talented with tools and sought after, but it took months before he could start repaying the debt. It took over a decade but he did it, gaining the respect of Vanessa's family and of the community. That lessened when his stepmother landed a job as a nurse in a clinic in Timmins, again when he moved to Toronto to find more work and got married, but revived with his return with the twins.

As if Heather had been reading his mind:

"Did you ever find out what happened to your kids?"

"They could be anywhere."

"I saw them, you know."

"You did?"

"A year after you stopped looking. They came here."

"Why didn't you tell me?"

"I thought by how they acted they were on their way back to you. They described where you lived, as if they'd been there."

That caught Ken off guard. Maybe this was the time to share everything with someone. Who better than Heather? As he was about to speak, he sensed a presence from inside the house. He glanced at Heather, she seemed to have noticed too. They let a few seconds pass. Nothing.

"Maybe we should go inside. Check on those two."

"Sure. The stew is close to being done."

The stew was actually close to burning and they found Otto taking it off the stove just in time. Ken asked him to get Monica but he hesitated. Heather offered to do it and left them. Otto grabbed Ken's arm.

"Who are the twins?"

"So you were listening to us."

"I can ask Heather."

"No, I'll tell you about it. Just not right now."

Thankfully the women descended quickly. Once more sparing Ken opening up about the biggest failure of his life.

Otto led Monica, with deference, to the seat next to his own. Not unlike a doting boyfriend. Heather looked pleased as they ate the tasty stew, more when complimented on it by Monica.

"I was saying to Ken it's nice to have company, how I wished you all could stay longer, so I could get to know you two."

Otto looked annoyed, which made Heather laugh.

"I know you two aren't like that, Otto. Forgive my implying so. I wanted to test you. To see if you two can pull it off."

"And?"

"Needs a little more effort."

"So you agree with Ken and her that it's necessary?"

"It doesn't hurt."

Otto accepted this with a sigh but still acted displeased. Is he upset with me? Ken wondered. He certainly wasn't annoyed at Monica anymore. Indeed, a bond had developed between those two that wasn't there on the road. It seemed to get stronger with every exchange. Whether a quick comment about their book, or passing a slice of bread, or Otto refilling her bowl. Meanwhile, Heather kept glancing out the window between spoonfuls. The strange aura subsided with the ice cream dessert.

"Such a long way for you three to go."

"Three, four days. Unless there's a bus."

"Not up here. I have an idea, though it will mean you staying another day. Don't give me that look, Ken. Give it a chance."

They followed Heather behind the dwelling to a wood garage, Packer dutifully following. Together Ken and Otto opened the large double doors. They creaked but were more unwieldy than heavy. It took his eyes several seconds to adjust to the dark and to spot the rusted blue compact Chevrolet bearing a nameplate Ken didn't recognize: Diversity. Dusty and well worn, it looked at least twenty years old. A hybrid.

"Always been a poor driver, you can tell by the dents. Which is why I get my groceries and essentials delivered. I only keep it for emergencies."

"Are you saying you'll let me have it?"

"Borrow it. You can leave it in Kapuskasing where my cousin can get you to Driftwood and bring it back."

"That's wonderful, Heather. Thanks."

"Is it hard getting electricity?"

"Yes. The engine won't go five kilometres without a recharge. You're better off with gasoline. There's enough in the tank to get to Kapuskasing, if you keep under sixty clicks an hour."

"Where can you get gasoline?"

"At truck stops. It's free. Most truckers don't mind folks filling up a puny car like this."

"Great. Where are the keys?"

"Hold on. It needs fixing first. Even a super mechanic such as yourself will take at least a day."

"Do you have tools?"

"Some."

"Go get them. I'll start right away."

"Is it reliable?"

"More reliable than anything brand new."

"That makes no sense."

"Otto, my dear, there's a saying: 'If it's new, good luck to you; if it's old, it's gold,' that applies to cars as much as anything. It's because all the people who knew how to fix things are dying or decrepit or, like Ken, just gone."

"And is this car new or old?"

"Kind of in between. You'll quickly see Ken that you can only do so much to it now. So do expect breakdowns along the way. Just remember that if you stop for gas or any reason, don't take on hitchhikers. Be especially wary of solo travellers. No matter their sincerity."

"Great. Now where are the tools?"

12

They made great time while in motion, but the frequent stops to identify then fix issues made Otto wonder if they'd be better off on foot. Ridiculous, of course, but a reminder of how he missed the water. Bracing potholes and ruts in tense anticipation of the next issue, he found himself pining for wildlife and the curving variety of the waterways. How that calmed him, how the fresh air helped pace his strokes. In a car he felt constrained, annoyed at not being in control of his movements, and weary of Monica's complaints how it smelled like Heather's dog.

That was in his head and stayed in his head. If he brought it up, no doubt Ken and Monica would point out that without the car they'd be forty kilometres back, less than halfway there. The car saved strain on their legs and backs and he had to admit he found the lights and digital readouts absorbing. At least until a certain red one brightened, foretelling the squealing brakes Ken kept promising he'd address the next time.

Of course, just as he thought it, the light flashed again, lasting several seconds before turning solid red. Usually it was possible to let the vehicle glide until they found a spot to pull over, away from traffic. This time the car jerked and it took Ken some effort to keep it under control. Somehow he did and, luckily, right at an empty dusty gas station. Otto and Monica pushed while Ken steered it fully off the road. Ken pulled the latch from inside the car before going out to pull up the hood and use the thin rod to keep it in place. He put his hands on the front of the car, only to quickly yank them away. His curse startled Monica.

"You all right, Ken?"

"Engine's too hot, I singed my finger. I'll need a few minutes."

She went to see and Otto felt an urge to join her but a stronger one to stay put. This was a moment like at Heather's when Otto experienced an instinctual resentment towards Ken but couldn't determine its cause. Maybe it was Monica, how she'd said fixing the car and chauffeuring them was Ken's chance to be heroic, again. She'd said it to tease Otto, he knew, but it still grated.

She returned to Otto and pointed at the dark puddles between the pumps, adding Ken asked them to check if they were fresh. She got the gas can while Otto walked to the pumps, shaded by an overhang, drawn by the chance to get out of the sun.

He slowed at seeing a dilapidated structure that showed no indication of life. Instinct told him to stop, to wait for Monica. Then he heard a foot shuffle, followed by a strong sensation of the presence of fear, human fear. A man emerged, a large pack slung over his shoulder, gesturing to show he had no weapon. He was at least thirty, possibly forty, with a face even paler than Monica's. His slight scruff indicated he'd shaved recently. His clothes were clean, un-tattered. Monica had caught up by now and noticed the man. She looked back at Ken, as if to make sure he could keep them in sight. Otto approached the man and she followed quietly but more deliberately. He wasn't afraid but his pulse quickened when the man smiled and spoke, his deep bass voice contrasting his small frame.

"Need help? I'm handy, especially with electric cars."

Monica stepped forward to wave the gas can.

"We're using gasoline."

"I hear those are pretty useless now."

"He'll fix it."

Monica's self-assuredness surprised Otto as she went to try a pump. The man intercepted her to point at the far one.

"I know that one works."

"Thanks."

"Assuming he fixes it, what direction are you heading? Maybe you can squeeze me in? I can be quite useful in other ways."

Otto watched him as he watched Monica fill the can and come back to stand next to Otto. His gaze wasn't lewd but Otto didn't like it. He did like how Monica ignored it. She tapped his arm.

"Let's go, honey."

The man grinned and repeated his request. Monica smiled at the man in a way Otto couldn't assess and coyly asked:

"Which way are you headed?"

The man chuckled, as if playing an amusing game.

"Same way your car's pointing. famCoch. Driftwood would be great, though. I'm Randall, by the way."

"I'm afraid we're going the other way, Randall. We turned the car around for a better look at the engine with the sun."

"That so? Don't encounter many girls like you running away from civilization. Especially with a dark-skinned one like him."

"Fiancé. That's my father, our chaperone. If you must know, we are on our way to our engagement announcement."

Randall put a hand to his mouth but his smirk was evident.

"Good looking, I'll grant, but he seems rather young for you. I suppose his skin colour makes that irrelevant, right?"

Otto felt offended at the disrespect of the man talking about him that way in the third person, but more upset at the ease in which Monica was telling outright unnecessary lies. She made it worse when she pulled him close as if about to kiss him. Before their lips touched, Ken's voice came through.

"Done. Let's go."

"Sure you're heading west? He doesn't look like he's turning to come get you."

"Positive. Sorry. Come on honey."

The exchange left Otto stunned, made him feel like a child. It was the first time he'd knowingly participated in blatant lying. Lies instantly exposed when Monica told Ken to put the gas can in the trunk and fill the tank later. Ken didn't argue. They were off and the dust raised obscured Randall's reaction.

"Who was that you were talking to?"

"Some traveller who wanted to hitch a ride with us."

"His name was Randall."

"What did you tell this Randall?"

"Said we were going the other way, to put him off."

"You did right."

"I know. He wouldn't have fit, anyways."

Monica's excuse didn't help. In fact, he felt worse that Ken, his hero, complimented Monica's deceit. Declining the ride didn't trouble Otto, but why give a reason, why not just say the truth, that there was no room?

The countryside didn't change much but the road got busier, marginally smoother. They passed apartment buildings, homes, businesses, abandoned and working factories, industrial plazas, silos, gas stations; their pace had quickened. Anticipation grew equally fast within Otto. He assumed the other two shared his excitement, that they were as thrilled as he was they'd gone so long without stopping.

The moment Otto thought this they slowed again. It wasn't for the red light, it remained dim. Ken steered the car to the side of the road. The squeal wasn't from the brakes but from Monica who pointed up and to the right at a billboard.

"Bring family Values to Kapuskasing. Make it a NewKapu."

Ken's speaking it aloud echoed Otto's mental reading. Monica let out a gasp as her hand pointed to another Ken read aloud.

"family Values: Preserving your progressive kin."

"We had the same signs. The same slogans. It's here."

She said it with regret but Otto didn't understand what made it bad. He found the artistic drawings of fancy buildings, sleek trains, freshly paved roads, colourful foods, and smiling people under bright blue skies appealing and inviting.

"It's a nice sign, it looks like a good thing."

"They're expert at marketing themselves, at showing the good things while concealing the negatives. In other words, lying."

You lie too, Otto wanted to blurt out. He instead asked her to specify what was negative. She didn't respond. He didn't know if he was being ignored or she hadn't heard.

They drove on but travelled only a few kilometres before the car slowed at another one. Identical except it'd been vandalized, white paint crossing out most words to make it say:

"Bring . . . Kapuskasing . . . a New . . . mayor."

13

Entering Kapuskasing felt oddly anticlimactic. Until he passed the cemetery across from the airport that had been converted to a combined solar/wind farm. It looked desolate and he hated to think they'd relocated Vanessa's grave to service progress. They passed rows of motels, several still in operation. His heart filled with melancholy as the river came into view. The familiar single steeple lost in a skyline of modern glass towers. A gleaming he never expected so far north. A facade of prosperity not reflected in the city core where the streets looked much the same, just less well maintained. No new traffic lights, nor signs of increased traffic. How would all the new people get to and from work or other activities? Walking? He did see more pedestrians than normal, not many. Was there to be some sort of subway system? As they passed newer buildings it became evident most were under construction, unoccupied, blocking the late afternoon sun from town. Each adorned with the family Values logo he'd first seen on the drink coasters at George's.

"Those buildings are housing for migrations. They wouldn't build them until certain the town is about to transition."

Monica's words filled Ken with gloom.

"How many more people will come?"

"In Cochrane the population had doubled, maybe even tripled by the time Wesley and I left."

In the town centre Ken found the changes—other than the reduced sunlight—less dramatic, amenable to indulging a little nostalgic tourism. He drove past his elementary school, slowing at street corners where he'd trade hockey cards, sports fields— many now converted to solar farms—where he'd play lacrosse, baseball, football. Places he hung out with friends, the spot by the river where he'd take girls. He avoided the neighbourhood where he'd lived his early years with his mother and sister. To Ken's surprise, the tour had perked Otto up; the boy was rarely curious about Ken's childhood before.

"Did the twins live here?"

"Twins? What twins?"

"I asked Ken, not you."

"Yes Otto, of course the twins lived here. I was their father. If you can be a little patient, I'll tell you all about it once we settle in. Then Monica can relax while we talk elsewhere."

"I want Monica with us when we talk."

"Maybe she doesn't want to."

"No, I'd be interested. If you don't mind."

Just as well, Ken thought, she might help keep the discussion from going sideways or becoming maudlin.

"As long as we don't encounter any Sirens."

Ken had no idea what she meant but resisted asking when he heard those two chortle. He reached into a shirt pocket for the address. It didn't take long to find. He'd once dated a girl who'd lived at the same house. It felt weird parking in his old spot, on the road, despite the empty driveway. He had Otto and Monica wait in the car.

He rang the bell and was answered by Jack, Heather's cousin, who'd agreed to lend them his home for a few days. Apparently that girl still lived there and Jack was her husband. He knew of Ken by reputation, but not of that past relationship, thankfully. And she was at work. They exchanged car and house keys. Jack promised to return in two days but didn't say anything about driving them to Driftwood. Ken didn't want to push it, pleased they'd have the place to themselves.

It was a modest, two-bedroom home, smaller than Heather's. There was food, the appliances worked. And there was a canoe in the backyard, near a path to the river he knew well. Too late in the day to take it out now. Everyone was content to stay in and wait until tomorrow to hear about the twins. Otto found a cupboard of games and Monica pledged to teach him checkers, after finding the television, like at Heather's, received no signal.

Seeing them playacting alternately as a couple and as siblings revived a dormant fear that Ken had done wrong by raising the boy away from the world. Otto was adapting to Monica and got along nicely with Heather. Better late than never? Perhaps this journey could be considered as correcting a wrong.

Ken was to take the small bedroom, so Monica and Otto could get more space on the larger bed. But once he reclined on the sofa Ken fell sound asleep and didn't wake until dawn. So Otto ended up sleeping in the master, Monica the smaller bedroom. It was tempting to put off the promised discussion by going out in the canoe on his own.

Instead he stayed put and prepared a hearty breakfast of eggs, pancakes, and sausages. He ate his while he inspected the canoe and found the craft in terrific shape, possibly never used. He then fetched Otto and Monica. They were groggy but Otto was quickly energized at the chance to get on water. Monica wasn't as keen but had no desire to stay behind by herself, once Otto pointed that out. Ken wondered: would the boy have chosen to stay with her if she didn't go?

While it was great to see them friendly with each other, Ken also found it disturbing in how it highlighted a new fear: if he didn't come clean with Otto about what he suspected about his origins, he could lose him as he'd lost the twins.

14

The farther they paddled the happier Otto was that Monica had come along. Since stopping at the gas station—notwithstanding the lies—he felt they'd gotten closer. Her joining them when he thought she'd want time alone affirmed this. Even better, it also assured him she saw Otto as a brother, or cousin, nothing more.

It was just after noon when Ken at last told them they could stop paddling, in the middle of a thick, seemingly impenetrable forest. Ken was serious when he guided them towards a narrow slit between two peninsular bits of grassy beach jutting out into the river. Far too small for a canoe, yet Ken steered them that way. Close up, as in a fable, or optical illusion, the entry spread open. Anyone unaware of it would have paddled by.

Once inside, the passage narrowed to a small channel but one in which it was possible to propel forward by oaring against the slope. Fifty metres in it ended at a muddy beach. No need to tie up the canoe, easier to dam it with a large chunk of wood. A ten minute hike led to a cabin larger than any previous camps. A lot fancier inside too, three rooms, and a separate toilet area, all in good shape due to the secured door and windows, which they discovered only after Ken's long search for the hidden keys. A curious Monica opened a trunk filled with children's toys before she inspected the rest of the cabin.

"This is a house. I can't believe you built it all yourself."

"It needed to be a home for my son and daughter, my twins."

Otto wasn't sure why he found Monica's surprise gratifying.

"So you do have your own children. Where are they?"

"I don't know. They left me."

"But how? Why?"

"Let's get our food and I'll tell you."

Monica seemed confused by Ken's matter-of-factness. No sign of sadness or resentment. Otto was used to it, but her question did send his mind spinning. Hadn't Ken cared for his children? Or had so much time passed his feelings had petrified? Otto kept quiet, glanced at Monica to get her to do likewise as they unpacked the bacon sandwiches they'd made from the breakfast to eat at the river. He feared Ken was hesitant to talk, so the less they interrupted, the better. Thankfully she took the hint.

Some sadness and resentment could be detected as Ken told them how he and his wife, the twins' mother, had separated and mutually agreed to have Ken take them out of Toronto. Both felt taking the twins—barely two at the time—out of a locked down city during the pandemic would shield them from turmoil. But the pandemic in effect only shielded a deteriorating relationship and their assumption of an end to the pandemic in a few weeks turned into months, then longer. Ken never saw her again.

"How could a mother do that? I know how I felt when I lost my child. You never sought her out?"

"It seemed impossible under the circumstances."

"Why?"

"It really was up to her . . ."

"But why was it up to her?"

"I have to admit, that's not so clear to me anymore and I regret that now. Not trying, that is."

"Do you?"

Otto asked sincerely, not as a challenge. Ken nodded.

"It's easy to look back on what you've done, or haven't done, through a filter of regret."

That satisfied Otto who was anxious for Ken to go on, as there clearly was more. Monica sighed but thankfully kept quiet.

The first weeks after the separation Ken lived with Vanessa, his stepmother, in Kapuskasing. Not far from Heather's cousin's place. The kids adored Vanessa. However, Ken knew it wasn't a permanent solution, just as he started to see going back might not be possible. That compelled him to build this cabin for the future, just in case. He retrofitted this retreat for a small family and they moved in. The twins saw it as an adventure at first but boredom quickly set in. Each toy Ken bought placated them for only short bursts. Unlike Otto, the twins had zero interest in fishing, hunting, canoeing, anything outdoors.

He took them back to live with Vanessa, who got them into a reservation school when they turned five. A good solution until Vanessa died and he found out how much his standing with her clan depended on her. They did not want him to continue living there without Vanessa. It forced him to try again with the cabin. He improved it by adding comforts and expanding it to appeal more to the twins. Giving each their own bedroom, for instance.

Their being older, along with their dislike of Vanessa's family, who they encountered all over town, helped them adapt. They still didn't care for nature or the outdoors but Ken was happy to do the work. It brought peace and a drop in complaints. Which ought to have warned Ken, but he remained oblivious until one day after their fifteenth birthday when, returning earlier than he had told them, he found them in bed together, wearing nothing. Ken was at a loss what to do.

Ken paused to let them absorb this. Otto wasn't clear why but Monica nodded, as if grasping something Ken hadn't said. Otto wished he had the letter as it could have provided a clue. It was back at Heather's cousin's house in his bag. Ken glanced at them both before continuing.

"Once it started, no matter what I said, how much I appealed to them, they didn't stop. I couldn't spend all my time watching them, I had no one to turn to, and could only chastise whenever it happened. Eventually they got sick of my being sick of it and ran away. I haven't seen them since. Heather just told me they'd visited her a year or so later. That's what you overheard us talk about, Otto. Then I moved to the camp where you turned up."

Monica glanced at Otto strangely, as if he was a creature she'd not seen before. He didn't like it. During the ensuing silence he wanted to challenge her but couldn't think of what to say.

"I'm going to take a swim."

Monica stripping in front of them no longer shocked Otto but she didn't this time, instead finding a concealed spot. Ken went to start a fire, evading Otto's stare, but also as if waiting for Otto to ask a question. A hint the story was incomplete in some way.

They were like this for an hour. Birds called to each other, the only sounds in addition to the breeze or occasional splash. Then the splashes stopped. Monica was out of the water, the sunlight complementing her soft pale and bare skin.

"Ken, what were the twins' names?"

"Felicity and Felix."

"And your wife?"

"Esmeralda."

Esmeralda. The addressee. Hearing Ken say it reignited Otto's intent to find this Esmeralda and deliver the letter. And not tell Ken until he did and heard her version.

The strong current made for hard, silent paddling back. They got back to the house by dinnertime. Monica uncovered an old beat-up barbecue Ken played with and got to work. Monica dug out four hamburgers from the freezer and two large pork chops from the refrigerator. They were too hungry to wait for burgers to thaw and cooked the chops. Ken had returned to his usual self. Monica's side glances at Otto continued but she directed a few at Ken too.

A variation of Otto's dream of the woman came to him that night. It consisted of wavy and essentially motionless images, as if the world had paused on one leg, and no matter how hard he pressed, nothing straightened.

Next morning, after breakfast, Jack strolled in without ringing the bell or knocking. He and Ken conversed and it looked to turn into an argument but eventually calmed. Apparently, Jack was only willing to take them to Smooth Rock Falls. From there they would be on their own to Driftwood.

15

The relief of having opened up about the twins yesterday had reinvigorated Ken's spirit, and his body. At times he wasn't sure if Otto understood it all, for he did talk around things a bit, for decorum. But he didn't ask, he seemed content. Pressing him to ensure he'd grasped it wasn't wise, in Ken's view, considering it was such a delicate matter.

They were on foot again and would be for a similar distance to what they'd covered to reach Heather's house. While the darn thing broke down too often, Ken missed the car, even fixing it. Strangely, this road was less lonely, yet eerier. Plenty of other travellers who, like them, kept to themselves. Personal vehicles were rare, as Jack had predicted. Heather's was the last they'd seen going in their direction, maybe half a dozen the other way. Driverless commercial rigs, lugging up to four trailers, and the odd family Values car with barred, tinted windows frequently raised dust, but were otherwise ignorable.

One difference between this walk and the earlier one was the availability of food. It was plentiful and cheap, once in a while tasty. Heather and George had each given them a universal toll card, politely refusing the obsolete cash Ken offered in return. Otto found the purchasing process fascinating, how the card lit up when they picked up an item to show its cost and remaining balance, doing the reverse if the item was put back. A tourist thriving on new experiences.

At the same time Monica had withdrawn. Ken could not help wondering if this was due to sharing their story with her. What did she think about it? Then again, why would she think of it? If anything, her mind would be preoccupied by approaching her home. Her pace showed no hesitation, she was as intent as Otto to reach Driftwood without delay. Thus they overtook groups, even the occasional lone traveller.

Just before Driftwood, traffic bunched at a large construction site. A complex of buildings stretching a kilometre or so on the north side. Along the south, billboards proclaimed famCoch as having achieved Stage Two of its family Values transition and endorsed a rapid transition to Stage Three.

Between two billboards a lane led to a gravel parking area full of parked buses and a sign promoting a shuttle service between Driftwood and famCoch. The open air vehicles looked safe and anonymous. Ken asked a driver about the cost. Pricey, but they could afford it. He had to decide quick, the driver said, because his was nearly full and was the last one today. He rushed to get Otto and Monica but found them speaking with a small Asian woman in her forties, stoking their apprehensions.

"Don't believe the billboards, they make it look peachy keen. It's a mess. Protests can get violent. Worse than previous cities. I ought to know, I was in Barrie before it became famBar. You're better off going through Timmins if you're in a hurry. It's a free zone, anyone can go through and it's as safe as NewTor."

"Do any of these buses go to Timmins?"

"I'm afraid you'd have to get there on foot."

"How far is it from here?"

"Actually, you can take this bus to an intersection where it'll stop to let you off. You won't be the only ones. I'm not sure how far it'd be from there, though."

"Is Timmins where you're going?"

"I work in famCoch. But on the outskirts, so I avoid the nasty stuff. For now."

Ken made his presence known and asked the woman if these buses were safe and reliable. She nodded.

"The drivers are apolitical and ensure their passengers are too, while on board."

"You said there's no buses at the intersection for Timmins?"

"Oh no. No vehicles on that road. Not even automated ones. Just migrating people on foot. In both directions."

"Why?"

She laughed.

"Why? Any car would be swarmed within a kilometre."

"So the road's dangerous?"

"Not if you mind your business and keep to your side. But do bring supplies. There are no places, and I mean zero, where you can buy anything. You'll find water if you're resourceful or you know where to look. There are several lovely campgrounds for sleeping though. They're abandoned, but in good condition."

She added that altercations occurred but were rare. That they were more likely to see people travelling in opposite directions recognize each other, even exchange house keys after a brief negotiation. Sometimes the transactions were prearranged. Ken wanted to ask more but she had to rush to catch her bus as it was about to leave. He swore. Otto asked what was wrong.

"That's the bus I wanted us to take."

"We have to work out our plans, with Monica, first."

"But it was the last one."

"It wasn't. The woman told us there are several still today. The driver you spoke with probably lied to beat out the next one."

Ken reproached himself for this reminder of his naïveté, that where he was going honesty might be the exception.

"People seem to lie a lot."

"They do, Otto. You two may need me for a while."

"What are you saying?"

"I'm saying I'm going to Timmins with you. I don't think I'm ready to face whatever's going on in famCoch."

Ken was glad to see Monica's mood restored, thrilled to hear she'd go with them to Timmins, possibly all the way to NewTor. She told them she'd thought of returning to Wesley but it'd be a lonely journey.

Another bus would leave in an hour, enough time to shop for supplies, including new shoes and a used tent, after learning it would be a three-day walk to Timmins.

A roofless red and blue vehicle pulled in and a few people got off. A curvy orange bench wrapped around the sides with small benches in rows in the middle. It reminded Ken of the top of a tourist boat but on wheels. There was a line to board but it was orderly. He found a seat near Otto and Monica who sat next to each other, but they were too far apart to talk inconspicuously. Amongst the mix of people it was easy to spot those who were going to famCoch and those who would join them on the trek to Timmins by the types and amount of baggage they carried. Ken saw it was becoming more natural for Otto to act as a partner to Monica. Which was good since there were many more couples than solo travellers.

The countryside was as barren as Ken remembered the entire way to the drop off point at the intersection. They disembarked with a dozen others while forty or so continued on to famCoch. Monica took an extra moment to watch the bus raise a plume of dust on its way towards what was once her home. When the air cleared Ken noticed Otto, he was running after the bus.

"Where's he going?"

"I don't know. He saw something and bolted."

Otto slowed on reaching a billboard then suddenly stopped as if halted by a trance. Monica joined him and Ken followed, but froze at seeing the giant image of a lovely black woman flashing an alluringly taunting grin Ken knew well. The signature smirk of Esmeralda, his wife, the mother of the twins.

The face. It was her. Having stared at it, then blinked and re-stared, Otto was convinced: this was the woman in his dreams. Not as glamorous, but more real. And she even had on a robe of varying colours. More subdued pastels, less intense. The skyline didn't dominate; in fact it was inside her palm. What was bigger was her smile, which conveyed an attitude he couldn't define. The image mesmerized him. Even with Monica's unique, fresh aroma announcing her presence. Otto kept his eyes fixed on the picture, as if afraid it would disintegrate if he looked away.

"Gorgeous, isn't she?"

When Monica got no response she chuckled.

"You two look like you've seen a ghost. You know who she is, don't you?"

"It says: Doyenne of family Values."

"Ha ha, Otto, I know you can read."

He hadn't intended to be funny. He didn't want to reveal this woman had dominated his dreams the past year or so, and was his main inspiration for their journey.

"Who is she, then?"

"She started family Values, she's the one who wrote the paper that formed its foundation almost thirty years ago. The paper all students had to read at school. I didn't understand it at the time, but I do remember it became a thesis that gave rise to the family Values political movement."

Otto recalled researching the essay he'd left for Ken to see and how he'd meant to put it in, but then left it out, which now felt auspiciously intuitive.

"Is she still alive?"

"She is the Doyenne."

"Where does she live?"

"In NewTor, of course."

"What is a Doyenne?"

"A leader, like a queen, not fully in charge. There's a word."

"What word?"

"It's slipped my mind. She's more like a revered symbol."

"Does she have an actual name, this Doyenne?"

Ken had been silent to this point and his sombre interjection startled Monica.

"It's Esmeralda."

Again Esmeralda. Again the name on the letter. Otto tapped the bottom of his bag where it was, he hoped, safely concealed. Never had he felt such a sense of purpose.

"Wait. Are you saying that's your Esmeralda?"

Ken slowly nodded, but in a way that didn't invite questions. Good thing because Otto didn't know what to ask, he couldn't even summon an expected reaction to match Monica's. Luckily, neither looked to him and he started to walk off. Ken seemed to be relieved to follow and so they went on.

By now the others from their bus were far ahead, out of sight. That left them alone on the southbound side, though the other side was busy with people scurrying to catch their bus before it continued on to famCoch. While there were no stores to acquire food, they had plenty of options to pitch their tent before dark. They needn't share a site, and the weather cooperated. The only complaint: adapting to the new shoes, made with a supposedly blister-proof material, according to Monica.

On the second day they saw a young couple verbally accosted by a northbound man. The wife did her best to restrain her man and was succeeding, until the other crossed the road, ready for a fight. Her partner went to meet the man, but as they got closer they slowed, and stopped a few metres from each other before giving up. It was bizarre, until Monica suggested it was possible the three were working together and the encounter was staged to induce Ken or Otto into a fight. Though she couldn't conceive of any purpose for it.

They were doing well with food but water was running low, with no sign of a pond or small lake. Then Otto alerted them to someone approaching from behind. They decided to break the code of non-interruption to ask about water as he passed, which he was about to do. Monica became agitated, she whispered:

"It's him. Randall. From the gas station. The one we told we were going the other way."

"You told him, Monica. It was your lie."

Otto regretted his response when it made her slow and then pout, allowing the man to catch up.

"I remember you folks. Weren't you heading west?"

Their speechlessness prompted Randall to laugh amiably.

"No hard feelings. I'd have done the same."

Randall removed his hat to shake Ken's hand. He and Monica reacted well to his good nature, ignoring Heather's advice. Otto couldn't relax yet due to the same aura of fear emanating from the man Otto had detected at the gas station. This time, though, he couldn't suppress his misgivings.

"You lied too, saying you were going to famCoch."

"Otto."

"He's right. It was a lie. Most people go to famCoch. I figured you would too. Especially if you two are a couple as you claim."

Otto felt defeated when Monica laughed and invited Randall to walk with them in a way that made it difficult for anyone to protest. Ken seemed appreciative for someone who might help find rainwater that didn't need purifying. For a few kilometres, he and Randall discussed trivialities like weather and distances. Then Randall abruptly stepped into a narrow path leading into some trees, presumably to relieve himself.

"Why are you so nice to him? Remember what Heather said?"

"Oh Otto, relax."

"You like him. Is that it? We're supposed to be a couple."

"At least you don't need to work on acting jealous."

Otto sucked in his breath, then Ken put up a hand.

"Look, we can't stop him walking alongside. Better we behave friendly with him for now. Otto has a point. Both of you need to act like a married couple that wants to be together."

"I told him we're engaged. That you're our chaperone. A little flirting could expose any bad intentions he might have."

To Otto's dismay Ken nodded. The awkwardness was broken by Randall brandishing a full water flask.

"Still fresh from the storm the other night. Better get it fast."

He guided them into the same path that after a few minutes brought them to a hill. Around it they found a cistern outside a quarry that looked abandoned. The paw prints looked to belong to domesticated dogs, not wolves or coyotes. The absence of any wildlife was sad, to Otto. Only two people could fill bottles at a time. Ken and Monica went, leaving Otto alone with Randall.

"You're suspicious of me, aren't you?"

"I'm suspicious of everyone."

"A safe way to approach life, not always the best."

Otto shrugged.

"Being on edge all the time wears you down. I guess in your case you can't avoid it."

"What do you mean?"

"Your skin. It's not black or brown. It's certainly not white. At the gas station I thought it was an average of all of them. Seeing you up close, it's something else."

"Something else. Like what?"

"You know when you zoom in so far on a computer image it turns into tiny shady square pixels of different colours that are sometimes nothing like each other? Only much finer, and with some pixels seemingly in the wrong spot. Do you understand?"

"Not really."

"Between us, you're not really that girl's fiancé, are you?"

"It's none of your business."

"Despite your skin colour, I do think you're Ken's kin, though. He acts fatherly, but he's too old to be your father, isn't he?"

"You don't know what you're talking about."

"So how do you and Ken know each other?"

"It's a long story. Let me tell it, Otto?"

Otto jerked his head at Ken's interruption and slipped away to fill his bottle to let Ken talk to Randall. He was glad Monica was still at the cistern. She asked what he and the strange man talked about.

"Ken saw you and thought you looked upset."

"It was nothing."

She pressed him until Otto shared Randall's assertion he and Monica were faking their being a couple. She shrugged.

"Who cares what he thinks? He's testing you, testing us. Don't worry about it. He did get us fresh water."

While Monica's certainty comforted Otto, it exposed his lack of preparedness. If it was like this here, what would Timmins be like? Or NewTor? He filled his water and they returned to find their bags but Ken and Randall were gone.

"I guess they went ahead. Let's go."

"Hold on, Monica. I want to ask you something, in private."

"Sure."

Otto paused to take a drink, uncertain how to share what had been troubling him since Kapuskasing, and bought another few seconds by pausing to let her do the same. Instead, she crossed her arms. When he admitted not understanding what Ken said about the twins, her demeanour transformed from impatience to benevolence, as if she precisely understood his concern. She uncrossed her arms and took his hands. He pulled them away.

"Just don't answer me like I'm a child."

"All right. You do know what incest is?"

"No."

That seemed to surprise her and she took a moment to think before continuing. Her tone was gentle as she shared her belief that Ken believed Otto was his grandson, that it was the twins who'd left Otto with Ken and then ran off out of shame.

"Shame?"

"Incest is shameful, it can lead to deformities."

"Is this what Ken thinks?"

"Maybe he has no proof and can't be sure. I suspect he hopes to find them as well."

"Find who?"

"The twins. Your parents. Theoretically."

What was most surprising about this was his lack of surprise, as if she'd merely but properly rearranged particles of what he already knew into what made sense. He became silent and for a while, amidst the emptiness and broad blue sky, the remoteness of their situation and environment almost overwhelmed him. It helped to shut his eyes to absorb it and in doing so he found in it a stark fragile beauty so hypnotizing he jumped when Monica tapped his arm. He opened his eyes to see her looking sad, sad and empathetic, unaware of his brief joyful experience.

"Believe me, I know all about learning hard things."

"No, it's . . ."

"Want to know the real reason why I chose not to go back to Cochrane and to come with you and Ken?"

Otto said nothing, letting her say it.

"Because I feel my own shame, my own guilt, letting my little baby die. I'm not up to facing my family. I kind of understand why the twins, who were much younger than me, did it."

She let out a heavy sigh and Otto was about to say something to comfort her when a loud echoing crack pierced the sky.

17

"Are you all right? What happened to Randall?"

The panicky questions were expected yet that didn't make it any easier to appear calm and above all suppress the details of the last few minutes. What did help was seeing Monica's terror, which bought him an extra moment.

"What's the matter with her?"

"What do you think? The gunshot. It sounded like one of—"

He was being too calm, Ken realized, it seemed to alarm them more. But it would be impossible to try to be otherwise; he was not that good an actor.

"Of course. It's fine. It came from across the road."

Otto rushed to the packs, feeling them all, before looking back at Ken, glad for yet another few seconds to polish the deceit.

"The guns are gone."

"I left one at Heather's."

"And the other?"

"Randall took it. Stole it. Then went on ahead."

"He must have been the one to shoot it."

"I assume so, yes."

"Why would he do that?"

"Said he needed a quicker pace to meet someone."

"Okay, but why steal the gun?"

"He didn't know I knew he'd stolen it."

"You just let him?"

"Well, according to Monica we'd have to get rid of it sooner or later, right?"

Otto frowned, looked sceptical, perhaps disappointed at Ken's vagueness, but seemed to have exhausted his questions. Monica had composed herself but her face gave no indication of what she felt. Ken had feared she'd been charmed by the drifter, a problem if she made it an issue. But if there was one thing to be said for the girl, and there was plenty, she'd never let emotion trump practicality.

"He's got a gun. What if he comes back to kill us?"

"That's not a concern."

"Why not?"

"Because I'd removed the bullets, except the one you heard."

Ken reached into his bag to show the two full boxes of bullets before counting out the loose ones he'd removed.

"You didn't bring any I don't know about, Otto, did you?"

"No."

"So that's all then."

Their hesitance to accept this was understandable but made it tough to now retain his external calm. For he was rattled inside, no doubt about it, not sure how long he could avoid showing it.

"You said it came from across the road. Should we go see? In case Randall's hurt and needs our help?"

Monica's question paralyzed Ken, her suggestion made sense and could not be brushed off casually, but it had to be brushed off. He couldn't relive the confrontation, the crying, the risk he'd taken. Then explain it. Impossible. Luckily Otto interjected.

"He did steal the gun, he could be dangerous."

"Otto is right. He was probably testing it and found out it had only the one bullet. That might make him angry or scared. We'd be wiser to move on instead."

"Maybe we should keep a rotating watch at night."

Ken nodded at Otto's suggestion though he knew in his heart it was pointless, that there was no threat. He had to play along, continue suppressing what happened indefinitely, ride out the extra guilt of deceiving Otto.

Prior to this accursed road, Ken had never lied to the boy. He had feared going back to the civilized world might corrupt him, he didn't expect it to happen so fast. Re-corrupt him; he was no angel before he left that world. But lying was a price he'd pay to preserve Otto's incorruptness. A small price compared to what he'd just paid to get rid of a tangible threat. A bargain.

The sun was lowering, a gentle breeze picking up when they reached Bigwater Lake campground, which Ken had frequently visited on camping trips with his stepmother and her cousins. It was on the other side of the road, which made them hesitant to cross. Exhaustion compelled them to try.

The crossing was uneventful and they found a secluded, tree-covered site fifty metres from the water. Otto caught three fish they cooked over a fire they extinguished right after eating. The sudden cold left them no option but to get under cover to sleep. Ken benefited from Monica's body heat first as Otto kept watch.

He only managed an hour's sleep before she got up as she did at least once every night to relieve herself. Her absence created a chill that didn't go away when she returned. Now he had to go. Ken rose, paused to let his eyes adapt to the dark, so they'd then orientate his position and locate Otto at his post, before walking the other way towards the road. The eerie silence was comforting until he heard a shuffle of feet as he zipped up. Otto.

"Ken, I need to ask you something."

"If it's about Randall . . ."

"No. About the twins. And me. I talked to Monica. She said you think I'm their son and . . ."

It struck Ken that Otto hadn't grasped fully all he'd revealed about the twins after all. Ken had been too satisfied letting it go, trusting the boy would fill the gaps and make the connections, not ensuring what he'd said was properly interpreted. Oddly, Otto bringing it up revitalized the faint hope he was mistaken, resurrected old rationales: no unequivocal evidence; the boy not taking after Felix or Felicity in an obvious way; his self-reliance, strength; most encouragingly, there being no apparent physical or mental abnormality.

"There's no proof, mind you."

"Proof? Like a deformity?"

"Precisely. You're as perfect as any kid could be. If there was an issue it would have come out long ago."

Ken's smile punctuated the lie efficiently with a truth. The boy was an ideal male specimen, human specimen for that matter.

"But you can't say it's not true, can you?"

"No."

"What if it is, what if the deformity is in my head?"

"What do you mean?"

"I have dreams, visions. Of a city, or my imagination's idea of a city. In front is a large woman. Not fat large, but a giant who could crush a city or swipe it away."

"All dreams are strange."

"Her face is the one on the family Values billboards."

Ken was grateful for the darkness, not trusting his reaction to the image of Esmeralda flashing in his mind. Spooky. She could be the boy's grandmother.

"How long have you had these dreams?"

"She was your wife, right? If it's true she's my grandmother. And she's famous. Important."

"Yes."

"If you know her, maybe we can see her. Maybe she can verify my identity. Unless you two hate each other."

"No. There was never hate."

"So she would help you? And then help me?"

"I don't know."

"We can at least try."

"I suppose."

Ken realized he and Otto had arrived at the same level, that he needn't hold back anymore. About that. Of course, Otto did not suspect a thing about Randall, didn't need to know.

"How about I take the watch, you get some rest."

They were groggy in the morning and almost forget they had to cross the road again. A quick reconnaissance showed no one had slept near them last night but they saw two separate groups of northbound people entering the park. They waited until the newcomers settled before exiting.

A mist obscured the view of the road ahead. Ken estimated they'd reach Timmins by noon. An hour later the road widened and they came upon hundreds of long, flat buildings Ken didn't recognize. It reminded him of their arrival at Kapuskasing, but as if that city's towers' floors had been un-stacked in three- or four-storey sets across the landscape. Also, these were occupied and full of activity, including many vehicles.

A sign welcomed them to the city of Timmins with the motto: "Ideology free since '33" emblazoned under a digital board with red numbers like a stock ticker incrementing to two million. The wider road had to be shared with cars now too. An unexpected rush of nostalgia hit Ken seeing streets and buildings associated with the anticipation of visiting his stepmother, of staying at a clean house to enjoy her simple but delicious cooking.

It was still a small city in the core. It hadn't grown upward, it had sprawled outward. Impossible to distinguish from the city of thirty, even forty years ago. Except the people. A marked lack of Indians, but plenty with dark skin. Ironically, Otto might feel strange in a place where his skin tone wasn't unique. The boy showed no indication of it, only saying he was hungry.

They came upon a donut shop, rather what used to be one. In fact, the one at which he'd dropped off Esmeralda that one time. Esmeralda. Funny how she kept resurfacing. He gave Monica a toll card to place their order while he and Otto found a table.

"What do you think?"

"I've seen all kinds of people, but no Indians."

So Otto had noticed. It was strange as there were plenty living there at one time, including many of Vanessa's relatives. Monica came by with a tray of donuts and cups of fruit juice. The sugar infected the youngsters with new energy, and launched another book discussion.

To distract from that, Ken tried to recall that encounter with Esmeralda. He'd been young, maybe twenty. He'd had plenty of girlfriends but was always ready for more. Seeing the gorgeous black girl he'd met briefly at school in a clinic made him ignore the obvious reason she'd be there. Especially after she'd let him drive her to meet her friend here. Too bad he hadn't pushed to stay in touch. If they had then, instead of reuniting later . . . who knows?

On a screen above them a black man in a fine suit was being interviewed by a reporter. Superimposed under the interviewee was a name, James Carson, and a title: Town Counsellor. An old red building Ken recognized stood in the background.

James in Timmins? Of course. It was at Vanessa's funeral that James told Ken he was moving to Timmins with a husband with a name Ken couldn't recall. And hadn't James, long before that, revealed his family owned a cottage around Timmins? Perhaps James was the friend waiting for Esmeralda. Funny that neither had ever discussed it. Ken urged Otto and Monica to wrap up their talk and finish eating. He wanted to find James.

They passed hotels and homes offering rooms, but Otto and Monica kept quiet until they stopped and Monica said:

"This isn't a place to stay, it's the city hall."

"I may know someone here. Wait for me."

It took several minutes to convince the receptionist to call up James, seconds for the call to end. She smiled at him.

"Councillor Carson will be right down."

Her words ought to have been a balm for Ken, but instead he was struck by a dilemma: what the hell would he say to James, how would he explain Otto and Monica?

18

The home belonging to Ken's old friend, James, was the fanciest Otto had ever seen. Set back from a sprawling but pristine front lawn, on a quiet dead-end lane, it had a large backyard with a kidney-shaped pool surrounded by a wraparound deck several metres from a pair of French doors. A wooded area prime for hiking or hunting lay beyond. Monica was in the pool, in a borrowed red bikini that barely fit her, splashing around with another girl named Desirae who was spending a few weeks in

Timmins with her dad before school. Otto assumed James was her father, until learning it was Roscoe, James's husband, a lawyer still in his office near city hall. Otto had never heard of a marriage between two men before.

The girls kept prodding Otto to join them. He wanted to since it was hot and he loved to swim. But real swimming. They were only being silly, splashing and yakking. But the real reason he didn't was the realization this had to be the James in the letter, when Esmeralda's name came up between James and Ken, then discovering they'd all actually met in school as teenagers.

"She's really the head of this family Values thing?"

"Esmeralda is the Doyenne, a figurehead. Her influence is not what it used to be and her actual powers are limited. But she is the originator."

"She could still help us, right Ken?"

Ken frowned and Otto couldn't understand why. They agreed to avoid mentioning Wesley, Cochrane, Randall, the twins, but not questions about their destination. That wasn't secret, was it?

"Help you? With what?"

"Get to NewTor and find out about my parents."

"I see. So that's where you're headed."

Otto wasn't sure if that was a question but then James stepped away to replenish Ken's beer and his glass of wine. He offered to top up Otto's lemonade, but it was still full. He'd only sipped at it to savour its tangy sourness. James returned with drinks and a large plate of nachos with a variety of dips.

"You going to NewTor, Ken. That surprises me."

"He's only going because I asked him to take me."

"I see. It's been what, twenty-eight years, since you were last there? How much do you know about the changes?"

"You mean family Values?"

"Yes."

"We've picked up pieces here and there. Maybe you could fill the gaps for us."

A smirk from Desirae who had climbed out of the pool to get a towel was matched by James.

"Desirae's right. I'm not the best to tell about it. She is, though. Honey, maybe you can put together something for our guests."

"I'd love to."

Otto found it fascinating how Desirae and James seemed to be in disagreement yet still fond of each other. They respected each other. He also found himself more interested in what this family Values truly was, beyond posters, slogans, or vague arguments. She ran into the house, followed by Monica.

"At least tell me, James, what's changed in Toronto?"

"For one, it's now called NewTor."

"I did know that."

"Where to begin. Remember the office buildings? Now they're all residences too, people living and working in the same place, reducing but not eliminating the need for more. Main streets are not used by personal cars—they don't exist anymore—but have been re-engineered for exclusive use by transit and other utility vehicles. Hence the smaller streets are packed with people and at times the congestion is unbearable. The need for housing is so great homeowners are converting their garages into rental units or suites for relatives. There is better breathable space due to the control of motorized traffic. Of course there's the elimination of the police as well as the homeless as so much is managed by a centralized entity you'll hear about from Desirae."

"Is it the thing called *arbiter*?"

"Very good, Ken. So you've learned a little. Although *arbiter* is much more than that."

"I have a question, Mr. Carson. Why aren't there any Indians here? Ken says he used to know lots who lived here."

"Indigenous nations have negotiated control of rural zones at the cost of living in urban zones. Hence, you won't see Indians here or in NewTor or any city that's reached Stage Two, unless as part of a diplomatic mission. Politics, you know."

Ken scowled but Otto liked that word: politics. Of course, he didn't grasp its true meaning, but hearing it generated an innate feeling pushing him to want to know, despite an equally strong instinct doing so would annoy Ken. Before he could ask another question, James patted his shoulder.

"How about you take a spin in the pool while Ken and I talk?"

Despite his eagerness to hear more, Otto was glad to be alone, cooling down with leisurely laps. Swimming was a distraction, he felt himself tiring quickly, realizing it had been exhausting getting to this point on a journey that so far had been long with extended periods of tedium, that nonetheless was turning out in ways he'd never expected.

In truth his expectations weren't clear at the start, but he saw them gradually becoming clearer, although attaining full clarity still felt remote. He might have been dejected by that at the start but he now accepted the possibility he himself needed to absorb it all, and grow to process it fully. There was a lot he'd learned so far, and with each phase—setting out, meeting Wesley and Monica, staying at George's, bonding with Monica at Heather's, what Ken said at Kapuskasing, the trek to Timmins—more was added. No single person or place could reveal the entire picture to him, he had to piece things together himself to come to his own understanding of the world and of himself.

The vagueness of his goals, of what he was seeking, remained, and he was fine with that. It was enough to keep going as long as it took. Ken's and Monica's motivations were irrelevant to his and Otto started to sense his would go beyond theirs, that there would come a point when he'd be fully on his own.

Otto heard the steps with his head under water, and peeked at the wooden stairs leading to the deck, expecting to see Ken. Instead, a stranger in a pinstripe suit with the look of someone expecting to see more people, holding two large cloth bags, a slight stain at the bottom of one. He nodded at Otto and smiled, then introduced himself as Roscoe.

"You must be Otto."

"Pleased to meet you. Thank you for having us here."

"I hope you're enjoying it."

James's husband was tall and thin, unlike James whose build was stockier. But Roscoe was as cheery as James. And younger, despite a silver beard and slight limp, with no wrinkles around his eyes, and the same wide smile he saw in Desirae, whenever she let it out. Otto felt as welcome here as he had at Heather's. Roscoe excused himself to bring the bags inside.

19

Since Otto came into his life, particularly after moving to the last camp, months, even years, might pass between contact with friends. Now, in a span of just two weeks, this was Ken's third visit with someone important from his past. But unlike Heather and George, who were always on his side, James had one mark against him: introducing Esmeralda to that bastard Baxter, the man who convinced Ken's wife to forego her finance degree for one in sociology. A decision that ultimately led to the breakup. Yet Ken respected James, didn't blame him for it, had assumed his actions came from a good place. So how could he explain his trepidation following James into the basement? Perhaps it was a latent resentment making him fear the ensuing discussion could shatter his image of his friend. Or vice versa.

A large irregularly-shaped recreation area with ceiling-high shelves packed with books and only books. Lights came on with their movements to brighten the space and keep it from feeling subterranean. Some of the volumes took on a glow.

"Don't let Otto down here, he'd never leave."

"He likes basements?"

"No, books."

"Is that so? Well, you know who else likes books?"

"Are we going to talk about her already?"

"You're right, let's relax first."

James bid Ken to sit in a large recliner while he pulled open a thin drawer from a mahogany desk, removed two cigars and an ornate lighter, and took them to the other recliner. A small oval table separated them. They lit the cigars and took a few puffs.

"Are all these yours?"

"Roscoe's. He's an avid reader but a more avid collector."

"Impressive."

"Yes. And in NewTor, illegal."

"Books are illegal?"

"Physical books. In NewTor or any family Values city. Not so much because of their content but because they unnecessarily take up space. Every book, movie, musical recording, and other media is stored in *reservoir*, a subset of *arbiter*, that Desirae will talk about. They're accessible via personal devices called Values tokens people wear all the time. You'll get a temporary one on arrival. These are directly linked up with *arbiter*, through which they have access to *reservoir*."

"It sounds convoluted. Is there a reason for telling me this?"

"Just trying to prepare you for the various changes."

"I appreciate it."

James's demeanour mystified Ken. He was uncertain whether the man was being supportive or contrary, whether ready to aid Ken and Otto on their journey or intent on sabotaging it. Either way it tested his trust of James. Fair enough, because apparently James was ready to test his trust of Ken.

"Who precisely are these young people with you?"

Ken had already decided to share with James all he'd shared earlier with Monica and Otto. That experience eased the telling now. James kept sombre, save for a few expressions of surprise, only interrupting to console Ken about the twins, which helped prevent Ken mentioning the encounter with Randall. When he'd finished, James walked to a decanter and poured two scotches. The bitterness at first was awful, yet wonderfully nostalgic. The alcohol made him woozy, but calm.

"Quite the story. I remember your twins at the funeral . . ."

"And?"

"Actually it was Roscoe who noticed they were a little close. You've not seen them since?"

"One of my friends, Heather, did, long ago."

"Everything was long ago, wasn't it?"

"Time isn't a big factor in my life. Things come to mind, not dates."

"Uh huh. I still feel a tug of guilt for introducing Esmeralda to Baxter, my part in her changing the course of her studies, her life, and yours. But each time I indulge in such thinking, I come to the conclusion things would've turned out as they did with or without my interference. Over time."

"She'd have made an awful accountant."

James chuckled.

"Generous of you to say so, Ken, but if I could have foreseen the difficulties for you and those kids—I guess this is my way of apologizing."

"Those events are done. I'm living now."

"I like that. Elliptical yet direct. So typically Ken."

"It's all in the past. Today is today."

"Right. Speaking of today, the past, have you been in NewTor, since it was renamed?"

"No."

"You'd be a current day Rip van Winkle."

"Except I'd be aware of the changes."

"On the surface. What I'm trying to convey is I'm unconvinced you're up to it. That world's passed you by. If you perceived it as hostile before . . ."

Ken was silent. The cigar was making him ill. He put it down, had a few sips of scotch.

"If the objective is verifying Otto's parentage, that can be done here with a simple DNA test. It can prove beyond doubt you're his grandfather. Or that you aren't. It'll confirm if his biological genes are from siblings to confirm or contradict your suspicion. That's all you really want, isn't it?"

"We're intent on going to Toronto. NewTor."

"But why?"

"Otto should meet Esmeralda, his grandmother, if it turns out she is his grandmother. Then she should meet him too."

"Hmm."

Ken shut up, sensing he was being goaded into admitting an ulterior motive. James smiled knowingly.

"You see my concern for you?"

"Not really."

"Going back to a world you left, which has not only changed beyond what I think you'd expect, but has changed largely due to Esmeralda. I saw how deep it got between you two. Which makes me unsure you want to, or should, go there."

"You think I want a reconciliation? After all these years?"

"If you did, what would you expect from her?"

"Are you saying she'd reject me?"

"I have no idea about that. I suspect she actually would like to see you, to see how you are now. But she's rather isolated, so I can't be certain."

"What about Baxter? I assume they're still together."

"As far as I know. A more tangible obstacle you'd be better off avoiding."

This conversation was frustrating Ken. He finished his drink and wanted to end it to get back to the pool. Outside. Fresh air. Only when he started to rise, James asked him to stay put, while he refilled their glasses.

"Tell me, Ken, be honest. Are you hoping to reunite with her and to rekindle—?"

"Definitely not."

Ken's conviction cut off James pursuing that avenue to instead get to the point. Which was proposing that Desirae be the one to accompany Otto to NewTor, not Ken. She could return to school early and help Otto access the family Values academy's library and other resources.

"And what about me?"

"Stay here as long as you like, or go back."

The proposal was like a gateway opening to an outcome Ken desperately desired, but hated for the guilt of abandoning Otto. That guilt passed on realizing his presence, filled with bitterness and prejudice that inevitably would surface, could actually be a hindrance to the boy. Ken nodded slowly.

"Would she be willing to do it?"

"She's ambitious. The idea of travelling with the grandson of the Doyenne would be irresistible to her."

"It's not as if he can go to Esmeralda and introduce himself."

"Desirae knows that. What I'll propose to her, if you and Otto allow, is to make Otto the subject of her thesis on say the culture shock of a family Values on someone who's never been exposed to it. She's clever, she'll figure out how to word it for herself."

"You mean treat him like a savage."

"I'll understand if you don't approve."

James pointed out Desirae was highly knowledgeable about the regulations, protocols, bureaucracies they'd encounter. She, unlike Ken, wouldn't let those procedures rile or upset her. Ken could stay with James and Roscoe. Monica was welcome to stay in Timmins with Ken.

It was hard to argue James's points. Furthermore, the appeal of living in this large house until Otto returned was undeniable. They enjoyed another drink while finishing their cigars to work out specifics. Including not trying to notify Esmeralda, trusting that at the academy an opportunity for incidental contact would arise. James's primary concern was Desirae, whose ambitious impatience might compel her to initiate contact prematurely.

"She's pestered me all summer for an introduction letter. I've resisted because I don't think it would help since Esmeralda and I are no longer on speaking terms."

"What? This is news to me."

"It shouldn't be. I mentioned it at your stepmother's funeral."

"That's right, but you never explained."

"You remember me showing you the paper she'd written, the one inspired by our class project in Grade Eight?"

"Yes."

James took a breath and told him it began when her paper got promoted to a thesis with the intent to actualize her ideas. She refused James's recommendation she release her connection to it by admitting she'd written it in jest to lampoon social media. He threatened to expose emails in which she'd said as much. Baxter van Leer got wind of it, got ahead of the situation by planting it as a rumour, such that if James were to make a fuss he'd look a fool and possibly get censured or even fired. The professor even created a faux anti-family Values movement that vanished once James left on his own to be with Roscoe in Timmins.

"She and I haven't spoken since."

"Are you and Baxter still friends?"

"No."

The terseness of his response felt good to Ken. As did hearing James say he was "cancelled" by Baxter not due to Esmeralda or her paper, but for being critical of one the professor published on a controversial topic. For some reason, Ken knew its subject had been racial blending, but felt no desire to confirm that.

"It happened before I saw you at your stepmother's funeral. It was a blessing in disguise for it was soon after that I met Roscoe and we decided to buy this property in Timmins. Remember?"

"I do."

"Don't worry about Baxter. He's not as evil as you or I like to make him out to be. Besides, other than stopping the trip, Otto is out of your control, isn't he?"

"The boy's eighteen, you're right. But he's naive. He trusts that people won't lie."

James smiled.

"The world has changed in unusual ways. One thing I will say is it's no longer physically dangerous. The only true danger is in cities in transition, where borders aren't yet well controlled. I'm sure Otto will be able to handle himself."

"And Desirae is still only a student."

"On that point, tell me Ken, do you have regrets in life? Not specific events you'd want to change, but general perspectives?"

Ken shrugged, never one for abstracts.

"You've lived an unusual life, Ken, one that correlates to that kid I met in middle school. It wouldn't surprise me to hear you truthfully say you had no regrets. That's a compliment."

"What about you? You have regrets?"

"Sure. And you mentioning Desirae's youth brings a specific one to mind. That all my life I treated adults as adults, children as children. Before realizing that our world had reached a point when it should have been the other way around."

20

Otto joined everyone gathered in the kitchen, circling a gigantic island with a patterned quartz counter covered to its edges with dinner plates of food. On the floor to the side, the bags Roscoe had carried, stuffed with emptied Styrofoam containers.

"I'd have cooked something nice."

"I know Des, honey. But neither the stove or oven is working."

"What? Since when?"

"Since this morning when I tried to fry some eggs."

It was fine with Otto. He enjoyed the salty, greasy ribs, pizza, chicken wings, and fries, even though they made his stomach ill at first. Ken had it worse and ate only a tiny amount. Same with Monica. Both did better with the vanilla ice cream Desirae had made the day before. While the hosts cleaned up, the travellers each went to a bedroom for a nap. It had started raining, with thunder and lighting that made the sleeping easier.

They assembled an hour later in the large living room. Roscoe opened several bottles of wine, which everyone drank, except Otto who opted for a fizzy raspberry ginger ale. Monica was her old self but Ken struggled to stay alert. The talk stayed polite, general, prosaic, until at some point it dovetailed into a primer on family Values, facilitated by Desirae who revelled in the role. Her ambition for a career in family Values administration was evident in her enthusiasm and professionalism. Such a different girl, or woman, from the silly one splashing around in the pool with Monica. For a tiny person her presence, aided by a husky voice, exuded command and instilled confidence and interest in Otto.

"family Values began humbly with the kernel of an idea from the Doyenne while attending university in 2020. It was a bizarre year ruled by a pandemic, racial issues, ideological issues, and the seeds of the political civil war in the United States still going on, which might never end in our lifetimes. In this environment, Esmeralda Williams wrote and published her seminal work that became the foundation of family Values."

Desirae paused when James held up his hand to nudge Ken who seemed to be nodding off. While to the rest it seemed Ken was drifting off, Otto guessed he was alert, deliberately trying to contain any reaction. James motioned Desirae to go on.

"She published a paper called *filial Values* wherein she laid out an abstract resolution to the ideological divides plaguing the world then—gender, race, identity, social, etc. Her proposal set out a general way to arbitrate conflict with algorithms all could agree to that would allow all humans to live their lives based on individual choices: leftwing, rightwing, anywhere in between.

She saw all conflicts as superficially rooted in loss of individual identity, based on the tendency of people to identify more with identity groups, or resist on that basis. If the identity group was tamed, she hypothesized, people could achieve a constructively fresh understanding of human conflict. Either outcome to her was preferable to the status quo."

"I have a copy of the original, if you're interested, Ken."

"Maybe later."

Ken's voice was weak. Otto noticed him shiver. He'd never looked this bad, Otto thought, not even during that deep winter before the last warming. Ken also looked as if any suggestion he go rest would not be received well. Monica raised a hand to ask to read it. Otto was glad she did, he wanted to as well. James nodded for Desirae to continue.

"It's such a bedrock for family Values now but her paper was not widely read at first. In fact, it lay dormant until 2027 when she was encouraged to develop it into a full thesis. It started as a thesis, but it quickly evolved into a design, supported by ideas from a large staff of technical consultants.

"What prompted this was the invention of a method to access people's physiologies via biologically attachable devices that by osmosis tapped into one's RNA, DNA, blood, biology—I'm not a scientist so don't ask me the specifics. It was developed at first to manage vaccinations for pandemics but it enabled the critical element of her paper: the Values badge, or Values token as we now know it, renamed after filial Values was rebranded."

Otto noticed Desirae put her hand to her chest at this point, but then pull it away quickly, almost self-consciously.

"filial Values—the original name of her idea—might still have remained a thesis indefinitely if not for the changes occurring in the world, primarily the severing of the provinces from Canada, the civil wars in the United States, and escalating global threats from China's growth, and Russia's expansion to the polar north as it became cultivatable. Weak national governments combined with weaker provincial ones led to the establishment of Quebec, including the capital area, and Nova Canada, and its annexation of Ontario's north-western parts, as separate nations."

An image of the school report he'd written seven years earlier came to Otto, and it made him cringe, how childishly simple it was. Lucky he hadn't brought that with him, how embarrassing it would be for someone as smart as Desirae to see it.

"The United States was concerned and it started talks to have the rest of Ontario join America as a state. Complications from their civil war made it untenable politically or logistically. Also, they didn't want to risk antagonizing Quebec or Nova Canada. The escalation of global tensions all North America feared had to have a solution as a weak Ontario posed a threat to America. Esmeralda's mentor, Professor Baxter van Leer, then proposed rebranding filial Values as family Values, as a vehicle to get the US to fund its development in exchange for the right to bolster our borders with their military protection. They loved the idea but insisted it receive democratic approval from Ontarians first. Thus her thesis also became a political movement."

"And made her ideas veer from their original intent to suit the political ambitions of van Leer and others, don't forget that."

James's interruption almost sounded like an apology. For Ken, who remained still. Desirae gave James a wry smile.

"Naturally the paper had to evolve and expand to support the larger scope and incorporate artificial intelligence components."

"Come on, Des. That artificial intelligence component, *arbiter*, is wrought with ideology, corrupted to exploit pandemics and natural disasters, tilt elections, justify wars, enable corruption, steal property. Nothing in Esmeralda's paper, nor in any record, indicates with what rules and algorithms *arbiter* gets seeded."

"*arbiter* works. People are happy with it."

"Happy? It's so bloated now it's the primary cause of frequent, prolonged power outages, water shortages, contaminations, and so on."

Desirae rolled her eyes.

"That's your opinion. It's true, those things happen but they're temporary and quickly fixed. They're acceptable disruptions in life people have become used to. For most, family Values gives them a good enough existence."

James then pointed at Ken, Roscoe, and himself.

"What people think is good enough now would be considered practically destitute in our time. Never mind the freedoms lost to those electronic leashes, the Values tokens."

"A small price to pay to be rid of police and wars and sickness and homelessness and other threats. Prisons. Nuclear war."

"And James, to be fair, you often tell me how wonderful it is to have the world no longer run by oligopolies and saturated by their ugly marketing campaigns."

"That's right, thanks Dad."

"Hold on, Roscoe. We were around in the 2030s at the start of *arbiter* absorbing private corporations. We both know it wasn't to eliminate corporations but to mine their talent because of the incompetence rampant within family Values. We witnessed the potential crumbling, wishing it, only to see them replenish their executives from those companies. In essence the poached talent was conscripted to infuse *arbiter* with the skills and manpower to monopolize its potential alternatives."

James then turned to Desirae and smiled.

"My dear stepdaughter, while I'm grateful to not be assaulted by onslaughts of advertisements, I doubt the cost was worth it."

"You mean the Values tokens that the Doyenne, your friend, envisioned?"

"No, I mean the loss in variety, in quality that, unfortunately, has rippled up here too. While I won't call it communism, this is similar to how people in Soviet countries lived a century ago. I admit, there has been a resurgence in small shops and private restaurants offering different cuisines, but these will eventually die out or get integrated until everything is homogenized."

James paused, his expression turning grim, yet still remaining avuncular and supportive.

"Forgive this old man lamenting what's lost, especially since it is for what you and Otis and Monica never had, and will never miss. I will add Esmeralda never envisioned the tokens turning turn out so powerful or comprehensive."

Desirae scowled but didn't contradict the assertion. The gap it left in the discussion was oddly fascinating. Otto attributed it to the absence of anger in their arguing. James's goading was more to tease or test her than convince her, he guessed. James meant what he said, he wasn't acting, as Otto did detect frustration at times. Each time accompanied by a glance at his old friend, then after no response from Ken, a softening of tone.

Monica asked why family was in lower case. Otto couldn't care less about that, but found James's response interesting.

"To promote a preferential distinction for groups, or family, in an ironic way. Most are unaware Esmeralda's paper was crafted tongue-in-cheek. She never expected it to be realized, let alone turn into what it did."

Desirae's face enlivened slowly until it displayed a dark grin, with a tone to match that of James.

"That's only a rumour. It only sounds convincing because you once knew her. Did she tell you so explicitly, in person? Funny. I ask you all the time to use your connection to help me and you say it's not worth it because you two had a falling out. Yet you claim to know her intent?"

James sighed as if regretting the discussion going this way but with no desire to concede.

"I'm talking about her original intent. You read the paper. She called it filial Values, not family Values. She defined *filials* and *filiations*, not *familyars* and *fams*. Badges, not tokens. I could go on and on."

"Semantics. Besides, she wrote the thesis with those changes, didn't she?"

Otto was impressed by Desirae's poise, yet also felt this was going in circles. He wanted to know more.

"*filials*? *familyars*? What is that?"

James leaned back. Perhaps as a peace offering, he put out his palms to let Desirae continue uninterrupted. She then explained individuals in family Values cities are either registered or not. If registered, they are *familyars*—*filials* in the original paper—and belong to one or more *fams*—*filiations* in the original—while the rest are *Indos*, linked only to *arbiter*. Different restrictions, rules, and privileges apply depending on one's designation.

"For instance, I'm a *familyar*, the only one of us in this room. You'd all be *Indos* in a family Values city. I had to register with a *fam*—in fact I'm registered with three—and become a *familyar* to attend the academy because they don't allow *Indos*."

"So if you didn't go to the school you'd still be an *Indo*?"

Desirae looked uncomfortable. Roscoe stood up.

"I think we're losing them. At least for now."

Everyone except Otto agreed. He liked the way Desirae talked and wanted to learn more. She was smart but not too smart. Her voice did get nagging at times but was generally fluid, bright. Precisely the type of voice he'd imagine from the woman in his dreams. It was possible Desirae was deliberately emulating the real voice of her idol, the Doyenne. Alas, she too was content to wrap it up. Just as Roscoe rose, a question came to Otto.

"So when is family Values coming to Timmins?"

"Never."

Roscoe and James said this in unison and Otto sat up.

"Why not?"

Roscoe explained that long ago Timmins had insulated itself from family Values by adopting opposing strategies to provide an alternative. Such as keeping open borders and letting people freely come and go with or without vaccinations or quarantines. A freer alternate society built on the will of a citizenry with like-minded folks such as James and Roscoe, kept free of ideology.

"Timmins has become a sanctuary for those unhappy with the restrictions of family Values, or Quebec, or Nova Canada. Those unsure can stay here without fear of recrimination for whatever way they choose. Timmins is a sort of way station for those who do know too, a safe stopping point, and that provides revenue for our businesses. This is an exciting place, constantly in flux, a haven for individuals willing to abide by certain principles: to always think for oneself; champion the individual, eschew the group; let dignity rule over fear; never cast oneself as a victim."

"By individual, Roscoe doesn't mean the capitalized *Indo* of family Values. That's a different beast . . ."

"Right, James. But let's clarify that, regardless of our personal views, we don't hate family Values or have an opinion about it. We're open to all ideas. Our city is like a Switzerland, neutral in an ideological sense. We only resist anyone trying to enforce an ideology or obligating others to combat an ideology. We believe in individual choice and exist to provide an environment where people are free to consider and make those choices, then to stay or move on."

Otto was impressed and could see it impressed Monica too.

"If family Values is so powerful, won't they assert themselves physically?"

James answered her by saying Timmins was unforeseen by family Values. They didn't expect so many citizens would refute their beliefs, let alone assemble in remote Timmins to transform it into a major city almost overnight.

"Now it's too late for them to act. Since family Values takes an exorbitant amount of energy and resources, they've had to fully outsource their forces to the United States. Even if the US could spare resources from its civil and international conflicts, beyond protecting Ontario they'd have little desire to instigate conflict within Ontario. In fact, they see Timmins as useful as an outlet, helping stem or divert internal revolt."

Otto noticed Desirae lift her eyebrows, but she said nothing.

21

It was only accumulated exhaustion from travelling exacerbated by personal concerns, some open, others Ken, with great effort, kept to himself, ailing him. Until something contradicted that, he'd refuse suggestions to consult a doctor. The cool basement would do as a sanctuary, never more so than now as the others prepared for a fishing trip, during which James was to share his idea that Otto continue to NewTor with his stepdaughter, and without Ken. He longed for a spell of solitude but would settle having Monica around in case his health deteriorated. They'd have gone by now but James got an urgent call delaying their departure, that led to a sudden need to speak with Ken. Instinct told Ken to get all the rest he could prior to this discussion, that he'd need it. He felt ready now so this time he sat up on hearing the steps.

"Good, you're awake. Hope you feel better, stronger. Because there's something we need to talk about."

"So I gathered. Sounds serious."

"It appears a corpse was found, shot dead not far out of town. Found by migrants at a campground. One you three might have stopped at around the estimated time of death."

"Yes. And?"

"He's a male family Values *Indo* but they can't identify him as he was found without his Values token."

"That's that thing Desirae talked about, right?"

"Yes. His was a wrist bracelet, like a watch."

James's grim smile troubled Ken. He was beginning to feel as he had at George's, that he was about to be cast out.

"How would they know this corpse was a—what was it you'd called it?"

"A family Values *Indo*."

"I don't understand. Don't they have DNA, stuff like that?"

"They do. But individual DNA data isn't available to humans, by design. For privacy reasons. Its designers didn't consider the possibility of anyone separated from their Values token."

Ken sat up but had to slow himself down to not give away his interest in this. It was possible this could pass. He repeated the question.

"They smelled the fam-elixir expunged by the corpse."

"fam-elixir?"

"It's an injected fluid that activates the Values token to connect biologically to *arbiter*."

"You're kidding. People inject themselves—I guess if they're willing to take vaccinations and boosters . . ."

"That's right. In fact, it was during the development of a new vaccinations about twelve years ago a method was discovered to tap into human blood this way."

"What way?"

"Well, that's never been shared. Never will be shared."

Curiosity almost overcame Ken's instinct to stop talking, as he was coming close to incriminating himself, evidenced by how James studied him while continuing to explain.

"Because of the odd situation, the discovery of a family Values corpse with no Values token, it was reported to the Exceptions Office, a department of family Values. They're about to launch an investigation, I may be asked to participate. You and Monica may be interviewed as potential witnesses. I expect to be back before then but, just in case, I wanted to let you know, if I can't be here. And to see if you had anything to share now."

"We never saw or heard anything, I assure you."

"So you're okay being interviewed?"

"It's fine by me. But I've got nothing to share."

"Okay. Oh, one other thing."

James went to a bookshelf, pulled out a binder, and from that he extracted a small stack of bound paper, which he handed to Ken, who read the title aloud.

"filial Values. What's this?"

"A copy of the paper Esmeralda wrote."

"It looks academic."

"I know, I wanted to show it to you since it's the cause of my rift with her. If you read it, you might understand better."

"Understand what? family Values? Or why in one instant you seem against it and accepting at another?"

"Maybe both. I get your confusion, I feel it too. It seems over time I've lost my urge to fight such things. Which I think is a reason family Values has become endemic. Everyone against it has been worn down. Maybe I'm holding a hope your reading it might reinvigorate my old resistance."

"I don't know. I'm not sure I want to get into that."

"That's fine. If not, give it to Monica. She said last night she wanted to read it."

"Sure."

"Remember me saying Esmeralda's inspiration came from that project the three of us did in Grade Eight?"

Ken couldn't help smiling melancholically at that memory.

"So what mark did we end up getting?"

"A+."

Once James left, Ken set the paper aside and reached into his pocket for the item he'd taken from Felix's body. He smelled it, it had no trace of any odour. It had to be what James described, an elixir or something like that. He'd have left it if not for a buzz it emanated and the spasms that made Ken search the corpse. It took some time to find it and then remove it from Felix's wrist. Once he did the body stopped moving.

Funny, when he'd taken the heart-shaped pendant, it flashed a series of colours, starting with a fading blue that reddened but then suddenly went purple. Now it was colourless.

22

This was the first time Otto had been without Ken or Monica since she'd joined them, yet he felt at ease. He liked Desirae. She was a lot like her father but better at catching fish. Not as good as Otto—three to his five—but close. No one could match James and his half dozen, though. Impressive, but of course it was his connection to Esmeralda and Ken that Otto found intriguing in James. He tapped his pants pocket to ensure the letter was still there, anxious to show it to James, to ask his advice.

"There's a keeper. That's dinner. That's enough."

It was Roscoe netting a large rainbow trout Desirae had just caught. Everyone took in their poles, as if done for the day, and they pulled anchor. It was odd being on a small yacht, gliding effortlessly with such speed, arms motionless. Otto didn't much care for the jostling and also felt it was cheating to get to prime fishing spots so quickly. James steered the boat towards a tiny island and anchored a hundred metres offshore. Desirae pulled down her shorts and removed her top, revealing a bikini with pink swirls. Roscoe already had his swimsuit on and without a word they jumped in the water and swam off. Otto asked where they were going and James pointed towards the island.

"That's where we'll camp tonight. It'll be less crowded. They'll scout a spot for us."

Otto saw two strong but different swimmers, Desirae's brash strokes versus Roscoe's patient smooth ones. She held a lead the first forty metres but he caught her and stayed in front. James dug into a cooler to grab two cans of cold lemonade. The bright sun compelled them to put on baseball caps before opening the drinks. By then Roscoe and Desirae had reached shallow water and were wading in.

"I sensed you wanted to talk with me, to perhaps fill in gaps. Ken isn't one to reveal a lot. Do tell me if I'm wrong about that."

"You're not. I'd like to know more about Esmeralda. Ken too."

James motioned Otto to sit back, to relax. He waited until the others reached shore.

"The people we believe are your grandparents were deeply in love once. I won't bore you with details of the romance. I doubt that's of much interest to you."

Otto nodded. James's voice was smooth, a politician's voice as Ken would say. His description of Esmeralda added substance to the woman in his dreams. A personality to match the image. A personality that was human, individual, not assembled by his imagination. Not heroic, not like a Penelope. It became evident James was purposely trying to paint a realistic picture, in case Otto met her, not a fanciful one. It was also obvious that James adored her and Ken, and that his adoration stemmed from their coming together at school nearly fifty years ago.

"Esmeralda is lovely and full of charisma, with an accent not quite British. She was born in Durban in South Africa. She was rather spoiled as a child, especially by her father, but possessed enough independence to not let it ruin her. Other than that she didn't share much about her youth in Africa and was humble to a fault about her success in beauty pageants there or in Ontario, when her mother got a job in Toronto, and her father found one as a computer programmer to work on Y2K."

Otto had never heard of Durban or Y2K but didn't interrupt. Like catching a strange fish he'd figure out how to debone later.

"She and her family had moved to Toronto only a few months before Ken and his father. We three ended up in the same Grade Eight class. I knew other students but they were both alone. We had to work in pairs for a project and she and I paired up. We had an odd number of students so I convinced Esmeralda to let Ken join us. We struggled but finished it and in the process we established a solid friendship. Then Ken's father died and he left Toronto. She and I stayed friends but didn't hear of Ken until she saw him on a dating website."

"What's a dating website?"

"An archaic way to introduce people—it isn't important. What is, is it reunited those two. They were almost thirty and had few prospects for marriage."

To Otto the idea of Ken being on something called a dating website was preposterous. But he didn't press for details. James excused himself and was gone a couple of minutes. Otto looked to the island but saw no sign of Desirae or Roscoe. He assumed they were foraging amongst the trees. He was anxious to swim over and contribute. Or grab a pole to catch more fish, even if only to toss them back. James returned with a plate of chocolate brownies, took one, then handed it to Otto who declined.

James described how Ken and Esmeralda were shy with each other at first but bonded with the tragic death of her parents in Africa, a year after they'd moved back and left her to live on her own. Ken accompanied her to the funeral and she relied on his support emotionally, then financially, because she lost her job soon after when her firm bankrupted. Ken was doing well with his contracting business so the loss of her income didn't prevent them marrying before she received her inheritance. A generous inheritance but full of conditions. Her parents had bemoaned Esmeralda's quitting university and designed their will to fund her studies. It meant putting off having children.

That's when James came back into the picture. At the wedding he learned about the will and the university stipulation, and her uncertainty about studying Finance as her parents wished, as it wasn't in her heart. He introduced her to a colleague, Professor Baxter van Leer.

"The man Desirae mentioned last night?"

"Yes. And with that, I probably changed their lives."

Otto noticed James's mood drop, and began to wonder if this discussion was more about James confessing than Otto learning.

"I'm sorry, sometimes I indulge in my guilt. Trust me, all that happened after I suspect would have happened regardless."

Otto nodded, not wanting to hint what he might or might not want to hear. James continued.

The professor impressed Esmeralda tremendously. Enough to convince her to devote her education to progressive studies like Critical Race Theory—James's aside to explain it had no success. The professor took Esmeralda under his wing and, under his guidance, she blossomed academically. Their closeness annoyed Ken but he was too wrapped up in his business to act on it. And for James it was too delicate a situation to intervene.

"Truth be told, it became evident Esmeralda and Ken, though drawn together romantically, were ideological opposites. A rift opened, it grew correspondingly to the long evenings she spent at campus. Eventually it dawned on Ken those two were having an affair."

"Were they?"

James took a moment to reflect before saying he didn't think so then but couldn't be sure now. Otto didn't like this dark story but appreciated James's candour.

"They were heading towards a separation when news came of the professor accepting a visiting scholar residency in Asia that would take him away at least a year. It disappointed Esmeralda at first but her perspective changed when she discovered she was pregnant. She always feared being barren so it thrilled her to hear she was having twins, inspiring her to be less political, more wife and mother. Unfortunately this wasn't in her nature. A caring person, just not in a family sense, which is rather ironic considering the way things turned out."

"What do you mean?"

James shook his head to brush off the question.

"She struggled with the twins. One was belligerent, the other docile. They obeyed Ken, but he was away often due to a boom in his business. She gave it an honest effort and I thought she'd break through, until Baxter announced his return. She told Ken she wanted to go back to university and hire a nanny, but made no mention of Baxter. Ken was sympathetic to her difficulties and thought a nanny was a good idea, though it meant dipping into their savings, the inheritance money having been used up.

"By then I was with Roscoe and my recollection of events are murky. Except to know she and Baxter started an affair that Ken didn't discover until the lockdowns in 2020. That triggered their mutual realization of how much they'd drifted apart. The kids staying at home from school was too much for Esmeralda. They decided to separate but not divorce, and for Ken to take the kids to Kapuskasing where the lockdowns weren't as severe, and his stepmother could help raise them.

"Only none of them—Ken, Esmeralda, the twins—foresaw the separation would be permanent. That communications between them outside administrative matters would turn silent and each would virtually disappear from each other's lives, let alone that she'd be famous for a paper that became a thesis that became a movement in which she became Doyenne. I did see Ken briefly at his stepmother's funeral years later, but that was the last time before you three showed up here."

Otto felt overwhelmed by this, but also appeased by how it corresponded to what Ken told them in Kapuskasing, and to the letter. A letter he decided then he would not share with anyone other than its intended recipient. And if unable to do so, to give it back to Ken. Then an idea that had been in his mind but had not yet formulated into a concrete possibility until this moment burst out. Otto felt himself blush while asking:

"Do you think Ken is still in love with Esmeralda?"

The question didn't surprise James at all.

"I asked him. Or rather, I asked if his objective on this journey was to see her again to maybe reunite. It's been their pattern."

"And?"

"He's adamant he's only here for you. I believed him when he accepted my recommendation he not go to NewTor."

"What?"

"Relax. You're still going, assuming you want to. Just a change in plans I want to propose. Let's load the dinghy and paddle to shore. The current's picking up, the quicker the better."

James then stood and waved towards the beach. Roscoe and Desirae waved back, then beckoned them over. They loaded the provisions and took the oars last. Otto looked forward to giving his arms a good workout.

23

Ken still felt weak but the fever was receding. He ate and kept down several candy bars for energy before returning to work on James's stove, as therapy if anyone bugged him about it. Luckily that wasn't an issue because the house was empty.

It wasn't easy convincing Monica he'd be fine while she went to the hotel on the card he'd found in Randall's pocket. He knew she wouldn't find Randall, but might find the sister. Ken capped his water and returned to his task. A similar model to the first stove he and Esmeralda owned, he'd manage without a manual. It took him twenty minutes longer than it might have before, but now, with only a few nuts to tighten, it was ready to test.

Monica returned from her errand in time to not let Ken bend down to plug it in, and then to help shove it back. She gave him a stern look but didn't lecture him for not resting. He turned on the first element, then the rest, before trying the oven. The heat came on for all. He was rewarded with an admiring smile.

"It's true what Heather said about what's old is gold."

"It's true."

"You should take it easy still."

"Forget that, what did you find?"

"Interesting question, Ken."

"Why?"

"I expected you to ask if I found Randall, since you assumed that's why I went."

"That is why you went."

"It was. Only when I got there I saw this black woman around his age talking to the clerk. She was agitated, holding back tears, kept repeating 'You're sure you have no Randall here?' as if the next time would bring a different answer. Then she cried: 'He told me he'd be here, he's never late,' before collapsing on the lobby sofa in front of everyone, whimpering. Pathetic, but I felt sorry for her."

"Good work."

"That's who? His girlfriend?"

"No, his sister. Felicity."

Monica took a moment to make the connection.

"But she was black, skinny, looked nothing like him."

"Of course. That's why Otto is the colour he is."

"Oh, right. Anyway, she called herself Vanessa."

"Oh geez. Really? That's . . ."

"That was your stepmother's name, wasn't it? Come on Ken, you know why she was upset, don't you?"

"I hope you believe me that it was self defence."

"Self defence? What are you saying?"

Again, Ken paused for the answer to come to her.

"So it was a lie? About Randall stealing the gun?"

Ken nodded, and disclosed how at the cistern Randall said his real name was Felix. Which he'd let sink in before also revealing he knew who Ken and Otto were, had known since they were at Heather's.

"He said he was one of your twins? You believed it?"

"Who else would say something like that?"

"I don't know."

"Trust me. I knew once I recognized the wildness in his eyes. They're commercial truck drivers and he'd spotted us before we got to Heather's. He found a place to park his truck to follow us on foot to avoid cameras and other tracking devices. He meant to kill us after we left her house."

"Kill us? Why?"

"After leaving me as teens they went to NewTor to find their mother, Esmeralda. Only to be rejected. They blamed me for it. Our getting a car disrupted his plans. He couldn't go back to his truck and he arranged a ride to catch up. He got lucky when we broke down at that gas station."

"How do you know all this?"

"He told me."

She took a moment to process this, perhaps to decide whether to pursue it and risk disrupting his uncharacteristic frankness.

"I guess we messed it up for him by going the other way."

"That's right."

"So how did he find us on the road to Timmins?"

"He didn't say. I think it was luck, I think he was only there to get to his sister in Timmins. He wasn't confident confronting me with you two around. Which is why he had to wait until he and I were alone. Perhaps he had no intent to harm Otto. Or you."

"I'm confused. Did he steal the gun or not?"

"He didn't. I gave it to him."

"Gave it—so why didn't he shoot you?"

"Only he could tell you that."

"You mean he's still alive?"

"No."

"What then?"

Ken knew he was frustrating her but he wasn't intentionally trying to be vague this time. Truth was, what happened was so horrific, his instinct was to block it from his mind rather than figure it out. If Ken didn't understand himself, how could she? Still, he had to tell her, even if she deemed it implausible.

"While you and Otto remained at the cistern, Felix asked me to cross the road, to show me something. The coyly cryptic way he asked made me get the gun, but remove all but one bullet."

109

"So that part's true."

Ken nodded, glad for the interrupting question, a chance for a deep breath to steel up his nerve to relive that moment.

"After he said his piece, I was riddled with guilt. Most of what he accused me of was defensible, much of it could be pinned on Esmeralda, but there was enough to shame me and compel me to do a stupid thing. Give him the gun."

Monica's head jerked back, but she kept quiet.

"I gave him the gun and told him if he really hated me, and if his sister did too, here was his chance to act on it. It was insane, I felt another persona had overtaken mine. Then the combative recalcitrant child I'd raised broke down. Cried like his sister. He stopped when I took a step to comfort him. The old Felix came back, hateful as ever. I was convinced he was going to shoot. He ordered me to turn around, but I kept facing him."

The emotion was welling up inside Ken. Monica put an arm around him, for which he was grateful.

"Felix was upset but calm, holding the gun without shaking. He said: 'You want me to kill you to make you a martyr and live on in the memories of others. Ha. I'd rather you be as miserable as possible the rest of your life, carrying the guilt of bringing the gun that killed your son and ruined your daughter.'"

"Then what?"

"Then he shot himself. In the mouth."

Saying it helped Ken regain his composure, just in time to put out his arms for Monica who looked ready to faint. She didn't. He saw her mind racing in her eyes. What she was thinking, he had no idea. He kept silent, waiting for her to settle herself, to speak first. She asked what he did with the gun. When he said he'd chucked it far into the lake, she scowled.

"Why didn't you just leave it there? With the body?"

"I was afraid they'd identify it as mine."

"But they'll find it in the lake. When we saw you, you weren't wet so you couldn't have thrown it that far."

She was right, he realized, that was stupid. The suicide would look like a homicide. If he'd left the gun and it was found to be his he could always say the twins had stolen it long ago. A panic threatened to consume him but he then figured if he had left the gun, it would have his fingerprints on it, and Otto's, so unless they could forensically confirm it was suicide by how the gun fell, suspicion would fall on them both. A terrible situation all around. The only possible way out was to stick to the story he'd just told Monica. Story. It wasn't a story, it was the truth. He had to be careful. If he started calling it a story, a time might come when his fading memory betrayed him to doubt what had actually happened.

"How did you know about the hotel?"

He described searching the body and finding a card with the name of the hotel, but skipped mentioning finding the bracelet, the Values token, and was glad she didn't ask.

"I wanted you to go see if Felicity might be there."

"Why, so you could give your daughter the same offer?"

Ken chose to ignore her tone.

"It's Otto I fear for. Right now James is telling him it'd be best to go on with Desirae, without me."

"I see. Where does that leave me?"

"You could go with them. Desirae would like that."

"It really has no appeal for me."

"Then what would you want to do, Monica?"

"I don't know. I do think about Wesley."

"Help me watch Felicity until Otto and Desirae are gone, I'll take you to Wesley. I'd watch myself but she'd recognize me as easily as Randall did."

"Are you sure you want to let Otto go? "

"I've taken him as far as I can. I'll miss him but it's important for him to continue the journey."

"How much of this have you told James?"

"You're the only one I trust now, Monica."

She smiled at this, then asked more questions, raised issues he hadn't considered, justifying his confidence in her, and a resolve to be honest with her about all else.

"Tell me, did you and Esmeralda ever divorce?"

"No."

She gave him a stack of paper. Esmeralda's paper.

"Where'd you get that?"

"I found it on the floor by you earlier and picked it up. James said I could read it, so I did. It's . . . interesting."

"So I've been told."

"You haven't read it?"

"Nope."

"You should. It might help you understand the type of world Otto is going to. Meanwhile, I'm going for a swim."

Monica abruptly left, giving him no chance to decline. His inclination was to stash the pages out of sight but he kept them at his side. He refilled his water glass to join her by the pool to read it. Only he found himself quickly become alternately bored and confused, putting it down several times. What helped him persist was recalling James saying it was sparked by the project they'd worked on in Grade Eight, then relaxing and indulging in something he rarely did: looking back.

Ken and Esmeralda

24

It was a distinct thrill when his elbow accidentally grazed her forearm as he took a seat at the rear of the Grade Eight class, her skin the smoothest he'd ever felt. So dark. Ken tried to relive the sensation in brushing his knuckles against her upper arm while adjusting his backpack on the floor. He missed but, struck by a faint flowery aroma too subtle to be perfume, clipped her elbow as he rose to sit upright.

"Sorry."

The slow shift of the girl's deftly oval face, with lips delicately blushed by pink lipstick, half a round ear sticking out of a thick mane of hair falling far below her shoulders, compounded his sheepish infatuation. He blushed at her welcoming smile, which lifted a pair of exquisite cheeks highlighting lovely brown eyes. A clear, slightly British sounding voice as she offered her hand.

"Hi. I'm Esmeralda Williams."

The teacher called the class to attention, sparing this gorgeous girl one of the silly lines that worked up north but undoubtedly would fail miserably with someone so classy.

It also meant he'd lost his chance. A student was in the wrong classroom and had left. Mr. Sampson invited Esmeralda to take the vacated seat at the front, leaving Ken to himself. A situation he'd have opted for to start, now heavy with disappointment.

She rose as gracefully as she had spoken. Her height took Ken aback, more so seeing she wasn't wearing heels. Her steps were purposeful but the swaying folds of the yellow dress that fell to her calves made it seem like gliding. At least her new seat was in his line of sight to the teacher, however, allowing his gaze to take in her exotic profile, hoping to see it turn his way to signal mutual regret.

This was nonsense, what was going on? Up north he was the girls' target, the rugged, athletic kid who charmed mothers with his manly features and impressed and occasionally intimidated fathers with his knack for tools and mechanical things. Ken felt a sudden intense resentment for the move to Toronto. Not even Toronto, North York, a suburb, or borough as they called it just a few years ago, stuffed inside a classroom of thirty students, none he knew. It was logical to assume he was the sole new kid, that his current classmates all knew each other. Esmeralda was likely relieved to sit next to someone familiar, likely smarter, of her own social status. To make it worse, Mr. Sampson was now getting everyone to introduce themselves—pointless if they did know each other—and share a few words about their life, their hobbies, their families, etc.

James, the lucky bastard next to Esmeralda now, was black as well, but not as dark. Not as foreign. If not for his short afro and urban manners he could be one of Ken's Indian classmates from elementary school. James wore an incredible smile as he shared his father was a Baptist minister, his mother a Vice Principal at a secondary school. It surprised Ken to hear James's favourite activity was fishing, and his family had a cottage near Timmins. The guy adored his sister and two brothers, all younger. He was articulate, intelligent, charismatic. Esmeralda looked impressed too, and oddly that didn't bother Ken.

But it did increase his dread for when his turn came up. Did he want to concoct a story? Or speak the truth: his father was an alcoholic deadbeat whose violence towards Vanessa caused his stepmother's family to run him out of town; who then, perhaps out of spite, forced Ken to move to Toronto to live in a dreary, cockroach-infested high-rise. How he and the old man lived off unemployment insurance, with most of the cash ending up at a liquor store. As for siblings, why not tell about his young sister living with his biological mother in the Maritimes, whom he'd not seen since they left when Ken was eight? It was tempting to escape to the bathroom. Ken even lifted his butt, but then heard Esmeralda speak and settled in.

She was captivating, exhibiting a poise and grace that didn't only validate her claim of winning beauty pageants in Africa, but did so without it sounding like boasting. Her mother was a doctor, her father a computer analyst at the same hospital. She was an only child. Her family had just bought a house walking distance to school. She stood out for herself, not for her upper middle class status, as others easily topped it with their parents' vocations and personal achievements in clubs and sports teams. Sports. There was something. Ken played hockey for Rep teams, until it was no longer affordable. What else? That he was a year older, having to repeat Grade Four the year his mother left? Or, to impress other boys but likely antagonize the teacher, that he'd possibly gotten a girl pregnant back home and lived in fear for paternity news? These kids weren't the kind to care about his mechanical abilities; if anything, they'd think he was bragging or full of it.

Somehow Ken was able to keep vague when his turn came—it helped that it seemed no one was listening—saying he grew up in the north where the nights were beautiful. About his family he only said he lived with his father and didn't mention Jeannie, his father's pleasant but erratic girlfriend, especially not how she was putting them up rent-free, which sounded pathetic. Mr. Sampson thankfully didn't press for details. Ken had to wonder if the teacher knew his circumstances and had deliberately let him off easy.

"Thank you all for that. I hope it wasn't too uncomfortable for anyone. I for one am pleased to find such a diversity of students in my home room class this year."

The teacher smiled as he let it sink in. It sank in with Ken who hadn't given it a thought until then. He glanced around. For every white kid, a kid from Asia or Africa or the Caribbean. The only non-whites Ken had encountered before this were native Indians. None of those here. The teacher was Jewish.

"Esmeralda, you said your father's a systems analyst. Does his work by any chance involve Y2K? As I'm sure you are all aware, that's only a few months off."

"Yes, that's precisely what he is working on."

"Terrific. It may give you an inside track on your assignment."

He'd been speaking at Esmeralda's desk but now returned to the front to address the full class.

"Yes, an assignment. Day one. What is it? A paper speculating on the new millennium, what the world might be like, based on your opinion on whether people like Esmeralda's father succeed or fail. The assignments will not be marked until next year, after Y2K. You'll submit them in envelopes, sealed, to be opened next semester. Assuming no dire predictions come true."

Several kids chuckled, including Esmeralda.

Ken knew electronics, but computers befuddled him, he had no idea what the fuss was about. It didn't help hearing they'd be working in pairs, then seeing James waste no time recruiting the obvious choice. He waited for someone to approach him, which always worked before. No one did. Instead of letting that bring him down, Ken decided he'd be better off on his own. After all, computers were only machines; he'd figure them out.

"I'm sorry Ken, I forgot that Sharon leaving means we have an odd number of students in the class."

"I'm fine on my own."

"This is very much about collaboration, about synthesis, the sharing of ideas and thoughts."

Esmeralda raised her hand, a gold bracelet dangling from its wrist. Aside from a tiny gold ring on her pinkie finger on the other hand, the only jewellery she was wearing. No necklace, no earrings, a naturalness he found enticing.

"He can work with us."

Ken checked James's reaction, expecting a frown, but his face was turned away. Later Ken discovered James was the one who had suggested it, that Esmeralda had been the doubtful one.

Being in Esmeralda's presence that hour of each weekday to complete the assignment sounded like bliss, but in reality was torture. As the days went on it became obvious she and James had much in common. Both had emigrated from large cities in Africa—Esmeralda only recently, James when he was six—and as they discussed sundry things like clothing, films, books, TV, etc., the social gaps between Ken and them became evident.

The only thing all three shared was an obliviousness to Y2K. Even Esmeralda, whose parental advantage wasn't of much use. Her father's volume of coding and testing meant sixteen-hour days and exhaustion when he came home late at night. She was hesitant to bother him to answer the questions they'd compiled. They were destined to miss the deadline, but then Esmeralda's mother suggested inviting the boys to their house the Saturday before the assignment was due.

Her home was the opposite direction of his from school in an area called Willowdale. It was a terrific autumn day on which Jeannie and his father slept in. Ken decided to walk the several kilometres and not bother them for a transit token. Amidst a din of cars, buses, taxis, he strolled the wide sidewalk of the main road, passing a hospital and countless plazas, hating it all until he reached her neighbourhood and the noise died off. He was fascinated to see such large houses, fancy cars, trimmed front lawns. Neighbours were talking over the rhythmic buzzing of lawnmowers, weed cutters, and leaf blowers, while several kids played ball hockey. Welcome sounds compared to the angry ones from the arterial roads. It took no time to find Esmeralda's street and Ken slowed on realizing he was almost an hour early.

He was admiring the two rhododendrons when a tall, slender black man emerged from the bungalow's garage, lugging a red toolbox to a blue Toyota Cressida, its hood already open. Next to it, a sleek but old tan Mercedes Benz. Ken was about to turn away to kill time and cool off before he got too sweaty, but was then distracted by a crude clank, followed by much cursing. It was coming from the same man who Ken guessed was trying to change a spark plug, clearly with no clue what he was doing. It was painful to see. Ken had to go back to see if he could help, before any damage was done.

"Ken, is that you?"

Esmeralda's voice made Ken stop. She was on her porch at the top of the steps, her black skin accentuated by a white summer print dress sparsely dotted with pastel flowers. Unlike at school Ken could make out the shapes of her breasts. She was striking in her pose, making it awkward with her father there. To Ken's relief, she rushed over, introduced them, invited Ken in, waving off his apology for being early.

The house was sparsely furnished, dominated by the aroma of freshly baked cookies, triggering a pleasant recollection of his stepmother. Esmeralda told him their belongings were still on the Atlantic in a crate. An old folding card table covered by a plastic tablecloth held a small carton of milk, one of fruit juice, and a stack of white plastic cups.

An elegant woman in a pleated mint green dress, a mature, more confident version of Esmeralda, entered and introduced herself as Isabella Williams. She set a tray full of white chocolate chip cookies on the table. Esmeralda poured a glass of milk for Ken, one for herself, while they waited for James.

"Mom, how long before Dad fixes the car to join us?"

"He said to call him when both classmates are here."

"Really? I'm afraid if he gets too far into it . . ."

Isabella's laugh belied a shared lack of confidence in the skills of Mr. Williams. Ken felt bad for the man and offered to help, adding he'd changed plenty of spark plugs. They jumped at his offer in time. They found Mr. Williams, the true baker, in a curse-storm of frustration that Ken feared could only worsen when his pride was assaulted by this teenager. But in fact Mr. Williams was as grateful as the ladies and yielded instantly.

By the time Ken finished James had shown up, wearing a pair of Dockers and a stylish shirt. Ken's hands and part of his t-shirt were stained by grease and oil. He took his time to clean them but was embarrassed at not getting it all off.

Her father joined them at the card table to explain Y2K. Ken got the general gist but James grasped it rapidly and impressed Ken and her father. Esmeralda too, but not to the same extent as the growing admiration Ken sensed in her towards her father. It made him envious to witness this blossoming respect in the girl. Something he'd never have with his father. It seemed fresh too, as if she was just discovering what he was about.

"I never realized how much we depend on computers, Dad."

"It's only going to increase as populations increase. Efficient and predictable systems are the way we'll support them all."

"If systems are to be predictable, don't the people using them have to be predictable too? I mean, won't they have to conform to how a system expects things are done?"

"What do you mean, honey?"

"Won't that spoil the uniqueness in people."

"Esmeralda, people will always be unique some way."

His assurance seemed to satisfy her. Mr. Williams left so they could absorb his input and brainstorm how to use it. Esmeralda invited her guests to sit in the backyard around a patio set with its plastic wrapping still on, to share snacks and cans of Fanta. They, but really only James and Esmeralda, had various ideas, in the end choosing a scenario in which Y2K efforts failed, opening the door for successful shadow efforts to overtake and monopolize industries, making governments impotent to stop it. Silly, Ken thought, but probably good enough to pass.

The session ended and James made a call to get his mother to come pick him up. Ken regretted having told them he'd walked there when James insisted giving him a lift home, but was glad when the drizzle turned into a downpour. His regret came back when, on arriving at his building, she had to manoeuvre past an awkwardly parked police cruiser with an officer inside. A dark instinct made him linger until they were gone and out of sight before he went inside.

Ken found the apartment in the same mess as he had left it. Empty beer bottles littered around stacks of dirty dishes in the sink and covering the stove, a full ashtray with a half-finished cigarette. The kitchen was his father's job to clean; Ken's to look after the bathrooms. Jeannie took charge of all the other rooms. Those were tidy as usual, save for a cigarette butt smudged by lipstick next to the phone. Ken called out for his father, then for Jeannie, no response. Under the ashtray, a note that struck Ken as angry, fed up.

"Couldn't wait, had to get him to the hospital."

Jeannie's note didn't specify the hospital.

Not the first time his father got so drunk he needed medical help, but the first time since moving in with Jeannie. At least he assumed it was because he'd gotten drunk. Ken couldn't dwell on it. Better to get busy, stay distracted. Ken organized the sink, turned on the hot water, pulled out the dish soap, and set to cleaning up. He owed Jeannie that much.

25

Esmeralda felt cocooned with her emptiness and loneliness in a corner of the waiting room, an empty chair on one side, a rack thick with coats on the other. A half hour of anonymous peace before calling James to get her. It was a pleasant room, if not as posh and warm as her doctor's office. Modern furniture, clean powder blue walls, and carpeting with geometric patterns that effectively helped pass time as something to stare at. Her cell phone was useless because her parents paid for it; she dared not turn it on in case they could access her location. Her mother had already shown signs of knowing something was up.

She shifted as the entrance door opened, to protect the empty seat. But on seeing a handsome young man, close to her age, she instinctively shifted back. He stood as if to consider taking that seat or take off his coat. He did the latter, then the former. The tiny thrill it gave her was packed with guilt and shame for why she was there, what she'd just done.

Esmeralda reached for a magazine on the glass table. In doing so she brushed her arm against the young man who'd rolled up the sleeves on his flannel shirt. A powerful forearm. And warm. Or was she cold? It startled them together, their eyes met briefly before she dropped hers to the magazine, flipping pages but not finding anything interesting. Then he spoke.

"Excuse me, didn't we go to school together?"

"I don't know. When?"

"Seven years ago. In Willowdale."

"Sorry."

"Aren't you Esmeralda Williams?"

She looked up. His dazzling azure eyes had a glint that was familiar, but the trim beard seemed out of place. As out of place as she felt as the sole African-Canadian person there. Esmeralda chose to shake her head instead of trying.

"I don't think I remember you."

"So you aren't Esmeralda?"

The easy lie was tempting but she couldn't do it.

"That is me, but who are you?"

"Ken Neilson, we were in Grade Eight together, briefly."

"Uh huh."

"I never expected to run into you this far north."

"I'm visiting . . . a friend who lives around Timmins."

"Victoria?"

Together, Ken and Esmeralda looked up at the receptionist, before glancing about the room. Esmeralda sighed, took a deep breath, then rubbed her palms down her thighs and approached the desk. The receptionist handed her the pain prescription. Out of her peripheral vision she saw he was minding his business. It gave her a chance to look at him, which was when she realized this was the boy who'd suddenly and inexplicably left school.

As she retook her seat, self-conscious, she glanced at him and saw him looking away. Surely he'd noticed her using a different name, her middle name. Would he assume it was a fake name?

What was his story? Why was he here? Had he knocked up a girl? His face was absent of guilt but also bore no judgement. A face that relaxed her, at least partially.

"I do remember now. How are you, Ken? Healthy, I hope?"

"Oh yes. My mother works here. I'm picking her up."

"Funny, I'm rest . . . waiting for a friend."

Her face became flush and Esmeralda felt sillier for her lack of poise than the actions that had brought her here.

"Yeah . . . say, how did we do on that assignment?"

"What?"

"The Y2K paper."

It was bizarre. For the life of her, Esmeralda had no idea what he was talking about yet sensed she ought to know.

"Remember, I came to your house? Your family was great. So was James. And you . . . whatever happened to him?"

The assignment. The one they did with her father's help. Her father, the last person she wanted to think about now. So again she shook her head.

"What about James? I thought you two might, you know."

"Why, because we're both black?"

"Uh, no . . . hadn't thought of that."

Esmeralda looked Ken in his lovely eyes and found no hint of insincerity. Perhaps because her parents were so successful, and her exposure to outright racism had been limited, she wasn't the best judge of such things. James was more racially sensitive, he often clarified race issues for Esmeralda, would know if it had been one. On the other hand, James had liked Ken too. But of course he would have, as it turned out.

"I'm sorry, I'm jumpy today. James and I did date a bit prior to high school. We drifted apart. I'd lost touch with him by Grade Ten. My parents were more upset than I was, I think, ha, ha."

"That's too bad."

The way he said it touched her, briefly tempted her to divulge her entire story, how she'd come all this way north to terminate an unwanted pregnancy from her summer European fling with that Danish boy, a fling her parents, who'd paid for the trip had no clue about; how she'd discovered the pregnancy the day she came home, and had roped in a friend to take her to his cottage on a fake weekend trip to his (lying to her parents that it was a girl); how that friend was indeed the same James who was now dutifully waiting for her at a donut shop.

Her chance to open up was quashed by the young receptionist when she out called Ken's name, in a rather alluring manner, to ask him to go into the back.

"Excuse me."

Ken's stepping away almost made her cry for being frightened and at a complete loss. She had to collect herself before rising to get him to rejoin her and not leave her as she expected. At least get him to give her a hug. She shut her eyes. When she opened them he was again sitting next to her. Esmeralda revelled in the strength of his presence, nothing more. It helped that he seemed oblivious to her circumstances.

"Looks like my mother will be a while."

"Guess we'll be waiting together then."

His nod released almost all her anxiety but she had to look off to the coat rack until her eyes dried up. If she could, she would have wiped them on his coat.

"I can get you tea or cookies. Probably not as nice as the ones your father made, though."

The reference to her father made her almost vomit. She stifled the urge, glad to see a wistful look in Ken's face, as if her father had made a good impression on him. She then remembered her father expressing admiration for the humble troubled white kid who'd rescued his car.

Now Esmeralda wanted to pry, find out why Ken left school suddenly, but sensed it was a delicate subject and her manners held her back. If she pried, it would also open the door for him to do so the same.

"No, no thanks. Besides, I should call my friend."

"I assumed your friend was picking you up here."

"Did I say that? No, my friend's at a donut shop."

"Let me drive you there. Better than hanging out in this place. I've got time, if it's not too far."

"It's at a Tim's, to the north of the town."

"I know it. Let's go."

The nurse's instructions to rest echoed but nothing could be more restive than spending time with this young who made her feel more at ease than Valium. It might expose her deceit about James, but she could always say, truthfully, she'd been frazzled.

She took his hand to help her get up and followed him along a hallway, then down two floors in the elevator to the now-filled parking lot of the busy plaza. He guided her to a blue pickup truck over ten years old, but rust-free. He opened the passenger door, helped her into the cab. It was a bit dilapidated inside, a tear in the driver's seat covered by duct tape, but spotless. It felt stark though, as if such a truck needed food wrappers and other trash on the floor. The ashtray was empty, unused. No garters or dice hanging from the rear view mirror. His work truck?

She asked what he did for a living. Construction work. Busy with new housing projects in the area. Good money but he was still paying off debts she assumed were student loans. She was wrong. He hadn't finished high school, had gone direct to work. This he offered without self-consciousness. As hardened as he was empathetic, she thought. So normal, compared to what she had just experienced. An ordinary conversation between a good looking guy and a pretty girl, a man and a woman, in their early twenties: how naturally pleasant that was.

Everything inside Esmeralda suddenly flew into turmoil, as if she no longer had control over what to think or feel and needed someone or something to corral and direct her emotion. With it that impulse to reveal everything to a guy who gave her a good vibe returned. Briefly. Again interrupted by something outside their impromptu bubble: the appearance of James's plain white VW Rabbit. Ken's face was expressionless, no idea their fellow former classmate was inside. It was imperative to Esmeralda to keep it that way so she could retreat to the safe company of the sole individual who knew her truth. Her brief reunion with this strange but likeable boy had given her energy to find a way to get past this situation and go on.

There was no awkwardness, thankfully, when he pulled up in front of the entrance door, got out, and opened her door. Again he assisted her down and rushed ahead to get the door into the donut shop. Respecting her privacy by not looking to see who was inside. Just giving a brief hug. She wanted to think it was shyness covering his being attracted to her, but assumed he was in a hurry to return to his mother. A pang of melancholy upon seeing him leave turned to relief on seeing James.

He was surprised to see Esmeralda, happy to not have to pick her up at the clinic. Esmeralda watched the blue truck drive off. Slightly disappointed but increasingly liberated.

"How did you get here? I was wondering when you'd call."

"I'm sorry. I met someone who gave me a ride."

"Must have been a good friend. This is the first smile I've seen on you in some time."

"Remember that boy who worked on that assignment in 1999, about the Y2K?"

"Ken Neilson? That was him?"

"Uh huh. His mother works at the clinic."

"So he knows why you were there?"

"I didn't tell him. I guess he'll find out from her."

"I doubt it. They're discreet—but why didn't you invite him to come in? I'd have loved to see him. Is he as handsome?"

"If anything, more."

"Geez, Esmeralda."

"Sorry, my mind was on other things."

"Of course, of course, but still . . ."

"Can we go home now? Get some takeout on the way back? I may sleep in the backseat. I'm starting to feel a little sore. The nurse gave me some pills."

"Sure. How are you feeling? Any pain?"

She nodded. While it was true there was pain, it was nothing beyond a bad month. The real difficulty was not being alone.

How bizarre running into Ken, how unexpected. Thinking of him, his solid lanky build, his sturdy yet kind face, provided an amusing distraction from the fear of facing the truth of what she had just done. Funny too him asking about that assignment. She probably still had it stashed away in her memory crate; maybe she'd dig it out after she got home and re-read it.

A restful sleep ensued. Esmeralda didn't wake until James pulled off at a rest stop to fill up. Only then did she remember her phone had been off all this time. Esmeralda turned it on. A few missed calls, fortunately none from her parents. If her luck continued, James would pull in while Esmeralda's parents were out to dinner or shopping. James got in the car and Esmeralda jumped when he closed the door.

"You all right there, girl?"

"Just thinking how I might avoid seeing my parents."

"Really, Es, you're twenty-one. An adult."

"Not in their eyes. They paid for my Europe trip. You won't say anything to them, James? Promise?"

"Relax. You made a mistake, you fixed it. Life goes on as long as you don't dwell on it. Besides, what can they do?"

"Please promise me, James."

"I promise. I promise. What kind of friend do you—?"

"I'm sorry, you're right."

"Just relax, let me drive, okay?"

Relaxing became easier the closer they got to the city where traffic was accumulating due to an accident that, according to the radio, had closed two lanes. For Esmeralda the slowdown was a welcome reprieve to put off seeing her parents.

For the first time since returning from two weeks of seeing family in Durban, then two months travelling south to north in Europe, then coming home to discover she was pregnant, then to today and what had to be done, Esmeralda Victoria Williams was ready to resume her life with her parents. However the lie would remain. Significant because Esmeralda had never lied to her parents before. A little extra time to suppress the lie and the guilt associated with it would help.

26

The face. It was her. A little older, a few lines. The lipstick still a subtle pink, the cheeks a little puffed but still bright, the smile a tad wizened. Esmeralda. The name echoed the identical electric impulse of his youth. Her name modified, slightly: Esme. With no accent on the last letter. Es-may, Es-mee, Es-muh? With the shortened name, a short haircut too. The hand slapped his back before he could put down the laptop screen all the way.

"Pretty slim pickings, eh Neilson?

Doug flipped up the screen.

"Who you looking—ah, didn't know you liked black girls."

"I recognize her. From school."

"Right . . ."

Doug was getting on Ken's nerves lately, and the little chuckle punctuating his taunt prompted Ken to put on his coat.

"Hey, you're not going for a drive, are you? It's snowing, the roads'll be hell. Join me at the pub."

Ken grabbed his keys, ignoring the advice and his better sense to engage his memory to guide him to that neighbourhood.

The first few kilometres carried a sense of adventure, but that dwindled as he passed the apartment where he'd lived with his father. It redirected his school recollection to the other time he'd seen Esmeralda, at the medical clinic. That was seven years ago. Odd her being there. Ken had asked about the black girl, but his judicious stepmother only gave a curiosity-snuffing stare. She didn't ask so he didn't share his connection nor that she used a different name. What was it? Veronica?

Unfortunately, his memory detour blocked his efforts to recall their first encounter in Grade Eight. Covering up a memory like the pristine hardwood underneath the tacky laminate flooring at their new client. Esmeralda's current life could be yet another unfortunate layer. It felt unseemly for such a beautiful girl to be trolling the Internet for guys, out of character.

Thick snowflakes fell, forcing him to turn on his wipers, and then turn around on seeing the banks of red brake lights ahead. Ken took the next exit to escape, lucky to reach it in time, albeit frustrated at abandoning his quest.

Doug was out when Ken got to the house they shared. But his truck was still there, he'd walked to the pub. It was nice to have the house to himself, not be assaulted by Doug's country music, never mind his crooning. But there was nothing on television either and Ken suddenly felt lonely.

128

It was rather childish how anxious she was to get in her studio apartment. Not one, but two alerts. She almost dropped a bag of groceries on her way to open the laptop on the kitchen counter, letting it power up while she refrigerated the meat.

Two men checked out her profile, only one requested a chat. Young, mid-twenties at best. Baby face. She liked that. Oh no, a web programmer, according to his profile. Sorry bud, no coders for this gal. The second guy, this Doug Parsons, was one she'd scrolled by often. He must have done the same with her. White, rugged looks, tanned, two years younger. Construction worker. No contractor. Preferred blondes, so why did her profile draw his interest? Maybe he'd clicked hers in error, she'd done it with others. She hesitated to check his profile. If he was a premium member like Esmeralda, he'd be notified it was her.

She glumly put away the other groceries, resigned to another dead end, but pleased how she took it in stride. Before putting away the Gouda, she cut off a chunk to enjoy with the Cabernet she'd opened last night. Better to acknowledge desperation than fall into despair.

Was it a mistake to dismiss the only hits she'd gotten the last two weeks? If not, what was she doing on such a site? While she had aged since her high school pageant days and her face and body showed wear of, of . . . life experience, Esmeralda was still pretty. With a respectable job. No professional, no accountant or engineer or lawyer or anything that needed a university degree, but doing fine as assistant manager and bookkeeper at a family-run furniture store. She liked them, they liked her.

What kept men away? Her divorced status? Her friends said to leave that blank, but it wasn't in her nature to embellish or to deceive. She insisted on using a recent photo, instead of the shot from that last pageant. Could people see accumulated baggage in a photo? So be it. Then again, what if the guy had just been shy all this time? Couldn't hurt to Google him.

Several images popped up of this Doug partying it up in a bar with guys wearing the same baseball shirt. Also a hockey team photo. Then she spotted one of a housing development, and he was posing with a starkly handsome man. Thumbing their tool belts like old gunslingers. Excitement returned and grew upon realizing why this Doug Parsons had contacted her, rather why, to be more accurate, his profile had.

Ken had grown to like the bar, a far cry from his initial reaction when Doug first took him there to celebrate their getting a large house with a big driveway to fit their trucks. While it was part of a chain restaurant and noisy, he found he could block out the sound by facing the bar and keeping his back to the restaurant. The staff was friendly, competent, and it didn't take long to get comfortable there.

Good thing he'd come back when he did because the sky was now thick with clouds; for once the artificial brightness inside was welcome. Usually Doug sat at the bar but today he was in a booth with a guy they'd met at the client's that morning, there to do some electrical work. Doug beckoned Ken to come over after he got his now regular pint of Molson Ex.

"You met Tristan, right Ken? He's joining our hockey team."

"Great."

"Ken here was almost a pro."

"I wouldn't call playing Rep being a pro."

Doug brushed this off.

"Anyway, Tristan was telling me about moonlight gigs, tricks to earn extra bucks. So what was this one again?"

"You ask for cash on the spot. If they ask for an invoice, tell them you'll send it later. Then don't bother. Most won't notice as long as you did your job well enough."

"What's the point of that?"

"The point is you charge HST, but keep it for yourself."

"Don't people complain?"

"If they ask, just put them off. Say you sent it and act confused as to why it never arrived. Though there was one persistent guy who kept at it a few months before dropping off. Kept pestering me for my HST number, which of course I don't have."

"Why not?"

"Not worth the trouble. All the forms, the filing. Only to give your money to the government?"

"The guy just stopped?"

"He talked about calling the tax people. Never heard nothing."

"You need to get us hooked up into some jobs on the side. Ken here is a whiz at anything."

Ken smiled at the compliment but kept quiet, annoyed at how Tristan reminded him of his father and his troubles for which Ken had paid plenty. He avoided slick guys like Tristan.

His roommate was preoccupied with his cell phone, nodding. Then his eyes widened before he let out a guffaw and directed Ken to read the text message.

"Just a school friend, eh?"

With each hour of no response or even acknowledgement of her note to this Doug Parsons, Esmeralda grew less anxious. To be honest, she recalled little about the guy beyond his being great looking and that he'd made her really comfortable in a difficult situation that one time. In fact, she wasn't sure she'd recalled his name right. How embarrassing if she'd gotten it wrong. No, his name was Ken. Short and blunt.

Esmeralda opened a new Cabernet and poured a full glass to jog her memory of the school assignment. But it was interrupted by the more recent memory of sitting in that clinic waiting room next to him. It came with a physical sensation in her gut. Not a painful one, more like a sensation of barrenness. A feeling she'd experienced often. She'd equate it to regret, although rarely was there an emotional aspect. Cold regret. Same this time. To be candid, a reminder Esmeralda wasn't destined to have children.

Why didn't she think of that before sending the note? Surely it would come up if they were to meet again.

The last thing she needed was to rehash that period in her life, especially when she was doing well otherwise. She was lucky to have found this small, expensive, but cozy condo to rent. Close to the train, the lake, the town centre, she could afford it by not having a car. The commute downtown was busy and long but she was used to it. Her parents had settled in back in Africa and no longer encroached on her life. No need to disturb all that by opening a potential Pandora's box from the past.

Esmeralda topped up her glass and took it to the dining table to look out the empty balcony, its two chairs and small folded table bungee corded together against the window for winter. It was tempting to undo them and watch the sun gleaming on the water, highlighting small waves. She realized it was Valentine's Day then. A dubious choice to contact someone this way.

There were still boxes of personal items sitting on the floor of her bedroom and in the closet, unpacked. Her yearbooks would be buried too deep but she might have her class photos nearer the top. Sure enough, she found the one, a 4x6 portrait slotted into four openings in a cardboard frame. There she stood, back left, tallest of the girls, her hair still long and flourishing, freshly puffed up from a pageant at which she'd been ill but still placed fourth. She scrutinized the faces. Most she remembered, but not all their names. Except of course James. But no Ken Neilson.

That's right. He'd have been gone by then, so suddenly, to be forgotten unless fate intervened. Which it had. Twice. Possibly a third time if he responded. Third time's a charm? The wine was affecting her, she was always a weak drinker, she had to stop. Had to make something for dinner before she fell into a routine of constantly checking for responses, vacillating if what she had written was too forward. Or not forward enough.

27

Ken hoisted the last box onto his truck and took a deep breath before lifting up the tailgate to push it shut. He looked at the window and saw Esmeralda watching him, her long lavender dress blending almost seamlessly into the light purple drapes, which were pulled back. Their eyes met. A last brief moment to convey his confusion about their family, beyond the pandemic turmoil everyone had to deal with. All he got was his confusion reflected back. Ken opened the door to climb in, but stopped on seeing his wife coming to him. His wife. Esmeralda. Mother of the twins. He hung his left arm on the opened window, perhaps defensively.

"It's the right thing to do, Ken. For both of us."

"Uh huh."

"And for the twins."

"Maybe."

"Maybe? Even more for them. Felix needs to calm down and stop being so protective of Felicity."

"Yes, but I'm not sure how this will help."

"Vanessa, your stepmother, she can help with that and maybe even help Felicity be less docile. Didn't you always say what a calming influence she was for you?"

"That's true."

"The lockdowns are awful for them. Worse than it is for other kids."

"How's that again?"

"I'm not—I just know they can't be home while I'm locked out of university. Also, your work is more restricted here and less so up north."

"No point repeating it. I don't disagree. It's just that, whenever you summarize it so tidily, I presume it's because *he's* back."

"We've been through that, it's a coincidence."

The silence of his doubt, versus her certainty, and her fear of him testing that certainty. He sighed. This was a stalemate.

"The pandemic, the lockdowns, hurt us all."

"You know that's not what I'm talking about. I suppose time will tell. Actions will tell."

"What does that mean, Ken?"

"Maybe that's the problem. I say actions will tell, you ask me to explain it to contradict that."

"I guess we've always been different, haven't we?"

"That's not the point."

"I know. When this all passes we'll reassess where we stand. I don't want a divorce, nothing like that."

"If it takes months, a year, more?"

"We'll see, won't we?"

"It's important, Esmeralda, you be the one to come find me."

"I understand."

Ken's mock scowl of resignation prompted a sad smile from Esmeralda that became one of relief when he got in the cab and started the ignition. The truck's engine sputtered before roaring to life. A blast of cool air from the AC reached her temple. Ken backed up slowly, allowing her knuckles to brush his forearm while it still hung over the window, before he pulled it in.

She stood there, long after the truck was out of sight, letting a flow of emotions parade like a fashion show put on specifically for her, as if she had her choice which to wear, yet was unable to decide and bought them all.

Her state of mind was too brittle for studying. Yet the house was empty, tedium imminent. She didn't want to call James. It'd also be disrespectful to the terrific man she'd just sent off to call the other one. Even the thought of wine was distasteful.

Then she was reminded of the irreverent piece she'd started. It was a lark for now but she had a feeling it turn into more. What, she had no idea, and maybe that blindness was the key, to allow her to let go and create.

The sound of a horn that sounded like Ken's truck startled her but the street was empty. The interruption created a vacuum in her mind that quickly filled with ideas, including a title, for that irreverent piece.

filial Values

by

Esmeralda Victoria Williams

Beyond Social Media

Who today in 2020 can enjoy a classic like *The Odyssey* without
the pall of the part it plays in enabling power structures behind
the subjugation, persecution, and marginalization of so many?
The same goes for cheering a sports team with an anachronistic
nickname or watching a movie starring an actor who declares or
accidentally exposes an unfortunate political stance or attitude?
Never mind the ability or right to unselfconsciously share one's
political leanings or utter criticisms or mildly facetious remarks,
without first gauging any risk of so-called cancellation.

Social media allows individuals to express themselves to ever-
widening audiences. Beginning with friends and family, then to
associates and coworkers, eventually involving strangers one is
unlikely to ever meet because they remain anonymous or are, in
fact, fabrications. With each new inclusion one's individuality is
whittled down by echo chambers to eventually gravitate to the
lowest common denominator of group acceptability. Creativity
and individual perspective get homogenized as they yield to the
joy of belonging to a group by emulating the group. All dissent
risks one becoming ostracized or "cancelled" after an assault of

abuse: shaming, doxing, ghosting, censure, accusing, firing, if one persists in maintaining a contrary position. It's no better for those who capitulate, only to find themselves in rabbit holes of apology giving or approval seeking, leading to self-cancellation, in a less dignified but less dramatic fashion. Those sympathetic to dissenters waste no time to virtue signal their conformity, squeezing out the individual within. This can turn into an ugly business that can warrant abandoning social media, even justify banning it altogether. Only social media has become so big its universality prohibits such drastic action.

The political impact of social media is irreversible and cannot be undone. People increasingly identify with or find support in marginalized groups, championed by saviours belonging to the fortunate groups. As variations in race and gender and religion increase, they cannibalize each other. Racial purities for instance are vanishing, albeit gradually, as mixed-race couples who bear children are more common. Humans in practice are connecting more and more by ideology than biology. Aligning with chosen *filiations* rather than involuntarily nature-assigned families.

Social media starts with individuals and evolves into groups. Its support for progressive values is good but its impact limited, due to this rooting in individuals. What can help is something that complements social media platforms, that can neutralize the vitriol contaminating those platforms by shifting focus to groups, not individuals, and by empowering groups, ensure the objectively fair treatment of the marginalized. Similar to labour unions of bygone days but with a scope that's more universal, that activates equality of outcome tangibly by emphasizing filial connections between humans as it rationally adopts and adapts its values to promote progressive ideals. And doing so without indiscriminately and irreversibly discarding prudent traditional values worth retaining. In other words, provide a positive sum alternative liberating us from the zero sum paths we are on.

Proposal

This paper proposes *filial Values*, an approach, philosophy, or programme targeted at progressive urban zones to de-politicize human interactions, clearing paths for positive social change. It circumvents social media pitfalls to encourage people to openly share values without recrimination. It phlegmatically advances social justice by disempowering the vitriol and hatred cluttering social media, hindering its ability to enable progressive action.

One use case is streamlining an organization's diversity goals and removing bias by using an algorithm that ensures a mix not favouring a particular identity group. The algorithm objectively compiles cumulative values scores, an aggregation of individual values, and monitors and reports diversity progress. Those not achieving a minimum score would pay premiums for supplies, licences, or face restrictions, boycotts, even decertification. They could avoid these by hiring *Indos* (non-filial Values participants akin to today's contractors) in the short term but that would be a prohibitive long-term strategy since such personnel command significantly higher wages that, unlike today, would be subject to exorbitant, almost punitive tax rates.

Goals and Principles

The goals of filial Values are: redefine society with progressive values while accommodating those who don't (yet) share those values; bolster itself with a robust technical infrastructure such that its absence would render filial Values impotent.

The above organizational diversity example illuminates a core principle of filial Values: to always opt for passive methods or approaches to sway human behaviour via positive motivation. Avoid badgering, threatening, enforcing, punishments to avoid inciting dissent or revolt. Allow for exceptions with short term relief but long term consequences that give parties time to come around willingly and peacefully.

Other principles will evolve but basic ones include voluntary and transparent participation, ensuring RNA, DNA, or any data retained within filial Values is only accessible to machines that are hack-proof; that all filial Values components are state built, controlled, operated with costs borne by taxpayers. No revenue is to be taken from advertising or any sales of data or assets to private interests.

filial Values is a self-contained superimposed template that sets a moral foundation to universally apply progressive values equitably. It empowers no individual or single group to ensure it remains impervious to being exploited by any entity.

The rest of this paper describes the elements comprising filial Values, illustrated below. filial Values is conceptual at this time and is dependent on capabilities that do not exist yet, or are not yet advanced enough.

Elements

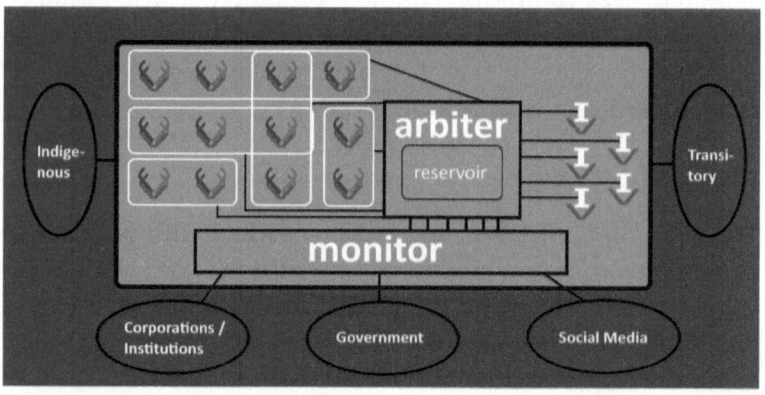

Everything inside the rounded rectangle comprises filial Values while outside entities are those with which it interacts. External entities can be machines, groups, or individuals. The diagram is intentionally simplified to establish context; it is not a schematic or blueprint. Starting from the outside:

Indigenous designates native peoples. filial Values focuses on urban zones and part of its mandate would be to revert ancient rural lands to Indigenous nations in exchange for claims within cities. This is not a goal but a step, pending the agreeability of Indigenous peoples to partake. It could happen fully, partially, or not at all.

Transitory refers to individuals not (yet) part of filial Values who may potentially express an interest or intent to join. When inside a filial Values zone they are treated as *Indos* (see below). Outside it they are unknown to family Values.

Corporations/Institutions, Government, Social Media interact directly with filial Values via *monitor* (see below), but are not part of filial Values. filial Values can influence these, and relies on their data, but does not require they become redundant.

filials (represented by the main logo) have the highest status within filial Values, the highest privileges. They join *filiations* (see below) and must join at least one *filiation*. They are free to travel with occasional limitations. *filial* is always lower case or lower case first letter if all caps. *filials* are linked to other *filials* within their *filiations* but not other *filiations*, nor *Indos*, unless the *Indo* has been specially invited and accepted into that *filiation*.

Indos (represented by the capital I logos) are a lesser category, but hold a subset of privileges available to full *filials* once they register. *Indo* is always capitalized. *Indos* cannot belong to any *filiation* (see below) but can become *boosters* (not pictured) to elevate their standing if they subscribe to and follow all rules of that *filiation*.

Transitory Indo (represented by the same capital I logo) is a temporary designation for outsiders who may at some point join or register. It is the most restrictive category in terms of what they can do and where they can go. They are monitored constantly. *Transitory Indo* is always capitalized.

filiations (represented as white-circled groupings) are sets of *filials* who are either assigned to a *filiation* or accepted into one.

filiations generally correlate to marginalized identity groups of which there can be sub-*filiations*. All *filials* interface with *arbiter* through their prime *filiation*. This is different from *Indos* who interface directly with *arbiter*. Each *filial* must belong to at least one *filiation* and adhere to its code, restrictions, obligations (i.e. voting). Membership is approved by *arbiter*, which can also expel or cancel a *filial*, but only based on clear, provable, exact circumstances, not arbitrarily. *filials* link to other *filials* within a *filiation*.

Once a *filial* is vested in a *filiation*, that *filial's* contributions to polls and voting follow those of the *filiation* in areas where a *filiation* has registered a position within *arbiter*. As it is possible to belong to multiple *filiations* that hold conflicting positions, a protocol exists to determine which position wins. Depending on the context, three things can determine the outcome: an *arbiter* algorithm, a split of the vote, or the *filial* makes a choice.

arbiter governs filial Values, applies its rules, and resolves all conflicts. It is like a coached artificial intelligence engine. It is seeded for each city by a management council. After an initial period, determined at the outset, it becomes self-operating, and inaccessible to humans directly. Its rules can be recalibrated but not changed by governments to reflect political will. All such changes are transparent to ensure people instantly see if elected officials keep their promises. *arbiter* reports changes and advises on impacts to affected *filials*, which could be everyone or a subset (i.e. a *filiation*).

Within *arbiter* is **_reservoir_**, a centralized media access store akin to those found on the Internet. It is organically accessed by Values badges (see below) that connect with screens or other instruments to interpret content. A sensory feature may one day be developed that can allow a Values badge to effactually act as one's eyes ears and eyes. This could potentially obsolete such devices as mobile phones or personal computers, and even the Internet and myriad of cloud computing services.

monitor is closely linked with _arbiter_. It processes filial Values data, always in aggregate. It never holds data about a specific individual (i.e. DNA). It functions as an ongoing census of filial Values. It constantly updates and tracks aggregate activity. For instance, calculating _filiation_ membership counts or organization equality scores, and any other processed information that might be useful. Its value lies in gauging equality and then influencing _arbiter_ to recalibrate for holistic changes; i.e. should a time come when other races dominate, Caucasians might be favoured.

Values badges (not shown in diagram), are devices an _Indo_ or _filial_ registered with filial Values must wear at all times. They store personal data accessible to the individual and _arbiter_, but no one and nothing else. It has no input method, only lights and audio signals for various alerts. _Transitory Indos_ get temporary badges they must wear and return upon exiting.

The data retained is of two types: fixed assigned (DNA, blood type, birth data, social insurance number, race, etc.), or unfixed unassigned (religion, gender, political leaning, _filiation(s)_, etc.). Data retained varies between _filials_, _Indos_, and _Transitory Indos_, and varies depending on _filiations_ too. Raw data is processed by _arbiter_ to calculate values that are maintained within _monitor_.

Values badges provide a physical link between humans and filial Values; in tandem with _arbiter_, its functional core. Some of the proposed functionality is available now in various forms on clunky Smart phones. Those implementations are disparate, the devices themselves flimsy, and too easily lost or broken. Values badges must be robust and tightly linked to _arbiter_ in such a way that should the link experience a disruption or separation, an alarm (odour, pain, noise, combination) is generated.

Encrypted Values badge data cannot be intercepted, altered, or hacked, but must be readable by _arbiter_ via dedicated input devices. A verifying device would match an individual to their personal Values badge, and detect organisms in an area without one. If it finds a discrepancy it activates an alarm. Alarms can trigger a distinct combination of light patterns, pain, odour, until the issue is rectified. Values badges constantly self-check. Biological mismatches produce an alarm. Possessing multiple badges simultaneously activates an alarm. The ability to effect pain as an alarm via a biological link between an individual and *arbiter*, unavailable now, promises to actualize the full benefit of filial Values one day.

As noted above all changes to *arbiter* are broadcast via Values badges. These changes will be highlighted if deemed too radical for one's *filiation*. The ability to identify personal thresholds for notification will be incorporated. Values badges provide an easy method to contribute to polls or votes and choices are forever stored and tracked by *monitor*, available to *arbiter* to administer family Values objectively and transparently.

Application

How the elements could work together depends on the quality of the biological link between Values badges and *arbiter* that at the time of this writing isn't near what is envisioned. That need not deter speculating on potential applications currently topical, two of which are quite feasible today and can inspire others.

The first is the one cited above to assert equality in hiring (or admitting, casting, etc.) with objective *monitor* scores favouring *filials* who ought to be favoured and identifying organizations that lag behind.

The second addresses social media ills. With filial Values, an individual possesses a distinct, secure anonymous identity that is accountable. One and only one. Fake accounts are impossible. With this identity one can act as one pleases on public forums without fear of recrimination from others. Abuses are deterred as they are detected by *arbiter*, logged, and exposable. "You are you, you are your identity," could be a guiding mantra.

Thirdly, a pandemic has rocked the world and one reason the impact has been severe is a lack of confidence in vaccinations. It is unlikely this is a one-time event and future pandemics can be potentially deadlier. The anonymous identity features of filial Values make it ideal to manage contact tracing to keep affected people apart in the short term, as well efficiently manage the distribution and dispensation of vaccinations, even customizing them to best correspond to an individual's biology.

Fourthly, a widespread adoption of filial Values can eliminate police departments without radical defunding by utilizing its blend of anonymity and specificity as a deterrent. Criminals can be objectively and quickly pinpointed. Once it's understood by potential culprits how little actual investigation is required by *arbiter*, crime will diminish. Once crime diminishes, policing is redundant. As well human surveillance and accompanying big brother fears. Another example of utilizing passive behaviour modification instead of brute enforcement.

Road Map

This paper is theoretical, it assumes biological and technological advances not yet available, none implausible. With dedicated focus they can be achieved more rapidly than one might think. Especially with a roadmap specifying the foreseen development phases and implementation stages.

The development phases entail the design and construction of early versions of physical components—*arbiter*, *monitor*, Values badges—concurrently with registering data for *filials* and *Indos*, and defining a base set of *filiations*. The design must be robust and realistically consider what can be implemented directly and remain effective through the final stages. This is ***Stage Zero***.

Each incarnation of filial Values (i.e. each city) goes through a Stage Zero assessment to identify scenarios requiring tailoring. The subsequent stages must receive unanimous approval from all contributors and stakeholders to proceed, as they all depend on each other. This stage is highly dependent on comprehensive data collection.

Once the development stage is approved, **_Stage One_** begins. This stage has the loosest controls, making it the one most likely to invoke (as well as best to reveal) any resistance that can pose problems for subsequent stages. Values badges are basic (cards, chips, other dumb devices), that are machine readable, but not yet connected to _arbiter_. Emphasis is on data security, reliability, and usability for easier applications like the hiring and social media ones above. Only _filials_ must have badges on their person at all times during this stage. _arbiter_ and _monitor_ remain inactive except to accumulate data.

Stage Two brings _arbiter_ and _monitor_ to life, along with the operational Values badges connected to them. The connections need not be fully reliable or consistent yet and this can be seen as a beta stage to identify issues and resolve them. Sophisticated features like pain giving, even if available, would not be used yet. filial Values is in essence a technical solution but it is critical to be mindful of human factors. Hence, marketing campaigns targeting the unregistered are a priority. Registered _Indos_ must carry badges, unregistered ones can still go without, but life will be harder for them. Pandemic management functions such as contact tracing ought to be implemented at a minimum.

Stage Three is the most volatile, when it is both possible and desirable to eliminate police. It is the technological summit with all Values badge, _arbiter_, and _monitor_ capabilities at their most reliable. A city cannot be certified Stage Three until this is tested and verified. Everyone must be attached to their Values badges, save for rare exceptions. Border access is restricted and borders are heavily guarded, with physical barriers if possible. To ready for an end to policing the existing force is temporarily bolstered as needed—even doubled or tripled—to exhaustively eradicate lawbreakers once and for all. This means police work will exist until the very last city enters Stage Four, providing job security for decades in law enforcement. Stage Three is the longest of the impermanent stages by far, and can be indefinite.

Stage Four is the nirvana of filial Values, its purest form. No one can enter or move about the city without a fully functional Values badge. *arbiter*, and only *arbiter* (i.e. no human), is aware of all movements. As all processes would be in place by now as part of the prior stage, this stage can focus on refining technical infrastructures, perfecting processes, and social advances.

Risks and Impacts

The risks of a program like filial Values are difficult to ascertain while it remains theoretical, for each risk can be countered by a corresponding risk to not implementing it. Hence, it would be counter-intuitive to identify (guess) at this point and to instead make it part of each phase or stage to do a full assessment. Most risks will be associated with resistive actions and addressing the strategies they concoct.

One can speculate more confidently on impacts, such as the inevitable migrations. filial Values is a solution that's rooted in progressive values. Those unwilling to adapt are bound to leave during or before Stage Three. Offsetting this are progressives living in places where they feel constricted, who may be drawn to filial Values. There will be disruptive migrations both ways, but in the end the risk of a population imbalance should be low.

Final Words

A programme such as filial Values may take decades to evolve. But if a focused effort to overcome its technological and political hurdles is given, the promises of filial Values can not only be achieved but exceeded. This will require patience. If rushed, the effort will inexorably become convoluted, leading to stagnation. Hence, while it's designed, developed, and implemented, filial Values must humbly continue looking beyond itself. A humility symbolized by the lowercase first word.

Esmeralda and Otto

28

The message displayed on the Doyenne's kitchen screen bore a terse subject line—"it's me, help"—that ironically highlighted it amongst the long-winded missives she hated as part of her role in academia. Obsequious platitudes to the Doyenne that once energized her now made her cringe. The meek appeal also woke a latent fear Esmeralda had carried for almost two decades: the threat posed by Felix and Felicity. Until now their interactions had been rare, impersonal, inconspicuous—maybe fortune had had enough. Esmeralda halted the class for a brief break.

The full message was more dire: "in Timmins. Felix supposed to be here 2 days ago. don't know what to do. hate to bother but you said in emergency to contact you."

Unlike Felicity, Esmeralda knew what to do. Message Grace, get her assistant to inquire about strange events near Timmins. Grace's pragmatic reply was unsurprisingly frustrating.

"It's unseemly for the Doyenne to seek information about non-family Values cities. Particularly that one."

"I heard something I need to confirm."

"Your inquiry will be logged and reviewed, of course."

"Mix it in with others, make it too routine to incite curiosity."

"Of course. When do you need it?"

"What do you think?"

Esmeralda hated being blunt with Grace, especially when her assistant's concerns were valid, but she'd have faced resistance if Grace knew this was linked to the twins.

What a shock that day they arrived at the NewTor border—it was still famTor then—without warning, after having left Ken. Their hatred for her husband was incompatible with her own recollections of a man she'd loved and on whom she'd saddled so much. What she did to Ken was unfair, she'd betrayed him. Small consolation to discover their hatred was due more to their inability to adjust to a rough, simple life up north than to any sense their mother had abandoned them. Ken, who was capable at anything he tried, had met his match raising the children. A result she might have predicted, but had chosen to ignore. They had failed their children together.

Despite that, Esmeralda's unexpected joy seeing them made it harder to hide their existence from her partner, yet keep them close. She lodged them in Grace's unit. A tumultuous stay that lasted barely a week before her assistant found them in the shower together. A disgusting crime for regular citizens, for the Doyenne incest meant utter collapse. Esmeralda had no choice but to send them off before Baxter heard about it. Undoubtedly, Felix and Felicity were ill-suited to live in a world changing the way famTor was changing. They'd never become *familyars* and live within those bounds.

Returning to Ken wasn't an option. Luckily they didn't protest when resourceful Grace found them jobs as commercial vehicle drivers in North Bay, with training, as well as an apartment. An apartment Esmeralda never saw—how cold she was then—as it was out of sight, out of mind. It allowed them to be together in their way, despite Esmeralda's warning their actions could lead to their being sent to separate education camps if caught. And if not careful, if they had a child, it'd be taken away, possibly even terminated. Her lecture had affected them enough to assent to sterilization in a way mothers—sadly, not hers—might suggest and help arrange birth control. Esmeralda had felt a strange mix of relief and sadness to see them readily agree to such a drastic step, then to again see them leave, possibly permanently.

Repeating her pattern with Ken. Three times their paths had crossed in life. The first two, at school and the clinic, they were only kids. The third, after the awkwardness of meeting through that Doug fellow, was ideal. Then it wasn't.

For a long time Esmeralda assumed there'd be a fourth. But as she sent her children off for a second time the reality hit home: the notion of her and Ken as star-crossed lovers was an illusion. Part of her missed his down-to-earth honesty. But he struggled in her world, despite his sincere efforts to adapt. Until the day, approaching three decades ago, they agreed it was best he take the kids to his world. Presumably to ride out the pandemic, but in all truth, she'd known otherwise. He must have too.

Esmeralda glanced out at the city, trying to reminisce how it looked back then, with her husband. Imagining away the tallest, newest structures was easy, it left most of the office buildings the same; save for those used by family Values administration and its university, most now combination office/residences. Ken always complained about traffic. Now personal cars were gone, along with their noise and pollution. The highway parallel to the lake, clogged with cars in daylight hours, torn down. The dedicated avenues for utility vehicles were a nuisance at first, but people got used to them, as they did with the smaller streets filling with humanity in motion. It was mesmerizing to observe the seemingly choreographed masses from forty-three floors up, still following archaic social distancing conventions.

Whenever asked to name her proudest achievement of family Values—as she often was—she'd cite the gradual elimination of police as envisioned by her paper. Unlike those rash politicized attempts of the early 2020s. However, as they discovered during those turbulent early 2030s, this was only achievable with a city cleansing involving a concentrated, protracted police presence in Stage Three some equated to police states. A difficult concept to convey, the essentiality of temporary hard policing before a city could graduate to peaceful Stage Four. Counterintuitive to many to take a seemingly backward step after working hard to reduce policing until then. The results were often unpredictable, making the process debatable. Those for pointed to encouraging results in famBar and famKing; those against exploited issues in famSud and famCoch. Easy to explain to these students in her current class, politicians with experience transitioning between stages and personal examples to consult; whereas the younger, idealistic ones struggled to test their ideologically pure minds to accept this harsh practicality.

Esmeralda returned to finish the lesson, then hurried back to her office to wait on Grace. However, she found Grace waiting, wearing her unique grim frown. Directed at the Doyenne from anyone else, it would get its wearer punished.

"I know I ask a lot of you, Grace."

This diminished but did not erase the frown.

"What did you find out?"

"It's not good. The body of an unidentified *Indo* was found on the north entrance road into Timmins. Murdered. By a gun. But the weapon wasn't found."

"A gun."

Grace nodded. Esmeralda was unsure what to say. The only gun she'd ever seen was a sleek German one Ken had let her try on the sole trip she took to his hometown, Kapuskasing. Where she'd met that delightful Vanessa. Guns were still legal then but were now as good as extinct. Even in a corrupt and lawless zone like Timmins, being shot by one was unheard of.

"Their officials are being cooperative and haven't publicized anything. They assumed the victim was an *Indo* by the ringed mark on his wrist. No Values token, though. No identification."

The chill coursing through her told Esmeralda it must be him. It was too much of a coincidence.

"So they can't confirm who it is?"

"Not yet. It means the Exceptions Office will be involved."

Esmeralda shuddered. Baxter headed that department and it would be only a matter of time before he got wind of this. She had to get Felicity to hurry back.

29

Desirae was new, different, with a volatile energy. Not someone he'd want to be around a long time, but perfect for this trip. She also didn't talk as much as Monica, nor try to figure him out, unless it had to do with her project. He still wasn't sure he liked being a project, her taking notes about him and his reactions to family Values. It'd depend on how she went about it.

The two were dissimilar in other ways. Desirae was tinier and slimmer obviously but it went beyond that. Monica treated Otto as an equal while Desirae made it clear she was the experienced elder, full of practical confidence Otto found tolerable. Such as how she explained the trip details, how he ought to behave with strangers, how best to pack his small duffel bag, then inspecting his bag and telling him to leave his utility knife behind. Luckily he'd kept the letter in his pants pocket and stuffed it in just before leaving. Monica, on the other hand, had a motherly tender way Otto often found cloying.

Roscoe was driving them to the departure point; Otto wished it were James. He'd enjoyed the talk on the boat that carried on into the next day when they got back to Ken. Otto understood it was best for Ken that James stay there and his concern for Ken convinced him to agree to be Desirae's subject. She was excited by it too, though it didn't stop her griping about James refusing to provide her with an introduction letter to the Doyenne once again. The patience of her father on this topic was impressive.

"Honey, I'm with James. This approach is better. Such a letter might do more harm in the long run."

"No reason I can think of that we couldn't do both."

When Roscoe didn't respond, Desirae winked at Otto. He had no idea what it meant but suspected she'd look to him to fill in as her connection. He felt for the letter in his pack, as if called to share it with her. He didn't have a chance for they had arrived. Roscoe slowed the car while Desirae unbuttoned her blouse.

"What are you doing?"

She flashed open her palm to reveal a flat, metallic, circular object with several needle-thin pins underneath. Its surface bore the heart-shaped logo that was on the coasters at George's, on many buildings in Kapuskasing, but nowhere in Timmins. He watched Desirae manoeuvre the item inside her blouse towards her shoulder, scowling several times shifting it until she relaxed and re-buttoned her blouse.

"I swear one of these days I'll get an implant. Make my boobs big at the same time."

Roscoe jerked his head back.

"Don't you dare."

"Only joking, Dad."

Desirae noticed Otto staring. She smiled and unbuttoned just enough for him to see the tiny scar. She pulled at it and a flap of skin opened to reveal the item attached in her shoulder. A light pink throbbing light stood out in the darkness of the car.

"First time you've seen a Values token, I bet. I'd have shown it to you last night but . . . actually, I'm not sure why I didn't."

"We just ran out of time, everyone was tired."

"Right."

"Why is it pink?"

"It shows it's biologically connected, working. It'll get brighter and stop flashing once it links to *arbiter* in famBar. Even more in NewTor. The flashing indicates it's charging. It feels weird, as if your blood or something is slithering inside."

"But what's the point of the light if it's inside you?"

"I'm not sure, they're just made that way. I suppose it helps to identify someone in case they die."

"Will I need one?"

"Of course. You'll get it soon enough."

"Otto, yours will work differently. Internal bio-charging is an expensive feature, only for *familyars*."

"You're right, Dad. Thanks for reminding me."

Roscoe launched into an explanation of how Otto's token will use his internal body heat to generate power once injected with a special liquid called fam-elixir.

"But Desirae didn't inject herself with anything."

"fam-elixir is for the temporary token you get as a *Transitory Indo*. Permanent tokens worn by *familyars* like me and for fully registered *Indos* generate it internally. A real convenience."

"It's imperative you get injections on time too."

"What if I don't?"

"You will. You can't really function otherwise. Besides, you'd be breaking the law."

"But what if I forget? Or don't feel like it."

"As a lawyer, I can assure you it's not a law you want to test."

"How will I know when to get them? Or where?"

"That's why I'm with you. To show you."

At the drop-off Otto witnessed a long sweet goodbye between father and daughter, even more emotional than the one between Monica and Wesley. It embarrassed Otto until Roscoe drove off. The crossroad reminded him of Driftwood.

Here too were private buses, lots of them. No hesitation from Desirae who knew the correct one to board. And what to say to the driver after she and Otto separated and the driver, a bulky, powerful woman in her forties with a hard face, waved a metal stick over his body and scowled. She looked about to deny Otto access but Desirae convinced the woman she was his escort and the driver had no choice. Somehow they managed to get a seat together, allowing Desirae to explain to Otto that as *familyar* and family Values academy senior student, she could take any form of transport and was also authorized to escort *Transitory Indos* like Otto. She seemed to be waiting for him to acknowledge this and when he did, Desirae groused the driver should've known better, before falling into a nap.

They had been travelling just over an hour when the driver announced they'd reached their terminus. The bus left the main road and pulled to a stop in a large open area with only a stark metal-frame building, in front of which a few dozen people had lined up to catch this bus back north. He and Desirae followed the other passengers to a waiting zone. Through the large glass windows Otto saw the building's facilities were meagre, barely enough for a snack. Most passengers didn't bother, staying near a metal tower centring rows of poles with tiny screens. It was strange seeing so many mouths move and hearing not a single voice. All the blank screens. Desirae explained they talked using their Values tokens. For *familyars* the connection was encrypted, invisible and muted to others. For *Indos* it was open, and if they wanted privacy they had to shield the screens with their hands. Otto asked to try but she pointed out he didn't have a token and the one he'd get wouldn't let him see anything more than advertisements and basic information. She left him for a screen to update her father back in Timmins.

At last a bus arrived, empty. The driver apologized for being late, explaining he needed to recharge at another location. His contrite manner shifted abruptly as he rudely hounded them to board quickly. He didn't ask about Otto's status. At one point, Otto scratched his side and his shoulder nearly touched a man across the aisle. Desirae gave him a light slap, then pointed at a sign overhead. Outlines of two people and a line with an arrow at each end between them, an X over their mouths. The drive was longer this time, a good ninety minutes, but it seemed to go faster. For the first time since Timmins, Otto saw the tops of buildings, the low floors concealed by a massive concrete wall, its wide opening the sole break in the grey expanse.

The bus didn't enter the opening, but instead turned right and then stopped at an entrance to a gravel lot enclosed by a chain link fence with signs indicating it was electrified. A uniformed man boarded and walked to the back, pointing at people along the way, including Desirae and Otto. She rose and gave Otto a gentle shove on the shoulder.

"Come on, we get off here."

Two men bearing rifles met them to direct them along a path into a long building. She excused herself to visit the bathroom. Once she was out of sight two guards approached and told Otto to follow them into a room, ignoring his protest he should wait for Desirae. He gave in when the woman promised to retrieve her shortly. The man added that if Otto didn't go with them he would go to the back of the line of all the buses and likely have to wait until tomorrow.

The room was painted beige, with brown tile floors, a single chair the only furnishing. They motioned for Otto to take it and then stared at him. Two lights shone from the white ceiling and seemed to shift like the tiny light from the scanner earlier. The room was refreshingly cool after the hot, humid buses.

"My friend should be back by now."

Both guards glanced at each other in hesitation, then shook their heads.

"I'm afraid that as famSud is transitioning from Stage Two to Stage Three, we are bound by new policies. This one requires us to interview *Transitory Indos* apart from their escorts."

"Really? I think she'd have told me about that."

"This is new. Had you come last week . . ."

"Never mind, let's start. First, tell us, who are your parents?"

"I'm not sure. I'm going to NewTor to see if I can find out."

The guards huddled, unaware their lowered voices could not escape Otto's excellent hearing.

"The detector says he's speaking the truth."

"It would explain why his DNA doesn't match anyone in the database. Not why it was flagged."

"Too simpleminded to be a Quebecer or Nova Canadian."

"Sure as hell can't be a Yank. Maybe a refugee, a true one you hear about time to time."

"Are we overstepping? It's confusing, these stage transitions."

"I agree. If there's no issue with the girl let's let them through to famBar. They're fully Stage Three, better equipped to handle exceptions like this."

They let him go and he found Desirae. All the way to famBar she griped about the incompetence of the staff at famSud. How they weren't out of Stage Two and prematurely applying Stage Three rules. For them to wait to get Otto until she'd left him was proof of poor training. Her knowledge impressed Otto but also bored him. He tried to amuse himself with the screens wrapped around the bus with variations of the image of the Doyenne. All advertising. University programs, public events, bio implant surgery, countless family Values approved everyday products.

Outside the empty wilderness was often broken by buildings, roads, and treeless tracts of land with concrete foundations that fanned out in symmetrical patterns, ready to be built upon in orderly fashion. Fascinating. But Otto found greater interest in spotting occasional dense forests or pristine lakes that reminded him of Ken, and of the rewarding exhaustion of paddling. Such reminders were flashes and didn't challenge his appetite for the new. This was like paddling rapids: at some point you've gone so far the best way to go back is to finish first. Otto was just as committed to this journey as he'd be on white water.

It was dark when their bus arrived at the next stop, the third of five, an intrusion of the modern world into nature. A shared stop, busy with dozens of commercial trucks and a complex of buildings full of travellers and workers making arrangements, purchasing supplies, or engaging with screens of which there seemed hundreds. A longer stop, a more intense identification check, requiring Desirae act her diplomatic and persuasive best. Her interrogator was kind once Desirae told him she would be studying at the family Values academy. That got them through to be among the first to re-board the bus. Only to find their seat occupied by a nervy, frailly thin woman with hard hair tied in a bun, thicker than Desirae's, more like his own. Her skin blended in the darkness, might have made her invisible in the unlit bus, if not for her bright red lipstick.

Desirae sighed the way she did when preparing to argue with an official. No words were required this time, just a glare, to get the woman to shuffle to a seat across the aisle, one row behind them. The incident forgotten until Otto felt a tap.

"Sorry about your seat. I only boarded here and didn't know."

"It's all right. I'm—"

An elbow to his kidney shut Otto up. He leaned back when Desirae reached across his lap to address the woman with a soft but unconcealed phony voice.

"Don't fret over it. We do need to catch some sleep before the next stop."

"Of course."

The woman sat back, eyes ahead. Otto wasn't tired, content to take in the countryside. Whenever he glanced across the aisle his peripheral vision caught the woman staring. Unnerving but intriguing. He checked Desirae; she was asleep. Otto turned to the woman, her eyes holding him with captivating intensity. He couldn't resist when she beckoned him over.

"Your gal shouldn't mind if we chat, I bet she'll appreciate the extra room."

Otto was about to correct her assumption but recalled James saying it was wiser to be the one asking rather than answering.

"Are you travelling alone?"

For a moment her eyes glazed over. She stared ahead several seconds, then back at him, now smiling grimly.

"I lost someone dear to me. I'd be grateful if you sat with me until the next stop. Or until she wakes up."

"Where are you going?"

"Young man, even I know it's improper to ask that question."

"I'm sorry."

"It's all right. Handsome boys like you can get away with it. You're not all that familiar with family Values protocols, I bet. I must admit, I'm still adapting as well."

The woman word's made Otto uneasy for their familiar tone, then the way her left hand slipped around his neck as the right rubbed his thigh. He wasn't sure what to do when she grabbed his neck towards her. She was stronger than she looked.

"You are quite handsome."

She kissed him, muscling her lips to pry his open. The effort to keep them shut prevented him from freeing himself without exerting force. It took a furious hiss from Desirae to do that. A few passengers stirred.

"Why are you sitting there?"

"We thought you wanted to sleep."

"I didn't ask you, lady."

When the woman didn't react:

"You're old enough to be his mother."

This made the woman gasp, then skulk to a seat all the way at the back. Desirae tugged Otto and made him take the window seat. A strange feeling of empathy grew and stayed within him until they stopped early in the morning. Otto was happy to see Desirae relax when there was no sign of the woman.

"I only sat with her because she looked lonely."

"Is that so? I have a question: When you and Monica acted as a couple, how far did you two take it?"

Otto shrugged. It was disappointing to see this childish petty side to her. He hoped by keeping silent it'd teach her a lesson. But instead of goading her, the silence calmed her, allowed her dignified demeanour to return, but with a trace of melancholy.

"I'm sorry I asked you that."

"Are you jealous, Desirae?"

"I'm not jealous over you."

As the words came out of Desirae, so did her toughness, and that bewildered Otto even more than what she'd said. He didn't know what she was talking about or could be implying. He felt as he had after Ken told about the twins. Only this time, it came to him as a light from a building shone on Desirae's face, which bore the buoyant expression she'd had in the pool with Monica. A different uneasiness to this conversation compared to the one with the woman but still an uneasiness. Fortunately it was time to board the last bus to famBar.

Exhaustion overcame him and he slept the entire way. Except for brief excerpts from his Doyenne dream, as he'd begun to call it, occasionally rousing him those last thirty kilometres. He felt refreshed as the bus pulled into the terminal at famBar behind several rows of other buses.

30

"I've never seen such a lovely home. Much nicer than your other one. The views must be spectacular. If only I wasn't so scared to look. And the furniture. So plush and more comfortable looking than that minimal stuff."

The mothering instinct in Esmeralda had lain dormant all her life. That was the only explanation she came up with to account for her sentimentality with Felicity, now uncharacteristically chatty, without a trace of insincerity. Maybe grief was making her daughter cling to Esmeralda so strongly. While Esmeralda shared Felicity's loss—Felix was her son, after all, as much as Felicity was her daughter—hers was offset by relief at the termination of their incest. Having them sterilized had resolved the offspring threat, but not that of discovery. Most frustrating was Felicity's inability to explain being in Timmins, beyond her brother instructing her to meet him there. Esmeralda suspected Felicity of holding back at least a guess as to why he needed to see her with such urgency. Until Esmeralda knew, Felicity could not stay at the penthouse. And Grace would understandably be reluctant to host again. Willowdale was an option only it was so far it'd be difficult to keep tabs on Felicity. Esmeralda was even uncertain what to do with her for the next hour.

"I'm glad you like it, but I'm afraid you won't be able to stay here. At least not now."

"What? Why?"

"Until I know—we know—what happened to Felix."

"You're not going to make me stay with that Grace again."

It was evident Felicity, despite being in her thirties, was still a self-absorbed child, incapable of appreciating what Grace, and others, had done for her. And did she need to wear that garish makeup? And so much. Or the cheap costume jewellery, which only highlighted her unkempt hair?

"You won't. Get your things. We need to leave."

"I honestly don't know what happened to Felix. I'd tell you."

"Well, we need to figure it out. Just not here. Not now."

Esmeralda managed with difficulty to persuade Felicity to go down a floor to wait in her office while she contacted Grace for suggestions. Her assistant had a great one: let Felicity audit the introductory lecture Esmeralda was about to give. It was a brief, rather ceremonial overview for prospective students to meet the Doyenne, to prove to the sceptical ones there truly was a human behind family Values. Even better, that day's class consisted of leaders from small cities close to NewTor, none of whom could possibly know Felicity. Nonetheless, Esmeralda deemed it wise to have her daughter sit in the back where it wasn't well lit, and have the roughly three dozen attendees fill the front four rows, where no one would notice the fretful black woman.

Esmeralda transformed into lecture mode to introduce herself, but got no applause or reaction. A group not enamoured by her stature. There was a time she'd be hurt by this but she now saw it as auspicious, a sign of serious intent for implementing family Values in their city. Also pragmatic questions and attentiveness. Even Felicity was sitting up, alert, judging her dangling bright yellow diamond-shaped earrings.

"family Values. What is it? Well, that is akin to asking what is life? The inquiry may be academically interesting but in practice such questions and attempts at their answers are irrelevant and ignorable. The ability to distinguish between academic abstracts and practical application is fundamental to the success of family Values cities. The irony is what I share with you today about the origins of family Values and the paper that started it, is abstract, but with the practical aim of illustrating this distinction in order for you to recognize it and avoid getting lost in the abstract, as can and does happen. As city administrators, your bureaucratic powers apply to the practical and attempts to apply them to the abstract inevitably backfire. Grasp this and you too may become the next famBar as opposed to a famSud or, far worse, a rogue entity like Timmins."

Esmeralda scanned her audience for any reaction to Timmins. A good indicator of the public support for these bureaucrats, or of renegades within. The greater the disdain hearing the name of that city, the better. This class was quiet, hard to tell. She was also interested in and possibly distracted by Felicity's reaction, if she'd suspect Esmeralda mentioning Timmins had to do with her. But it was too dark to see her daughter's face.

"Most of you aren't old enough to remember 2020 but I'm sure you've all read about the pandemic that indelibly reshaped the world and spawned the vaccination obsessions that eventually led to the discovery of the fam-elixir that enables Values tokens to be so effective. A tumultuous era marked by an increasingly binary divisiveness across politics, gender, race."

163

She paused again, as she often did at this point, before going on to provide examples of the world of that time. Only so much had changed not just in its reality but also its history. If honest, Esmeralda would have to admit she wasn't certain anything she told them was true in fact, or opinion, or even relevant. Which was why she tended to rush through this section, but didn't this time because of Felicity. For that was the year she and Felix had left with Ken. But Esmeralda's audience was not Felicity, it was those immediately in front of her, wherever they were from; she had to focus and not stray. Be the Doyenne, not mother.

"The lockdowns gave me time to observe the world, where it was going, and it became clear to me these binary divisions, like the universe, would continually expand, never contract. Instead of fighting this, I felt we needed to adapt by first accepting the differences. Focus on mutual respect and exploit what we share as humans rather than indulging and enforcing personal views in the zero sum environments fostered by social media.

"My challenge to myself was to design a method attractive or even desirable to all and document it. That's how family Values began. With a paper I wrote while studying at university. I will assume you read it prior to coming here. It laid the foundation for the application of technology by smarter minds than mine to develop the world upon which you are embarking. A world in which urban behaviour is governed fairly for all."

So far so good, she thought, before articulating the differences between her abstract paper and the reality of its evolution, like renaming filial Values as family Values, *filials* as *familyars*, *filiations* as *fams* and correlating her theoretical foundation to the experience of actual implementations. She was proud how close her vision was to reality, though it didn't seem as close today. In fact, the gaps seemed wider. She was too professional to dwell on it, but it could trouble her later. No one drifted off and the session concluded with satisfaction at having met her objective: ripening them for what was to come.

"Doyenne, after all these years, do you still believe in it and all the tenets that comprised your original filial Values?"

"Of course I do."

Not the first to dare such a question, though this time she felt her voice was unconvincing in providing her usual explanation. That she trusted the design but granted certain implementations created doubts, though those doubts were usually attributable to local circumstances, rarely universal.

"What about racial blending? Don't some aspects of this add-on contradict the principles of opting for passive approaches as well as the 'voluntary and transparent participation' one?"

Esmeralda hesitated, unable to gauge the questioner's tone. A male voice from where Felicity sat interjected. Esmeralda fought to conceal her horror seeing Baxter next to her daughter. Right next to Felicity, when he could have taken any seat or joined her at the front.

"Firstly, racial blending is no add-on, it has been connected to family Values conceptually since inception."

Baxter then stood up and continued speaking.

"I'm Professor Baxter van Leer. You'll see plenty of me in your time here, more as your city graduates through the stages. It is such questions for which I can provide answers. And please do not withhold them. As to contradicting the principles, it's naive to think an expansive program such as family Values can retain an entirely yielding approach and stay effective in reality. As the Doyenne concluded in her paper, it must continually look beyond itself. That includes scope and methods. Which is the case with racial blending, which builds on the success of family Values to eliminate racism. Most of you are too young to recall how it was twenty or thirty years ago, hence prone to repeating those errors. Thanks to family Values, discrimination by race is possible to overcome, if there are no pure races."

Esmeralda could kill Grace for not reminding her of Baxter's habit of showing up at her classes to screen (scout, according to him) new students. Couldn't she have prevented him attending this time? Then to let him sit so close to Felicity? Did they talk? Did he know who she was? Or vice versa?

"Do you really think that can work, Professor?"

"It will take time, but I'm certain of it. Especially if voluntary sterilizations increase. Before you ask, let me address famCoch, which as some of you may know, volunteered as a beta site. It's true we are facing difficulties there and have endured setbacks. We were perhaps overambitious for such a remote location, but it's taught us much. You'll find here in NewTor that support for racial blending is virtually universal."

Despite her irritation Esmeralda was grateful for his coming to her aid on that question. Was it instinctual? Had he sensed a level of discomfort in her? Unfortunately it would be impossible to get an answer from him because he just as abruptly gave her the floor and left. Once the class ended and the room emptied, Felicity rushed down the aisle to greet her.

"You were wonderful. I never imagined you were so smart."

"Why, thank you."

"I wish you talked more about how it began. The time Felix and I went away."

"Yes. The man who next to you, who spoke up at the end. Did you talk to him? Did he say anything to you?"

"No. He just sat there. Who is he?"

"He's my . . . partner."

Felicity looked perplexed, as if the idea of her mother with a man other than her biological father was inconceivable.

"He's nothing like my father. He seems meaner."

"What makes you say that?"

As Felicity pondered a response, Esmeralda wondered if the question was positive about Ken or negative about Baxter.

"I don't know. Is he why I need to stay elsewhere?"

"You know what? I've changed my mind about that."

31

Otto fiddled with the flesh-coloured bracelet tightly attached to his wrist. A constricting nuisance. He'd never worn jewellery of any sort, not even a watch like Ken sometimes wore, didn't care for it. He especially hated how visible it was, a detail omitted by Desirae and Roscoe. The fam-elixir injection wasn't fun either, but it was painless, better than the dozen vaccination needles, and the boredom of waiting up to an hour between each shot. Otto found amusement in observing others' bracelets, their light pinks and blues of varying shades. Not all had bracelets either; some had rings or necklaces; others, like Desirae, must have had them inside their clothing. It was also fascinating to survey the variety of places people wore them. The shoulder was popular but many put them on chests, necks, stomachs, thighs, ankles. One woman her cleavage. He recalled a bus advertisement for two-for-one implants that included breast enlargement.

This was their second day at famBar. Once again they'd been separated, since this morning. Last night they slept in beds next to each other but divided by thick glass to block conversation. He'd been told to expect this, but still found it discomfiting. At least they could move around the facility while inside the cubes. It helped kill time and a couple of tours confirmed the woman from the bus was gone.

Yesterday they'd seen her again, in the cavernous processing room. Otto wouldn't have noticed if not for the sigh of disgust from Desirae, followed by a glare in the direction of the cause. It looked as if the woman was being taken somewhere, but not as if she was in trouble. She noticed them too, he could tell by the way she averted their gaze. He expected Desirae to chastise him for looking but didn't notice his travel partner had gone off to another area. He'd have liked to have been told. He'd continued to watch the odd woman until she'd been escorted to the buses.

Desirae's (and the woman's) absence exacerbated the hollow feeling of the glass cubes. Cold. Sterile. So many people, yet so eerily quiet. As if all their voices had been sucked in a tube and concentrated into a high-pitched buzz. Most were engrossed by a screen in the cube, oblivious to others. Also calming, in a way, due to the soft pastels of the floors and plastic seats.

Otto noticed a lot of attention given to a cube near him, where a man he assumed was a vagrant lay down, his wrist flashing a dark red. It stopped flashing as two guards opened the cube to let two officials in white remove what looked to be a corpse. The drama ended as quickly as it began, everyone returned to minding their business. Otto checked his wrist, became a little concerned to see it not pink like Desirae's had been, but a solid deep blue.

When he looked up again the same officers who'd come to the dead man were at his cube. They led Otto down a corridor, to a white-walled lab filled with shiny steel instruments. The same instruments that yesterday had poked, prodded, and probed his body. He had no desire to experience them again.

"Otto."

He turned, shocked to hear his name. No one had mentioned it or asked him to state it. It could only be one person.

"Desirae. Where've you been?"

"Secluded. Until your token activated. Let me see."

He assumed that was what the blue light meant and showed her his wrist. She nodded, satisfied.

"How many vaccination shots did they give you?"

"I lost count at twelve."

"Wow."

"I thought I was going to be here forever."

"There was a time when you'd have to wait up to two weeks if they didn't know you. At least now they can tell if you've got an illness or virus right away. Did they ask questions and use these instruments on you?"

"Yes. I had trouble with some questions. The woman got quite frustrated with me."

"Oh? Like what?"

"What is a preferred pronoun, for instance?"

The door opened. A man entered, didn't say who he was, just that he needed questions answered to release them.

"Your companion doesn't seem capable of answering these."

"So he's fine physically?"

"Indeed. Spectacular specimen. Heart and body functions as good as any I've seen pass here. A surprising lack of ailments in a body that's never been vaccinated. First time I've seen it in—I can't say I've ever seen it. First time ever with no ill effect from the shots either."

"So we're good to go?"

"Once we gather the last data."

Desirae acted like a proud parent answering for him. Parents (unknown), race (undefined, probably mixed), diseases (none), birth data (unknown), *Indo* or *familyar* (*Transitory Indo*), Gender leaning (male), Preferred pronouns (he/him). Otto felt insulted, like a child, but appreciated Desirae making it go fast. The man told them to wait and it'd be only a few minutes.

"He was nicer than the woman from yesterday."

"He was nice, wasn't he? You know Otto, I'm getting the sense we're being treated differently."

"How do you mean?"

She didn't answer because the door opened. The man handed Otto a shiny thin metallic card to be used for fam-elixir injection refills. He said the card also gave access to thousands of public video terminals on which he could access *Transitory Indo* Values token rules and other non-secured family Values information, such as city maps and guides and books and so on. Desirae kept nodding, which was reassuring to Otto.

"Any questions?"

"Why is my light so blue while hers is pink?"

"Well, the elixir detects you as male. You haven't altered . . ."

"No, he hasn't. I just forgot to tell him the colour indicates the degree of sex one is. I'll explain everything to him as we go."

"All right. Any questions, young man?"

"Yes, how do I remove it?"

"You don't need to. Remember, you must always be in contact with it."

"Even to shower? Or do heavy work?"

"You can wear it anywhere. They're as sturdy as anything."

"If he leaves a family Values city he has to return it, right?"

"He wouldn't get far with it if he didn't."

"So there is a way to remove it?"

"Of course, Otto. be patient."

"I don't mind showing him, ma'am."

"Okay. In fact, it might be good for him to experience the risk of being apart from it." .

The guard smiled then grabbed Otto's wrist to turn it over. He slid his thumb over a thick section until a pin emerged, then he pushed the pin into a tiny hole. The bracelet sprang open.

"Is that the only way to do it?"

"No. It does come off on its own, if it detects you're dead."

Then he pushed the bracelet away with a ruler and motioned Otto to back out the room and keep his eyes on his token.

He did and saw the blue shift to orange as he moved towards the door and felt a dull pain stab at his stomach that slowed his pace. The pain increased each half-step. He was able to open the door but not get past the threshold before he doubled over in agony. Desirae helped him back but made him work to grab the bracelet. The instant he touched it the pain diminished and the colour gradually returned to blue.

When the man left, Otto practiced taking it off and putting it on. Not to be a rebel but because he liked the feel of the smooth heavy metal in his hand.

"How did it do that? Create the pain?"

"Values tokens are constantly scanned by machines inside all family Values facilities. If they detect a human without a token they generate a sonic signal to cause pain."

"So that's why people get them implanted?"

"That's the main reason. The fear of misplacing it."

"Or having it stolen."

"Actually, they're theft proof. Tokens constantly self-check if near a monitor. If there's a mismatch it'll create the same result. Having two is especially painful. That's why I couldn't hand it to you. Stealing them can actually be deadly."

Desirae described this with enthusiasm yet Otto didn't see the benefit. He recalled James calling them electronic leashes and it was clear what he'd meant by that now.

32

Esmeralda remembered a time when one could challenge such a report by challenging the precision of DNA measuring devices, but those flaws were fixed years ago. It was correct, despite its absurd implications. A *Transitory Indo* with DNA matching the Doyenne's. How was that possible?

Esmeralda was heartened at first at the prospect it was Felix, that it wasn't his body found near Timmins. Except the report was clear the subject was eighteen and had arrived without any vaccinations. Felix would be thirty-three. Felix also had to have had his vaccinations because he had an *Indo* Values token. With no other biological family connections, Esmeralda could arrive at only one conclusion: The twins had lied.

It'd been only a couple of days since Felicity moved in but the girl—Esmeralda couldn't stop seeing her as a girl—had been acclimating well, except for the vertigo that kept her from her mother's penthouse balcony forty-three floors up. She even got along well with Baxter. It seemed prudent to be honest with her partner about Felicity's identity so as to let her stay with them. She'd never have guessed he'd react so warmly to her presence. Maybe he saw in her a contrast to the stuffy academicians and bureaucrats filling his daily life. Maybe he found her appealing. Odd that he expressed no curiosity about Felix. Lucky too, for it indicated he knew nothing yet about the event in Timmins. That would change if Esmeralda's fearful conclusion came true. She had to suss it out first. Now was her chance.

Baxter had gone to his room for his video meetings, providing an opportunity to prepare a breakfast for mother and daughter. Only Felicity was a heavy sleeper, with a poor appetite, and the smell of eggs and pancakes didn't rouse her nor did Esmeralda's deliberate clumsiness with the cookware. She had to be patient. She had no classes today, she could work in the home office, so there was no hurry. What a luxury to have an entire penthouse floor in addition to an office eight floors below and the separate suites for guests, when most people had to combine all three in one tiny space. One of many perks for being Doyenne.

Esmeralda took her breakfast to the balcony and left the door ajar. She preferred to sit close to the exit where she could see the lake and avoid looking at the tightly packed buildings, a vision that churned her stomach if she looked too long; this vertigo was hereditary, her father had had it too. Once in a while she'd see fireworks in the form of bombs bursting across the sky from the interminable American conflicts.

The sun was breaking through a thick mist, promising a fine summer morning. It'd be hot in an hour but it was relaxingly cool now. Felicity should be enjoying this. Yet Esmeralda wasn't able to summon the nerve to wake the girl. Even after the coffee cooled, Esmeralda remained affixed to the chair, chained by her uncertainty-induced procrastination.

She worried the ring around her index finger, an annoying tic, according to Baxter. More when she removed it and rubbed it in her palms as she did now. She'd never dropped it she'd say, to which he'd respond that just brought the first time closer, then nag her to get an implant, that she set a poor example not doing so. His nagging got her to stop fidgeting, not his logic. What she wished he'd understand but didn't want to explain was how its design meant a great deal to her so she liked to keep it in view. The soothing pink glow amid two small f's to represent *filial* and *filiation*, the capital V for Values.

filial Values. What she'd originally called her pride and joy. True, family Values was more impactful, less clinical, but didn't truly and fully represent her original intentions. Get the original name tattooed, Baxter would say. It wouldn't be the same. She twirled it another time before leaving it be.

Esmeralda's heart skipped at hearing footsteps. Felicity, in her mother's pyjamas, which hung loose on her too thin frame. She looked different without makeup. Prettier, in Esmeralda's view. A resemblance to Ken's features. Esmeralda rushed inside to fix another breakfast. Felicity followed behind her.

"Don't bother, I'll just have coffee."

"You've got to eat . . . dear. I can make French toast."

"I don't care for anything with eggs."

"Ham, bacon, plain toast. Cereal?"

"Maybe later."

Felicity poured another coffee for herself, then sat at the far end of the island that faced the stove. She scanned the suite as she had the night before, as a resident, not an impressed visitor. Esmeralda liked to see her at ease. She opened a cupboard, from which she retrieved a bag of caramel cookies and put most on a plate. Felicity didn't hesitate to help herself.

"Those are Baxter's favourites, save a few for him."

"My favourites too. I like Baxter. He's cute. Funny he's smaller than you. I usually don't go for men with goatee and paunches."

Esmeralda couldn't believe it. Was she really speaking about Baxter as if he was romantically available?

"Don't forget he's much older."

"Who cares about that if he's attractive? I don't know what it is, maybe the turtleneck, the tweed sports coat. So ainch."

"Ainch?"

"Ancient. You know. But in a good way."

"You are aware he is my partner. He lives with me."

"Oh, sorry, that's right. You two don't seem like that."

"Felicity, I'm confused."

"Confused? You? About what?"

"I thought you and . . ."

"Felix? Yeah we were . . . our jobs keep us apart for weeks. We agreed to be with others . . . now that he's dead . . ."

She's no child, can't treat her like one, Esmeralda told herself. Her lack of emotion over the loss of her brother—it had to come from Ken. No, that was wishful thinking on her part. Ken was different, his stoic facade never concealed an underlying caring nature. Esmeralda detected real indifference from Felicity, even relief, that Felix had died. Or was that more wishful thinking on her part, the wish for an emotional accomplice in moral guilt?

Esmeralda showed the report to Felicity, taking pains to be as clear as possible to ensure no misunderstanding. She needn't have bothered. Felicity clued in instantly, indicating maybe she wasn't as simple as she came across.

"Otto. That's why Felix wanted to see me so urgently."

"Who is Otto?"

Like a little girl, not unlike how Esmeralda was herself once, her daughter became obstinately taciturn. Esmeralda repeated the question forcefully, which Felicity clearly didn't expect.

"Otto is our son."

"But how is that possible? We had you . . ."

"We had him before we came back to you."

"You lied to me then."

"We hated doing it, we tried to fix it."

"Fix it? What does—? No, start at the beginning."

Felicity repeated how they hated living with Ken, how their mutual inability to adapt to his lifestyle and rules drove them to run away. When they conceived a child they got scared. Felicity didn't want an abortion but after having the child realized they couldn't raise it either. They returned to Ken for help, but found him and his canoe and fishing gear gone. They scribbled the name Otto on a card and left the baby in a basket. They got to Kapuskasing to catch a bus. The fear Ken might not return for days compelled them to go back. Just as they arrived they heard Ken's paddling, and ran off for good.

"Then you came here?"

"We didn't know what to do, only that we had to be together, wanted to be together, away from Ken."

"You hated your father that much?"

"Didn't you? I mean he left you and took us."

"I've never hated him."

"But you never came to find us."

"You're right. Circumstances made everyone do—oh it's much too complicated to get into now. I promise I'll explain it to you some time. Just not now. It's important you tell me all first."

Hesitation returned to Felicity but she didn't protest. It was a shock to hear the resentment the twins held towards Esmeralda for manipulating them to move north. Rejecting them, in their eyes. That resentment festered and spread to blame Ken and, by extension, Otto. They subsequently surmised that if the kid was out of the picture, they could come back and Esmeralda would accept them. Felicity slammed her palm on the table, causing Esmeralda to spill some coffee, her eyes wide open.

"That's why Felix wanted to meet. He'd found them. And they killed him. It had to be them. Oh my god. Oh my god."

"Them?"

"Ken and Otto. One of them. Or both."

"Do you think Felix provoked them?"

Esmeralda couldn't read Felicity's evasive shrug.

175

"But the report says he's travelling with a young black woman to NewTor. A student at the academy, which explains his ability to get this far without being noticed."

Felicity stared at Esmeralda with impossible-to-read eyes that glistened, as if ready to tear, but stayed dry.

Another reality struck Esmeralda. She had assumed Ken had raised Otto. What if he'd recruited others to do it? He knew lots of folks, especially Indians, who'd help. Ken wasn't likely to let an eighteen-year-old travel by himself all this way—maybe the dark-skinned woman was a step-cousin? Could she be the one who'd killed Felix?

She knew this speculation was to avert the unthinkable: Ken killing anyone, let alone his own son. Her husband was still an old wound that throbbed with sadness those rare moments his memory came up. A particularly deep sadness if those thoughts led to her thinking Ken might be dead.

"What made you give him that name, Otto?"

"Felix saw the name. We both liked it."

"What would they be doing near Timmins, of all places?"

Another shrug, this time as if expecting her mother would be in a better position to answer this.

33

Something had been nagging at Otto ever since famSud, but he hadn't been able to pinpoint it until Desirae made that comment about being treated differently: it was getting easier the closer they got to NewTor, not the opposite. Here he was a stranger, a nobody, entering increasingly restricted worlds. Yet no one had challenged him to ask his business. He could be a criminal for all they knew. They were happy as long as he openly displayed his token. He wasn't Otto, he was a token. Anonymous.

"Desirae?"

"What is it?"

She'd become irritable the past few hours, less willing to show interest in his questions. He sat back. Maybe she was too tied up with her own concerns. If he could figure out fishing, hunting, making fire, camping with Ken, why would it be any harder to learn what he wanted to learn by just observing and copying?

"Never mind."

"Sorry, just in my own thoughts. What is it?"

"Nothing, go back to sleep."

"I'm up now. Tell me."

Otto paused to ponder a different approach.

"All right. It's just, I thought everything would be different."

"Different? From what?"

"Different from Timmins, or Kapuskasing. I expected it would be more modern, grander. It's all flat, so much farmland with no skyscrapers."

"Is that it? It'll be different in NewTor, trust me."

Not a satisfying answer, but Otto couldn't bother pursuing it. He refrained from sharing the comparison to his dream of cities filled with gleaming buildings connected by aerial tracks and vehicles travelling at high speeds. From what or where his mind concocted those images he had no clue. He'd never read science fiction or watched futuristic stories and had written his Ontario report based on old, probably outdated photos. Nothing around them came close. Not even the newer buildings in Kapuskasing or NewSud or NewBar. This world seemed grimy, dull. Desirae could be right, the horizon could change suddenly to match his vision, but nothing had indicated that to this point. In fact, little had changed except for this road, it was wider, much busier at points. The bus would get up to a good speed for a ways only to slow to a crawl or even stop as it did now.

"What's happening? Have we arrived?"

"Just a traffic jam."

He smiled, recalling Ken's story when he himself was a little boy, how he'd relate the concept of traffic jam to the homemade blueberry jam his stepmother would sell at the market. How it made people laugh when his stepmother shared the story. Otto had to cover his face to prevent a laugh he knew would annoy Desirae. Funny, she rarely laughed. Unlike Monica who would get down at times but whose moods were more often cheerful. He was starting to miss that girl's chatter.

"Are you angry with me, Desirae?"

"No. But stop saying my name out loud."

"Why are you so moody?"

She put an index finger to her lips, then leaned in to whisper.

"Next stop, when I'm sure no microphones are present."

That seemed ridiculous to Otto, he'd only asked about their destination, nothing sensitive. He might have pressed but they started moving quickly again and didn't slow until the next stop and last connection. They exited the bus and were immediately taken aside by two staff members who waved a device at them, then nodded to each other as if confirming they'd gotten the right people, before guiding them to a limousine.

"This was prearranged. Special treatment. I can't tell if that's a good or bad thing."

"You look worried."

"Maybe it's nothing. Be cautious, avoid saying anything about my uncle, or James, and especially about Ken."

"I'm not going to lie to anyone."

She gave him a strange look, then grinned.

"All I ask is that you say nothing unless they bring it up. Can you do that?"

"Yes."

This vehicle was like a car but bigger, longer. It was also very nice inside. They could sit diagonally opposite each other, lots of room for his legs. Despite her misgivings, Desirae made herself at ease. She pressed buttons and opened tiny doors until finding one dispensing tiny bottles of water, juice, soda. Other than disappointment at no wine, her mood vastly improved. He sipped from a box of orange juice while looking out the tinted window. Not much to see, except hundreds of cars and trucks around them. Then it appeared. A skyline. Desirae smiled, as if she knew what was captivating his attention.

This was similar to the one in his dreams, only not as majestic, or colourful. In fact, mostly grey due to the grim clouds above. The car was moving fast; at times it felt as if the buildings were coming at them. Vertically rectangular, geometric shapes at the tops. Spikes of green from what he guessed were little forests or maybe gardens on the rooftops. Cloud breaks released rays of sunshine to reflect on window grids, their glare often obscuring neighbouring buildings. This was more like it. Otto expected to see the larger-than-life face of the dream woman any moment, but of course that didn't happen. This was reality, not a dream. Wonder turned to panic when the car dipped down into a dark tunnel engulfing them in darkness. It braked to a near stop then bumped into something with a clunk, before being lifted. They began to move forward again, this time faster.

"This isn't the way we're supposed to go. Oh my goodness."

Otto's determination to not let her fear affect him was being tested. Instinct told him to grab her hand, expecting that to snap her out of it. To his surprise, she held on, and even crossed to sit beside him and keep hold of him until the car stopped several minutes later.

She tightened her grip on his hand when they got out the car and were met by a small, formidable woman who introduced herself as Grace. She led them into an elevator and had them stand on spots marked by footprints. She pressed a button. Two perpendicular glass panels slid out from each side to keep them apart. One had to pause until Desirae let go his hand. They rose rapidly. Seconds later the panels slid back and the door opened onto a marble foyer. Grace nudged Otto to exit first.

There stood the woman from his dreams, slightly older, more elegant, with the smoothest complexion he'd ever seen. Her hair was golden, her expression inviting, her presence imposing. He was mesmerized by the colourful swirling swaths of her gown. He started to step forward but, just like his dreams, couldn't get himself do it until he heard her speak:

"Welcome to NewTor, Otto."

34

The shock both exhibited at hearing the Doyenne address Otto by name gave Esmeralda a moment to assess him. Good looking boy, strong, powerful, medium length hair that needed cutting. Most jarring, his skin colour, a mix of black and white that you couldn't say was a mix. Yet one couldn't be sure which. Perhaps an effect of his birth circumstances? He appeared normal in all other ways; if he had a deformity maybe it was advantageous. He had a disarmingly humble and graceful confidence too. He looked rugged in face and posture, beyond travel wear, which could be attributable to Ken's genes. Though Otto was broader, leaner, a good four inches taller than Ken, thirty pounds heavier at least. Oddly, she could find no resemblance to the twins. A little to herself, but not enough to guess a biological connection. Even to keen eyes like Baxter's. Were the DNA tests wrong after all? And his skin colour? Hard to determine how much its tone was natural, how much a product of his having travelled so far. A jarring thought: Baxter would see Otto as an ideal outcome of racial blending.

An attention-seeking cough from Grace alerted her to the girl with Otto. She looked nervous.

"Forgive me. I'm Esmeralda, the Doyenne. And you are?"

"I'm Desirae, ma'am. I'm a student at the university."

"You don't know her name but you know mine?"

Esmeralda flinched. Interrupting the Doyenne was a rudeness warranting a rebuke, only his voice had caught her off guard, it sounded like Ken. More than flawless DNA reporting, this told her he was Ken's grandson, hence her grandson. Family. Still, it wasn't decorous to be seen challenged by a teen, or anyone for that matter, regardless of biological connection.

"I am the Doyenne, young man. It is in my purview to know about anyone of importance."

"What makes me important?"

Esmeralda smiled, her instinct to admonish his impertinence transforming to amusement at two things: the boy's gall and the shock on her assistant's face.

"I want you to be my personal guest for the time being. Look upon it as an honour, nothing more. As to your importance, that will be divulged soon enough."

"What about Desirae?"

"You're a student? Then you must have housing arranged for yourself."

"Yes ma'am."

"Well then."

"But her housing doesn't start for a week."

"Otto comes from a rural area and is participating in my thesis to study the culture shock, if any, of family Values on someone with no prior exposure to it. So I decided to come early."

To Esmeralda it sounded plausible and ridiculous at the same time. The sort of rationale Baxter would concoct, and fall for.

"Where did you intend for him to stay? I know the housing units for students are limited."

"We still have to arrange that. I still have to arrange that."

"I see. Then you are welcome to stay here too, Desirae."

"If it's no trouble, ma'am."

"So polite. Grace, please prepare the suite on thirty-six for our guests. But first start us some tea? Thanks."

Esmeralda led her guests onto the balcony. Streams of rain fell vertically over the lake but the city was dry. She pointed to four chairs at a small table. Desirae sat immediately but Otto went to the edge to look onto the street below. He seemed taken aback by the swarms of people but wasn't scared. No fear in him as far as Esmeralda could tell. Unlike his escort who kept fidgeting, until Otto sat next to her. Only to jump at a sudden boom.

"Relax, dear, just a power outage."

"But your lights are on, your kettle sounds like it's working."

"A benefit of being Doyenne is access to the same electric grid keeping our Values tokens functional in such instances."

The water had boiled. Esmeralda granted her guests a private moment while she poured tea, taking her time to select a mug for each, amused to find herself deliberately avoiding ones with family Values logos. No snacks, Felicity had eaten all Baxter's cookies. She didn't want to call Grace back. She put the cups on a tray she carried out the door that opened as she approached. Otto and Desirae were together at the rail now, watching busy streets made more hectic by the confusion from a power outage taking longer to restore than usual.

Otto and Desirae quietly retook their seats like good guests or dutiful students. Esmeralda wished they'd relax. It might help if she addressed what was likely on their minds, even if it risked a bit of plagiarism by borrowing from the girl's story.

"You're both wondering what my interest is in you, no doubt. It's rare to encounter arrivals for whom we have no data. Even more, a healthy unvaccinated individual capable of enduring an entire suite of vaccinations with no reaction. I am talking about you, Otto. I was alerted to this when you were at famBar. We've been monitoring you since."

Esmeralda took a sip of tea to let this sink in. She glanced at the clouds over the lake now moving to the south, to the USA.

"Are you suspicious of me?"

"Tell me, what brought you two together?"

Esmeralda addressed the question to Otto but Desirae was the one who responded, her self-assurance starting to emerge.

"I met Otto at my father's house where I was spending my last weeks before my third year at the academy. Otto was a guest of my stepfather, on a stop prior to coming to NewTor to research his biological parentage. His unfamiliarity with family Values made it logical for me to help him out."

A little too tidy to be true, Esmeralda though, but decided to give it the benefit of the doubt.

"That was kind of you."

"And of course to help me on my term paper."

"Right. You said that. How so?"

"He's lived his entire life up north. When I heard he had never experienced family Values, and was coming here, it made sense to write about his culture shock, his experience. And for that I'd guide him through the procedures."

"So he's to be your guinea pig?"

Esmeralda regretted her words upon seeing a pained look on Otto's face.

"I couldn't have made it this far without her."

"It's a fair question, Otto. He's not a guinea pig that I tell to do things, but a subject free to do what is natural."

"Nicely put, young lady. Now Otto, tell me more about why you wanted to come here."

"Like she said, for information about my birth parents. I'm an orphan, I never knew them. I was left in the woods at someone's cabin. They helped raise me until now. People said NewTor was the best place to find the information."

It took a great deal of self-restraint for Esmeralda to not let on who she was. She couldn't be emotionally reckless. His arriving the same time as her daughter complicated matters; the events could be linked. Also, he might not believe her. She nodded to indicate she'd finished questioning them. But he then leaned forward.

"I've dreamed of you. Just as you are now."

Esmeralda was taken aback. But not as much as Desirae.

"Tell me about this dream."

"You're in front of a big city like NewTor, wearing robes just like that one, and calling me to come to you."

"How extraordinary."

"You never told me this, Otto."

He ignored Desirae's clear irritation. Esmeralda chose to wait to pursue this until she got him alone and instead redirected her focus to Desirae. She was happy to learn the girl wasn't actually from Timmins, but famSud, and impressed by her ambition for a career in the family Values administration of that city. Baxter would like her. This could work out nicely. However, there was much for Esmeralda to learn first. She didn't yet suspect them of deceit but still had a sense she needed to be careful with both. Esmeralda was getting tired, a little overwhelmed.

"I appreciate you two sharing all you've shared and apologize for disrupting your plans. But I do think it'll be to your benefit to stay here as my guests a while. Desirae, I find your interest in family Values encouraging and I'd like to help you."

"Are you serious? I'd be honoured."

"And Otto, I'll make resources available to pursue your quest for information. But let me manage it. You are a *Transitory Indo* so I can't let you just run free."

"I understand. And thank you."

As he said this he flashed the loveliest of smiles and she felt a warmth in her heart. That spurred a small epiphany that unified her convoluted thoughts to one directive: separate them. Just as she'd pre-separated Otto from Felicity, his mother, by getting Baxter to take her daughter on a tour of the school.

Felicity would be back soon. She and Felix had wanted Otto out of the picture. Was that still the case? Would she be looking for revenge? Esmeralda had to isolate Otto from both women. A daunting task but one for which she was well-suited.

35

"The Doyenne is impressive isn't she? Getting us these clothes. That it's likely you're related to her, I just can't . . ."

Otto barely listened to Desirae who was in the other room. He was preoccupied by the clothes laid out on his bed. Much better than the pants and shirts he'd travelled with, but all in black or grey or muted colours. No whites, no primary hues. Four short-sleeved shirts with collars and a couple of pairs of jeans. A pair of khaki shorts. In the closet hung a dark blue suit with a tie slung around the neck, and a pair of black dress shoes on the floor. Two long-sleeved dress shirts as well. The drawer in the table by the bed held six pairs of socks and underwear. Never had he had so much to wear of such quality. He happily tossed his old clothes in the plastic bag labelled "laundry" on entering the bathroom for a shower. It took several frustrating minutes to remove his Values token bracelet.

The shower was hot and strong and he lingered in it almost as long as Monica would have. The towel was thickly lush and he was in no hurry to dry himself. He put on the black jeans and a medium grey shirt and knocked at Desirae's door. No answer. He said her name several times, then gradually opened it. She was gone. He stepped in far enough to see her room was like his but had a window. A bed, a night table, and an armoire took up nearly all the space. It reminded him of famBar and famSud, without the people. Where'd she go?

The suite's furniture was sleek and luxurious, yet welcoming, despite bland beige walls and a dull beige carpet. Put up a few pictures, add some paint, a few rugs, it might become as nice as James's home. A U-shaped leather couch faced a gas fireplace with a large screen above the mantle in the living room. How to turn it on? he wondered. No remote control on the drawer-less coffee table. A closer look showed it wasn't plugged into anything. It might have to do with the bracelet. He put it on—easier than taking it off—and waved it around. Nothing.

Small appliances covered almost all the counter space in the kitchen, with a tiny refrigerator underneath, containing drinks and snacks. Inside the cupboards, pots and pans and glassware. He filled a tumbler with chocolate milk, which he had once and remembered being delicious. Not as tasty this time, but filling, and he drank it in one swig.

The door opened, in walked Desirae. She wore a skirt—first time he'd seen her in one—and her hair had been cropped like a boy's. He didn't like it initially but gradually became fascinated at how it actually made her look more feminine. She carried in a bag of groceries and was on her way to the kitchen but stopped when she saw him waving his wrist at the screen.

"What are you doing?"

"Trying to figure out how to work this."

"You use your Values token."

"But how?"

Desirae set the bag on the counter and joined him in staring at the screen as he'd done. She then slanted her neck one way and the screen brightened to show an image identical to his bracelet and another he assumed would match Desirae's.

"How did you do that?"

"There are receivers in all screens and many other devices that connect to your Values token, which itself is connected to your physiology, if you allow. It takes practice. I suspect it may not work with your token type. Was there something you wanted to watch?"

"Not really."

She sighed, leaned her neck, and the screen went black again.

"Where'd you go?"

"Out shopping for a few things, girl things. It's nice out so we should go for a walk."

"I thought I wasn't allowed to 'run free just yet'?"

"Doesn't mean you're imprisoned. I know the zones, you'll be fine if you stick with me."

"Zones?"

"I'll explain after some fresh air. When we get back, I'll cook up this chicken."

They entered a different elevator, larger with dividers for ten people, each in use by the time it reached the ground floor to open onto a congested lobby. He was anxious to get outdoors, only to find the density worse. Otto's height helped him see; it must be have felt claustrophobic to Desirae, he thought.

She held his hand to keep him close, jerking him at times like a leashed dog before he understood it was convention to keep a distance from strangers. Two metres. No wonder it had looked so packed from far above on the balcony.

They walked a few hundred metres and reached a park by the lake. It was crowded but they found an empty bench. They sat as the sun was starting to go down and Otto found it lovely in its own way. Not as majestic as the northern lights, but brighter and sharper, orange and red, instead of purple and blue and green. The moon started to cast a soft faint glow upon the still harbour that diffused farther out into the artificial lights of US ships, according to Desirae. She added the port had expanded immensely since control was ceded to the United States, both for military and cargo, beyond the islands, leaving the inner bay for residential use. It wasn't how Otto had imagined it when he wrote his report, but wasn't far off either.

"They're our sole export partner, which is why we let them do what they want at our port. It keeps us protected from foreign threats like Quebec and Nova Canada."

"Why doesn't Ontario just join the US?"

"It was and still is in their interest to keep us neutral, because of their internal conflicts. If one side ever wins we might join. It makes sense for them and us to wait until then. We're a neutral, stable satellite. They invest a lot in family Values and it's paid off. In addition to facilities, food, and raw materials, NewTor is the vaccination provider for nearly all North America."

Otto wondered if Ken was aware of any of this, if he'd been around when it happened. Likely not.

"Desirae, do you think she knows who I am?"

"I don't think so. And we should keep it that way. Let her find out by accident. Or by natural research. Until then, we act as if it isn't true."

"I can't lie, though, that's my problem."

"It's not lying. It's an unconfirmed theory. There's no value in sharing a theory as truth until it is confirmed. That'd be just as deceiving, don't you think?"

"I suppose. But saying it might get to the truth faster."

"Then again, it might do the opposite. If it is true."

"How so?"

Desirae paused to put her words together properly.

"If it's true, if you are her grandson and the child of the twins, that not only means you're a bastard, but also a child of incest. Being a bastard isn't a crime but is shameful. Incest, on the other hand, is a serious crime that could get you deported and could ruin lives. Including the Doyenne's. Even if she knows, she just can't let it out, she has to protect herself."

Her explanation sounded reasonable. All he knew was that he knew little, he had to trust her. She had a point about his telling Esmeralda he was her grandson being a lie, regardless of how it felt true inside. He then realized something else.

"I'm not sure I agree with you."

"You think we should come out and share it all?"

"No, I mean, I don't think she's impressive.

"Oh?"

"Sure, she looks majestic in the fancy robes but that seems like only flash. In her heart I don't think she's at all powerful."

Desirae's quizzical look made him unsure why he'd said that. Ken often attributed Otto's feral sense of fear helping when they hunted, but potentially awkward socially. It had resurfaced at famSud and had been increasing since, reaching a peak with the "impressive" woman. He'd disregarded it, assuming it was just Desirae, but it had subsided only after leaving Esmeralda.

Desirae was right insisting they reveal nothing yet, not just for her reasoning, but the fear Otto sensed from the Doyenne. If she was so important, why not have an inferior like Grace deal with them? She feared something. If incest was a crime then she must keep it quiet. If she knew. Otto could be a threat to her, to her position. If only Ken were here to guide him. And what should he do with the letter? He couldn't give it to Esmeralda now, he ought to hide or destroy it.

The tap on his shoulder startled Otto.

"Speaking of not revealing anything, why didn't you tell me about this dream thing. Or did you make it up?"

"I didn't make it up."

Otto felt he ought to say more but didn't, then expected her to ask about it, but she didn't.

"Of course, that would be a lie. I'm starving. Let's go back and eat and rest. I think you'll like my chicken recipe."

They returned to find a note from Esmeralda inviting them to her suite for dinner, requesting Otto wear his suit, but it didn't say anything about Desirae, who said she'd wear the outfit she had on. He struggled with his tie and asked her to the mirror to help. She was amused, but only briefly.

"What are you—put your Values token back on?"

Otto found it on the bed. He carried it to the living area but instead of putting it around his wrist, he put it on the television and went to the kitchen. Desirae's panic subsided when she saw nothing happening.

"I took it off when I had my shower too."

"And no pain?"

"None."

"But you did have it on when were outside, right?"

"I did."

A knock at the door. It was Grace, ready to escort them to the penthouse suite. The old woman looked unhappy.

36

All was set for a pleasant dinner with guests. Convincing Grace and Felicity to go to the theatre, together, took some doing, but the toughest task was evading Baxter's desire for explanations. For that she had to summon (and test) her old charm. It worked, he was still smitten with her because he instantly complied with her wish to host the strangers and didn't question that Otto was no more than the academic thesis subject of a promising young, student. Epithets like "promising young student" often worked on Baxter who was drawn to new blood. Desirae had to deliver as he'd even blindly granted Esmeralda's request he include her on his famSud site visit. Getting Desirae to agree to go would be easy, doing so with Felicity would be tough. It was imperative she succeed, she couldn't let her daughter know about Otto, not yet, despite her qualms that to prevent their meeting was cruel to both. Felicity's unpredictability, including the risk she'd seek revenge for Felix, was the clincher. Since she and Desirae would each assume the other was another student there was no risk in putting them together.

Grace had Felicity holed up in her suite while she went out to retrieve Otto and Desirae. Baxter was in his bedroom freshening up. Now it was only a matter of playing it out. Her assistant's familiar knock sounded louder than usual. Esmeralda breathed in before opening the door to her guests. They looked reserved. Grace said nothing and just left.

Desirae looked smartly attractive in that skirt, even with that haircut Esmeralda would never dare. Lamentably the suit made

Otto look like a boy outgrowing his clothes. She guided them to sit across each other just as Baxter came in. He sat at the head of the table, closest to the balcony. Introductions were made before the meal was carted in by the catering staff. Cloches were lifted to reveal lamb in white wine sauce, roast potatoes, and mixed vegetables. A Cabernet Sauvignon imported from Niagara for the ladies, a glass of milk for Otto, a tankard of beer for Baxter.

"Did you enjoy your walk by the lake? It was a lovely sunset."

"Yes we did, Doyenne, it was lovely."

"How'd you know we were there? Were you following us?"

Esmeralda found Desirae's glare at Otto amusing. Baxter did as well, she noticed.

"No, we did not have you followed. All *Transitory Indo* tokens are tracked. We knew where you'd gone, Otto, not Desirae."

Otto was about to speak but Desirae interjected to ask why his token didn't work when he left it on his bed while showering. Esmeralda told them the pain function was disabled on floors belonging to family Values. Baxter coughed.

"Nonetheless, you are legally obligated to wear it at all times."

It was subtle, but Esmeralda again saw a twitch in Otto she'd seen earlier when he'd met Baxter. An aversion to males? That wouldn't be like Ken, a man's man if she ever knew one. Indeed, it'd be more like Baxter who, prior to balding and acquiring his paunch deemed himself a ladies man. Maybe he still did, based on how he not-so-subtly fawned over Desirae.

"Baxter's right. Had you left your floor to go anywhere except another such floor, you wouldn't have gotten far."

Thankfully, Otto's twitch subsided and dinner was pleasant, save for the occasional awkward moment. Such as Desirae's too often proclaiming she was a *familyar* in three *fams*, hinting at her lesbianism as if that might boost her diversity advantage within the academy. Baxter didn't point out diversity was irrelevant at the academy because the school indoctrinated cities regardless of who was involved.

The conversation grew to be dominated by family Values. The recent successes in famLon and famKing, contrasted by troubles in famSud. It naturally led to Baxter sharing his dream to build his Brasilia or Canberra version of a family Values city, to avoid transition stages and begin directly at Stage Four. Even hinting that Desirae, being from famSud, had a geographical leg up on others if she'd be interested. Which she directly and predictably declared was the case. Baxter at least had the good sense not to disclose the classified name and location of the endeavour.

Normally such behaviour by her partner towards a Desirae would be irritating, but today it played into Esmeralda's desire to get Otto alone. The young man made an impressive effort to pay attention, better than she'd hope from a *Transitory Indo*, but boredom was setting in, even a little disgust at Desirae for being so captivated by Baxter.

Esmeralda let them talk through career options for Desirae, as well as get into more detail about famSud's difficult transition from Stage Two to Stage Three, then the nuances of *familyars* in varying *fams* and situations that might cause cancellation of one or more. When racial blending came up, however, she decided to intervene, with a hard glance at Baxter. He grinned, aware of his obsession with that particular topic, and nodded.

"I hear you two came here together from Timmins. But Otto is from farther north?"

Esmeralda was impressed, as usually Baxter couldn't say that city's name, without overtly conveying his revulsion.

"He was passing through on the way here, Professor Baxter. A coincidence. A lucky one for me because, to be honest, I was at a loss for my thesis."

"So I heard. I'm more curious why he chose a route that went through Timmins and famSud. I ask because Timmins has a, let me say, unique status in our realm."

There was a tone of provocation in Baxter and Esmeralda was glad to see Otto deliberate his response. Even gladder to see the young man not intimidated by the professor, with a reluctance to let Desirae respond for him when she cleared her throat.

"At Driftwood I learned the famCoch route could be difficult due to violent protests there. Someone said it would be easier to go through Timmins."

"I see."

"But what is so unique about Timmins?"

Otto's question paralyzed Esmeralda but Baxter was ready for it with his stock, diplomatic response.

"Timmins is an option for people who are not yet convinced of the benefit of family Values. Until the entirety of Ontario has transitioned to family Values, much as I don't care to admit it, it is useful. What makes it different is merely that it's not like us."

"I read somewhere that certain Values tokens functions were built because of Timmins."

"I'm not sure where you would have heard that, Desirae, but that's not true. The essential functionality of Values tokens have been part of family Values since its start. True, experiences with Timmins influenced their evolution, but no more than with any other city. In early days, those unwilling to adopt family Values migrated to smaller cities like Barrie, Sudbury, Guelph, London, etc. As family Values expanded to those places, resistors would keep migrating to small cities until there were few options left. Timmins capitalized on this and developed an infrastructure to support rapid growth and in a few years was the largest centre of resistance to progressive ways. By then the impact to family Values was minimal, it wasn't worth doing anything about it. As I said, it became useful for us in other ways."

While Desirae was lapping it up, Esmeralda had to suppress a sigh at Baxter's propagandistic tendencies, how he was so full of it. Her partner hated Timmins and wouldn't stop hating it until it was destroyed or converted to family Values. She wondered what was going on in Otto's mind as he no longer looked bored.

"Honey, maybe you ought to share your proposal."

"Indeed. Desirae, you impress me and I don't impress easily. I took the liberty of speaking to your instructors who universally affirmed my sense that you possess a unique aptitude for family Values. Furthermore, that you could benefit from experiencing firsthand a transition from Stage Two to Stage Three. I'm taking a class to an inspection first thing in the morning. Interested?"

"In coming along? Absolutely. May I ask where?"

"famSud. Mind you, it won't be luxurious. We're going there on a bus of mostly tactical transitions officers. Possibly a crude experience, but a lesson you'd never receive in a class."

"I noticed problems there when we went through."

"Did you? Excellent. You can show me."

"I would love that. Thank you. But are you sure I'm ready?"

"Desirae won't be the only new person, right Baxter?"

"That's right. There'll be another less advanced than you."

"While you're away, I'll show Otto the city as we try to locate information about his parentage."

"To be shown around by the Doyenne. Quite an honour, Otto. Much better than me doing it."

Despite a detectable grimace at Desirae's obsequiousness, the boy seemed pleased. Esmeralda even caught hint of a genuine smile distinct from his polite ones.

"Doyenne, we don't see billboards with your image anywhere in NewTor? But we saw them everywhere else."

"My dear Desirae, you've touched upon my partner's singular flaw as the leader of family Values: her humility does not allow her to gaze upon her own image. You'll notice very few mirrors around here too."

"But you're so beautiful."

Otto looked up with a slight nod as if affirming what Desirae said. No compliment could have meant more to Esmeralda in that moment, but he then continued eating and she couldn't be sure if instead his reaction was to mock Desirae.

"Thank you."

The dessert tray arrived, filled with bowls of ice cream and chocolate mousse and a plate of blackberry cheesecake. Other than the tiny piece Baxter took, Otto ate all the cheesecake and happily took the uneaten ice cream with them on leaving.

An hour later, when Grace and Felicity were to have returned, Esmeralda went to her daughter's room, but found it empty. She hadn't taken her token and only saw the alert from Grace after she returned to her suite. Felicity had been involved in an incident at the theatre. Grace had not joined Felicity to visit the washroom, and had waited in lobby. After thirty minutes Grace sensed trouble and found Felicity in a washroom stall engaging in sex with an *Indo* male. Too late as they were caught by a staff member. Grace begrudgingly consented to stay until Esmeralda could arrange for someone to get them.

A disturbing situation, but also one she could use to compel her daughter to go to famSud with Baxter and Desirae.

37

The famdrone glided just high enough to clear the tallest of the vehicles. Its wobbly fragility made Otto wonder about the type of damage it could cause in a crash. These machines were rare, only for top officials, with a family Values logo underneath. He felt honoured riding above the citizens in between the buildings with Esmeralda next to him at the front as she received dutiful waves from *familyars* raising their heads on hearing the whirr of the airship's engine. Esmeralda's cheerful responses did not reflect her mood, which was darker than last night. Her voice didn't sound as full, she seemed distracted, even troubled. He was glad to have Grace there—Otto admired the woman's stern steadiness—not Baxter who would be in famSud with Desirae by now.

Otto didn't like Baxter. He couldn't pinpoint anything Baxter had said or did, probably just the sense he'd gotten from James, aggravated by Desirae's silly behaviour around the man.

What struck Otto from this vantage once they flew beyond the skyscrapers was how the grids of streets below reminded him of the checker pattern on the tattered tartan blanket Ken liked to have by the fire. Each square's streets filled with people, each space occupied by structures split by alleys. Four perimeters—occasionally three or five for misshapen "squares"—dedicated to and packed with fast-moving vehicles. Small trains on rails and trucks, an occasional conventional car. At intersections barriers would rise in symmetric sequence blocking one direction or the other to let and protect pedestrians across, shuttling them as if in a horizontal elevator that symmetrically rolled along while its counterpart did the same. People then swarmed out to blend in with others lingering near the intersection like free range fowl not willing to venture beyond familiar surroundings. Once clear the barriers dropped into the ground again to release traffic.

Grace explained the exponential growth in population due to migrations had led to housing people where they worked—for most, office towers, but other buildings too—it being prudent to segregate humans and vehicles to avoid accidents and clogging. Arterial streets were dedicated to transport and this design of distinct grids evolved. There were growing pains until the grids attained equality in providing amenities for life or leisure, thus reducing the draw to other grids for something unique. Which reduced or even eliminated the need for most to cross.

"The key was commandeering the subways for distribution of goods, not transit. Except for emergencies and family Values use, of course. You and Desirae came in on the subway."

"It was fast."

"Because of the rails. Once your car rolled onto the railway car ramp it proceeded without interruption."

"I don't see bicycles. It's such a warm day."

"Cycling for leisure isn't viable with this system since you'd be waiting to cross into zones, and navigating crowds. A licensed few can use the arteries, but that's risky. Farther out, where the streets are bigger, you may see some. But because the demand dried up, the supply is low."

With nothing to compare it to Otto had no way to judge if this was good or not. He was fascinated and impressed, despite a latent longing for the people-less outdoors. Would Ken think this an improvement? Not the Ken who'd written the letter he'd left back in the suite. Grace continued:

"Everyone lives in one zone and while one is within that zone, Values tokens are mostly inactive, except for basic functions like ensuring its owner remains in contact with the token, financial transactions, access to *reservoir*, vaccination monitoring, social networking, ensuring votes are registered, so on. Once a token and its owner leave a zone, tracking kicks in. Tracking millions is costly, it takes enormous amounts of energy. Therefore only having to track outside one's prime zone is efficient. New people suffering from wanderlust soon discover the satisfactory existence that can be had within their zones."

"Grace's longwinded way of saying people are content with the life they have here in NewTor."

"But you tracked me within the same zone, didn't you?"

"Because you're a *Transitory Indo*. For the time being."

That sounded like an invitation. Possibly this excursion was about seeking his approval of family Values so he'd become an *Indo* or *familyar*. It seemed logical and practical, but he had to wonder if such a choice would trap him in the city, in a block of a few square kilometres. That didn't appeal to him at all. Yet Esmeralda and Grace saw it as paradise. Did they truly believe it or were they acting? Or fooling themselves? He wished his mind wouldn't think that way, but after Monica's lie, and others since, he couldn't help it. The conversation ended as they glided through the last complex of tall buildings and saw open air.

The famdrone lifted to float above a massive, domed building. They hovered until its roof parted, then slowly descended into a giant expanse of cubed areas where people in white lab coats operated blue and grey machines, similar to the computers he once used at school. They landed in a marked area. He followed Grace while Esmeralda stayed inside. Otto found the immensity of the machinery overwhelming. A white-grey forest of blinking lights to assault one's eyes, a loud, oppressive hum explaining the earmuffs worn by most staff. He regretted having put on the khaki shorts and golf shirt as it became chilly the instant he left the vehicle, the chill accenting his unease in this sterile building. He was glad to not be alone.

He admired Grace, who was fiercely competent. A doer, not a talker. Otto felt comfortable disclosing the few details he had of his birth. His age guess, the date he was found, and Kapukasing as his likely birthplace. Grace told him this building housed the largest database of births in Ontario, including all from family Values cities at Stage Two or higher. How during transition this data gets centralized in NewTor, in this building, formerly the home of a professional baseball team, now a datacentre. He was about to discover the identity of his parents right here and the notion made him anxious.

Workers ignored them as Grace led Otto through a maze of wide aisles to a desk at which stood a frumpy woman. She and Grace hugged briefly before the woman left them alone.

"Is she a close friend?"

"No. We both have implants, it's a good way to link up."

"Link up?"

"It's how *familyars* transact, or interact. In this case to have her authorize my search based on your data. Luckily you were born before racial blending, which is bound to make future searches challenging. For now though, it's easy enough to refine searches to filter out same race couples and include mixed race couples only."

Racial blending. There was that term again, which he'd heard at dinner, but also before. The reason Monica left her home.

"Could I have come here on my own?"

"Oh no, this facility is privileged. You'd have to hire an agent to access the databases. That could take a long time, cost a lot of money, more than a *Transitory Indo* like you could get."

The woman returned, shaking her head. She handed a sheet of paper to Grace who glanced at it before passing it on to Otto. Two paragraphs of text, a chart, and a box: INCONCLUSIVE.

He was glad to get away from the hum, back to the car, back to Esmeralda. He offered her the sheet but she shook her head.

"Too bad, I'll have them keep looking. Let's make you a tourist now, instead of an orphan seeking information."

"Was this place really the baseball stadium?"

"Yes. Until the team moved to Buffalo."

"Why?"

"Baseball, like all spectator sports sort of died out as NewTor approached Stage Four and it became logistically challenging to host teams, the closing of our airspace being the primary issue, but not the only one. I'm no sports expert, but in my opinion I think our citizens are more interested in betting on games than actually watching them. Thankfully, we didn't let the facilities go to waste. If you think this is impressive, you'll have to see the hockey arena, how we refitted its refrigeration systems to store vaccinations, after the hockey team was dissolved. We reached a point where we can inoculate every *familyar* in NewTor within a week, and in addition export tens of millions units to the US in a matter of days."

Otto recalled Ken reminiscing about attending hockey games, saying he'd loved to have had the chance to take Otto to see his Maple Leafs one day, a rare hint of any regret for living freely in the woods. Apparently nothing for Ken to miss anymore.

"The development, distribution, exporting of vaccines is one of our largest revenue generators."

"Second largest, in fact, Doyenne."

"Thank you, Grace. See that little building with the revolving door? It's one of several thousand vaccine dispensing stations in NewTor. Filled within an hour with the newest vaccine tailored for you if your Values token flashes yellow. Though it won't be as often once we add vaccines to the water, like fluoride."

"I had to get a lot of shots coming here."

"Because you had to catch up first."

"That's right, Grace, and you had to start from scratch, if I'm not mistaken. It's summer, you should be good for a while now. Though you'll still need those stations for fam-elixir injections as long as you remain a *Transitory Indo*."

Again, Otto got the sense of invitation, that Esmeralda wanted him to stay permanently. He didn't much care for the shots, his arm was still sore from them, nor the fam-elixir injections. Was that enough to keep him away? Likely not. He was starting to find the rest of it intriguing.

"You say vaccinations are your second biggest industry. What is the largest revenue generator?"

"Why, family Values, of course."

"How's that?"

"Baxter and Grace can explain it better, but it costs a great deal to implement family Values. And NewTor owns the monopoly. Only we can grant, or retract, franchise cities. The latter has yet to happen, thank goodness. Whenever cities transition from one stage to another, four times at least, we are involved. For that we charge a premium. The more cities that transition, the larger the profits for us. For NewTor, I mean."

"NewTor must be very wealthy."

"That day is coming. The initial costs to develop family Values were enormous, we're still paying them off. Also, we're limited by a lack of bright, skilled personnel—people like your Desirae once trained—limiting the number of cities we can transition at a time, and how quickly each can get through each stage. But as long as we get young, positive people—I'm repeating myself. Who knows, if the US ever finds internal peace, we'll expand to the south. Some American cities are already expressing interest by sending students to attend classes. Right, Grace?"

"That's right, Doyenne."

The car lifted and continued to new places. Areas alternating with rows of houses and blocks of industrial buildings. Shades of brown all over it seemed, including the thousands of people, but no buses on rails. An occasional patch of green with trees, tiny and geometric: triangles, squares, a few ovals. Plenty of tall buildings that used to be residential only but now also acted as offices.

Grace did most of the describing and answered his questions, but Esmeralda pointed out landmarks like the conspicuous and isolated family Values Tower not far from the lab, which they circled as people waved from its elevators and restaurant. The greyness proliferated after Casa Loma, aided by cloudy skies. A large rectangular area between two giant streets and crossing another stood out for its greenness. Mount Pleasant Cemetery, according to Grace, designated an *arbiter* free zone, where one's Value token had no effect, as with all cemeteries. This was the largest. Its sombre aura made it popular as a launching point for rallies that connected *familyars* across *fams*.

"What's that?"

Otto pointed down to a small clearing at a group of about two dozen people moving in choreographed motion, each wearing a pink or blue or red shirt, and when finished made a pattern that looked liked just like the symbol he'd been seeing since Monica pointed it out at George's. He got the sense Esmeralda found it silly, even annoying, when she responded instead of Grace, and with a wistful tone.

"There was a time, in my youth, our youth, right Grace? when people assembled for demonstrations or protests. They still do, but not in NewTor or any advanced family Values city. But of course due to the realignment of the streets, there are no large spaces for real protests anymore. The intersections are too busy, too controlled. Nevertheless, the spirit still exists in this form of what I call anti-protests."

"What are they anti-protesting?"

"They're actually called pro-tests, with a hyphen between the syllables, indicating they're pro- or for something. To encourage something. In this case, it looks to be—"

"Thank you, Grace, enough on this topic."

It became slightly uncomfortable as Grace got still. Esmeralda then, as if to ward off the growing awkwardness, spoke again, her voice once again upbeat.

"Would it interest you Otto, to see where I'm from? Where the Doyenne lived before she was Doyenne?"

He sensed a baiting in the question that put him off, or was it the peculiar disapproving grunt from Grace? But of course, this was precisely why he'd come. Did Esmeralda know as much? If she did, maybe she'd try goading him into saying so first. A cat and mouse game. Oddly, the fear he'd detected in her earlier was gone, as if never there. He nodded.

Grace uttered a command without looking up and the vehicle gathered speed as it whisked them away from the lake to where roads were wider, zones larger, with far greater space between pockets of buildings. He even spotted a few bicycles.

The futuristic look was more sporadic, many buildings looked decrepit. Neighbourhoods with rows of brick structures rising high with vertical stain streaks. Few waved here. Otto recalled Ken once describing how he'd lived in Toronto in what he'd called a high-rise. Maybe one of these was the one where Ken's father had killed himself.

38

What did Otto think of this? she desperately wished to know. What did he have to compare it to? As far as she knew he'd never experienced any form of civilization. It was hard to tell if he approved or disapproved. Or was he indifferent?

There were few landmarks of note this far north and all was silent within the famdrone until they slowed again.

"We are here, Doyenne."

"Thank you, Grace."

Esmeralda watched Otto's reaction. He remained impassive. They slowed to hover over the home where she'd first lived in Toronto, instantly recognizable by a pair of rhododendrons she had nurtured as a teen now tended to by professionals. Along with the swimming pool the old couple who'd bought it from her parents had torn up the yard to build for their grandkids. That was, of course, before family Values eliminated inheriting real estate for which Esmeralda held a tinge of guilt because, as Doyenne, she was able to lay a claim on it. Unoccupied now, it had served as a potential sanctuary or haven if NewTor faced attack or rebellion. A definite possibility during those turbulent early family Values days. Once past the copyright challenges to the name, ironclad agreements with the United States, Quebec, Nova Canada, and Indigenous nations, they would be secure so long as they kept neutral. The Switzerland of North America in a sense, free from wars and global turmoil, albeit at the cost of some borderlands. She didn't come this way often because with the guilt also came sadness at seeing it unlived in. Baxter's idea to transform it into a museum celebrating family Values was an intriguing one, but only if she were alive. She didn't want it to be a mausoleum. Of course, it could soon lodge Felicity to keep her from Otto until it came time to reunite them. If all turned out well with Otto, it could then again become a family home.

"Are we stopping here?"

"No. I wanted to show you my humble Willowdale origins."

"Doyenne!"

"Relax, Grace. It was called Willowdale in my day but is now Zone . . . what zone, Grace?"

"Eight."

"Willowdale sounds nicer to me."

"That's what it'll be for me always, it'll be our secret."

"Doyenne, please."

"It looks fancy compared to other areas we passed. The whole neighbourhood looks wealthy."

The remark perturbed Esmeralda, even more for not grasping why, maybe because she was struggling to figure him out. Otto was clearly pondering something and she stayed quiet, in hope he'd break his silence, yet also dreading what he'd say.

"I'd like to hear about your life. Before you were Doyenne."

This instantly lifted her spirit. She had Grace guide the car to the school and set it down on a field. No students were around, it was closed for summer holidays.

"Few people know, Otto, that I'm not married to Baxter. That I'm married to a man I first met at this very school. At the end of 1999, just before this millennium. Like you, he was from the far north and had just moved to Toronto and didn't know anyone. He was shy but very handsome. The teacher assigned a project, to me, him, and another boy, about the next millennium. It was hard until one day those boys came to the house and my father helped us work on it. The next week he left school after finding his father had killed himself. Forced to return north to his town to live with relatives."

Otto listened ardently but betrayed no sign any of it sounded familiar. Assuming he knew Ken, it was possible Ken had never shared this. Likely even. Then again, Esmeralda could conceive no other reason for the boy's keen interest or the tenuous yet warm bond between them, despite their physical separation. If she revealed Ken's name, he might keep it in, she had to wait for him to do so, or at least ask her to say his name.

"The third student and I were sad we'd never see the first one again but the third one and I remained close long after. He even drove me to a clinic—not far from Timmins as a matter of fact—for a procedure I could get done there for certain reasons. I had him wait elsewhere because I wanted to keep anonymous. I was sitting alone, resting in the waiting room after the procedure, feeling sad and sorry for myself, when I saw that boy again. He recognized me, we talked briefly, and he offered . . ."

Esmeralda paused here, troubled by something, but couldn't identify what it was without stopping her story.

". . . offered to drop me off at the spot I was to meet the third friend. I accepted but had him drop me off only, not reuniting them. In all the years since I never told either about this. So you can imagine my shock seven years ago when I spot the first boy, now a man, on a picture on the Internet. I reached out and we began to date, eventually married, and had twins."

Otto was as good as Ken at concealing reactions but guessed the boy's head was spinning. It puzzled her why he wouldn't pounce on her clumsily avoiding saying Ken's name.

"What happened to your friend? The one who helped with the abortion?"

It wasn't the question she'd expected. The disappointment she felt was intense. Thank goodness for the barrier providing her a chance to collect herself and fabricate a smile prompted by a nice memory.

"He was still my friend and we were all friends for years, until my husband left with the children. It was a mutual decision, I should add. Then some time after my other friend and I had a misunderstanding too and he left NewTor for . . . you'll never guess."

"Timmins?"

"How did you know?"

"You said he was from there. Maybe he went back."

"You're right, I did say that. I'll share a secret with you I doubt even Grace knows. That project the three of us worked on? It was the seed for the paper I wrote over twenty years later that led to family Values."

"I did know that, Doyenne."

"Of course you did, Grace."

"Everyone does, they learn it in school."

Esmeralda bit her lip, she knew too, but had forgotten. Maybe her mind was going. She then starkly saw what she'd hoped to gain from Otto. Not compliments, not approval. What she truly desired, perhaps even needed, was to have her grandson truly hate everything about family Values, as Ken would hate it. And that his doing so would not be a rejection, but a liberation. This both exhilarated and frightened her because it made no sense.

"There's a message, Doyenne."

"It can wait."

"It's from the professor. He says it's urgent."

Esmeralda skimmed the message feeling it would be about Felicity. It was. She tried to think of a way to put the issue off, to continue the tour, but knew she had to treat Felicity, or rather the risk of Felicity, as priority. Which meant disengaging that instant and exposing the fact she was in her suite and that he'd been communicating with a remote human.

39

Esmeralda's story about Ken touched Otto but it also made the game less fun. Too near deception. No point in prolonging his mission, time to reveal the letter, just hand it over, without any awkward preamble, give it to her. Only when he turned to face her, Esmeralda was gone.

"Where did she go? She just vanished."

"She didn't. She was never there. She rarely actually goes out."

Grace explained his grandmother had been in her suite all this time, that it was her image with which he'd communicated. In other words, he said to himself, a lie. That killed his desire to be forthcoming.

"It was her you were speaking to, just not her person."

"But why? She seems healthy."

"As healthy as you and me. She just feels safer at home. The roof and balcony provide enough fresh air."

Otto couldn't understand why anyone so beloved would coop herself up. Maybe she didn't care for the world she'd created. It made Otto recall James's comment that the reality didn't match what she'd intended, or something like that. If James was right, maybe she was ashamed of the outcome.

"Can you tell me why she shared so much that was personal?"

"Honestly, it shocked me. I've never seen her like this."

So the trusted assistant wasn't trusted with everything, which meant, what?

"But you're real, Grace?"

"Ha ha, yes, of course. You saw that at the lab."

"Right. Why did she leave then? Did I say something?"

"Nonsense. Trust me, she enjoyed it a great deal and would not have ended it abruptly if the message wasn't urgent."

Grace asked if he wanted to see more of the city. He shook his head. She directed the vehicle to return via the identical route. Seeing the crowded streets again felt odd, even uncomfortable, with people waving, unaware they'd been waving at an image before. Or did they just wave at the logo underneath?

Coming back, the city looked different too, its towers forming a thick t-shape that looked impenetrable from their perspective, like a filed off mountain range. From the lab building they went towards the lake. Once clear of all buildings, the true size of the US presence became evident. Beyond the set of small islands, a flotilla of ships bearing the stars and stripes, commercial and military. A giant complex of administration buildings flying the American flag dwarfed the modest airport, which was jammed with jets and helicopters. They had to slow while Grace spoke to inform someone of their intent to glide by. While awaiting approval she explained airspace was restricted, even famdrones required permission to pass through. For the first time he could remember Otto wondered what life was like beyond Ontario, a notion prompted by a sudden awareness of the impossibility of leaving.

Grace made a point to tap him on the shoulder to prove she was real when they got back. She escorted him to his suite and demonstrated how to use his Values token to open it. He hoped to see Desirae but knew the suite would be empty. Grace left him no instructions, plans, regulations, or dinner invitation. He welcomed the opportunity to fend for himself.

Otto took a can of soda from the refrigerator which he drank on his bed. Starving, he then remembered the leftover ice cream and had that. He wished Desirae was there so he could tell her about his trip. No doubt she was doing well, doing what she wanted. That only exposed an emptiness of purpose on his part. The goal of finding Esmeralda had been achieved easily, but figuring out when or how to give her the letter was hard. They could go back and forth indefinitely in this game until someone gave in. He enjoyed her company but what would happen if or when it ended? If only he had a way to contact Desirae or Ken or James. The Values token likely could do it but he'd need to be shown how. And he'd want to talk in private. Here he was only private in his thoughts.

All the while Esmeralda related her love story without saying Ken's name he felt she was prodding him to ask it. He almost did when she mentioned James, but luckily recovered from his Timmins slipup. If he hadn't, she'd discover who Desirae was. Otto had to prolong this deception, much as it troubled him. For

Desirae's sake. For his own, he'd reveal who he was because he liked Esmeralda. The tie between them was similar to what he had with Ken, yet different too. As if she was a mix of Ken and Monica and something else.

As Otto drank another soda the dreams and vague curiosity that inspired his coming to NewTor coalesced with his current thoughts into a singular objective: to bring Ken and Esmeralda together. The letter could be the means, but it'd only work once, so he had to figure out how best to apply it. While this sated his mental craving for purpose, it left a physical one for food. What was in the suite wasn't appealing and the ice cream hadn't been enough. There was the chicken Desirae had bought but he had no confidence trying the appliances. He was about to search her room for cash but then recalled the money was in the token. He couldn't find anything on which to scribble a note for Grace but of course the token would reveal his location, if they needed to know. He was starting to see why it was called a Values token. He changed into a pair of jeans and a grey pullover. It had long sleeves but was of a comfortable thin silky material.

Otto exited the suite and walked down the hallway to the elevators. No one stopped him, his bracelet quiet. Once out the revolving door and in daylight, he felt a buzz on his wrist. He looked at the blue light, it was flashing. It stayed that way as he left the property and merged into a row of pedestrian traffic. It stopped flashing but remained blue.

Ground level was a sharp contrast to riding above. Mere air separated him from people, not glass, yet it was harder to hear voices. People spoke softly into their tokens, which were located on various parts of their bodies. Otto stood out as one of the few with a visible bracelet. No one spoke to anyone, not even those with them. Sounds were intermittent, mechanical from vehicles he didn't see, or musical from shops with their doors open.

Finding a place to eat was Otto's priority but proved difficult. For one, they only had flags to indicate the type of food. He saw green-white-red, blue-white-red, black-yellow-green, none he'd be able to match to countries. It didn't matter because most had official-looking signs with family Values logos, indicating they wouldn't serve *Transitory Indos* or *Indos* at all. Underneath some, handwritten cards politely stated this wasn't by choice, but due to family Values rules. He tried one place when he saw it nearly empty inside, started to enter, only for the greeter to point at his red blinking token to confirm the sign's message. If the token told you, why was the greeter there? To make you feel bad in person with rejection? Otto asked where a *Transitory Indo* like him could eat but received only a grim headshake.

At last he found one. He'd have missed it if not for spotting blue and pink dots of light at an intersection of a small alley and street. There was a line-up at least forty people deep. Again he received looks. Less suspicious and fearful, more curious. The man ahead of him turned to face Otto.

"You're not a plant, are you?"

"Of course he's not, he's got a bracelet. A *Transitory*. Forgive Phil, he got so hungry he decided to eat his manners. My name is Kennedy."

Otto stepped back when Kennedy put a hand out to shake, but then relaxed and clasped it. Not as firm as Ken's but close.

"What did you mean, asking if I was a plant?"

"Your skin colour. You kind of stand out here."

Otto looked around. Almost all the people were pale. The two with dark skin were also looking at him but no one was looking at them, indicating they all were familiar with each other.

"How long will it take to get inside to eat?"

"At least an hour."

"The other places I tried are empty, but won't let me in."

"That's just the way it is. *familyars* don't eat out much. There are places closer to the intersection without lines."

"How far?"

"Go see. If no luck, come back and eat with us."

40

Neither the light emanating from the suites in hundreds of high buildings spread in front and beyond her, nor the glow from the streetlamps below could dilute the reflection of the moon on the lake, which in turn couldn't allay Esmeralda's anxiousness once again over the impending arrival of her daughter. At least she had these moments to enjoy the calm of sky on water before the dark storm of Felicity.

Terrible thought.

Esmeralda wished Grace were here to reproach her for it, but her assistant needed time to herself. She'd earned it. Esmeralda had been annoyed at Grace for leaving Otto on his own earlier but, as Grace sensibly argued, it'd be good to see him manage without Desirae, Grace, or Esmeralda. How far, if at all, might he venture on his own? She knew he couldn't get in trouble in this zone. Even if the impossible happened and Otto got into an altercation, his size would deter any threat. Besides, at any time she could instantly locate him; albeit doing so could spoil what had been a terrific day with mistrust. For he'd likely guess the reason his token was turning yellow. He might resent that. She wanted to earn his trust. Needed to. Just as she needed to focus on Felicity, separately, and not let the joy of Otto prejudice her against her daughter who'd done enough herself. How had Ken managed them? Poorly, as it turned out. But honestly, could she have done better?

Esmeralda scanned Baxter's message once more, but it wasn't any less troubling. How Felicity tried to seduce a woman on the ride but was rejected. How she fled to the rear of the bus where, after waiting to not be conspicuous, Baxter went to console her. Only to see her under a blanket with two male officers. Little he could do short of raising a disruptive fuss until they reached the facility. By then everyone was composed when they assembled in the hall for an orientation of the border operations. That was short lived. Felicity returned to flirting at lunch, almost ruining the afternoon session. Baxter summarized by declaring Felicity as pathologically promiscuous and lacking the character and discipline needed, concluding with the news she was on her way back to NewTor this evening.

Esmeralda left the balcony and realized she once again hadn't put on her Values token ring. It was still next to the wine bottle, between two glasses, and she found it flashing in the pattern notifying of a visitor. She put it on and had it open the elevator as she went back inside. Felicity stood at the entrance meek and humble, patiently waiting to be invited in.

Something about her was new, beyond a demureness that was uncharacteristic. Calmer, more mature, not like what one might label a "pathologically promiscuous" creature. Her face looked fresher; was it merely due to wearing so little make-up?

"Come in dear. Want a glass of wine?"

"Yes, please, Doyenne."

"Don't call me that. Not you."

"What do I call you? Esme—?"

"You can call me, Mom."

It felt as if their hearts simultaneously skipped a beat.

"All right, Mom."

"It's on the balcony. The moon is lovely over the lake."

"I'm afraid of—it's too high."

"We can go to the middle of the roof. Watch the sky."

Esmeralda held out a hand and Felicity took it. They stepped into a small hallway at the end of which was a door. Esmeralda kept holding her daughter's hand while waiting for the door to open to the stairway. They climbed to the exit. On the roof, in the centre, past building equipment and a loud fan, a simple but large patio with a massive barbecue and a wooden dinner table surrounded by eight chairs. Felicity sat on one facing the lake as if drawn to the moon.

"There, not so bad, is it?"

"It's okay. You were right. The moon is gorgeous."

Esmeralda poured Felicity a glass before topping up her own.

"Often on nights like this, if Baxter's home, we open a bottle of wine and stay until we finish it. It's been a while, I suppose."

"Can we not talk about him just yet?"

"Sure, honey. Let's enjoy ours a few minutes."

Barely a minute passed before Felicity exhaled a sigh, then another. Esmeralda ventured a matronly smile at her daughter.

"We can talk now, if you're ready."

"You mean about what happened in famSud?"

"Yes."

"What do you know?"

"Only what Baxter told me."

"Which is?"

"How about you tell me first, in your words?"

Another sigh before Felicity spoke. The disparity between her oral version and Baxter's written one was alarming. Felicity did admit to flirting with a girl. Desirae, based on the description, a peculiar omission on Baxter's part. She also confirmed she was under a blanket with two young men but they didn't do more than kiss, adding Baxter had raised the blanket and saw this.

"If he said otherwise, he's a liar."

"Easy now, that's my—"

"Maybe he's saying so to cover his failure with—"

"What? Failure?"

"With that girl. The one I tried—you know what, she looked familiar. I hardly saw her or Baxter afterwards because they sat together at the front. Close, you know?"

"Are you saying he tried to seduce Desirae?"

"That's right. Wait, how do you know her name?"

"A third-year student—never mind. What you're describing is very serious."

"I saw what I saw. Don't you believe me?"

Felicity's petulance only compounded Esmeralda's frustration with her partner. No matter how numb one got from betrayal, it still wounded one's pride. But it wasn't really jealousy. Baxter's infidelity had peaked years ago, along with his physical appeal, meaning his attempts usually failed. No, it was more than that.

"Don't get upset. It's just hard for me to hear this."

"I'm sorry. I don't know if it matters, but that wasn't what sent me back. At least I'm pretty sure it wasn't."

"Oh?"

"No, it was an incident at the famSud facility that didn't even involve me. I'm not sure what caused it but suddenly he and this Desirae decided it was best that I return right away."

"Desirae? What part would she play in such a decision?"

"Because she was involved in the incident—oh my God, now I know who she is. But that's weird."

"Felicity, just tell me what happened."

"Can I have some more wine?"

Esmeralda obliged and Felicity settled back in her seat, eyes on the starry sky, except for an occasional glance at Esmeralda, perhaps to check for a reaction. Felicity began by reiterating her claim the encounter with the two officers was innocent, and was over long before they boarded the van to the detainee centre.

"Outside the building was cold and stark but tidy. Inside, it was a complete shambles. Total disarray. It surprised Baxter to see how bad it was. There was an older man, old as Baxter, with a young woman. Big girl, pretty, very blonde. The man stood to walk towards Desirae and Baxter as if he knew one or both. I didn't catch any of it because a guard steered them away. Baxter was pale, more than usual. Guess who else looked alarmed?"

"Felicity, please."

"All right. It was this girl, this Desirae."

"Did she know the man?"

"Sure looked like it. Shortly after, the officer who'd taken him away told us the man had called her by name."

Compose yourself, Esmeralda told herself, can't get caught up in the dramatic way she's speaking.

"How did this Desirae react?"

"Mom, is there something you're not telling me? You seem to know a lot about this girl."

"Just go on, please?"

"Her face didn't change, she was in shock. Baxter's face was red. I think he was angry at the guard for saying it in front of us instead of to him alone. He took the guard and Desirae aside a few minutes, leaving us wondering what was going on. Desirae left with the guard while Baxter led the rest of the students to a room to teach his class—deadly dull by the way—and he didn't stop even when Desirae came back in and sat down."

"I don't see what the fuss is then."

"After the class, I saw Baxter and Desirae talking very closely. Just before he told me it wouldn't work out and I'd have to go back. Strange, isn't it? Or was until I figured out where I'd seen Desirae before just now."

"Where?"

"I think you know her too. Don't worry, you don't have to tell me. If you believe I didn't come back because of my flirting. I'm glad to be away from famSud. It's awful."

Felicity sat back to take in the stars, as if having released the stress Esmeralda now bore. Her first priority was locating Otto, getting him back here. It would be difficult with Felicity in the picture. She couldn't be left out of sight anymore either. With more wine Felicity might tire and sleep. Then Esmeralda could locate Otto and have Grace bring him back, and keep him busy until Felicity was elsewhere.

Esmeralda was alone, lonely, trapped in a world of her own making. One with an imminent threat of crumbling.

Where the hell was Otto?

41

A horn sounded, then a repeating bell. Otto pursued the sounds and their echoes. Occasionally he passed sets of concrete stairs descending belowground, blocked by iron gates with the family Values logo and warnings to keep out. He stepped close to one but retreated on noticing his token flash pink. Then he recalled Grace saying the subway, like all major streets, was restricted to commercial and governmental use. Otherwise it'd be impossible controlling the movement of people between zones.

The traffic sounds got louder when Otto came upon a wide street with embedded railway tracks and a rapid, constant flow of trucks and trains full of people in both directions that made it impossible to see the other side. Signs indicated a crossing zone for pedestrians. He found several people standing, frequently glancing at an electronic sign counting down minutes until the next crossing. Forty minutes for this one, too long to indulge in curiosity about the horizontal elevators, even if instinct told him there'd be better food options on the other side.

Otto abandoned this idea when he spotted an eatery with no line, and a sign saying *Indos* were welcome. Inside it was full of patrons at long numbered bench tables. Otto wriggled his way through backs until he found an open spot between two men. The blond brush-cut man in his forties had a wispy moustache, while the face of the clean-shaven red-haired one was freckled. Slightly older than Desirae. They interrupted their discussion to shift for Otto, then resumed talking. Otto tried to listen for an opening to ask how one ordered food.

A machine rolled up, a container loaded with a stack of thin computer tablets. Otto guessed he should take one. He guessed right, it displayed a menu. Not much variety. He tapped at fish and chips. Nothing happened, no highlight or other indicator to confirm his choice. Yet a large board at the front did change to show his table number and order. Could it have known from his Value token like Desirae had described? He placed the tablet on the table. The men halted their conversation and the blond one pointed to a slot in the table.

"In there, table's small enough as it is."

"Thank you, I've never eaten here."

"Every place works the same in NewTor."

"I've only just arrived here, my first time."

The red-haired one pointed at Otto's token, it was green, but they didn't seem alarmed by that. Otto said nothing, hoping it meant he'd successfully paid, but wary of confirming it.

"A *Transitory*. I remember wearing one of those."

The men were eating quietly now. A box arrived that smelled of food. He had no idea how to open it. Maybe he hadn't paid. His token had gone back to blue. He touched about the box and suddenly it opened to his meal, turning itself into a place setting with napkin, cutlery, and an empty cup. His portion was puny and already cut up, hence the lack of a knife. Others used their hands. Not much different from eating with Ken by a campfire. Except for the meagre amount. He forked a piece of fish, ate it. Dry. He noticed someone press a button under their table that caused a tap to rise. Otto did the same, filled his cup with water, drank most of it, then refilled it in time before the tap retracted. Chewing slowly made the food moister and even taste a little better, but not much. He recalled Desirae or James saying food in family Values cities contained less protein because of citizens gradually developing lower metabolisms. That hadn't been the case at Esmeralda's, where he'd enjoyed the richest, tastiest food of his life.

"So that's it. Another three months and I'm off."

"It's uncertain out there. You're better off getting a dark girl if you want babies. Or just eliminate the complications."

"You mean get sterilized like you?"

"Sure. Why not?"

"Because I love Ashley, she loves me. We want children. Our own. No surrogates or criss-crossing with another couple. Just natural, you know?"

"Enough to give up the benefits of being an *Indo* in NewTor? We can talk freely, we're paid well. No police."

"But at what cost? In Timmins—"

"You and Timmins. That's a myth. It's no different from other cities. They'll be off-whiting soon enough."

"I'm not so sure."

"I'll bet by the time you get there they'll announce a transition to family Values. Like famCoch and all the rest."

"No they won't."

Otto's words came out muffled due to his dry mouth. He had to drink some water and withstand their bemused glares until he swallowed and could repeat it. The younger red-haired one was interested, the blond sceptical.

"What do you know about it?"

"I just came from there."

"How old are you? Under twenty, I'm sure."

"Forget that. Were you really there? What do you know?"

"About family Values, not much. I saw enough in Timmins to tell you it's not like NewTor. NewTor is a shock to me, Timmins wasn't. It'll never be like this."

"So where are you from?"

Otto hesitated, but felt a good vibe with them and described the basic parts of his trip truthfully, without mentioning names, including his own. They were fascinated.

The younger one introduced himself as Josh, who'd emigrated to NewTor at Otto's age, with his parents, as refugees from New York City. He shared how he'd felt awkward at first and didn't trust anyone. Lloyd on the other hand was a native Torontonian and had experienced its transition to famTor, then NewTor. The two men had met after a subway crash involving two trucks.

"That was a bad one."

"That's right. It disrupted food supplies for days in two zones. A major panic. Josh, an ace electrician, was troubleshooting the cause, while my job was to get the trucks driveable to clear out. Officials and bureaucrats would come by every fifteen minutes, it seemed, in pairs or groups of three, to check progress, never saying good work or anything, only talking or arguing amongst themselves. Then it got dark from a power failure, it split a pair. The nastier one came so close I heard his breath. He told me to rush or he'd report me. I "accidentally" elbowed him. He cussed at me. Josh intervened to tell him we'd slow down if he didn't shut the hell up. With no witnesses, he skulked off. Josh and I laughed about it and agreed to share a drink after work and became friends. I doubt we were reported."

"Even with a witness he'd do nothing. That's the irony. *Indos* are the skilled workers while *familyars* are bureaucrats one and all, or so it seems. Full of arrogance and fear. And more keep on coming, especially from the US."

"But we make more money."

"True, Lloyd, but we have less to spend it on."

"Food, beer, women, what else do we need?"

"Yes, but at some point you'll want someone too."

"We'll see. We're in good shape, that's what I'm saying, Josh. The infrastructure is deteriorating, new people have no skills so they become *familyars*. We'll never run out of work, it's a cash cow. A cash cow you're giving up for sentimentality, for a girl you could one day lose to off-whiting."

"If that's so then I have to go when I can so we can be together as long as we can."

"True love, I suppose."

"I know someone from Cochrane, I mean famCoch, who left because of that."

"My, my, our new friend is a fountain of information."

The table flashed bright purple and the table number showed on the large screen. The men weren't alarmed and told Otto it was the signal for them to leave to let others use it. They invited Otto to join them after he ate to go someplace for a drink.

"Maybe you can tell us more about Timmins."

Otto felt his nerves twitch softly.

"Looks like someone's trying to locate you."

Lloyd was pointing at Otto's wrist, at the bracelet, which was flashing yellow in a strange pattern. They explained it meant an official wanted to know his location. Tokens had different flash patterns and colours he'd learn. Otto was inclined to ignore it, wanting to spend more time with these men, but they acted as if he should address it. To his relief, it abruptly stopped.

"Could have been a mistake."

It was dark when Otto exited the eatery, the streets busier and louder. As promised, the two men were waiting. He followed them through small lanes and alleys to a stairwell descending to a heavy wooden door. He grabbed the wrought iron railing as if needing to steady himself, a feeling he was going somewhere he shouldn't, somewhere forbidden. He glanced at his token: still blue. Josh was looking at it too.

"You're eighteen, right?"

Otto shrugged, which satisfied Lloyd.

Unlike the eatery that, despite its crowded confusion, was clean and bright, this establishment felt dingy, oppressive. The thumping arrhythmic music coming out of unseen speakers so loud. A yellow theme—dull from candles on the tables, harshly bright from banks of ceiling lights, a lurid mix from the stage where two women danced—had a numbing effect. Grey plumes of tobacco smoke obscured their motion, delayed his realization the dancers were naked. They reminded him of Monica. Except these women were naked to be naked, and they wore pendants with tiny pink lights around their necks that jumped as they danced. Like little strobes. Once seated it got dark and eerily quiet save for glasses tinkling.

"Guess you'll be called in shortly, Josh."

"Only a brownout. I can tell from the brief gasp coming from the walls. Shouldn't last more than a minute."

Josh was right, the power returned moments later. Along with a waitress, clothed, to take their order. Otto wanted nothing but agreed to share the two pitchers of beer. He got self-conscious when a dancer made eye contact and grinned at him. He turned to see Lloyd leering at her and Otto hoped his new friend was the object of her interest.

"Are power outages common?"

Lloyd shrugged, distracted, and nodded at Josh to answer.

"Common? That's an understatement. A dozen a day, easily. Used to be four or five. Depending on your zone you could go a week or two and not experience one. It's these Values tokens to which they keep adding functionality requiring more energy."

"Josh, your tone. Someone might overhear."

"Ah yes, can't speak ill of family Values, can we?"

"Come on, man, you'll get us kicked out."

"Wouldn't be the worst thing to happen."

The waitress refilled their glasses and took an empty pitcher away. Lloyd raised his glass. Josh did the same so Otto did too.

"You my friend, won't have to deal with this for much longer. Best of luck to you, and Ashley."

"Thanks."

"Still can't see why you're going. Want to know what I think? I'm thinking of how in Russia they used to send prisoners to the remotest parts of Siberia to suffer. To me, you going to Timmins is like a prisoner volunteering to go there."

Lloyd exhaled from the cigarette he just lit and continued:

"And rumour is your internal systems won't fare well outside NewTor with it's vaccine-loaded water. Inverted colonialism in which the settler catches disease, especially in filthy Timmins."

At this, Otto had to interject.

"Timmins isn't filthy. Its people aren't sick. There's not much different in fact, except the buildings and houses are spread out

221

across the land instead of vertically. And also people drive their own cars. And no one wears Values tokens."

Lloyd took this in quietly, but then pointed to the stage.

"See that dancer, Josh. She's new. That body. I bet she'd make a terrific surrogate."

"Keep it up, Lloyd."

"Come on, you know I'm kidding. I adore Ashley."

Otto was looking at the girl, she was as pretty as Monica, and her eyes seemed to share the same melancholy, but were more hardened. He turned as their eyes were about to make contact.

Too late. She came over, fully naked, to stand between Lloyd and Otto while Josh leaned back to sip his beer. She told them to call her Jasmine. She kneeled to put an arm around each, then glanced left and right, before pulling away the arm from Lloyd to put around Otto's neck to clasp her other hand. Otto didn't stop her as she pushed out the table to make room to sit on his lap. She pointed at Lloyd.

"Got a girlfriend? Maybe the four of us can do a little blending criss-cross?"

Lloyd's eyes widened until Josh nudged him and he shook his head.

"I'm afraid I'm fixed."

"What about you? You've got the look of someone in love. We can help each other out."

She was pointing at Josh now, who looked briefly frightened, but then pointed to Otto's wrist.

"He's a *Transitory*."

"So am I. We can help each other become *familyar* by getting familiar, if you know what I mean."

She laughed at her pun, then shifted Otto's hand to her breast as her mouth pressed on his lips. Her hands slid down his chest to his groin, where she moved it about, her voice emitting an exaggerated cooing. Eventually he tired of it and shoved her off. Jasmine was lighter than expected and fell to the floor several metres away, her back hitting a chair, arms dragging through a puddle of spilt beer. As she tried to shake it off two men rushed to help her to her feet. She stormed off. Lloyd slapped Otto's shoulder.

"Why'd you do that?"

"I didn't like what she was doing."

"We better leave, Lloyd."

"Yes. Come on."

Otto needed no encouragement and relaxed once outside and breathing fresh air. He followed Lloyd and Josh to another lane until it was clear no one was following. Still, they decided it was best to go the next zone. Curiosity stoked his excitement almost as much as the sign indicating they had twenty seconds for the pedestrian window and he joined Lloyd and Josh in their rush to join a crowd of several dozen others.

A raucous, impatient rumbling from the idling buses, trucks, vans, and other vehicles to his right and left. A grey barrier rose on both sides, blocking any view of the vehicles or the street. He heard the shuck and click of the horizontal elevator as it locked into place. They waited for people to disembark before stepping into the enclosed space. Another barrier rose behind them once the last person got on. Josh and Lloyd were laughing about the incident. When Otto asked about it, Josh explained the bar and dancers were part of the racial blending program to entice white *Indos* like he and Lloyd.

"Then why was she bothering me?"

"She was looking for a racial blending criss-cross in which two couples—one white, one black—switch partners until they both have a baby."

Otto didn't fully grasp what Josh said, only that it sounded disgusting.

They completed the crossing and he suddenly felt woozy. His token twinkled, flashed red. It became a constant red after they cleared the large square and he felt his pace slowing.

Josh and Lloyd were ten metres ahead when his steps froze. His muscles contracted. All he felt was fam-elixir pulsing in his bloodstream like a boat wake, before settling. It was impossible to move any part of his body now. He couldn't even fall down.

"Hey kid, why are you stopping?"

"I forgot, he's a *Transitory*. He's out of his zone."

"What do we do? We can't leave him."

"We have to. I can't risk my chance to get out."

Otto tried to plead with them to stay but no sound came out. Other voices quietened as space opened up around him due to people avoiding his presence. He saw them, smelled them, and their fear. The fear didn't emanate from an individual, nor from himself, but instead was a cumulative meekness that struck him as mass whimpering. Bizarre, as he was the vulnerable one, not them. They were free.

Soon he was alone. Once he felt hands on his body, searching his pockets, but the invader cursed at finding nothing.

A bang as the power went out. All around darkness, save for the moon, stars and, high on a tall building to the south, thin bands of billowing lights, alternating in blue, green, violet. Or was that too a product of his Values token?

42

A warm relaxing evening breeze combined with a soft haze had transformed the city vista from Esmeralda's balcony to present a different angle, one from the island ferry the day he asked her to marry him: the granola bar in her hand now an ice cream cone; the lilac and yellow silk sari she'd put on after her shower, roughened to feel like a terrycloth towel with the Canadian flag, modestly draped around her bikini bottom; the other Canada Day celebrants on the busy ferry as isolated from her that sunny day as those living around her now where Canada Day was an anachronism. Only then a gust cleared the haze and both vistas turned black to provide a panorama of a starry sky, the reward of another brownout, before a light above blinked to signal the generator kicking in while those around her stayed dark.

What was happening to her? This nostalgic indulgence could do nothing to resolve her only concern: where was Otto?

It made no sense. She'd never heard of this before, doubted Baxter had either. An untraceable Values token. As if it stopped working. They never stopped working, not even in long power failures, longer than this one. It was absurd.

Esmeralda was startled by the creak of the balcony door, more at seeing Felicity approach carrying the tea tray. The plain skirt that went to her knees was better at making her figure not too thin. It calmed Esmeralda to see her like this, shifted the context of the others on her mind—Ken and Otto—in a way that was summed up in a single word: family.

"You've been up here some time, Mom. Thought you might be up for a pot of tea."

"I'd love that."

Esmeralda watched as her daughter poured the tea, her heart filling with emotion, and purpose. She'd enjoy her tea first, stare into the darkness, not fret about the power failure—she always felt guilty for not being affected, a feeling that stayed until the power came back—but instead wait it out.

It returned sooner than expected and Esmeralda's hand shook as she put down the teacup, took a deep breath to announce:

"Otto is here in NewTor. I've met him."

As Felicity continued to sip her tea, Esmeralda moved to pat her daughter's arm, but withdrew seeing her eyes flitting.

"He is? Where?"

"First, tell me the truth about him."

But Esmeralda's authoritative tone had no effect. Felicity was adamant. Esmeralda had to admit Otto had been staying there but she hadn't seen him since the tour and only knew that he'd gone out on his own.

"You mean he's lost?"

"We know where he went. But he's untraceable."

"We?"

"I'm going to get Grace to—"

Felicity abruptly stood and stepped to the balcony's edge, as if choosing this moment to conquer vertigo. Her frail frame shook at first but steadied by grasping the railing with both hands, her thin arms spread wide.

"As I was saying, I'll get Grace—"

"No. Let me find him."

"You don't even know what he looks like."

"I do know."

Felicity turned around, keeping hold of the railing, her back to the city. Her shoulders trembled but her eyes were calm and lucid. Esmeralda experienced a touch of pride at her daughter's resolve to overcome this fear.

"Remember me telling you I recognized that Desirae?"

Felicity explained she'd encountered Desirae and Otto on the bus to famSud. It was dark but she'd recall his youthful face and large frame. She then admitted, to Esmeralda's dismay, she'd been sexually interested in him at first.

"Relax. Even if Desirae hadn't interfered I wouldn't have gone through with it. Something about him, some feeling. If I see him again, I'll get the same feeling. I'm glad to know he's still alive."

Felicity's matter-of-fact demeanour triggered regret. Why did she let on about him to the girl who only days ago had deemed him responsible for Felix's death? Was Felicity looking to cause him harm? Was this an act?

As Esmeralda explained how Otto came to NewTor, it became clear those fears were groundless. Furthermore, that Esmeralda had no one else on whom to rely. Grace might be too tempted to involve Baxter. Also, as an Indo, Felicity was ideal to follow the trail. She could visit Otto's last known location recorded by his Values token without being conspicuous. Finding the boy was paramount, sending Felicity an unavoidable risk. Besides, Otto could easily defend himself against a tiny creature like her if she did have other designs.

"All right, Felicity, as long as you're candid with me and tell me all that happened from before Otto was born until you left him with Ken."

"Can I ask you something before answering? It's important, it might help me to understand things too."

"All right."

"Did you really love Ken, did you two love each other?"

"Yes, I did. We did."

"Why did you separate then?"

Never had Esmeralda faced this question, not from James, or even her own conscience. Perhaps she'd feared discovering the truth. Had Felicity asked because she truly wished to know, or to put off what Esmeralda wanted to know from her? Now her token signalled an incoming urgent message.

"It's Baxter. I'll take it inside. Finish your tea."

Esmeralda rushed off and shut herself in her bedroom. It was unusual for her partner to contact her while away on business. His message said there was to be an impromptu conference for a large delegation from New York and Pennsylvania. He asked that Esmeralda arrange it, and also attend.

The distraction of a conference was the last thing she wanted, but it affirmed her decision to recruit Felicity. Even better, it'd keep her daughter and Baxter apart. While Esmeralda ached to hear Felicity tell the whole story about Otto, she was not as keen to respond to questions about Ken. Maybe the conference was a good thing.

Tomorrow she'd have Grace compile Otto's Values token data for Felicity. In a world without police, it was up to the Doyenne to recruit her own investigation team. And include herself.

Esmeralda felt no compunction going into the guest suite for clues to where Otto went. There was nothing in the suite itself, except his bag, lying on the floor. It pained her to pick it up, as if a force was fighting her muscles, reminding her of her spiteful reaction to that time her parents searched her room and found the condom a friend had given her, just in case, prior to a date, that hadn't even been used.

This was different. It wasn't suspicion driving her, but sincere concern for her grandson's safety. She unzipped the bag and felt around until she found an envelope. No name or address. She opened it and read the letter inside, dated fourteen years ago.

To Esmeralda

Dear Esmeralda,

There was a time when fate would bring us together one way or another earlier in life. Looking back on those years is painful because I no longer see them as about the two of us coming together, but instead us coming apart. We've been separated over fourteen years and all hope for an event like before has faded, along with any hope for you to reach out to me now.

You may challenge me that I never reached out to you. I could BS many reasons but really I felt it was necessary you be the one to come to me, based on the circumstances of our separation. If I initiated anything, I felt, it was likely to result in rejection. And if not, there'd be doubt about your motivations and sincerity.

Vanessa passed away a few years ago and James came to the funeral. He didn't explicitly say anything to get me to conclude this but his visit confirmed you had no interest in seeing me or the twins again. That our temporary separation was final. As is the case with the subsequent one, I fear.

For they've left me.

I don't know where they've gone. For the past three years I have searched for them and failed. Just as I failed in raising them, failed miserably. I won't speculate on why they left. I now fully realize taking them from the city was a mistake. But then their leaving me is also a mistake. They were fifteen when they did, I doubt they've matured much the past three years. They're legally adults, free to make their own decisions, which they always made clear was what they desired. They've gone their way, you've gone yours, and it's time for me to go mine.

I will not be alone. I have taken charge of an orphan I found as a baby almost three years ago at the camp where I was living. His skin is a mix of black and white that's hard to describe. He often looks sickly as if with a fever, but he is the sturdiest child I've ever seen and he's never ill. I have an idea where he came from but can't prove it. I'm not a spiritual type but I like to think his arrival was meant for me to keep him pure, i.e. away from your world.

I apologize if that comes across as critical. It likely reflects my fear and ignorance of a changing world I've been told has a lot to do with you. It sounds like a world I need and want to avoid and even run away from, as I'm doing once again.

I wasn't sure whether there was a point writing this but now that I'm doing it I think it will help cleanse me of my bitterness. It may fortify me for the solitary life I'm destined to live. I have enough money and knowhow to build new camps, or homes, as needed. That's not meant to be defiant, but to assure you, if you care (which I believe you do deep down), I'll be all right. We'll be all right.

I'm not as confident about our twins. They couldn't adapt to life out here, a reality I stopped deluding myself about far too late. For a time Vanessa helped, before she passed away in 2027. It's possible they will seek you out. I can't help that nor control what they'd say. They're efficient liars. Anything they tell you is disputable. Except perhaps for the hate they feel for me. I accept that. If you encounter them—actually it won't matter what you believe or choose to believe.

This letter can be taken as my attempt to go forward to live a simple, honest life and raise this boy as honourably as possible. I hope I'm doing what's right but I'll admit I'm not entirely sure.

A potential regret is that Otto won't meet you. And you won't meet him. His name is Otto, by the way, I don't think I said that earlier. That was the name on a handwritten card I found inside the basket with him. He was malnourished at first but you'd be impressed how healthy he is. He's a natural outdoors, already learning things at only four. He catches fish, lays traps, starts fires, etc. So unlike the twins.

Now I'm not raising a wild child. I plan to enrol the boy in a school when the time is right. And when he gets older I'll share enough about the world to let him make his own decisions. I'll never lie to the boy, just as I'll teach him to never lie. Although that may do him more harm than good.

I will let that be my final cynical remark to end on what to me is a positive note: That I love you, have always loved you, since the day we met. I doubt I should share that with you, so I doubt I'll send this letter. Likely it'd never get to you, or if it did, you'd ignore it. Writing this serves one purpose: it affirms my decision to withdraw and live "off the grid" is one I make with an inner peace I think you'd recognize in me, maybe even appreciate.

I'll leave it to fate to determine what happens. I'm not yet fifty, plenty of life ahead to see if you and I are cosmic magnets that life knocks about, drawing our positives and negatives together or pushing one the other way to repel us. I can't take credit for the analogy, James came up with it. I forget if he was describing us, but it fits, doesn't it?

With love, Ken.

May 15, 2034.

Ken and Otto and Esmeralda

43

Ken remembered being imprisoned as a youth in Kapuskasing, at a party that turned into a brawl. He was put in a cell with five tough Indians who came to his aid when a white kid repeatedly called Ken "Indian lover" after Vanessa came to bail him out. He had to come to the white kid's aid upon realizing his cellmates knew his stepmother and were actually fighting on her behalf. That was his one and only jailing.

Until now.

True, it was a stretch to call this facility in famSud a prison, it was too chaotic, the detained too orderly. The one prison aspect was the inability to leave of his own accord. Monica no doubt was in a similar two metre by two metre glass cube in some other hall. Moving about was possible but odd. The raised cube walls hovered just over the floor and, like transparent shields, followed you as you went about the large room. No privacy but you could talk to others despite the glasslike material inhibiting physical contact. Though most only did briefly before switching to a concealed device. It agonized him to imagine unsavoury men accosting Monica. That almost made him regret ceding to her entreaty she accompany him to assuage her guilt for having lost contact with Felicity. Of course, if he hadn't given in, she'd have told James who'd have found a way to stop him.

It added to the urgency he felt following them. Now he had to admit he'd needed Monica to get this far. Confusing rules, slow, bumpy buses, dreary stops, clumsy transfers, patience-testing lines—if he'd known, he'd have charted a water route—and his reliance on her was as necessary as Otto's on Desirae. Or so he'd thought, as to the latter.

He didn't want to believe it but there could be no doubt that had been his nemesis Baxter, leading a group with Desirae. And no sign of Otto. He'd been too hasty confronting her, it got him ushered here, thankfully without Baxter noticing. Still, now he was separated from Monica whose "be patient," as she went off with Desirae was all he had to maintain his sanity. But for how long? What was Desirae doing with Baxter, how had they met? Had James set something up for her after all? Not likely. Maybe it was chance. Or ambition made her resourceful.

Reading Esmeralda's paper, which he'd barely grasped at the time, that sounded like her but didn't sound like her, had only muddled his mind further. It made him wonder how she and that professor ever got together, though it dispelled James's fear about Ken's motivations. If his goals had anything to do with Esmeralda, it would be to increase distance; he truly was doing this solely to fulfill Otto's wishes and keep him safe.

Unless this was about Felix. Ken felt awful for his son but his remorse only went so far. Felix would have killed him and Otto, possibly Monica too. He could find small comfort in that Felix was the troubled twin, Felicity the tamer. He had gotten sore at Monica for losing track of her at first, but she did gather Felicity was on her way to NewTor, likely pursuing Otto.

"What the hell are you doing here?"

Ken couldn't tell where the voice came from? Everyone close to him was engaged with their screens. His cube had one too, he realized, and tapped it. Desirae's face emerged, an expression of anger on it that softened when he asked where Otto was.

"He's fine. He's with Esmeralda in NewTor."

"How did that happen? Does she know who he is? And what are you doing with that Baxter fellow?"

"Slow down. This is not a place to talk. Listen to me. You must get away. Before they discover who you are. I discussed it with James and he agreed. Please, do as I say."

"Promise to answer my questions?"

"At the earliest opportunity. I swear."

Ken relented and listened. He was to get the attention of an official and say he wished to withdraw his application to go to NewTor, to return to where he'd come from, and only say it was Timmins if asked. Then get on a shuttle for the entry gate.

"There's plenty of them. I'll meet you at the taxi stand."

"That's it?"

"The rest I'll explain then. In person."

"What about Monica?"

"I left it up to her if she wants to go with you or if she wants to stay here and continue on."

"What did she decide?"

"You'll find out when I do."

The plan was too vague for Ken, he didn't like that it entailed going in reverse. He was no longer sure he could trust Desirae. The absence of an alternative, boosted by the appeal of leaving the facility, convinced him. He tapped his cube until an official came by. The sheepish woman looked displeased by his call but happily obliged after hearing his request: one less individual to process, Ken figured.

Outside was bright daylight despite the sun being behind the building. He boarded a shuttle bus along with two officials. It drove less than a kilometre at golf cart speed before stopping. He was told to get off and walk left. The bus and its passengers continued through a gate into a restricted area.

A lonely pleasantly empty paved boulevard, with young trees in boxes like those one sees in cities in front of him. He passed a red brick building, a high school turned administration office.

Ken's languid stroll became a cacophonic experience as several buses rolled past him to park in the semi-circle drive just ahead, disembarking people in varying uniforms who dutifully formed lines that walked around the building to its football field, which was packed with Quonset huts, into which lines of passengers disappeared like trains in tunnels. An impressive efficiency, the human mass cleared quickly, the buses drove off, giving Ken an unobstructed view ahead to a taxi stand. Empty. Then a heavily tinted four-wheel drive SUV slowed ahead of Ken. Desirae was leaning out the passenger window, waving him inside. He took a seat in the rear, thrilled to see Monica there, smiling and calm.

"Okay, I'm here. Now tell me where's Otto? "

No response. Monica tapped the glass partition separating the front and rear seats.

"She can't hear us."

"Doesn't trust the driver?"

"She trusts the driver fully, he's her cousin. He doesn't want to hear anything, so he can pass a lie detector if necessary."

"What's going on? Who were all those people back there?"

"Transitions officers."

"What?"

"According to what Desirae told me, famSud is in the middle of transition from Stage Two to Stage Three. There's been a lot of violence, protests. Apparently it's normal to import police in the thousands to instil and keep order."

"Did she tell you about Otto?"

"She wanted to wait for you."

Monica's trust in Desirae was reassuring. Even after the car veered onto an unpaved road for a rollickingly unpleasant hour long ride. The road ended at an unmarked trailhead. Everyone got out. It was wonderful to be outdoors again, the air and sky so clear he almost forgot the circumstances. Desirae instructed the driver to return for her—not them—in an hour.

"What's going on, Desirae? Where's Otto?"

"Come on, follow me."

Desirae led them to the far side of a copse to another trail that was short and ended at a large rock seemingly in the middle of nowhere. Behind it a small pond that, beyond the reeds, looked ripe for fishing.

"This was a favourite spot for my cousins and me when our families would hold our annual reunion. Isaiah, who drove us, is a cousin. Sorry for the long ride, we're not that far from the city, we just doubled back a couple of times. He's just gone back to make sure no one followed. You can trust him."

"Trust? Sorry, it's hard to trust you when I see you with . . ."

"With Baxter? I understand. Baxter has no idea I'm with you. If he hadn't been diverted, I wouldn't have had a chance to get you out of there in time."

"And where is the good old professor?"

"On his way to Timmins."

Desirae's pause to let that sink in was deliberate, Ken felt. She was studying him, his reaction, exhibiting a shrewdness belying her youth.

"Guess that rules out going back to James for us."

"That's right, Monica, it does."

Desirae's explanation was troubling. She'd contacted James to tell him about seeing Ken and Monica and asking what to do. If not for Baxter having to rush to Timmins to investigate a death, James would have let them be. But he and Roscoe had to remain neutral; keeping Ken and Monica at famSud might expose their connection. They asked Desirae to get Monica and Ken out, and keep them out until everything cleared.

"It means you two will be on your own, indefinitely."

"Where do we go?"

"Nowhere. Stay in famSud. Things are in such disarray here, it's easy to be unseen. My cousin will help."

"I need to see Otto. Where is he?"

"As safe as anyone could be, in NewTor, with the Doyenne."

The matter of fact way Desirae stated it stunned Ken. What he deemed an inaccessible goal at the outset had turned out to be simple. He listened closely to Desirae describe their journey to NewTor. It helped restore Ken's trust in her when she candidly said she suspected they'd been singled out due to a DNA match between Otto and the Doyenne. She added they'd been treated well and suspected Esmeralda knew who Otto was but it wasn't confirmed. He glowered while she spoke of the professor with admiration and learned Esmeralda still lived with the man. His envy wasn't for a romantic rival, but for the boy. It helped to hear Baxter had shown little interest in Otto.

"I still don't like this. Being refugees out here."

"I don't like it either. I came to go to school, to start a career."

"I'm sure she didn't want to be caught in the middle, Ken."

Monica's interjection annoyed him. He hated being dependent on people, especially those he'd known briefly, while the one he trusted most was with his estranged wife. With no perceivable way out. He could still doubt Desirae but he had committed to trusting Monica. It would be foolish to abandon that.

"I need to speak with James."

"He wants that too, but it can't happen yet. We'll arrange it as soon as possible. Probably through Isaiah."

Desirae asked how they could have managed to get as far as they did without a Values token. Ken reached for the item he'd taken from Felix but instinct told him to hold back. Instead he lied to say the buses were so busy they were never hassled. She believed it.

They rushed back at hearing the SUV's engine call them to the meeting point. Her cousin got out the car this time. Isaiah, a tall, lanky young man with an afro, opened the passenger door for Desirae, but not the rear doors. He opened the trunk to retrieve a beaten cardboard box he gave to Ken, intentionally avoiding looking at Monica. Isaiah got back in, checked his watch to get Desirae to hurry.

She ignored him to grab the box and open it on the ground. It contained sandwiches, two filled water bottles, a tin of cookies, a large canister of peanuts. Underneath, a map of famSud with a key folded inside and a cruder hand drawn one.

"This is to an abandoned cottage my father's friend used to own. Continue along the trail for about a kilometre. Stay there until we get it all sorted out. There's a card loaded with money and another map with directions to an alternate spot if needed for Isaiah to communicate with you, and vice versa. Otherwise he'll drive up to the property."

Ken was impressed by her organization, dejected at having to hide again. It felt as if he'd merely transferred from one prison to another. Not that he was ungrateful, but it wasn't in him to express it. Fortunately Monica was there to do so. She also gave Desirae a long hug that included some whispering. He asked what they said after Isaiah drove away.

"She was just warning me that Isaiah thinks I'm hot."

Monica then admitted forgetting to tell him that one member of Desirae's group with Baxter appeared to have been Felicity.

44

Without warning and unable to stop it, Otto started urinating. Only it couldn't be urine, the texture was different, the smell too pungent. fam-elixir! Exiting through his pores. He exerted and pressed to flush it out. It was working, he felt himself releasing from the bracelet; only now his mind was becoming addled, the outflow creating disorientation as if also emptying his mind, his mental faculties swapped for muscle facility. The flow stopped, now he could move freely but wasn't sure of anything beyond a desire to go home with only a faintly echoing inkling home was north. The bracelet, that he remembered. He wanted it off. But pulling made it tighten. He relaxed his muscles to rid them of panic. This made him aware of the last of the fam-elixir. One final exertion. He flexed his wrist, the bracelet sprang away. He was too late to catch it, it bounced on the concrete then rolled on edge down a sewer grate. At least it was off and the fam-elixir smell receded. He recalled it had been much darker earlier, now it was more like twilight.

Otto took the first step. Painful. But the pain disappeared after several more and he looked ahead to a flat landscape of deathly grey concrete. Few trees. People slowed to observe him until he picked up his pace. Smell and hearing and a heightened sense of others' fear in charge, eyesight demoted. It led him to a park of mature maple trees and benches. Pigeons pecked at morsels only they could see on a concrete path ending at a playground, with two young girls on swings pushed by a woman who let up until Otto passed. The girls pleaded for five more minutes, but the woman told them they had to get to bed. He walked to them with quiet steps and unintentionally startled the mother.

"Sorry. Can you tell me which way is north?"

The woman kept still, gave him a nervous smile, then ushered the kids off without answering. Otto started to follow, thinking she hadn't heard; it only made her move quicker. He stopped at sensing another presence. An older man with a dachshund, its legs scurrying to keep up with the man's loping, a comical sight that made Otto grin. His eyesight started improving.

"Good evening, young man."

"Good evening, sir."

"Sir. Such language. Are you mocking me?"

"Mocking?"

"I may be British, but I'm no colonial."

"I'm wondering, can you tell me which way is north?"

The man studied Otto as if annoyed, but then flashed a row of bright white teeth that looked fake. Otto couldn't tell if he was friendly or not.

"Impertinent too. Now I know you're mocking me."

Otto was about to protest but instinct told him any response would be a wrong response. Could the bracelet he lost help him get the information he was seeking? It seemed important to be careful what he said to people, not let on he didn't have it. Otto wanted to get away, then heard a grunt, and a sharp bark.

"That for sure isn't north."

Otto turned around, trusting the man wasn't lying. If only he could be certain. The stars and moon were blocked by thick but unthreatening clouds. He continued along emptier and emptier streets as the darkness deepened. He went down streets without shops, only residences. Occasionally lights from windows drew his attention. Only for a blink, their shutters or blinds closing abruptly. He still felt watching eyes attuned to any movement he made. His own eyes had adapted well now, he was confident he'd detect any dangerous presence before it detected him. But he was the only human. The stray dogs, cats, raccoons, squirrels, all disregarded him.

Otto.

That was his name, a fact he'd been able to retain, though it'd taken great effort. He kept repeating his name to himself until confident it would stay.

Otto wandered through residential streets, parks, crossed two big streets of crossing vehicles before exhaustion hit and he had to stop. It was good to rest but it also brought awareness of his situation: nothing to eat, nowhere to sleep. He had no idea how long until daylight, until people would reappear. He didn't risk knocking on doors and frightening anyone. Everything looked alien, cramped. Houses nestled against each another, their tiny unkempt lawns of overgrown grass edging concrete driveways, most full of cracks, all with one to three huts on each. No cars. Fronted with mature equidistant trees trapped in boxes sliced out of sidewalks interspersed with ones more recently planted. Occasionally an apartment building of six or seven storeys.

Eventually he came to the end of the houses to find himself in a large park with what he had to assume were sports fields. It was pitch black here, no streetlamps. Engine noises, rumbling wheels on concrete over a hundred metres off the sole indicator of humanity. They lapsed once in a while to let him hear a plop or splash to imply a nearby creek or river. The idea of catching a fish suspended his hunger, even though he'd have to wait until morning. It was a pleasant night, cloudless and starless, no sign of rain. Making it possible to sleep in the open air.

Otto slept uninterruptedly until the sun had risen to shine on the parkland around him. On one side a skyline he felt should mean something. Sadly his memory hadn't returned beyond the time he'd lost that bracelet. He walked a few steps down a path before he again heard water. He went through a patch of trees and reached the river. He splashed his face and the icy wetness helped him to fully wake.

When he rejoined the path, a group of joggers was passing by. Their pace was synchronized but each wore a distinct outfit. He watched where they went until they slowed, as if to run uphill. That meant the river flowed the other way, which in turn meant the other way was north. It didn't seem right. Somehow, against his experience, he knew that here, wherever here was, the rivers ran south to a large lake. This potential connection to a memory excited him. Could he trust it? If so, he'd follow the joggers to go north. Which meant he'd been going south yesterday.

The joggers ascended a staircase, two-by-two, that took them over a narrow bridge to cross the river. Otto followed, picking up his pace. Good thing he did, because once they crossed, they took a turn he'd have missed. Here the path opened up and the sun had moved enough from right to left to confirm he indeed was heading north. That was satisfying but he still had no idea to what or where he was heading. Then there was his hunger. This path had no shops of any kind. He could climb to the city level but didn't trust his ability to not get lost again.

More people on the path now. He passed many walkers, was passed by more jogging by themselves. He felt conspicuous, but if he kept to the right side it was better. He was hesitant to stop to ask where to find food. The aura wasn't unfriendly but it did seem it would become so if he bothered anyone. This echoed his fear from a recent walking experience in a desolate area. Again a hopeful sign his memory was not lost forever.

A strange sound made him stop. Someone swearing. Strange, as it was the first word spoken by anyone all this time. He left the path and found a narrow one through brush to the river. A young man a few years older than himself was fishing. And not doing well. He looked ridiculous in colourful plaid shorts and a bright red t-shirt. Otto approached him.

"Can I help?"

"Damn reel, I keep forgetting how to work it."

He explained the reel he'd bought last week had fallen apart, forcing him to use his grandfather's ancient one. He had no idea how to work it. The fellow added he wanted to catch a salmon for his sashimi party.

"What's sashimi?"

The fisherman turned to Otto, as if surprised to see him there, but he was still smiling.

"Think you can really help?"

"I think so. Here."

Otto took the pole, inspected it, placed it on a picnic table, and without thinking about it, restrung the reel and took it back. He surveyed the water and farther up saw two salmon jump. As he cast the line he heard the fisherman's admiring sigh. A minute later he reeled one in to drop into a net the young man held out. He took the net to a cooler and put in the fish.

"It's small. I bet I can catch a bigger one."

"I bet you can. But this'll be plenty."

The young man twisted the fish in the cooler, inspecting it. He found it and brought the cooler to his chest, generating a beep.

"What are you doing?"

"Claiming the tag. Only one a month, right?"

"You mean they aren't here naturally?"

The fellow shook his head.

"Still tricky to catch, but not for you. I'm tempted to ask you to use your allotment but I really only have room for the one."

"We could start a fire and cook this one up?"

"Sorry?"

"I'm starving, I haven't eaten since yesterday, I think."

The perplexed look made Otto think the man wanted to run away from him. Instead he put out his hand for Otto to shake.

"I'm Rico."

"Otto."

"Hello Otto. Where are you from?"

"I don't know, I don't remember."

Rico was perplexed a moment, but then nodded, saying he'd heard of *familyars* having concussions or accidents, their tokens needing a fam-elixir restart, that he'd be able to help.

"*familyar*? fam-elixir?"

"Come. Follow me."

Otto followed Rico along the path to a small road underneath a giant roadway, then up an inclined road to streets with houses like those he'd seen the night before. A look back revealed the skyline that again triggered familiarity within. Rico nudged him to continue down several streets until they got to a large house, almost a small mansion. Rico had Otto stay put while he went to freeze the salmon. Instead of going in the house, Rico walked down a driveway to a shed with siding of a fake material made to look like the brick of the house. Rico went in and returned in less than a minute.

"Let's get you to a fam-elixir station to figure this out."

"I'd really rather get something to eat first."

"We'll do that too."

"Not the fish?"

"No, that's for later. You do know where your implant is?"

"My what?"

"Hmm. Never mind. Shouldn't matter."

More streets with packed houses until they came upon a wide road full of shops and busy with people and vehicles. Rico led Otto to a glass-enclosed shed with a door-less opening just wide enough for him. Rico pushed Otto to step inside and follow the directions on a screen. He wished he hadn't the instant the glass panel above and behind him closed. It was quiet, too quiet. The screen stayed grey. Otto looked at Rico who was looking away. The screen began to flash, emitting a low whistle that became painful. The door raised again behind him, then another one on the other side, a bright orange strobe light blinding Otto. He felt Rico yank at his arm and he let himself be pulled out. He could see nothing and trusted Rico to lead him away from a crowd he only sensed. Slowly his eyesight returned to realize he and Rico were in an alley, with the latter starting at the impression on Otto's wrist.

"Are you an *Indo*?"

"What's that?"

"Damn. You are an *Indo*. But where's your Values token?"

"The thing that was around my wrist? I lost it."

Rico let out a small laugh, not a humorous one. Otto thought he would run, but instead he took Otto back to his home.

45

The meeting floor's best feature was its versatility, provided by retractable movable walls. It could be a single, enormous room encompassing the entire fortieth floor of family Values HQ, or be parsed into up to thirty individual rooms with soundproofed walls ensuring optimum privacy and discretion. All week the setup was tailored for a delegation from the United States, one hundred ten in all, in a special arrangement of thirteen rooms as an ode to the original colonies, the largest overlooking the quiet, lovely harbour and beyond the islands to the flotilla of cargo, coast guard, and navy ships. On a clear day one could even see the skyline of Niagara Falls. Depending on her mood that could be a glorious view, or a sobering one for territory they'd ceded to support family Values. Today the view was irrelevant, her mind preoccupied with Felicity's efforts to find Otto, potentially inhibiting her ability to focus on this meeting.

While she expected her presence to be ceremonial, she had to attend in person, not as a hologram, which she regretted having done with Otto who would have found out regardless. This was an important session and needed her to apply sincere interest in its subject: Girdwood, Baxter's ambitious, grandiose endeavour to build a family Values city from scratch. One as progressively mature as NewTor, instantly in Stage Four. An alternative to the messiness of stage transitions. His Brasilia or Canberra, located in a remote area northwest of famSud. Its success would lay the foundation for a supreme northern defence, hence the American interest, if its development proved repeatable.

For her, this was the pure manifestation of her vision without the unpredictability of a second or third stage, what she saw as the path to restoring the original buzz she'd felt when she wrote her paper. Only her ardour was marred, seeing her partner had brought in Desirae as his personal aide. Bright girl, to be sure, but most certainly not primed for a session of such importance, one crucial to the actualization of their original aspirations.

Implementing family Values south of the border was a goal turned distant dream when the United States civil wars erupted and spread like a virus. A nation already engaged in conflicts in Asia and involved in the European struggle with Russia was prime for internal attack by a growing conservative contingent its liberal rulers thought suppressed. It put any plans for family

Values in American cities on hold indefinitely. Unfortunate, as its evolution would likely have been quicker there, and broader in scope. Paving the way for global growth akin to the spread of American culture in the twentieth century. Fortunately the US funding stayed and actually grew with Ontario's cooperation in providing fuel from raw materials and other key resources no longer needed by family Values cities as their infrastructures simplified. Letting the US manage and protect its borders made it easier for Ontario to focus on evolving family Values, without concern over the intentions of the new countries of Quebec and Nova Canada.

Before Baxter could launch into his proposal for Girdwood, he had to give a status and face questions. Her partner loathed this but tolerated it, a price to pay for their contributions.

"And these troubling reports about famSud?"

"Some kinks due to an ill-advised and unapproved alteration to the implementation. I'm confident it will be fully Stage Three by the end of the year or early next year. A new detachment of police was just deployed and is making an impact."

It surprised Esmeralda they didn't ask where he got the extra forces from. She was relieved on Baxter's behalf he didn't have to bring up famCoch, how those extra cops were available due to what in essence was a retreat from that city.

"Once stabilized, we'll harvest what we learned for next—"

"You've done how many, ten cities? Shouldn't it be repeatable yet? I mean, to consider doing this in America—why else are we investing so much?—it has to be repeatable."

"The original family Values as designed by the Doyenne is an abstract meant to be flexible. Experience from implementation is what we do to refine and solidify it. Flexibility sounds nice but there is no one-size-fits-all—yet—each city's uniqueness cannot be determined at the outset, only with actual experience. Plan. Learn. Adapt. As needed. Repeat the cycle enough and it gets easier and easier. But never the same."

This was Baxter's show. Esmeralda was content to keep quiet and provide moral support with smiles and nods, not opinions or clarifications. Stay in her abstract lane to let her partner deal with realities. Only then she caught his eye cuing her to add her voice. A tone she'd cultivated to convince and entrance. As long as she remembered what he'd coached her to say.

"Professor Baxter and I are grateful for the funds provided to this point. Your investment has paid off handsomely and family Values wouldn't be the success it's been without it. The setbacks we encounter ought to be viewed not as negative but as positive returns on those investments. For they evolve family Values to strengthen it, and to make it more comprehensive. Our troubles are ones you'll avoid when you choose to adopt family Values.

"As this is not a status meeting, let's put off migration figures, costs, budgets, and all the sundry details until the agenda calls for them in tomorrow's sessions."

She smiled at Baxter, long enough for all to witness their love, their intellectual love. It worked, it calmed the general aura, but more importantly set up her partner.

"Our experience in famSud illustrates well the potential risk, as well as the lack of risk to starting from scratch. Specifically, Girdwood. This project makes possible the concept of an out-of-the-box, one-size-fits-all solution that's impossible with existing cities. I'm talking about a family Values city beginning at Stage Four. It was once a pipedream, now it's a potential reality."

Baxter paused. Esmeralda could tell by his quivering lips he'd regretted saying potential. She scanned the reactions, but as usual with the Americans, they were muted.

"I would like to introduce this young lady here, Desirae. She is the newest, brightest addition to my team. I expect her to play an integral role in this project and accompany us when we tour the site."

Esmeralda glared at Baxter but he didn't acknowledge it, his eyes beaming on his freshly anointed protégée. She was used to

Baxter acting independently, but this was different and it made Esmeralda furious he hadn't warned her. What was she to infer from his promoting Desirae so quickly? It pained Esmeralda to keep quiet while stewing over this.

Her indignation simmered to nothing, replaced by excitement for Girdwood. He'd always possessed a unique seductive knack to persuade with his firm soothing voice. She saw the attendees' faces indicating they were beginning to appreciate its potential. Cities across northern Ontario with fixed populations of a half million adventurers coming to build, then live, in those cities. Experts and skilled labourers sourced by *Indos* from within the country attracted to a change in circumstances or incentivized, but primarily migrating from elsewhere. The US in particular, who'd send unwanted refugees from their wars, ideological and actual, but have them retain US citizenship to remain potential conscripts.

Baxter was essentially pitching American satellite cities they controlled to the level of their investment. Such investment was beyond the means of Ontario or family Values. The location was remote, requiring capital for roads, buildings and the reopening of air traffic while under construction. Opening the skies raised the threat of stoking foreign curiosity, but would accelerate the project. She doubted they'd go for this, opting for the project to take longer instead. She suspected Baxter inserted this element to create an object of blame for delays. He was doing well.

The one sour point tugging at Esmeralda was Desirae and her unearned privilege of being part of this. Seeing the girl smile in adoration, marvelling at the possibilities, echoing Esmeralda's joy, though not to the point of spoiling her elation.

To Esmeralda what Baxter presented was the embodiment of what she'd developed during the stultifying pandemic. In a way an honorary gift for her, nurtured for years in his head, to build a world she'd imagined—at least attempt to—unconstrained by historical, geographical, political, or other baggage. It took over two decades to bring NewTor to this point. It wasn't perfect, there were glitches. Here was a chance to do it properly from the outset; she couldn't be happier or more in love with the man describing what was in essence an ode to his Doyenne. This good feeling stayed until one delegate had the nerve to ask:

"Desirae, do you perhaps foresee yourself as a successor to the Doyenne someday?"

"I don't believe there can be a successor."

Cleverly diplomatic response notwithstanding, Esmeralda felt troubled by Desirae's status. This angst made her want to leave first when the meeting ended, but she willed herself to stay to shake every hand.

The last delegate left behind an awkwardly silent gulf. Then a mayor from some industrial town came back to ask about "off-whiting," generating a sternly measured response from Baxter.

"Racial blending."

"Racial blending, right. Do you see it working in America?"

Baxter's indignation vanished, he was the salesman again.

"Absolutely. In fact, your cities are my inspiration. The influx of black immigrants is a trickle compared to what is available in your urban centres. Racial blending isn't yet a formal part of family Values, though. We plan to ease it in."

"I look forward to seeing it in action. There are rumours of people pushing back in a small city farther north?"

"famCoch. Yes, but that was expected. A learning experience, a contributor to the end result, a profitable sacrifice."

"So the racial blending program is still evolving?"

"For established cities, yes, but for Gird—"

"Yes, but I won't be the mayor of Girdwood, or any new city."

"What are you asking then?"

"You see, some of us mayors might want to incorporate such a program, even if we can't yet adopt family Values."

It was rare for Esmeralda to see Baxter's face light up, actually beam; the only time she could recall was when she told him Ken had left. Baxter rose to follow the mayor out but Esmeralda had him stay seated.

"When were you going to tell me about her involvement?"

"Whose?"

"Don't play dumb. Desirae."

"We only got back late last night, remember?"

Esmeralda's anger subsided with the realization their absence would keep Baxter from Felicity. He hadn't asked about her yet. The appeal of avoiding that discussion trumped her interest in Baxter's interest in Desirae.

"If you have an issue, tell me now or wait until next week."

"Next week? You're going away again?"

"I'm taking several delegates out to survey the Girdwood site, to show them the need for allowing air traffic."

"She's going with you?"

"Like I said, if you have an issue . . ."

"No, no issue."

Esmeralda returned to her office to find Grace waiting with a message that Felicity wanted to see her right away. It came to her then that neither Desirae or Baxter knew about Otto. She felt it her duty to tell them he was missing. Baxter could find him, if anyone could, but telling him would only complicate matters.

"Did she locate Otto?"

"No, but she has news she wants to give you herself."

"I see."

Despite her anxiousness to know what her daughter came up with, it was better to wait until morning when Baxter and his acolyte were gone.

The wait proved interminable. Increasingly, Desirae occupied her thoughts during those hours, specifically how she and Otto coincidentally happened to come to NewTor together. The story they'd met accidentally in Timmins seemed contrived, the way they were with each other implied a different connection. Was Baxter aware of this, was this why he kept her close? In a keep-your-enemies-closer kind of way? That was silly, her mind was drifting. Nonetheless, it'd be worth getting Grace to investigate Desirae once she was gone. Meanwhile, Esmeralda could do her own interrogating.

The opportunity presented itself after the last session. Baxter invited the delegates to his favourite restaurant but left his staff, including Desirae, behind. Esmeralda knocked at the girl's suite and was invited in as if she'd been expected. Esmeralda walked to the bedroom. Desirae was folding underwear to place into a travel bag.

"Did you have any trouble getting my skirt clean, Grace?"

"It's not Grace, it's me."

"Doyenne, this is an honour."

"Not now. I want to know, who are you?"

"I don't know what you mean."

"I think you do."

"Look, if you think something is going on with your husband and me . . ."

"My partner. And no, that's not what I mean."

"I was telling the truth. I'm not into men."

Esmeralda could see Desirae getting upset and trying to hide it. The Doyenne could exploit that if she wished. Part of her did, part of her wanted to crush the young woman for a reason that wouldn't become clear in her current state.

"That wasn't what I meant."

"Then I'm confused."

"Why haven't you asked me about Otto?"

"I meant to, everything's happening so fast."

"So you don't know he's missing."

"What?"

Her shock was genuine, it added to Esmeralda's confusion.

"Where could he be? Didn't you track him?"

"It's a puzzle, but his token is untraceable."

"But that's impossible."

Desirae's eyes shifted slightly but not away. She wasn't afraid of the Doyenne. That troubled Esmeralda who inadvertently let out an exasperated sigh. Enough to give the young woman the upper hand.

"You know who he is, don't you, Doyenne?"

Esmeralda absorbed the part accusatory, part empathetic, and fully unexpected question before softly nodding.

"And you care about him?"

"He is my grandson."

"You've known this a while. It was no coincidence Otto and I were brought here."

Esmeralda nodded. Admitting it brought relief and awareness she had the power to do so restored her equanimity.

"Be truthful now, how do you know him? How is it you knew of our relationship? It wasn't Baxter, was it?"

It was Desirae's turn to be defensive. She insisted she'd really known Otto only a short time and his coming along was foisted on her. Esmeralda got the impression Desirae wished to be free of those obligations so she could exploit career opportunities in family Values. But also still holding something back. Esmeralda concluded Desirae wasn't against her. Nor for her. She left the suite intent on finding Otto, resolved to stop circumventing the truth, at least with her grandson, convinced Baxter's interest in Desirae, and vice versa, was platonically professional.

46

No running water but the well was only a hundred fifty metres away. The electricity from a small generator filled with gasoline supplied enough juice to operate lights and small appliances. A bedroom each ensured no awkwardness inside the cabin, since Monica had once again taken up doing everything nude around the cabin. This never irritated Ken as it had Otto. Insignificant compared to her lack of concern for the silence from Desirae. At least she'd put on her nightshirt when going to the pond.

A curious impact of so much idle time was a sudden thirst to know Esmeralda's reaction to Otto, and vice versa, that at times was unbearable. But as Monica continually reminded him, the situation in Timmins made him a fugitive, forced his patience, and dependence on Desirae and cousin Isaiah.

He was a young lad, pleasant and taciturn. He'd come by two hours after picking up Desirae to fuel the generator and guide them to good spots for fishing. He was coy with Monica and if she asked a question, he'd address his answer to Ken. Anything to do with famSud or how to act, however, he'd explain first to Monica so she could restate it for Ken.

The transition from Stage Two to Three actually made it easier to remain incognito due to a temporary relaxation of restrictions before famSud's forceful push to complete Stage Three. Anyone could go anywhere without identification until then. Thousands of extra police had been hired to instil and keep order. As long as they didn't loiter, offend anyone, or commit a crime they'd be free to explore, albeit under nervous watchful eyes of officials on the edge of action. Which was what they intended to do as soon as Monica was ready.

Ken sat at the rustic picnic table, playing with Felix's bracelet, twirling it while Monica refreshed herself at the pond. He'd had no success penetrating what made it work so far. She'd be gone a while, this was an opportunity to really go at it. Hence he was unprepared for her black nightshirt to block his sunlight. Ken tossed the bracelet under the table, too late.

"What's that?"

"I thought you were at the lake."

"I forgot to take some sham—what is that?"

Her hands were fast and she picked up the bracelet, examined it, and realized what it was on seeing the logo.

"Where did you get this?"

"Where do you think?"

"This is dangerous. We need to get rid of it."

"On the contrary, I think it could be useful. I want to see how it works, maybe even alter it."

"You're crazy."

"Go ahead, Monica, try it on. I'm sure it's deactivated but it might need human contact."

She hesitated, her curiosity battling her fear.

"Why don't you?"

"A little tight on my wrist. I think it'll fit yours perfectly."

Curiosity won out. Monica had to know it was harmless, yet she stepped back as if performing a rite, before slowly slipping it over her left wrist, holding it a moment, then trying to snap it shut. She was left-handed Ken realized. He motioned for her to try the other wrist. It snapped shut and fit nicely. He couldn't be sure but Ken thought he saw it flash blue, then pink, possibly the device trying to activate with a last bit of that stuff James said powered it. It stopped before she noticed.

Now she was admiring it as a piece of jewellery, but a smirk indicated she didn't like it. She took it off, went into the cabin to get her shampoo and left. He returned to his task but frustration soon drove him to nap. He woke to see her clothed and clean, hair tied back, ready to venture into town. To his surprise, she asked to wear the bracelet.

"I thought you found it ugly."

"It kind of matches my pink blouse. Besides, it might be useful once we're in town. Make me look like I belong."

It wasn't too far a walk, relative to their recent treks, just over five kilometres. The gravel and dirt roads had dried from the rainstorm that had kept them cabin-bound most of yesterday. A couple of pickup trucks slowed to pass them, but none offered a lift. Good ole boys checking out the shapely girl, Ken figured, cringing with a tinge of nostalgia.

As buildings started to appear they seemed to converge, the small streets and alleys blocked, funnelling incomers to a single entry point. They came upon an impatient but behaved crowd clamouring to get through, uniformed officers and others trying to keep it civil. Ken asked one officer what it was about, got a stern look, before the man pointed at a sign indicating this was a check-in station, a temporary border. Monica whispered.

"Should we go through?"

"We've come this far."

"I don't want to get stuck in another facility."

Ken shook his head to ignore the question. A relief when she didn't press the point. Just in case, he avoided looking at her as he held her hand to push through. At last they reached what to him looked like an amusement park entrance. He and Monica stepped up to a booth but found no one inside. They waited. He felt a shove from Monica. He turned to see her with a slightly alarmed look, as if she'd been groped. Ken took a breath, said nothing.

"Come on buddy, move it."

"There's no one in there."

"No kidding, it's not the checkpoint."

"You all right?"

Monica nodded. He let her hand go briefly to pass through a turnstile, then grabbed it again as they came upon an expansive but unfinished plaza of well trodden grass. He pulled her off to a spot by a muddied patch that looked to once have been part of a large park. He asked Monica if the man in line had groped her but she shrugged it off saying he wasn't the first. She also said it might be wise to move along because they were loitering. Her suggestion came too late. An officer, barely older than Otto, approached. Ken let go Monica's hand when he saw the woman frown.

"Anything I can help you folks with?"

"Just pausing for a break."

"If you're here to register, follow the crowds. Keep it moving."

The officer pointed to a bank of benign billboards extolling family Values virtues, mixed with sinister ones urging people to register immediately, as famSud's Stage Three declaration was imminent, and if not registered you'd face inconvenience at best or legal trouble. An implied urgency that didn't mesh with the general calm. Below the billboards, screens displayed counts of registrants but no percentages to gauge relative progress. One screen was playing a real time video of a construction site, with a superimposed counter of kilometres of border wall finished, how much to go in the corner, while another screen broadcasted a news feed. Monica pointed to it as if to show the officer it was their destination, her long sleeve shirt pulling up to reveal the bracelet. Ken noticed it had turned pink again, though it could merely have been a reflection of the sun.

"Is it okay if we catch up on the news first?"

"Of course. Why didn't you tell me you were registered?"

"Only me. He still has to."

"Good, glad to hear it. Stay out of trouble."

"That was easy. Let's see what's on the news."

Monica kept staring at the crowds lined up at the dozens of registration kiosks, jostling for position, on their way to the news screen. A gloom had fallen over her that was also affecting Ken. Now she had tears in her eyes.

"I'm sorry, Ken. This all makes me think of Cochrane, that it'll be just as . . . weird."

Ken nodded but said nothing. They stayed through the entire ten minutes of the news cycle. No mention of Timmins; in fact little news at all, the most informative piece a weather forecast. The rest mostly propaganda to exhibit the slogans in action via interviews with experts and happy citizens, including a bizarre but amusing clip in which people showed the novel locations of their internal Values tokens, and a brief, nagging piece showing *Transitory Indos* how to wear their bracelets to best reload fam-elixir. Unfortunately, too brief, too nonspecific to be useful for Ken's purposes. Then Monica smiled as a man approached.

"Monica? Is that you?"

Monica blushed as she hugged the man. When they let go she introduced him as Larkin, a friend of Wesley's, a former police officer too, who'd left the force for a different reason she didn't specify. His imposing muscular frame and brush cut were offset by an infectious smile and friendly face. Apparently, Larkin had provided a haven for she and Wesley within Cochrane for a few weeks until the coast was clear to leave. He was closer in age to Monica than Wesley. His reserved nature Ken attributed to his confusion about Wesley's absence.

Larkin said he was relieved to see she was safe, but saddened at the news of the baby. Monica caught him up with her life and then explained Ken's presence, at which point he relaxed.

Her joy at the reunion was cut short when he shared rumours, ranging from her being dead to assembling a revolt against the city. Ken wondered if she now regretted not going to Cochrane when they were in Driftwood. She offered a meek grin.

"Look, you have time to let me buy you a coffee?"

"I don't know . . . we have to . . . I mean . . . Ken?"

"Of course we have time for your friend."

Larkin guided them to a hoity yet quaint coffee shop of a type Ken would never enter on his own. He held the door for them. As soon as she crossed the threshold, Monica let out a groan, then collapsed in pain, grabbing her stomach. Larkin had to get Ken's help to lift her up and back outside where she felt better, except for a headache and queasy tummy. Larkin looked sick himself when he went to check her pulse.

"When did you get this?"

He was pointing at the bracelet, which now was a sharp pink, and flashing erratically.

"It's a long story."

"Come on. Let's get away to my apartment."

Ken trailed behind as Monica and Larkin walked together, as she was still woozy and might collapse. A handsome couple, he thought, tall and graceful, athletic. They got a few looks but no one bothered them as they crossed through the downtown to a boarded up storefront. Larkin opened a door next to it and led them up a flight of narrow, steep stairs into a large and open concept apartment looking out onto the street. The space would have felt roomier if not for stacks of boxes and suitcases. Larkin called out a name. No response.

"Good, my roommate's out. He's not a fan of company."

"Is he moving out?"

"Those boxes? No, they're mine. I'm leaving next week."

"Where to?"

Larkin didn't answer, perhaps hadn't heard on his way to the kitchen to make coffee. Ken sat in the armchair, Monica in the love seat while Larkin noisily took out mugs from a cupboard, a moment to collect his thoughts perhaps, because on his return with the filled mugs, his expression had become grave.

"What's the matter, Larkin?"

"When did you become an *Indo*? And why?"

"She's not an *Indo*. Monica, take that off."

She obeyed and, after a little struggle, set the bracelet on the coffee table with the family Values logo facing the window. The pink light had faded back to nothing. She looked better, except still alarmed. Ken was grateful she let him tell Larkin the story his way, avoiding any mention of Desirae, Felix, and naturally how he'd acquired the device. Larkin was clearly unimpressed with the lack of details.

"Your Uncle Wesley is in the wild and this Otto is in NewTor? You two are what, hanging around until Otto comes back?"

"To be honest, Larkin, our plans aren't set."

"famSud isn't an ideal place for uncertain plans."

"What about you? Where are you going?"

"famCoch."

How Monica's face lit up drained all suspicion from Larkin, his expression genial again. Ken sipped his bland coffee while he let them talk. It was great to see her smile. So pretty. Which filled him with an unexpected deep sadness.

Their visit ended an hour before dusk after pizza to give them enough daylight to get back. Ken suspected Monica would have stayed if he hadn't been there. He was pleased to learn the plaza they'd used to enter was the main transition registration point. Other options were available.

47

The woman is large, imposing, appealing, familiar. He knows her, but a resisting force prevents him identifying her. The more he desires to find out the greater the resistance, to the point he becomes frantic, and the scene switches to a memory of Rico, of catching a salmon. He longs to eat it not only to sate his hunger, but a hope doing so might help penetrate the resisting force.

"Well, well, man of a thousand dreams, you're finally awake."

Otto rose and saw only walls, this was the extent of the home. No bedroom, just two internal doors, one leading to a closet, the other to a bathroom. The pullout sofa he'd slept on, Rico's bed. His host calmly observed Otto from a kitchenette. No windows. A shelter, not a house. Yet it felt appropriately homey.

"How did you know I was dreaming?"

"I didn't. You've been out a couple of days. I imagine you had a few. Judging by your sweat. At least you're not feverish."

"A couple of days?"

"You must be starving."

"Can we cook up that salmon?"

"Ah, you remember that. Anything else?"

"Did I say anything in my sleep? Say any names?"

"Nah, you were quiet. From what I saw. I slept at a friend's so I was mostly away, just checking in from time to time."

"When are we going to have that salmon?"

"Still in the freezer. It's for later. I'll make you something else."

Two vents to outside provided fresh air until suddenly a new aroma filled the space. Coffee. But only briefly, before a strange more powerful smell took over that erased all thoughts of fish. Rico smiled at Otto's reaction.

"It's curry. Some leftovers a friend of mine, Aziz, whom you'll meet later, gave me. I'm guessing you've never had it."

Otto shrugged then shook his head. He put a hand to his face and it still had a trace of the salmon smell. He'd prefer that but was too hungry to be fussy.

"Remember anything? Like why you don't have a token?"

"I'm not sure I even remember what that is."

"See the mark on your wrist? You were wearing one."

"If you say so."

Rico frowned but said nothing and finished cooking. He told Otto to grab the plate and a knife and fork. Rico pulled the table from out the wall and dragged it over two stools. Otto set down the plate. Rico added a coffee mug filled to the edge and moved to lean against the counter.

"Enjoy."

Otto devoured almost half before the spiciness hit. He drank the coffee but it was too hot and made it worse. He asked for a glass of soda or juice but Rico only had filtered tap water. That tasted odd, but okay. Once accustomed to the flavour and heat, Otto finished it all and took his dish to the sink. As he rose he felt lightheaded. Exhaustion had returned, he desired more rest. Rico was agreeable, and felt that without a token Otto shouldn't venture out so it was just as well he stayed in bed.

"I've got friends coming by later who may be able to help."

Otto fell asleep to the sound of dishes being washed and the apartment being cleaned, an intermittent sleep full of dreams that mixed with the reality of Rico's movements and talking at a small screen on the wall above the table where he'd eaten. Otto caught snippets only, nothing that grabbed his interest.

The smell of raw fish got him to take notice. Rico was at the counter, his back to Otto, unwrapping uniformly cut pink slabs out of plastic wrap. He sliced them into small pieces and deftly removed the skin. It fascinated Otto who rose to observe as Rico trimmed off unwanted parts he set aside, folding the good ones in half. After assembling enough, Rico placed them in bowls. At this point he noticed Otto watching.

"Go freshen up and you can help me get the place ready."

Otto came back to find a dozen bowls with small fish morsels on beds of vegetables and lemon slices covering the counter. He helped Rico reset the sofa, then extend the dining table. Otto set the bowls in the centre as Rico got bottles of white wine and glasses and put on lively, joyful music, with instrumental songs that seemed to be missing vocals. Otto couldn't tell if he would be in the way or was to be the guest of honour.

One by one Rico's friends arrived, each refusing Otto's offer to share the sofa, except the last who arrived. Patty, short, bubbly, chubby with thin eyes shook his hand and then joined him. Otto thought she was native but learned she was Japanese. They all had foreign origins—Aniyah from Iran, Aziz from India, Rico from Peru—and all wore similar shorts and t-shirts.

Patty was the oldest, but strikingly cute due to her shortness, her medium-length pitch black hair, constant smile, twinkling eyes. The brown-haired girl, Aniyah, had an angular face that was only appealing when she smiled. Her dark green eyes often gazed at Otto. Aziz had a prim goatee, no moustache. He was sombre but seemed the most intelligent, most likely the best to dispense useful advice. Individually pleasant, but collectively morose and mutually unhappy with life, particularly their jobs. They didn't hate their work as much as they saw little future in it. Because of their low values scores and the continual influx of migrants from the United States, they would be passed over by others for promotions. When they said "others" he'd sometimes sense looks in his direction, as if to let him acknowledge or even apologize for their situation.

He didn't care for the wine and chose to drink water. It kept his head clear to observe their odd exchanges that seemed too personal at times, oddly remote at others, and they often would talk about each other as if the subject wasn't in the room. Like people might with a pet. When they did it to Otto he asked they stop. That was when their attitude towards him changed. Now treating him like an honoured guest, someone they wished to impress, not as if he owed them something.

The litany of personal issues continued—Patty's frustration at not being a schoolteacher; Aniyah's annoyance at having to do clerical work for idiots; Aziz's inability to advance his technical career due to political interference; Rico's near-abandoned hope of becoming a chef through regular means—all attributed to the lack of a disability such as poor health, lameness, weight issues, and more limiting them to a single *fam* and keeping them as low score *familyars*.

Otto got a feeling they'd become resigned to their situations, even found contentment living with their complaints. Nothing was said about what they'd do to fix it. With each complaint he felt they were pushing him to see his dilemma, his amnesia, as a private complaint to nurse, and that whenever he balked at that, a sense of resentment returned, with traces of envy. They were nice but confusing, unpredictable. Especially Patty who'd been shifting closer. He'd been making room but ran out and now she began to press against him with her soft fleshiness.

"Looks like Patty's found a way to avoid sterilization."

"Quiet, Rico. You're just jealous because it's too late for you."

"Are you kidding? Aziz and I are now free to be with anyone we want, black or white or whatever. You and Aniyah . . ."

"Not me. I'm going next week. I've given up hope."

"You're only twenty-five."

"Maybe you and Patty can share this one."

Aniyah then looked at Otto in a way that troubled and made him sad simultaneously. Their eyes locked a moment but then broke off when Patty pulled him closer and Aniyah left for the bathroom. The conversation waned and everyone heard her pee through the thin wall. That only increased Otto's discomfort. He relented this time when Patty offered a glass of wine. It tasted better, after the sashimi, and gave him courage to speak.

"I have to be honest. I don't know much of what you're talking about. Like what's a *familyar*? Or an *Indo*?"

"Hey Rico, are you sure he's an *Indo*. I mean, I can't recall an *Indo* with his skin colour."

"Aniyah has a point. No non-pale visitor would come to this neighbourhood."

"He could just be lost."

Aziz raised his hand.

"What if he's a *Transitory Indo*? It would explain his not even knowing such basic things."

"That makes sense. We can help him with that. At least make sure he's somewhat informed."

They all nodded at Rico's suggestion. It galvanized their focus on Otto's problem. They explained NewTor residents must be either an *Indo* or *familyar* and the latter had to belong to at least one *fam*. Which wasn't a biological family, but a set of people marginalized or victimized by race, gender, disability, or other basis by *Indos*.

"The bottom line, *Indos* are a lower status with fewer rights."

"For one thing, *Indos* can't own property, they must rent. All of us only rent because we can't afford to buy."

"We're at the low end of *familyars*."

"Which means we have to live among the *Indos*."

"Except Rico, he gets to live among privileged *familyars* with few neighbours."

"My diagnosed vertigo allows me to live alone, while others, like my friends here, get assigned multi-unit complexes."

"With the lowly *Indos*."

Otto's confusion overflowed. Yet the terms *Indo* and *familyar* had an empty freshness that strained his mind as he repeated them internally, hoping they'd help restore his memory. He had to keep them on this subject.

"Why would anyone choose to be an *Indo*?"

"It's not your choice. It depends on *arbiter*, of course. Which is always fair and so impossible to dispute."

arbiter. Another word he felt he ought to know.

"I don't know what an *arbiter* is."

"Right. *arbiter* is a centralized, automated agent that governs all aspects of our lives. Everything we're talking about involves *arbiter* to a degree. Like determining our famBI."

"If Otto doesn't know *arbiter*, he won't know famBI."

"family Values Benefit Income."

"famBI is a basic income we all get as registered family Values members. It's not enough to live on, which is why we're all also Gotcha Miners. Guess I need to explain that too."

"Why bother, Aziz? I doubt he'd ever have to do that."

"Easy, Aniyah. Be kind to our guest."

"I'll give it a go."

Patty took Otto's glass and handed it to Aziz to refill. She took over speaking to explain once Aziz handed the glass back.

"Before *arbiter* consolidated recorded human communications, they were dominated by social media of all kinds, mixing words and images and sounds. Social media is gone but everything it recorded was kept. As Gotcha Miners we sift through databases of stuff keying on Sensitive Search Words and Phrases: SSWaPs. These can also be acronyms or phrases or image elements or—"

"Patty, skip the details."

"Right. Anyway, new SSWaPs emerge every day, as databases of content are released. Hence the search data is endless. Gotcha

Miners keep trying combinations until they find offensive items they report to a committee. If deemed offensive, the offending party is reprimanded. That can mean anything from censure to outright cancellation, depending on the quality of the apology, if any, they offer. It can also be tabled for future action should a new directive impact its interpretation."

She paused and smiled weakly, but kindly.

"I'm confusing you more. Essentially it's for the betterment of everyone to hold others accountable for what might have been said or done in the past. For young *familyars* with no future it's an opportunity to correct wrongs and also advance status. Like a lottery, in a way. And the rules changed recently. We can now hold people accountable for what their dead relatives said in the past. I am confusing you more, aren't I?"

Otto nodded slowly, until a clear thought struck him.

"How do you know what was meant in the past has the same meaning now?"

The question bothered Patty, she got quiet, but Aziz chuckled.

"The past is relative my troubled friend. Let's not spoil Rico's success celebration with such academic pedantry."

This reanimated Patty.

"Yes, we're together now because Rico had one of his finds go to the committee. He could achieve the Switch."

"What's that?"

"Getting to the committee earns Values points and the further it goes he starts getting money and, possibly, the Switch. That's when you get to replace the offender. It's rare, but it happens."

"Don't jinx it for me, Patty."

"But then can't someone do that to you too later?"

Again Otto's question bothered them, including Aziz, whose smile looked forced. He recovered quickly to prompt Rico, who was eager to redirect the discussion to his success.

"It happened when I stopped by a restaurant to read its menu, to get ideas, you know. It struck me the meals had been named after characters from an old novel, *The Odyssey*. The owner/chef had even titled the menu Homer Cooking to be clever. Homer being the author of that book."

The others' faces went blank. None seemed to understand the issue but deep down Otto sensed a mental click within. Homer. Odyssey. These names meant something to him, a visceral link to his memory onto which he could latch.

"With the book banned and the chef not changing his menu in a reasonable time, he was ripe for reporting. If I'm lucky, I'll get his restaurant."

"I've heard of that book. I know I have."

The others exchanged quiet glances. Otto finished his wine in the silence, and felt lightheaded. The talk resumed but he found himself detaching, listening but not able to participate or object when they again spoke about him in the third person.

"I think he's getting tipsy."

"We might have something here. If we find out who he really is, maybe he can help us."

"What, by being such nice people?"

"I think Patty's got a head start on that."

"Quiet Aziz. Just open more wine. He needs some."

Otto struggled to process their words, intent on making sure his hands didn't spill his wine. This was a different one, not as sweet. It had a stronger effect he felt behind his eyes. He'd felt a similar feeling before, in a strange dark loud place with people he barely knew. If he had more wine he could identify it.

Patty then pulled him tight and mumbled in his ear, only he didn't understand it.

Otto got up too quickly to go to the bathroom, his head spun. Patty stood to help. He shrugged her off to manage on his own. They lowered their voices but he could hear them.

"A bit young."

"I have no other prospects. Even if he's not into me . . ."

"That's true."

"You won't stand in my way, Rico? You won't tell anyone?"

"On the contrary, I'll help you as best I can."

"You're a good friend. And if Aniyah's interested . . ."

Patty's voice trailed off when Otto returned. The sudden and conspicuous silence made obvious to them he knew they'd been talking about him. But Otto just grinned, he felt good, and even helped himself to more wine, getting a warm smile from Patty. Only then he realized all but Patty and Rico had gone. Just as he blacked out he heard Patty:

"I'll take care of him. Thanks, Rico."

He's in the middle of a suburban street of fine houses, all with broad lawns, wide paved or stone driveways. Homes for well-off people. All but one monochrome, basking in an aura of danger, while the sole house with colour—brown roof, reddish-pink brick, lush landscaping on the bright green grass, pastel blue shutters, a teal door ajar—invites him. The path is clear, yet he can't propel himself, held back by flesh. Or is he not letting go? The front door opens to reveal a large, shapely woman in a translucent white frock. She looks off to the left, the right, never at him, though mouthing something. Willowdale. He tries to call to her, but his voice is muted.

Otto woke from his dream naked, his body pressed against an also naked Patty, whose arms were around his torso. She pulled at his shoulder until they faced each other. Her hypnotic smile halted his impulse to leave. She put an arm around his neck and pulled. As their lips met she manoeuvred her hand down and up. Confidently. He remained still. Relinquished control.

48

The thunderstorms earlier in the evening had left a glistening mark on the city but now, with darkness setting in, a dense fog surrounded the suite, covering all the outside in a gloomy grey blanket. At first glance one might assume a blackout. Luckily not the case, and Esmeralda didn't have to endure the generator groan while poring over Grace's file of notes, before speaking to the man Felicity found who claimed to have seen Otto the night he left. Her one comfort was Baxter and his "assistant" were far to the north right now.

First there was the murder near Timmins, how the Exceptions Office had not yet identified the victim, exposing a loophole in *arbiter* in that people's DNA was only visible to the Exceptions Office in aggregate form and the logic within *arbiter* hadn't been designed for such a situation.

However, they'd been alerted to a brief use of a Values token not belonging to its wearer. It meant someone had found it and used it, not necessarily anyone connected to Felix, assuming he was indeed the victim, for which doubts were creeping in. More pertinent was an alert, prior to the one in famSud, in which a fam-elixir station in Zone 4 had detected the presence of a body without a token, possibly coinciding with the incapacitation of Otto's *Transitory Indo* token. Meaning he was dead or somehow had disengaged it. The former was likely, except no corpse had been found, making the latter feasible. She hoped so, but had to know before it escalated to the Exceptions Office head: Baxter. His involvement with Girdwood bought her some time, but not much. A *Transitory Indo* crossing into another zone was serious enough to draw his attention, the chance of one walking about with no Values token—theoretically impossible in a Stage Four city—would hasten Baxter back to investigate firsthand. Hence the need to breach protocol by accompanying her daughter to interview a man claiming he'd seen Otto just before his Values token stopped transmitting.

Felicity had done a tremendous job finding this fellow, since *Indo* movements were tracked but not logged within their own zones. Why would they be? She'd gone every evening the last few nights to where Otto had spent a half hour, a restaurant at which he'd dined, and checked out all the candidates and found Lloyd. He'd admitted seeing Otto but was hesitant to say more, until Esmeralda granted authorization personally by inviting him to assist in the search; a rash decision, but anything to find Otto before Baxter got involved. Because if he did . . . she didn't want to think about that.

Thinking of Baxter did remind her he had various tools in his office, including a scanner to locate defunct Values tokens over wide areas. The issue: he'd never allow Grace, let alone Felicity, operate the device. Meaning Esmeralda had to physically leave the suite. Early spring was the last time she'd ventured out, for a forgetful party to celebrate the anniversary of her coronation as Doyenne. The tricky part was getting Lloyd to the famdrone, with Felicity, ensuring her daughter didn't reveal her Doyenne connection. Potentially awkward and clumsy, which was why it needed Grace's organizational skills.

Esmeralda was anxious to do this last night but the weather had forced them to hold off until morning, after the fog cleared. Another lonely night, as Felicity had informed her she would be with Lloyd, making no effort to conceal the obvious implication. Yet Felicity's tone was respectful, even deferential, almost like a daughter valuing her mother's trust. Perhaps it wasn't a casual fling. Potentially concerning if he did learn of their relation and tried to exploit it. Another unavoidable risk made necessary by the urgency of finding Otto.

Esmeralda changed into pants and a jacket, hoping to remain incognito if possible. They'd take an unmarked service vehicle, less comfortable, but she wasn't up to waving today.

Grace was waiting at the launch area, alone. Felicity was on her way down the entrance path, but it didn't look like her. She wore a smart print dress, flat shoes. A mature woman to match the man with her in navy blue slacks and undoubtedly his best button-up shirt. They were flanked by two officers with sombre expressions that hid any reaction they might have to the honour of seeing the Doyenne in person.

Esmeralda made note of the contrast between the paleness of his skin and Felicity's smoky brownness. Side by side they were similar to the twins, despite the man being a decade older than Felix, and his looking about with boyish wonder.

Lloyd's wonder increased at being introduced to Esmeralda. An *Indo*, but he willingly obliged Grace's insistence he refer to Esmeralda as Doyenne. When Felicity did so too, without irony, it told Esmeralda her daughter had been discreet. When Lloyd left to use the facilities, Felicity revealed he believed Felicity had been specially hired to find Otto because she was an *Indo*, hence inconspicuous. Not forthcoming, not an outright lie. Esmeralda was impressed. She smiled when Lloyd returned.

"Coming here by subway must have been a unique experience for you."

"Actually, no, because I work on problems down there."

"Problems?"

"Accidents and breakdowns that cause power failures."

"Oh. Interesting."

She and Felicity sat in the rear to let Lloyd relax and provide Grace specific directions to the restaurant where he'd met Otto. On the way, Lloyd described how Otto came into the restaurant by himself and sat next to Lloyd and another man he asked to remain anonymous. A wish Esmeralda granted too readily for Grace's liking. How Otto was unfamiliar with the ordering process and needed their help. He'd kept to himself until Lloyd and his friend began talking about Timmins and then famCoch. Otto said he'd been to Timmins, and knew a girl from famCoch.

"Did Otto say anything else? Any names?"

"He never even told us his name. He didn't talk much, but he did say he knew someone who'd left famCoch because of the off—I mean, racial blending."

"Oh? Who was that?"

271

"We didn't ask. We were more interested in Timmins."

Esmeralda was intrigued by this famCoch girl. Neither he nor Desirae had mentioned her. But it had to wait.

"We? Does that mean you are considering leaving NewTor?"

"Not me. I'm too old for that. I'm content here. It was . . ."

"No, no, that's fine. You don't have to tell me."

Grace said they were close just as Lloyd put his hand out to point at an older three-storey building with a number of people lined outside. A few glanced up but most were focused on not losing their place in line. Esmeralda instructed Grace to hover the car so she could engage Baxter's scanner. Its faint splaying light drew looks from below but Esmeralda continued scanning until sure its negative response was comprehensive.

"Where did you go next with him?"

The man shifted, as if uncomfortable, until Felicity nudged him and assured him the Doyenne was unconcerned about the zone breach. Instead of saying where it was, he pointed out the route. Esmeralda kept the scanner operating. Minutes later they hovered near the zone's edge. Lloyd crimsoned. Felicity noticed and started laughing.

"It's okay. It's just one of those bars with the black dancers."

Esmeralda frowned. Not at Lloyd for frequenting such a place or even Otto for going to one. No, for Baxter who bought into this marketing idea of entertaining white men with naked black dancers to entice them to racial blending. Baxter didn't originate the idea but did see deeming such places semi-legal might make them enticingly risqué. A reputation that stayed even after they became legitimate centres for surrogate arrangements or for the blending criss-crosses between couples, a program for which the Doyenne still had reservations.

"We weren't there long. In fact, there was an incident."

"What sort of incident?"

Lloyd cleared his throat and told her one dancer was friendly with Otto and sat on his lap. She made a suggestion he partner with her for a criss-cross and then he threw her off and she fell on the floor, drawing the attention of bouncers.

"We left as quickly as we could."

"And where did you go?"

"We wanted to get away so we decided to go to the next zone. Over there. We'd only gone a few metres into it when he froze. I am sorry, we didn't think . . ."

Grace guided the vehicle across the intersection. The scanner's lights came on, it began buzzing. Esmeralda had Grace go left to get it to stop shaking before someone noticed, then back and forth until she found the precise spot. The device could record the coordinates, no need to linger. Grace would send a team to retrieve it later.

"This is it. This is where we last saw him."

"And you just left him?"

"We didn't want trouble. We panicked. I'm really sorry."

"Fine. Just make sure you keep this to yourself."

"I swear. I think Felicity will be able to vouch for me."

"Hmm."

This troubled Esmeralda and, by her silent scowl, Grace too. As they returned to the launch pad, Esmeralda began to think it would make sense to keep Felicity in contact with Lloyd in case he remembered more; in any case it would help keep him quiet to others. It was evident there was a bond between the two and Esmeralda was certain Felicity would readily spend more time with him. However, her daughter came back immediately after she'd escorted him off the grounds.

"He really likes you, dear."

"Yes, and I like him too."

"Then why didn't you stay with him?"

"Because . . . you may not believe it, but we're not that way, at least not yet."

Esmeralda ignored Grace's smirk and smiled at her daughter. A tiny but precious moment that prevented her raising the fear

Lloyd might be drawn to Felicity because of the Doyenne for a short cut to becoming a *familyar*.

"But you were with him last night?"

"I said that to test you. I was in my room and got up early to get him here in time."

"He doesn't know about our relationship, does he?"

"Definitely not. That's another reason I don't want to be with him in that way, in case I let it out. I want to go slow. Just now I told him I had to go back for further instructions."

"Good thinking."

"And before your mind goes thinking things, Lloyd has been sterilized. His interest in me is genuine."

That was comforting but didn't preclude the possibility he'd be operating on behalf of others. Esmeralda highly doubted it, but wasn't as confident about men as she once was. Felicity was in too good a mood to share these cynical thoughts, though.

"I think that's all, Grace. My daughter and I will go back to the suite for some lunch."

"I do have a message. From the professor. They'll be returning this evening. He wants to speak with you when he gets back."

"They? Oh, of course, Desirae."

"Desirae? If that girl's coming here I'd better stay with Lloyd."

There wasn't much for Esmeralda to say to that. Grace's news meant a change in plans. A home had to be found for Felicity, at least until she and Baxter sorted everything out between them. Only one option. She told Felicity to pack and then, after lunch, to go with Grace. When Esmeralda shared these plans with her assistant, Grace surprised her by saying she thought putting up Felicity at the Willowdale house was a great idea. Felicity was less enthralled hearing how far it was from the city centre, from Lloyd. She came around hearing she could use a famdrone to go see him or bring him there on occasion.

A mothering impulse compelled Esmeralda to take Felicity to her childhood home personally, instead of Grace, and taking the subway, the same route she'd take after her downtown outings with friends. It was often crowded and lively those nights; now just the two of them, riding the rails for an hour.

One thing Esmeralda had never put much thought to was the way family Values would change lifestyles. Once people were content to live inside their zones it made sense to repurpose the subterranean rails for the exclusive, hence efficient transport of freight and VIP human traffic for family Values or government-related functions. Securing these essential assets by walling off street access and enlarging elevator capacities to facilitate equal fulfillment for zones in variety and quantity. Complementing surface changes to apply the equality principles fundamental to family Values. It had demanded coordination with the removal and construction of buildings, parks, businesses, etc. to create a zone system fair for all.

Esmeralda enjoyed explaining this to Felicity whose interest was sincere. Unlike that previous tumultuous time with her and Felix when they were too young to appreciate it. It also passed the time as the train clunked its way north, frequently having to pause at an old station for a freight to pass; the subway a rare place in NewTor where the Doyenne was not top priority.

One station before they were to exit Felicity suddenly grabbed at Esmeralda's arm and pointed.

"That's where Lloyd said he'd been in the subway before. To remove a truck in an accident. It's where he met his friend, the one who's going to Timmins."

"So his friend is going to Timmins?"

"Shoot. I didn't meant to say that."

"Be careful with him, dear."

"Don't worry, I won't let anything else slip."

"No, I don't mean that. I mean about his motivations."

"You think he's faking liking me because of my skin?"

"Lots of *Indos* secretly want to be *familyars* and are inventive figuring out how. It's not only about having children."

Aboveground they were greeted by a driverless surface car. It drove along a major road lined with large buildings. Esmeralda couldn't remember the former name of the street and of course there were no signs. Her neighbourhood in her formative years, now unrecognizable, anonymous. A right turn onto a side street gave the first sight of the brick single-family homes. Other than a dearth of cars, not much had changed. Good-sized lawns, bay windows, sleek roofs, asphalt or cobblestone driveways ending at wide garage doors, all contributing to a calm suburban space. Funny, Esmeralda hadn't been here in at least a year and had now seen it twice in a few days.

The only thing tainting her nostalgic appreciation: those signs protesting so-called Driveway Homes, being adopted more and more in the suburbs. Practical but unsightly. With private cars a rarity, long driveways could lodge deserving *familyars* in tiny houses, of the kind Ken used to build on a single property. An issue she left for Baxter and his associates, seeing it in real life made her want to reconsider her position.

Felicity was in high spirits as the car pulled into the driveway. Esmeralda smiled, recalling an image of Ken as a boy going to help fix her father's car before they set to work on that project with James. A project that inspired . . . everything she was now.

"This was where you grew up?"

"Partly. My early childhood was in South Africa. We moved here when I was thirteen."

"Any memories in particular?"

The other memories seemed to drift off, as if to highlight one.

"Felicity, a while back you asked why your father and I didn't stay together. Let's go inside, get you settled. We'll discuss it."

Esmeralda knew it'd be a long talk, that she wouldn't get back home with enough time to prepare for Baxter. But the truth was overdue. Besides, it might be better to be unprepared for Baxter, who had a knack for anticipating her well thought out concerns and having polished responses for them.

49

Tomorrow Larkin was to leave famSud for Cochrane. Though Monica hadn't yet confirmed it, Ken knew she'd go with him. It was possible she feared he'd talk her out of it, but he'd never try to do that. He'd miss her greatly, but it pleased Ken to know he had fulfilled his obligation, to both Monica and Otto—albeit not as he'd imagined—getting each home, in a manner of speaking.

Each day since meeting Larkin they'd gone into town to visit him and have a solid midday meal. Then at some point Monica would hint for Ken to find a way to amuse himself. Larkin told him about the pub he was in now, where he'd wait for Monica, and they'd return to the cabin together. How long the wait was depended on Larkin's roommate, which was hard to determine. Ken couldn't complain, recalling his trysts up north and making Otto wait at George's indefinitely. The boy never displayed any impatience. Or judgement.

He was enjoying a fresh lager draught, sitting on the torn but comfortable stool he'd adopted as his favourite, like a regular, picking at a bowl of stale pretzels on an over-varnished bar. The nostalgic air was matched by a crowd consisting mostly of men Ken's age. Men finding refuge in its dank cosiness to brood on whatever. For him, today, after having exhausted all else, past, present, and future, it was time to give old Professor Baxter van Leer centre stage in his head.

Ken's first encounter with the professor occurred just over a year after he and Esmeralda had for the third time run into each other, indirectly via his old construction colleague, Doug. Third time's the charm. An acknowledgement of destiny, it seemed, as they fell in love. Older, more mature, the mutual attraction as fresh as ever. The romance was moving steadily, life was great, when her folks, who'd returned to Africa a year earlier, died in a car accident.

He insisted on accompanying her to Durban for the funeral. The gesture and trip quashed all doubt about fast tracking their relationship. They decided, en-route, she'd move into his house just east of Toronto, not far from the commuter line. That would save her money and it was barely ten minutes longer than her walk to the office. Then came the reading of the will. It revealed a larger sum would come their daughter's way if she re-enrolled in the same university to resume her degree in Finance. She saw it as an opportunity and didn't resent the condition. However, she needed to be close to campus. The rental market was tough, the cheapest apartment more than budgeted for by the will, but manageable if she sold her car. Making it hard to see Ken. Until they discovered their old classmate James taught there. He was happy to drive her to Ken's on Fridays for the weekend, joining the couple for dinner, or the entire evening. Then she'd take the commuter train back early Monday or late Sunday.

University life changed her, or maybe revealed what she truly was. His first shock came on discovering she'd transferred from her Finance program to something called Critical Race Theory, without telling him. Taught by a Professor Baxter van Leer. Her explanation was convoluted and Ken didn't know enough to challenge this decision. It didn't affect them much at first and she seemed to be enjoying it.

One day she invited Ken to a Christmas party where he at last met the professor she revered. Ken expected someone older but learned she'd met him her first time at university, that he was a year older than Esmeralda. He was tall, skinny, pale but full of bravado and apparently did well with the younger females in his classes. Naive types Ken never had any interest in. It tainted an already dubious view of the man. He was presumably highly regarded by his peers, although Ken detected tension in several exchanges he saw. His enmity towards the professor grew. The condescending smugness was one thing, Ken expected as much from an academic elite; not all could be classy like James. No, it was Baxter's poorly concealed disapproval of Ken's relationship with Esmeralda that stoked that opinion. Thinking of it now, in famSud, the professor's attitude might have been due to Ken's skin colour. He didn't disapprove of Ken the individual, but as a stereotypical Canadian white male, implying Baxter was some sort of special white male.

Again, there was no impact to their home life until Esmeralda invited the professor to their engagement announcement. He came alone, meaning she spent as much time that day with him as with other guests. When Ken brought this up, to his surprise it triggered a big argument that led to her staying downtown on weekends more often, blinding him to the widening ideological gap between them.

A break came with the news Professor Baxter had accepted an offer of a residency in Europe. It was annoying to have to attend his bon voyage party but Ken was glad he did. It confirmed the man would be gone. Best of all, she gave up the rental to move back into his house, commuting every day as her new courses weren't as taxing. Then she became pregnant. With twins. These little babies — white boy, black girl — little versions of themselves to love and with which to reseal their bond. But not for long.

Esmeralda deferred her education a year for the kids, but once September came around she started to resent them. Eventually she admitted she needed to return to school because Baxter was coming back and he was the best instructor. They hired a nanny when she insisted on having a place in the city to concentrate on her studies, taking a female roommate to save money.

Ken suspected nothing until the second term when he drove downtown to surprise her on Valentine's Day, only to have the door opened by a half-dressed Baxter, no sign of the roommate. It was over. An awkward but mercifully brief reconciliation for the children did little and this last chance to mend the situation was obliterated by the pandemic in 2020. They agreed to try a separation, for him to take the twins north. While he struggled raising the kids, Esmeralda and Baxter went off to change the world, and presumably had done so.

"Another, pal?"

Ken saw his glass nearly empty. He finished it and nodded. A hush could be heard, it made him turn around. He hadn't heard the door open but now it was closing and Monica, ignoring the attentions from the men in the bar, brushed off the stool next to Ken and sat down.

"Why do they keep reacting to me that way?"

It was the bartender who answered, after setting down Ken's drink. He said it wasn't lust as much as it was sadness. That the beautiful women were leaving, either for Timmins or NewTor. Ken ordered her a pint.

"Just a small one and then I want to go."

"You don't want something to eat? I'm hungry."

"Maybe you can grab something to go?"

"Everything all right with Larkin?"

"Yes, yes. Great, in fact."

Monica didn't elaborate and it was a quiet beer before a quiet walk that felt longer than usual on an unusually warm evening. Finding the cabin undisturbed was bittersweet, a relief from the safety standpoint, annoying for the lack of word from Isaiah or Desirae. Ken started a fire and sat alone until darkness set fully to reveal the array of stars. Eventually Monica sat next to him. Her long blonde hair dripped from washing.

"Sorry I was gone so long. I got so sweaty on that walk."

"So you're going with him tomorrow?"

"I hate to leave you."

"You'd have left us back in Driftwood, if you'd known how it really was in Cochrane. I'll be fine."

"You were a stranger then. You're a friend now. I worry about you. That's why I haven't been myself today."

Ken chuckled but stopped when she put her arms around his neck to kiss his cheek. Thankfully, she was clothed. Which, he now realized, she had been since meeting Larkin. They held on a long while. Ken couldn't tell if the trickles on his neck were tears or pond water. He didn't care. He let himself get swept up in the emotion until he felt his own eyes moisten, then let go.

"What do you plan to do?"

"Stick around, wait for Desirae to make sure Otto is fine. After that, who knows? Timmins? Home?"

"Come with us to Cochrane. So good to call it that again."

Ken shrugged noncommittally. She excused herself and came back with two cans of beer. She handed one to Ken, then sat on the other side so they could converse face to face, the flickering flames contorting each others' expressions at times.

"Stole them from Larkin's roommate. Probably warm by now but what the hell, better than nothing."

"Thanks."

Another long but satisfying silence, two friends enjoying each other's company, saddened by its imminent separation. A brief moment to honourably encapsulate their journey together. Only it was almost ruined by Monica's prying.

"I wonder at times why you came, and stuck around. You say it's for Otto, which I believe, to an extent, but I also believe he's fine and can manage on his own. I fear it's her you hope to see. I suspect you're not waiting for him as much as hoping to find an excuse to go to NewTor, to force yourself, if necessary."

This was the sentimental sort of thing Ken had come to expect from Monica, only she was dead wrong. Whatever desire he felt for Esmeralda had drained long ago. He wanted to argue it, if only to not let it fester and become concrete. But he didn't want to spoil the mood. He smiled good-naturedly.

"You've got romance on your brain."

She tossed Felix's bracelet across the fire to him. It seemed as if she was annoyed by what he'd said, but he couldn't be sure.

"You weren't going to give it back to me, were you?"

"I thought about hiding it."

"I'm glad you didn't."

"I'd prefer you threw it in the fire but that's not my choice to make on your behalf. You can do it, or you can figure out how it works. If anyone can, you can. Just be careful."

The next morning Ken escorted Monica for the last time to famSud, to meet Larkin at a bus station. Their route wouldn't pass through Timmins, instead via North Bay. Larkin's sincere reiteration of her invitation generated a slight tug of temptation. When the bus departed, Ken was left with an empty and deep gloom, similar to when he and his father went to Toronto.

A long stint in the pub was warranted but it was too early to be open. Too early for protests or other troubles too. Ken had the streets to himself, enjoyed listening to the metal clamour, or squeal of wiped windows as shops readied for business. He saw one store already open. A hardware store, tiny but packed with tools on peg-boarded walls and aisles of boxes filled with nails and screws. The proprietor, a balding man with a pair of safety glasses flipped up, came out from the back to ask if Ken needed assistance. He was about to say he was browsing when it came to him to ask for a jeweller's tool kit and magnifying glass.

"Sure thing. What sort of project do you have in mind?"

"I want to fix a special . . . memento."

The amount on the cards Desirae had given was running out. The tool kit he preferred would eat up the rest, leaving nothing for lunch, let alone a draught at the pub. He considered buying a cheaper set, but Otto was too important.

He was back at the cabin by early afternoon, pecking, poking, prodding the device, searching for a way to open it. Frustrating and seemingly hopeless. His hunger made it worse. Ken knew he had to eat. The pond fishing had been poor but he'd noticed rabbit tracks. He entered the cabin to search for a weapon and came up empty. Under his cot was a small box that hadn't been there that morning. A dozen cupcakes and a note:

"A small thanks for all you've done. Love Monica."

Ken had to wrestle the emotion welling up in him and ate two before making some coffee to wash it down. The combination of sugar and caffeine energized him for his task.

This time it didn't take long to gain access. It was pure luck, accidentally touching three points at once, keeping still enough as it happened to memorize which three points. He repeated the action four times in case the device had been designed to alter its method of opening. It was Larkin who'd made him think of that when he mentioned devices of all kinds existed, including devices that manipulated other devices. Then, as if blocked to this point, he recalled a term James had used: fam-elixir.

That was how it worked. A liquid injected in the bloodstream. The smell emanating off Felix's corpse was fam-elixir draining. That was why it'd stopped working. Monica's pain at the coffee shop didn't come from engaging the fam-elixir, it was generated by a device inside the building that detected her wearing one. It would be risky but he could still use the device to fake his way around as they had in the plaza. At least until NewTor where, according to Larkin, you couldn't enter without a working one. Even if you did, you'd get nowhere because every square inch in the city was monitored. If only he could activate it safely.

His elation, fuelled by sugar and caffeine, compounded his startled reaction at hearing the crumble of dirt underneath thick tires. He scurried to conceal the tools and bracelet but only had time to cover them when Isaiah steered his SUV past Ken to the cabin. Ken carried his coffee mug to greet Desirae's cousin.

Isaiah took his time exiting the car. He handed Ken a tray of items, including another money card but said nothing, looking around, until he asked where Monica was. Ken tensed up, not sure of the motivation behind Isaiah's concern.

"She's gone. She met a friend and she's gone with him."

The young man's face dropped, and Ken relaxed. Isaiah had no sinister motive, he had a crush. It amused Ken and arrested his desire to express his frustration at not hearing anything for days, even when Isaiah didn't acknowledge or apologize for it. The young man seemed frantic.

"I'm afraid you to have to leave. Right away."

"Leave. Why?"

"The Timmins investigation. There's been a development."

"What development?"

"I don't know. All I know is you must go. My family can't risk you being on our property."

"What risk?"

"Please."

The more Ken badgered, the more confused the ramblings of Desirae's cousin. It then dawned on Ken that neither Desirae or Isaiah had ever wanted him there, had only done so for James. Possibly James's influence was no longer enough. Possibly they could betray Ken if he didn't do what was asked.

Once again in his life, Ken found himself alone and uncertain where to go. Previously those moments had been daunting, but also exhilarating. Now, in his sixties, only daunting.

50

Willowdale.

A word he'd heard outside his dream but couldn't recall when or where or how. Instinct told him it was a place to seek out answers, despite pressure from Rico and Patty to not leave the tiny home after learning of a scanning search targeting a threat that was likely Otto.

When he'd entered the fam-elixir station the other day, it had raised an alarm. When not immediately resolved the public was notified of the "extremely remote" possibility a "token-less *Indo*" was roaming about. Any information or sighting of an offender had to be reported. If this didn't resolve the issue a widespread search would be initiated, encompassing all private and public spaces. If caught the individual and any aiding individual could be punished. It was deemed best by Rico and Patty for Otto to stay put while they figured out what to do. Patty agreed to stay with Otto at Rico's house while Rico stayed at Aniyah's, as her unit was on a low floor, while Aniyah agreed to occupy Patty's apartment. Otto was touched they'd do this for him, but staying cooped up at Rico's was not tenable even one night. Which was why last night, after he and Patty had had their sex and she'd fallen asleep, he'd ventured out into the dark city. The freedom felt good and, a little closer to dawn, he quietly dressed to do it again with anxious anticipation.

For last night's jaunt he'd avoided the building where he had raised the alert. This morning he was braver, though troubled at first when he didn't recognize anything until the first crossing road. There it was, surrounded by a temporary fence with signs saying it was out of service. Yet no one guarded it. He remained wary until the horizontal elevator gate closed behind him and the two stopped vehicles were out of sight.

The opposite side revealed a staggered horizon of buildings of varying heights and widths bundled together some distance off across a broad valley. The same skyline he'd seen before, but it resonated deeper this time. He'd traverse the valley if it wasn't so foggy, even for his keen eyes. He remembered the river from which he'd caught the salmon only had a few bridges. He didn't want to waste time getting lost and had no desire to get wet. Plenty to explore nearby on this side.

More people were about, most going his direction towards a busy road full of trucks and other large vehicles. A wave of self-consciousness came over Otto for being in jeans. He stood out in an almost uniform sea of well dressed men and women.

They stopped in unison at a screen filled with numbers and times, one counting down. When it reached zero an imposing tram stopped in front. No one got off and the majority of those waiting boarded calmly in single file. A staccato of beeps meant some coin or token was likely needed. Otto stayed where he was, to the dismay of two women who had to shove past him to catch it in time. A sudden sharp trill halted the boarding. Those not yet on the tram had to step back to allow the vehicle's doors to shut before it moved on.

It left Otto at the front of the pack for the next one. It would be awkward to retreat because the waiting zone was packed. He was tempted to board the next one because it could take him across to the buildings. Risky. How could he be sure where it would go? The other tram had no markings yet its passengers knew to take, or not take it. That baffled him. He had to use his size and muscle to push through the impatient crowd. You'd think they'd be happy to have one less in line but the grumbling only stopped once he reached open space.

"You look lost, young man."

Then came a chuckle from the porch of a decrepit house, from an old man on a rocking chair, sipping out of a large mug of coffee so fresh Otto could smell it from the street. The man's head was full of grey hair falling down onto his neck. He wore a long bathrobe that somehow made him look dishevelled and distinguished at the same time.

"Come, join me."

He hadn't liked Rico's coffee but the aroma was tempting. The appetizing tray of muffins the man lifted convinced him to take a seat in a wicker chair to which the old man pointed, once he'd selected a blueberry muffin.

"Haven't seen you here before. Some coffee?"

"I don't know."

"Of course you will."

The man poured a cup for Otto. It was hot and smelled great. Otto let it cool while he ate the muffin. The fog was lifting, the sun breaking out, the heat increasing. It agitated his need to get back to Patty before she woke. But the thought of that cramped space, inside, not much larger than this patio, urged him to risk it until he ate the muffin. And maybe another.

"I'm guessing you're not from NewTor."

"How did you know?"

"From America, perhaps? Unfamiliar with the trams?"

"I've never seen them before."

"A student at the academy? Too young to be a supervisor. By your clothes . . . don't tell me. I want to guess. I like to guess."

Otto took a sip of coffee to ponder whether to play along once the man guessed or tell the truth.

"And what do you do?"

"This is what I do. I watch. I watch the sun rise and the world decline. It is my purpose in retirement to last as long as I can in hope of discovering I am not a prophet."

The man explained he sat on his porch each morning to watch this parade of commuters, commuting in and out of Zones One and Two, ever looking for signs his personal prophecy might be wrong, but only finding confirmation.

"Prophecy?"

"That the expression, 'the meek shall inherit the earth?' is an accurate one. But that they shall inherit a meek earth. This daily ritual is a gradual but noticeable symptom of that descent into meekness, without anyone aware it's happening. Happily they go along, free of the need to think for themselves. Everything available in sufficient supply, desiring nothing more. Only you don't fit in."

"I don't?"

"You're different. I don't know, you just don't fit in."

Otto didn't know how to respond. He knew himself he didn't fit in but didn't think the man was talking about the same thing. Was this a trap? That anything he'd say could lead to this man reporting him? Maybe he needn't answer, maybe there was no question. A minute of silence passed and suddenly Otto wanted to tell the man his truth. The man put up his hand to shush him.

287

From the house came music with words sung by a singer. The man was nodding, his upper body in tune with it.

"What is that music?"

"Oh that? Don't listen to it, it's not acceptable anymore. In fact my house is full of the unacceptable—books, music, magazines, photos, films and television shows. My impermissible museum. I'm a ghost, invisible, no one will trouble me about it. You made me lose my train of thought."

"Sorry."

"Ah yes, I know what's different about you. You aren't meek. You're not docile, not like those lining up to pack into trams on their way to workplaces to spend hours on redundant recursive tasks for which they are simultaneously worker and task. On an endless cycle supervising one another supervising one another ad infinitum. A Kafkaesque spiral where the completion of any task spawns the subsequent creation of the same task. Dutifully observing protocols and processes for a grand objective they are unable to define if asked. Like all manmade abstracts brought to life only existing because of each other. Self-fulfilling. Nothing about the world would change if they were extinguished."

The man coughed and paused for a sip of coffee.

"But that's not you. You have a *familyar*'s skin tone, an *Indo*'s aura. My guess is you're from far away, not only geographically but also chronologically. So what kind of *familyar* are you?"

"I'm not a *familyar*. I do know that."

A pall fell over the man's face. Otto felt an intense but only momentary fear coming from the man, affecting himself.

"But how can that be? With your skin colour?"

"What does my skin colour have to do with anything?"

The man's face brightened and he was now grinning.

"Of course. I'm an old fool. So then tell me, what are you?"

"I don't remember. I lost my memory a few days ago."

"Fascinating. But it doesn't matter. The most unreliable thing is someone telling of themselves. Unless it's verifiable facts that in effect make the telling pointless. I can inform you my name is Pavel, that I was born in 1965 in what was then Czechoslovakia, that my family came to Canada for a freer life. That is verifiable, but of little consequence. If I claim to be a good person, or a bad one, I did this, or I did that, I believe this, I believe that, then I tell you nothing worthwhile and risk equivocating. My point is one ought to judge for oneself, meaning you ought to make and be allowed to make your own judgement. Not believe anything you are told. The more authoritative the source, the less you can trust it. That's how it was when I was born, that's how it is now, that's how it will be when I die.

"There were years in between, about forty of them, when I did experience a freedom of a type those my age are doomed to take to our graves. All gone, and to a certain degree I suppose it was never there. I am consigned to end my days as they began.

"But there is one difference: how we got here. The loss of my old freedom required a military to take over my country. Here, absurdly enough, the people invited it. Lifeless souls like these, willing to board crammed trams so they can dutifully follow or give orders they've been indoctrinated over generations to treat as sacred, intentionally by hateful souls and unintentionally by credulous ones, until they adapt to an existence of utter banality comforted by a cloak of mediocrity."

Otto was moved by the man's words, despite not grasping any of them. They resonated in an inexplicable way.

"Why am I saying this to you? Actually, I say it to anyone who might listen. What I like is you are the only one not reacting, not laughing at me or arguing. It shows I'm with an honest soul to whom I can indulgently unburden my wisdom, my folly. I wish you well on your odyssey."

That last word set made Otto turn his head abruptly, almost spill his coffee.

"Odyssey?"

"The word means something to you?"

289

"Maybe. But I can't remember. What is odyssey?"

"I will show you something?"

The old man rose. Even without his stoop he was short. Pavel went in and returned with a stack of books. He spread them on the ground after brushing away a leaf and a few crumbs. One stood out to Otto, one Rico had mentioned in his story about the chef. *The Odyssey* by Homer. He knew it in a deeper sense, knew it was linked to his lost memories. He pointed at it.

"I recognize that one. Only I can't recall from where."

The old man handed it to Otto, let him fan the pages, read the back and a few paragraphs. Little stabs in his head indicated he was right about knowing it. It was different with the three other books, from which he experienced no reaction beyond a visceral pleasure feeling the pages and seeing typewritten words. The first was *1984* by George Orwell. Franz Kafka wrote the others: *The Trial* and *The Castle*. Kafka. Kafkaesque. Ah, like Kafka.

"Other than *The Odyssey*, these novels are special to me. Each foretold futures so well they now depict the present. One day, perhaps, they'll depict the past. That makes them literally, and literarily, timeless. Sorry, an old joke I've been saving. *1984*, shows how NewTor would be with family Values while Kafka's books show how it turned out. *The Castle*, comes closest to what you might be experiencing, while for me it's *The Trial*."

"So they could help me understand this world better?"

"They're not manuals, you have to think it out, but perhaps."

"Can I borrow them??"

"Being in possession of these could cause you trouble. Better they stay here. You may come by to read them if you wish."

Otto nodded, though he knew it was unlikely he'd be back.

"If books are bad, won't you get in trouble for having them?"

"As far as anyone knows, I'm a ghost. While everyone eagerly let technology control their lives, I resisted. I didn't join any social media or buy fancy mobile phones or register myself for anything I wasn't compelled to. To put it succinctly, opting for individuality over aggregated anonymity. That's the key, at least for me: individuality. It's why I love novels. They celebrate the individual; whereas non-fiction, even biography, subsumes the individual into the general; hence the extinction of novels is a harbinger of the extinction of the individual. To you and those of future generations this is not a loss because there's nothing to miss, but it could become a rediscovery one day.

"I am not alone, thousands of others did the same. But we are dying out, it's why no one bothers with us. As long as we keep to ourselves and demand no entertainment beyond nostalgia or perversely observing the fulfillment of our prophecies."

Otto kept silent, unsure how to process this, or even what to ask, until the obvious resurfaced.

"Do you know a place called Willowdale?"

"That's a WASP name. Not a thing to say aloud."

"Wasp?"

"Not the pest. An acronym. White Anglo-Saxon Protestant in my day. White And SuPremacist later. Now merely improper."

"Could it be the name of a street?"

"There are no street names. Anymore. But why this name?"

"I don't know. I hope I'll find out when I find it."

Pavel produced a pen and a pad of paper and scribbled. Then he ripped off the sheet, folded it, and slid it to Otto.

"Speaking of names, young man, you haven't told me yours."

"It's—"

"Actually, no, don't. I've got one in mind for you, an apt one. I don't want the real one to spoil it."

"What is the name?"

"K. Single letter."

"What does it mean?"

"Come back and read *The Castle*. You'll see."

The man got up and took the books and muffin tray with him, giving the slip of paper a nudge towards Otto before stepping into the house. Hearing the bolt shut was Otto's cue to leave.

He went back the way he came, the streets now full of people, dressed in all sorts of ways, some even talking to each other. It didn't take long to confirm Pavel was right: there were no street names, because there were no street signs.

He quietly opened Rico's door to slip into bed, but Patty was gone. Otto unfolded the sheet of paper Pavel had given him. A skeletal map of lines marking Pavel's house, downtown at the bottom, a large WD at the top, Z8 in parentheses. Otto stashed the paper away in time before Rico entered, Patty right behind, respectively upset and relieved to see him.

"Where the hell have you been?"

"Rico, easy. Are you all right, Otto?"

"I'm fine. I went for my usual walk. I hoped to get back before you woke up, but took my time."

"Usual walk? You've left before?"

"The other night—it's too confining in here."

"Well, that won't be a problem a minute from now."

"Rico, what's gotten into you? Be nice."

"I've been nice, Patty. I can't risk losing my home."

Patty told Otto they received notification of a comprehensive search underway that would reach Rico's street within an hour. Otto had to leave before Rico landed in trouble.

It seemed to Otto the two were at odds, that Rico might prefer leaving Otto to his own devices but Patty wouldn't. His friend no longer a friend, Otto thought, then felt bad. How could he blame a man who'd helped him this much?

The idea was to get Otto to Patty's apartment in another zone to buy time, counting on the search going zone by zone instead of across all NewTor at once.

"So stop delaying and go already."

Rico spread his hands and turned, not saying goodbye. Patty grabbed Otto's wrist to pull him outside, scanning left and right to make sure no one saw them.

"Come on, we can go now. Keep holding my hand."

"You want to act as a couple?"

"Huh, I kind of thought we were a couple."

The squeeze from her hand was indecipherable.

"Which direction are we going?"

"North."

"Towards Willowdale?"

"Willowdale? I don't know what that is. My apartment is just across the border in Zone Six. If we get by the scanners without detection, we'll be fine for at least another hour."

"I don't want you in trouble at my expense."

"When we get close, we'll separate and cross individually. Just keep calm and, like you say, act like my lover."

They talked about little things on the walk. A smart girl, Patty had answers, including an explanation for the nameless streets and locations. So many names were spoiled by Gotcha Miners, it required too much changing. As the number of cars lessened and people spent their lives within their own zones, and Values tokens provided all the navigation needed, street and location names became superfluous and were eventually removed.

"That's why we wanted you to stay in Rico's house. Without a Values token, you'd get lost. Or worse, end up there."

She was pointing to a large cemetery, with hundreds of stones sticking out of the ground. The lawns were immaculate. Patty's pace prevented him from saying he'd like to explore it.

An hour later they reached the crossing, a busy one, to Patty's joy, as she stopped a hundred metres short. The timer indicated the crossing would open in ten minutes. Enough time for her to explain where to meet, intentionally not sharing where she'd be in case he got mixed up. It left time to buy hamburgers from a street vendor they enjoyed under a tree. When it came time for him to cross, she had difficulty letting him go, as if fearing she'd never see him again.

His crossing occurred without incident. Finding the meeting point behind a grocery store was easy and fast, he could wander about before Patty's crossing. Though not much to see except hi-rise residential buildings, one of which he assumed was hers. He got to the meeting point just as Patty arrived. She seemed overjoyed to see him, kissed him, grabbed his hand for what she promised to be a short stroll to her home. Her stride slowed as they came upon a row of tall structures that, up close, looked in need of repair. She let go his hand, but not before he sensed fear in her. Patty stared up at a vehicle hovering above. Underneath, the logo she had on her bracelet.

"Patty, I think I've been in one of those before."

"I highly doubt that."

"Are you all right? You look scared."

"Why would they be here, again?"

She told Otto to retreat to a bench in the small park while she checked her apartment. He watched her go to the door, but not inside, stopping to speak in the lobby to someone she seemed to know, once in a while looking back his way. Patty returned, her face flushed.

"Aniyah, that bitch. She reported you, they're with her. If she tells them about Rico, which is likely, they'll go there."

"Why would she do that?"

"I don't know. A reward?"

"Why don't I come out? I don't want to get you in trouble."

"Too late. We'd be in trouble for not reporting you earlier."

"I'm sorry."

"I can fix this, but you have to go."

Patty's certainty convinced Otto. He found it painful to leave her, and also felt guilty for having turned these friends against each other. But he knew he had no choice.

51

It was great to have her daughter back in her life, it felt natural, her settled in the house. Like the penthouse and other special family Values facilities, it wasn't tethered to *arbiter* so no matter what Felicity did there, where she went, who she hosted, she'd remain inconspicuous. Naturally, Esmeralda didn't share that with her. While trust in Felicity had grown, that unpredictable nature remained a concern, even after her calm reaction to what Esmeralda shared about herself and Ken.

She'd tried to leave nothing out, from their brief friendship at the school near the house and the project they'd worked on that led to Esmeralda's fame, to their separation. She did omit seeing him at the Timmins clinic as well as that ill-fated prior marriage lasting only a year to jump to the dating website story. Reliving the memories, mixed with wine, made her emotional about her past with him, their courting: Blue Jays games in a stadium that was a scientific datacentre now; Raptors and Leafs games in an arena now the North American vaccination hub; trips to Centre Island to swim on beaches now inaccessible due to annexation by a foreign power; romantic dinners at restaurants demolished for hybrid office-residences; his futile efforts to teach her to ice skate at city hall—the rink still intact—by the annual Christmas tree—no longer erected—spiking hot chocolates from mickeys of rum. Even that trip up north to his hometown that turned out better than she'd expected, though not enough to warrant going there again.

These reflections exposed her tendency to enhance memories like one might saturate colours in imperfect vacation photos to make them vibrant. Framing and hanging the modified versions while discarding retrospectively flawed ones. Likewise, she had chosen the most clichéd anecdotes, assuming they'd be the most appealing, even if that made the selection incomplete. It wasn't all self-editing; many negative memories didn't come readily to mind in enough detail. Vague recollections of arguments over children, her renting a condo apartment in the city. His justified apprehension of her staying there on weekends backed by her weaker and weaker rationale. Absences didn't make their hearts grow fonder, they seeded them with bitterness that led to her indiscretions.

Felicity's attention waned when Esmeralda mentioned Baxter. That made describing her university years self-conscious, even defensive with nothing from Felicity to encourage or discourage a particular description or anecdote. In a way Esmeralda had to be grateful having to navigate egg shells. If she'd been relaxed, the one thing she'd never told anyone, still hoped to never tell anyone, might have slipped. To the person who'd least be able to handle it. The deception, and betrayal, that could have ended her marriage instantly, rather than eroding it with an elongated ideological divide no passion could outlast.

If Esmeralda were honest, she'd admit she hadn't adequately answered the question why she and Ken had stayed separated. If anything, the talk only complicated it by taking the easy route in not sharing the complication of Baxter, not being ready to face reality: that it was her own doing. The one salvation was her daughter wasn't going anywhere. The two women had time to hash it out. Away from Baxter. Grace. family Values.

That evening had been helpful in taking her mind off Otto. It was ironic that Felicity kept Esmeralda from getting frantic. The dynamic between them had shifted, with Esmeralda relying on her daughter to support her. Until the evening had to end. After which Esmeralda again was on her own, her thoughts invaded by worst case scenarios, her intellect struggling to choose what to do with the information Grace had found about Desirae.

Esmeralda had returned home not looking forward to seeing her partner. To her relief Baxter was exhausted too, after several weeks of travel, and took an immediate long nap prior to eating dinner, after which he'd be host again. Exempting her from the grilling she'd expected about Otto. Desirae had opted for a nap too, then to dine in her suite and prepare for their next trip. Locking herself up to avoid Esmeralda? Had she learned about Grace discovering her relation to James?

After dinner, as promised, Baxter went out. Esmeralda took a bath—she liked to prepare for challenging conversations with a soak to mentally rehearse them. It wasn't effective this time; she kept feeling adlibbing was the optimum approach to take with Baxter's obsequious, secretive acolyte.

Esmeralda emerged from the Jacuzzi to rinse off the soap with a shower, keeping her freshly dyed gold hair dry. She towelled herself in front of the mirror, trying to ignore the flabby spots to not be displeased at the sight. Shortly she'd suffer compliments from Desirae and had hoped to pre-mock them, instead finding herself pre-validating them, which was preferable for a woman in her mid-sixties.

She put on one of her brighter saris, flowing with violet, blue and soft yellow bands that highlighted her hair. Along with the simple pearl necklace people thought was real but she'd owned since—wait, James had given it to her for her thirtieth birthday. Ken had been there too. The irony of wearing it was enticing, although Desirae wouldn't grasp it. To emphasize its meaning, to herself, she didn't put on jewellery. Except her Values token ring to express a possibly sardonic respect for Baxter. She came out of the bedroom to find reliable, patient Grace waiting for last minute instructions before going home.

"Where is Desirae?"

"In her suite."

She dismissed Grace whose momentary glance, intentional or not, prompted Esmeralda to realize she looked ridiculous, that it would be silly to confront Desirae dressed grandiosely. She changed into a plain tan skirt and light black blouse instead, but kept the pearl necklace. More hesitation on whether to summon

Desirae to the penthouse or go to her. She chose the latter. She wanted Desirae uneasy, but not overly so.

Her knock was met instantly. The joy displayed upon seeing the Doyenne impressed Esmeralda with its complete absence of fawning. Desirae's bearing was diametrically opposed to that of the young woman Esmeralda first met. No longer fearful, nor on edge, even when goaded by the somewhat glib observation she was on her own for once.

"I would have gone with the professor but he said I wouldn't care for it. Some bar with dancing women of a kind I might not appreciate."

"That figures. The climax of his racial blending tour, I bet. But it's funny, he told me it was your choice not to go."

"Oh? Maybe I said something about needing time to pack. I'm so glad I still get a chance to see you before we're off again."

Her enthusiasm at seeing the Doyenne was tempered by news of Otto's absence. Oddly, Esmeralda now found herself the one on the defensive for allowing it to happen, for mishandling the situation. But the disturbing topic wasn't disturbing enough to interrupt her packing. Esmeralda began to wonder about her efforts to keep Desirae and Otto apart, if she'd only been doing what Baxter had wanted.

"Would you have any idea where he might go?"

"I don't know him well, I do know he thrives outdoors. Maybe he went to find open space."

"I see. We found his Values token. It'd fallen down a sewer grate in Zone Four."

This got Desirae's attention.

"You mean he's separated from his token? He left this zone?"

"It appears so."

"That isn't possible, is it? Wait, they did have trouble when he got it, that they found him hard to read. Maybe all that time in the woods . . ."

"You don't sound as worried as I feel."

"Otto strikes me as responsible, resourceful. It wouldn't shock me if he'd figured it out. He'd have to have done so, right? Or you'd have found him with it?"

"I must admit, Desirae, Otto isn't the reason I came to see you. At least not the only reason."

Desirae looked Esmeralda in the eyes. Nothing like the girl of a few days ago. Relaxed, confident, as if comforted or reassured in the meantime. It retriggered Esmeralda's original fears about her and Baxter, but that had to be pushed aside. The only one to address about that was Baxter, if it mattered.

"What is the reason then?"

"James. My old friend, James."

Now Desirae was rattled. She stepped into the bathroom but didn't shut the door. She checked herself in the mirror, returned with a weak smile."

"I suppose it was only a matter of time before someone found out. I'm kind of relieved it was you."

"Are you saying Baxter doesn't know this?"

"He's never said anything. Everything I kept from you, I kept from him. And everyone else."

"He's probably been too infatuated—"

"Maybe at first, but I was clear about that, that I prefer—"

"Yes, yes, I know. But I'm sorry, I'm at a loss. Why else would Baxter put this much faith in a young woman such as yourself?"

"Can't it be because I'm capable? And support family Values as much as I do? That I'm trustworthy? Loyal?"

"Are you? You withheld your connection to James, you had to know about our friendship. What else are you holding back? Be honest with me."

Esmeralda saw Desirae turn away, as if about to sob. How she hated seeing from young women, she'd shed plenty on her own. Instinct told her this reaction was sincere, the girl wasn't being manipulative, but trying to unburden herself, armed with only the inelegant dignity of youth.

299

"You want to know about Ken, don't you?

Hearing the name made Esmeralda feel faint. Desirae let out a sigh as if she'd spoken out of turn but realized backtracking was not an option. It gave Esmeralda a moment to compose herself before asking Desirae to elaborate, at the same time wondering how Baxter could be ignorant of this.

Desirae began by stressing she barely knew Otto and Ken and had only met them when James brought them to the house with a girl named Monica. That she learned Ken and Otto had been living for years up north in the wild, then had decided to go to NewTor to research Otto's parentage. Monica had an inkling of family Values, but as she was white she wouldn't be much help. They decided—not Desirae's choice—that Ken would stay with Monica while Otto would continue with Desirae.

A plausible story, potentially clever, because it downplayed the girl's deceit. It also explained her behaviour, confirming she and Otto were independent. Esmeralda felt she could believe it, but it was a challenge when Desirae could not answer questions such as how or why Ken found James. Nor did she reveal much about Ken, giving Esmeralda the feeling she didn't care for Ken. She liked Otto, as Esmeralda had witnessed firsthand. And she seemed especially fond of Monica, corroborating her irrelevant sexual preference disclosures.

Desirae fidgeted while Esmeralda processed this, as if anxious for confirmation her audience believed her. Once again on edge. Esmeralda suspected there was more to tell and Desirae needed permission to tell it, a specific prompt from Esmeralda to let it out and, if properly given, could transfer Desirae's loyalty from Baxter, to herself. Esmeralda had no clue to the key.

"How is James?"

"James is fine. As you no doubt know, he's happily married to the man who is my father."

"What does James think of your career choice? Of you coming here? Of your views on family Values?"

"He supports me."

"Really. I find that hard to believe, considering he's living in a city like Timmins."

"So you two get along."

"Of course. He's wonderful. Though I did pester him to give me an introduction letter for you. He wouldn't. He said you two had had a falling out."

That stung. Their argument happened over twenty years ago but remained a sore point. A tender point. She respected James more than anyone and for him—no, can't dwell on that.

"Well, he said things, bad things about family Values, and my intentions. I see why he'd think it wouldn't have helped."

"Really? He is critical of family Values but respects my choice, as he would for anyone."

"Sounds like James. Always in the middle. Not on the fence, more like underneath it. Shaking it. A politician."

"He is a city councillor in Timmins?"

"Is that so?"

"I guess it's kind of how I feel with you and Professor Baxter. Except for the shaking."

"Are you updating James on your progress?"

"Like where is Ken?"

Hearing the name again with that question was unsettling. It also indicated the girl's desire to come clean and absolve herself of the familial complications of Ken, Otto, Esmeralda, Baxter, James, to focus on herself. Projecting a selfishness others might have ascribed to Esmeralda in her youth.

"You know where he is?"

"He's in famSud."

Desirae paused, presumably to let it sink in, as if famSud had special meaning for Esmeralda. Of course, famSud was where Baxter had taken Desirae and Felicity, before Felicity's incident. Esmeralda was curious to hear Desirae's version to compare to what Felicity had told her.

She had little to say about Felicity's behaviour, and nothing to contradict her daughter's account. Desirae's opinion of Felicity wasn't as harsh as Baxter's. Interestingly, Desirae didn't realize Felicity was the same woman with whom she and Otto had had an encounter before NewTor, which meant Desirae had no idea of Felicity's relationship to Otto and Esmeralda.

All that was forgettable, insignificant when Desirae described seeing Ken with this Monica girl at the famSud facility, just as Felicity had described. How, after Baxter returned to NewTor to meet with the US delegation, at James's behest she had gotten Ken and Monica out of the facility to a cabin in time to avoid being questioned for a murder investigation.

"Someone was shot to death, by a gun, on the northern road out of Timmins. An *Indo*, without a Values token."

"I am aware of the incident. What does it have to do with the two being at famSud in the first place?"

"No idea. It shocked me to see them. I tried to ignore them to not let Professor Baxter notice, then find a way to reach James to ask about their being there. That's when I heard of the murder. I assumed Ken was involved. They didn't tell me anything, only to get him to the safest place I knew. Our family owns a remote cabin north of famSud. I took them there, with Monica. Before I left on the trip with the professor. I've had little contact since with anyone since."

"He's there now?"

"I hope not. Apparently there was an alert indicating someone had used the same Values token in famSud. They were doing a full scan of the area. James figured it was best to get Ken out of there, which I arranged."

"But how, if you're here?"

"My cousin is a go-between. He's supportive of family Values and hates *Indos*. He resented Ken and Monica staying there and I suspect he'd have caused trouble eventually."

"*familyars* shouldn't hate *Indos*."

Desirae bit at her lip while nodding, clearly itching to escape this conversation. She suggested to contact James if Esmeralda wanted to know more about Ken. Or the professor.

The inclination to label Desirae self-absorbed, only interested in her career, was offset by a realization people had been unfair to the girl by putting so much on her.

Esmeralda returned to her suite to open a bottle of wine and calm herself on the balcony. There was artillery activity flashing across the lake, but far away, like lightning without thunder. It was quiet. Too quiet. The city seemed to have gone to sleep. She felt abandoned. The wine didn't help; in fact it only exacerbated her loneliness. Felicity would come if asked. No, she couldn't be sure of that, not if her daughter was with Lloyd.

A steady drizzle forced Esmeralda to retreat to cover, moving slowly to not let the humidity make her sweat. Several flashes to the west, followed by faint booms. She'd been wrong. It was a storm, not artillery, across the lake. It upset her, she felt herself shaking. Esmeralda took the ring off her finger but immediately put it back on, fearing she'd lose it in her state. She worried it in place, her fingers brushing back and forth over one "f" then the other, recalling what she'd never shared with anyone, not even Baxter: that she'd chosen the terms *filial* and *filiations* to honour her children. That she'd purposely chosen blue and pink for boy and girl and that, contrary to conventional thinking, the blood red represented her true family, not the biological link between family Values machines and humans.

Her fidgeting grew frantic until she forced herself to stop, by enclosing her fingers. She then burst into tears thinking of little Felix, sinking into a deep, hollow sorrow with the double-edged realization she had an eternity to mourn her son, and the fear it might not be long enough.

52

Ken loped in, two fish slung over one shoulder, the fishing pole against the other, delicately balancing to navigate a tree-rooted trail his bare feet hadn't fully gotten used to. He preferred it to the trodden path, it concealed him until just before the cabin at which point he could survey to see if the young man or anyone else was waiting. This time caution had paid off, as he spotted the cherry red of Isaiah's SUV. The young man was speaking to a box or screen inside the car, his back to Ken. Scrawny kid, that Isaiah, the type Ken hated to get embroiled with in his youth. The type who'd have a knife in a fight, cheat somehow or, if he didn't, who'd turtle to make the tough kid look bad for picking on someone weak.

Ken gently set down the equipment and fish before stepping closer. Twitching shoulders and a fearful tone indicated Isaiah getting upset with the other person.

"Okay, but when will you be here? . . . The kid who went with you? Disappeared? . . . Why should I care? I need help over here because I think he's back. The fire pit's been recently used, and I recognized one of his shirts."

Ken felt a chill, aware he wasn't wearing one. He'd taken it off because it was hot. Stupid. He yearned for Isaiah to leave before the kid thought to toss his cleanest shirt in the fire pit. No doubt he was talking to Desirae. The image of her and Baxter made Ken flush with anger. Had he heard correctly? Something about the kid disappearing? Otto?

Isaiah had given Ken only minutes to pack when he'd ordered him to leave, before dropping him off at a bus station. Instead of leaving, Ken walked into town, uncertain what to do, then went to the bar near Larkin's apartment and settled in. People were discussing the Timmins murder investigation, bringing up the challenges of identifying the body because of its missing Values token, until it was linked to an alarm in famSud that launched a wider search with more powerful mobile scanners. Nothing had been found so far. Of greater interest to Ken: hearing James was the lead investigator, again ruling Timmins out as an option of escape. Unless, and he did seriously entertain the notion, Ken surrendered. If only to draw out Baxter, or Esmeralda, let them confront him. A last resort. Ken had also pondered how to turn the token to advantage. That was when he'd decided to double back to the cabin to stay near it, if not in it, to wait it out and strategize. His time for that appeared to be up.

Until now he'd been left alone. No officials with scanners, no Isaiah or any sign of the cabin's owners. It had given him time to contemplate how to make it work. He was sure it needed that fam-elixir and had figured out how to obtain it, but not inject it. The day before, while leaving famSud, he'd passed a structure he'd previously assumed was a bank machine. As he got closer, he detected an odour like the one he'd encountered with Felix. He couldn't see anything through the tinted window and had to scurry off when someone arrived to use it. The more he thought of it, the more he felt he was close.

Isaiah, who'd been still a long time, got animated.

"Des, you have no idea what it's like here. Scanners and police all over . . . mercenaries . . . no, I'm a registered *familyar*, I can't break rules. Not just me, your aunt, cousins . . . no, I don't want to hold on . . . I want to report him. Today, Des."

Another long silence from Isaiah and he became calm.

"True. No evidence. I . . . yes, an intruder. I guess—but I'll get Values points if I . . . all right, for Uncle Roscoe . . . What? I was going to toss it in the fire pit . . . that's good thinking. I'll come back first thing in the morning. If it's gone or in a different place I'll know he didn't just forget it . . . okay, Des."

Now what? Ken wondered, as Isaiah stepped away from the car to shake out his shirt and place it near the cabin door where it had been. Isaiah seemed hesitant to go, as if hoping an extra few seconds might catch Ken out, and ended up waiting a good half hour before climbing in his SUV and driving off. He could return any minute, Ken figured. A steady chill grew in him but Ken couldn't risk retrieving his shirt just yet and left it there. He rushed into the cabin for a towel and retreated to the trail.

Ten minutes passed, no sign of Isaiah. Chilled and famished, the fish odour conspicuous, Ken came out. He was cold and had to put on the shirt and start a fire. If Isaiah or anyone came he'd rush off. The fish smell might conceal him long enough, it might even indicate a squatter. It would also mean leaving the token concealed until the coast was clear.

This was fine for a few hours but Ken knew he couldn't go on this way. He doubted the scanner sensors were so strong they'd locate him randomly this far out of town. Then again the one in the famSud plaza that had detected Monica was accurate. To be more precise, it had detected the token. Nonetheless, Ken opted to dig it up to keep with him as the diminishing light from dark clouds would make finding it impossible otherwise.

The fire, along with the fish, warmed Ken up. He would have loved to curl up in the bed in the cabin but couldn't risk it. He'd have to be ready to vacate quickly with no time to remove signs of his presence. It was beautiful by the fire, under the stars, with glimmers of waving bands, faint and lonely northern lights.

A shooting star disrupted Ken's indulgences, reminding him of Isaiah indicating Otto was missing. Ken knew what he had to do, he had to risk it. First, rearrange the camp to make it look as if it was a squatter who'd camped there. No reason not to rest in the cabin now, it would look more like a random person. It'd be unlikely anyone but Isaiah could surprise him tonight; Ken was confident he could handle the cousin.

There was no incident. Ken woke just past dawn, well rested but ruing the lost time. He double-checked the bracelet, wiped it even, hoping its puzzle might miraculously reveal itself and let him avoid the riskier route. It didn't.

The smell from the fish and fish guts was awful. It would help conceal evidence of his specific presence at the camp, but it was on him too. Ken hated to waste time bathing but had no choice. He also had to trim his beard. He barely finished before hearing Isaiah's SUV rambling up the driveway. It was tempting to stick around to spy, but Ken was committed to his other plan.

He avoided the trails in case Isaiah went looking for him on foot. It was possible the kid would be happy to see him gone, would convince himself it was a squatter, treat it as an out-of-sight-out-of mind situation.

The indirect route, combined with waking too late meant Ken didn't arrive in famSud until early afternoon. The streets were packed with people moving towards the town centre. The line at the fam-elixir station, however, was short. A smartly dressed woman joined it and he stepped in behind her. She was good looking, but haughty. Ken struggled to get the bracelet over his left wrist. It was extremely tight, but he'd withstand it.

"Pleasant day, isn't it?"

The woman smiled curtly. Probably poor etiquette to speak in line but worth it for any hint of what he was about to do.

"This is never fun. I hate needles."

The woman turned away. A lingering fish smell, Ken realized. He felt a tap on his shoulder, from a small older man who'd just lined up behind him, along with five or six others.

"Don't mind her. Probably her vaccination day."

Ken's confusion prompted him to reveal the Values token and to whisper.

"I thought this was for fam-elixir."

"Yes. fam-elixir and vaccination."

"I don't need any vaccination."

"Your token will figure it out for you, give you the right shot. Or shots, if you need both."

Ken sighed grimly, fearing what was about to be injected in him, but glad to have found someone informative.

"I never take the needles. Sure they inject more and last longer but I hate them. Give me the thumper injector any day. I guess you just got registered? This your first time?"

"Uh, yes."

"Don't worry, it's easy. Just follow the instructions."

"Thanks."

The line had moved quickly while they talked and now the woman was inside the booth. Ken could see her silhouette, how she raised her arm; he even spotted her bracelet. He shuddered seeing her body jerk, like someone treated for cardiac arrest. She exited the other side as the door slid open for Ken. He inhaled a deep breath and tried to ape the woman's movements. Nothing. He then realized he had to press a pedal on the floor. The screen lit up to display two options: needle or thump. Ken chose the latter and lifted his bracelet arm. For the woman the reaction was immediate, for him it was slow. A series of rapid beeps preceded the screen flashing yellow. An alarm? But then the flashing went green and suddenly stopped. A smack below his left shoulder, like a friendly fist. The bracelet was flickering blue. The door in front slid open and he stepped out, not feeling anything unusual.

Except his surroundings looked unfamiliar. Everything spun about, above, inside; he was losing sense of himself. He'd tried LSD as a teen, this feeling similar, but accompanied by nausea. It made him vomit in front of a crowd. Some stared in wonder, others in disgust, no one offered to help.

The vomiting paralyzed his muscles. He attempted mental tricks he'd learned from George. They helped, at least now he'd reoriented himself, he could see his bar, and with some painful effort he could move. He wanted coffee. The blacker the better.

"Hold on there, buddy, where you going?"

Ken didn't trust his voice and pointed towards the bar. A pair of police officers approached, affecting a look of authority, but Ken could see they were young and timid.

"Looks like a scrapper, step back."

Which they did. Ken waited for them to speak or let him go. It was a stalemate. Until one seemed to respond to a message.

"The protest is starting, no time to waste on this guy."

Taking it as permission to go, Ken rose. His stumbling caused each officer to pull out a taser. Ken couldn't remain still and his flinching caused them to fire, knocking him out on two sides, not before feeling electricity rush through his entire body.

"Why did you fire?"

"I did because you did."

"Let's get him away somewhere and get to the protest."

He awoke to find himself slumped over a Formica counter in a diner, a steaming cup of coffee he couldn't remember ordering on his left. It smelled terrific, tasted even better. The pain went away and now his mind was lucid.

A large middle-aged woman emerged carrying a pot of coffee, peeked his way, then went another direction to the booths at the back. Ken drank his delicious coffee. It calmed him enough to recollect and reflect. Morning at the cabin, the trek into town, a fam-elixir station with an aloof woman and helpful old man, the incompetent cops. The pain. Then the absence of pain. Could it be his bracelet was working? He looked at it and saw a bright, solid blue light.

A woman behind the counter—her nametag identified her as Edna—refilled his mug and stood, an unspoken question in the air. Ken thought of a cheeseburger and fries. Only Edna left as he was about to voice it. A minute later, with no interaction, his food arrived as he'd imagined it. It was pretty good.

He finished and called to Edna for the bill. She was speaking with another customer and nodded at him to look at the counter and its embedded screen. It showed his meal and coffees, how much to pay, and a button: PAY. He pressed it. A family Values logo appeared and a single five digit number. No decimal point or dollar sign. Did it happen with the device? He glanced at it in time to see it transition from green back to blue. Green. Green, as in successful transaction?

Ken left. No one prevented him. He walked slow just in case, disconcerted at how it felt as if his mind had been read. It had to do with the bracelet but how could it transmit mental thoughts? As he wandered he put together a theory: it didn't read minds, but instead reacted to and processed visual and aural cues, such as the combination of his looking at a cheeseburger and a sort of inner physiological signal transforming into an order. Bizarre but somewhat plausible. Or way off.

He found the bus depot where he'd said goodbye to Monica. It was busy, dozens of buses, the confusion daunting. Finding a bus to NewTor seemed impossible for anyone unfamiliar with the process. He saw people gathered by screens. The lines were long but screen use was brief and soon he found himself at one. He didn't have to do anything, as he hadn't at the diner, to get the screen to show he first had to travel to famBar to transfer to NewTor. The screen indicated a gate, time, and price. He had nothing with which to write it down but that was unnecessary. An image of his itinerary played in his head, it stayed with him like a guide until he found his gate. Then it was replaced by an indicator pointing to his seat. He sensed a tiny pulsation as the images faded out and his bracelet once again showed blue. Blue had to mean it was working. It thought he was Felix.

He braced for trouble but was relieved when the bus passed by the facility and went express to famBar, a town he'd been to once or twice when it was Barrie. The outskirts looked familiar but its centre had filled in with high-rises along the lake. The processing facility at famBar was larger than the one in famSud. Yet his bracelet let him bypass. Too easy it seemed, but nothing indicated it was unusual, and he wasn't the only one. No odd glances or pauses to distinguish Ken.

The wait for a bus to NewTor was long due to a large demand and short supply of vehicles. His not knowing where to go put him at the rear of the line. Nevertheless, Ken had come farther and faster than expected, he welcomed a brief respite. A chance to experiment with his fam-elixir-fuelled device. He discovered an area filled with dozens of kiosks like old phone booths, but with screens instead. Ken entered one and let his mind do what his fingers would have done on a keyboard long ago.

His first thought was to find out how much credit Felix had accrued. A surprising amount, the meal in famSud and buses making a negligible dent to the balance. Ken experimented and discovered how to conjure bus schedules, maps, even images of famBar and NewTor, shocked at the changes revealed by aerial photos, but more surprised by places still untouched, like the expansive cemetery of Mount Pleasant. It felt like the Internet, only less cluttered. No ads. More tailored to individuals, less for random casual browsing. Without a word or pressing a button, he got a soda and sandwich delivered directly to him, which he ate while perusing news items that meant nothing.

The screen then flashed to indicate he'd been assigned a bus and time for the last leg to NewTor. It'd be another two hours. Boredom prompted Ken to give in to curiosity, to explore what he could learn about Felix. What he'd bought, where he'd gone, what he'd communicated.

He wished he hadn't seen the messages between Felicity and Felix for they revealed what Ken had feared about them was in fact far worse. It brought about another urge to vomit. That this discovery could justify what he'd done to Felix brought him no comfort whatsoever.

The screen went blank, the booth became dark, except for the red flashing on his bracelet. Ken couldn't see but felt the booth, and himself, moving. Up, down, left, right, he couldn't tell; his eyes didn't adapt to the darkness. A few minutes after stopping, the light returned gradually. Just as his door opened a familiar, unfriendly voice spoke.

"Come on out, Ken."

Ken obeyed. As he exited he was grabbed by two strong men. He didn't resist when a hand, covered with a thick heavy glove slid down his forearm to his wrist, unlatched the bracelet, and tossed it on the floor. Ken flinched at a brief but intense stab of pain that passed just as the voice spoke again.

"You do remember me, I hope."

All the lights came on, confirming it was Baxter, dressed in a sharp business suit. He was skinnier, older, but still carried an intimidating aura that had annoyed and impressed Ken on first meeting the man. Now it inspired a bitter irony expressed in the tone of his response.

"Professor."

Baxter chuckled and came closer. Ken sensed the two men at his side tense up.

"You may not be aware but it's a crime to wear a Values token belonging to someone else. A serious crime. Even if that person is dead. I must admit I'm in awe you got it to work and did so without harming yourself. I recall you were clever with devices, now I've seen it for myself. I must learn how you did it."

"Why?"

"To prevent it happening again, of course. Such a crime is not comparable to murder, though. And once we match the bracelet with the corpse it belonged to, we will have caught a murderer, with the evidence to convict."

Ken said nothing.

"I believe you know a young woman named Desirae. And you know she and I have bonded. Not in the way you or my partner might suspect but, to follow an adage: keep your friends close, your enemies closer."

"She believes all the nonsense you believe."

"Yes, but she's also the stepdaughter of someone who's a bit of a sceptic. I speak of our mutual friend James. For you see, I've tracked her, you, and the girl named Monica, since you were in Timmins."

"And Otto. Where is Otto?"

Baxter's face dropped, as did the professor's bravado. It was a strange moment in which the animosity between them eroded. Both men, to put it simply, simultaneously acknowledging they were too old to sustain a rivalry. This kept Ken from jumping at Baxter when the professor humbly said:

"I wish I knew."

The implied shared goal of finding Otto motivated both men to agree to set aside hostilities, to compare notes, possibly even pave the way for a truce. It started poorly with Baxter trying to flex bureaucratic and political muscle, bragging he'd controlled everything since Otto acquired a Values token at famBar. How it led to Baxter discovering the connection between Otto's travel partner and James, and taking on Desirae as his personal aide to keep tabs on her.

"If I hadn't done that, I'd never have found you."

"Why wait so long?"

"I wanted to understand what you were all up to."

"Which isn't much."

"Apparently."

"Stop leading her along then."

"I'm not leading her along. She's very capable. An unexpected bonus in addition to her admiration."

"Admiration? For you?"

"No, for Esmeralda. I'll admit this, Ken, since you of all people might understand. Her admiration for Esmeralda matches mine in such a way that affirms my own."

Ken had never seen the manipulative Baxter so candid. Yet it didn't make him cringe, but instead revealed to Ken, simply yet wholly, the finality of his own detachment from Esmeralda. The professor can have her, she can have him.

At this point, the conversation matured, no longer between a pair of enemies, but two aging men with enough life experience, wisdom, and an honest realization of what was needed to fulfill their distinct lives; in other words, the suspension of pride. That allowed them to rationally discuss the events that led to Ken's departure without Esmeralda as filter.

Nonetheless, it was painful for Ken to learn his wife had been unfaithful more than once, but equally painful for Baxter to hear the history of Ken and Esmeralda and grasp the depth of a bond the professor could never achieve. Baxter's demeanour almost became maudlin, but recovered to restore its original sternness, albeit with a degree of empathy.

"There is something I must share with you. All along I'd never doubted Esmeralda and you about the twins until I went away. When I came back in 2020 there was uncertainty, the timing and all, but it seemed irrelevant once you'd left with the twins. Then when Felicity came to NewTor the same time as a certain young man . . . the coincidence. I had to delve into it, perform tests."

"Tests?"

"Yes. And I found Felicity's DNA matches mine, not yours."

"Your saying you're their father?"

Baxter hesitated a moment before nodding solemnly.

Ken felt an irrational urge to laugh, to blurt out that if Baxter had wanted the twins, he could have had them. He suppressed it due to a hollow sadness invalidating his enjoyment at seeing Baxter squirm. That made him angry, more than what he'd just learned, but it was what he'd just learned he had to attack.

"I don't believe you."

"I have a report, I can put it up on a screen."

"Reports can be faked. Especially by someone like you."

"These can't, but I take your point, and it would take too long to explain why they can't be faked."

"Why do you care if I believe it or not?"

"I shared this with you in good faith. Believe me, had I known before I'd never have let you get this far."

"But I did get this far. With someone else's Values token."

Baxter frowned, but tried to cover it.

"Aha, you're not sure either, Professor."

"Of course, I'm sure. "

"Tell me, if I'm not the father, how would Felix's bracelet have worked for me?"

"I already admitted that's a complication I need to resolve."

"There's a way to solve your problem and convince me."

"Which is?"

"Take me to Esmeralda. If she believes it, I will too."

It took Ken's last nerve to summon the courage to make such a proposition as the reality of this revelation, if true, hit home: that Baxter was Otto's grandfather, not him, and this step could confirm that with no turning back.

Baxter took a long time to respond, during which his manner, instead of submitting to Ken's resolve, became reinvigorated, as if he'd discovered something.

"Yes. We shall go see Esmeralda. Together."

53

Otto had loitered around Patty's apartment a few hours, hoping she'd emerge. Long after the official cars were gone he still saw no sign of her. Or Aniyah. He felt bad for the grief he'd caused and hoped the girls could stay friends. He was by himself, once again, alone in an unfamiliar world, his mind still emptied of all memories prior to meeting them. At times he felt it'd be easier to reveal himself but a powerful instinct convinced him to least discover what Willowdale was first. It became his beacon, albeit a dim one. He tried to figure out Pavel's crude map but it wasn't clear to him. He then recalled the large cemetery they'd passed prior to their last crossing. Perhaps he'd find an open space, free of buildings blocking the sunlight, where he could address his situation in the following morning.

His crossing was uneventful but felt conspicuous with fewer people around. Darkness came rapidly due to a swath of clouds that looked ready to burst, causing people around him to raise umbrellas. Otto felt the clouds would pass and be replaced by a starry sky he saw glimpses of far off. He was right.

The cemetery itself was empty. It seemed another world with no endless rush of pedestrians, hence he was spoiled for choice finding a place to rest. Plenty of fountains with fresh cold water too. Food could hold off until morning; he'd gotten accustomed to long periods without it. He spent that evening strolling the paths, inspecting names on tombstones, many defaced perhaps to obscure identities. His meandering got him lost at times but eventually he found his way back from where he'd set out. It'd gotten quiet, the only noises from scampering squirrels and fearless racoons attacking garbage bins. When he'd dragged away the bin nearest his spot they thankfully went with it and it only took minutes before he'd fallen deep asleep and the dream of the graceful black woman emerging out of the city came to him, more vivid than ever. He'd woken often, reaching to touch her, before falling back into the dream precisely where he'd left off. It might have been less exhausting to stay up all night. At dawn, Otto felt disorientated. It took time to find the fountain, it was behind him. He'd had a drink and watched the sunrise as he recalled the previous day's events, listening to the gradually increasing volume of the city around him.

Now he was starting to feel energized by the fresh day's sun, rejuvenated by a freedom he now realized had been suspended yesterday and all his time at Rico's. A little longer and he would set out to find some food.

The bench he chose looked out onto an arterial path and Otto found himself absorbed by a seemingly choreographed pattern of humans going to and fro. The ways in which they followed, passed, crossed each other knowing when to slow down, speed up—never stopping—with no words exchanged. The inevitable collisions never occurred. Each time the parties involved—even when encumbered by a baby stroller, shopping cart, backpack, rolled luggage—made the correct manoeuvre to keep the flow, while maintaining at least a two metre gap.

"Oh look, we're not the first, after all. Someone beat us."

"Good sign. Oh my, he's ca-ute."

"Don't get any ideas, Calvin."

"You know better than that. I'm thinking Polly or Helena, or a Persson sister, they'll go crazy when they see him. Won't that be fun to watch?"

"Maybe. Maybe."

"Of course it will."

Otto looked up at the two men approaching, holding hands, clearly unaware he'd heard them. The sun blinded him to their faces until they got close, then they were mostly concealed by oversized sunglasses. Each wore tight shorts in bright patterns, exposing muscular legs, but their shirts were an identical sky blue with two lines of white block lettering washed out by the sun. The short one held a duffel bag he dropped to the ground, then dug into to pull out shirts until he grabbed one for Otto.

"Extra extra large, I assume. You're lucky. There's only one."

Otto took the shirt. It was soft and smelled clean. It was black with a large X on the front. Inside the X was typed, in light blue letters: Criss-cross to stop population loss. The term criss-cross sounded familiar.

He pulled it over his head on top his own. Too snug, too hot, so Otto pulled it off to remove the old shirt, then put on the new one again. Better. Others arrived and each got a shirt. Some got black ones like his, others white ones, each with a slogan: "Join the race to no race." "Blending is mending." Along with some he found bewildering: "salt and pepper together makes the spice *arbiter* likes." Some slogans were in light blue like his, but just as many were pink. No one knew Otto but they all acted as if he belonged.

The taller of the first two introduced himself as Calvin, then welcomed everyone, and said he appreciated their being there. adding he'd expected more. As did the shorter one who seemed unhappy lugging a heavy bag of shirts. He took them a distance and at each of four corners set down a shirt. It took him some time as he needed to find stones or items to keep the wind from blowing them away. Calvin continued talking, emphasizing the importance of keeping peaceful, not to engage anyone passing through. Then he announced it was time to get in place.

Everyone headed to one of the corners, knowing which one to assemble at as well. Otto stood still, unsure, until a woman gave him a push to one corner with only four men. He fell into the back and kept still, watching, intending to emulate whatever they did. Everyone stood solemnly at the four corners. He then realized how they'd known where to go, and that the shirts had not been handed out randomly. He looked at his skin and it had never looked darker, and was nearly as dark as that of the men with him. The corner to his right was all dark-skinned women. To his left, all light skinned men; and only light-skinned women diagonally across. Five in each group.

A whistle blew twice from Calvin in the centre. Everyone took a step towards him, then another. It took a full two minutes to converge with the other groups, but they stopped just before. It had remained sombre to this point but the mood brightened as people from diagonal groups partnered up. He wasn't sure who to go to. It didn't matter, a girl with auburn hair in a pony tail came to him, grabbed his arm and pulled him to the middle and close to the others. To Otto, his own skin seemed to lighten to be more like hers. She didn't notice. Calvin blew his whistle and the coupled people, including he and the girl, hugged. He was hesitant, which made her cling to him as Patty had, without the kissing and other touching. They remained like this for a good minute until Calvin blew his whistle twice. Everyone separated and gave a cheer. Otto clapped too but was confused.

Calvin motioned for everyone to follow him. Otto stayed with the group until they reached the cemetery gate. Here he thought they'd exit. Instead, they walked to a set of temporary tents and tables where three of the girls were handing out signs with the same slogans, along with nutrition bars. His stomach growled. Otto took one sign and three bars. He ate one quickly and then a second, before walking amongst the others. He questioningly said the word Willowdale a few times, but got no response.

The purpose of the rally was never clear to Otto. It came to the point he felt it wasn't wise to keep asking about Willowdale, in case someone discovered he was a fraud and he got himself in the same trouble from which Patty had saved him. He enjoyed the fellowship, the food, and that was enough.

They circled another hour, after which there appeared another tent with food. This one was giving out small bags with salads, which looked appetizing after all the sugar. Otto joined the line and was waiting patiently when he was tapped on the arm. It was the girl with whom he'd performed the ceremony. Her face was like a ghost's, except for the attractive cheeks, her eyebrows and hair thick and lushly dark. He smiled at her and her face lit up. She grabbed his bicep and whispered to him.

"I thought you were new. Follow me, I'll guide you."

She moved around to the back of the tent. Otto followed her in, until a man stepped in his way.

"Hey, where are you going?"

"Oh, sorry, Hon, I meant for him to start a line here. Just wait outside, okay?"

Otto retreated to wait. He could tell the girl and the man were having a discussion. It might take a long time and he wondered if he'd have been better off in the other line. Then the girl came and handed him his salad. Her smile was as warm as Patty's but less intense and thereby more attractive.

"Sorry about that. He's just . . . I've never seen you before at a rally. Are you new around here?"

"Yes. No, I mean, this is my first . . . rally."

"Oh. I hope you'll come to more. My name is Alice."

She put out a hand to shake but pulled it back when the man returned. He was in a jovial mood now and even smiled at Otto.

"You're right, he could be a good candidate for us, babe."

"I told you."

"Fine, but stop flirting for now, get back to work."

Alice gave Otto a helpless shrug.

"My man, such a task master. I hope you'll stick around."

"Sure. But first, I have a question. Do you know a place called Willowdale?"

Otto noticed her glance to her left as her demeanour sank. Her boyfriend returned. She repeated what Otto said. He too looked to their left before pushing her to the back to face Otto.

"Are you here to make trouble?"

"No. I'm . . . no, what did I say?"

The man retreated. Otto knew it was time to separate from the rally. Their reactions disturbed him, but also excited him, as he suspected they knew Willowdale, and that it lay in the direction they'd looked.

He stole away to a clump of trees to eat his salad. From there he saw hordes of people entering the cemetery; another exit. He didn't want to wander around in their shirt outside the park so he went back to where he'd disposed his dirty one. The trashcan had been emptied. Wearing the current one inside out wasn't an ideal option but the only one. Outside the cemetery, he walked with his arms crossed. He did find a clothing store with a bin in its alley but all it contained was garbage. He didn't want to go in the store for fear of raising an alarm.

He crossed the major street again, suffered a moment of regret at recognizing where he'd rendezvoused with Patty, but didn't hesitate to continue, allowing instinct to direct his steps, only conscious of having to keep north and avoid human contact. It was surprisingly easier on this busier street. No one cared about him, only themselves, keeping their heads down except to find a shop or engage a Values token. Otto felt conspicuous keeping his gaze straight ahead until he learned to mimic their motions, to every so often act as if he had a Values token in him.

Then without warning the buildings and people gave way to trees lining the road, though the traffic remained as thick. It was more pleasant here and Otto found his pace slowing to match his inner calmness. It didn't last long. The approach to another major road brought more congestion. How many did he have to cross before he found something, or gave up and surrendered?

He went on until he reached another major road. It may have been his optimism but this time he was struck by a feeling he'd been near here recently. He slowed his pace to try and shut out the noise, to focus on trying to make that mental connection.

An unusual sound broke his effort, a whirring hum coming from overhead. He arched his neck and was at first blinded by the sunlight. His eyes adapted to let him see the source. A sort of car, like the one at Patty's but sleeker, was flying just above. Underneath it, that same logo. Otto altered his route to go in its direction, his attention split between street and sky.

The craft was out of sight but Otto could hear it and focused on following it by ear. It brought him to a different area where the commercial buildings were shorter, most no higher than five storeys. It didn't feel enclosed like where he'd been. He could move freely, less conspicuously; best of all, his feet seemed to know where to go. It didn't matter that the vehicle was gone, nor that his mind was ignorant beyond a certainty he'd passed here recently. This realization was accentuated by a throbbing that intensified when he reached a smaller street. He knew he had to turn here and the feeling strengthened when he reached a quiet wide street of large lawns, mature trees, and driveways, not filled by tiny homes like Rico's, nor any as close to their neighbours' lots. And one stood out due to its prominent lush red rhododendrons.

As he walked up its driveway, tall hedges bordering the next house made it feel isolated, private. He took a deep breath, then stepped onto the porch. He looked around while grasping the wrought iron railing. He was alone. He rang the doorbell, then knocked at the door, waited a minute, before knocking again. He tried the handle. Locked. Disappointment was about to wipe away the positive feeling accumulated to this point. He wasn't sure if he'd ever cried, but felt a strong impulse to do so now.

A movement across the street froze him, a woman emerging from behind a house. Otto kneeled low to conceal himself until he saw the woman enter her front door.

He waited until no one saw him, before walking to the side of this house and then towards the rear. There was a wooden gate. He approached it but slowed on hearing a voice, a man's voice. Then a woman's. Water splashing. A bit of giggling. Otto crept up to the tall gate and had to go on his toes to see over. He saw two people in a swimming pool that spanned the entire back yard, embracing. Her skin dark and smooth, his pale save for a red swath across the shoulders. He stared a long while before they saw him. Long enough to recognize them amidst a river of memory flooding his mind.

Life with Ken in the wild disrupted by his wanderlust fuelled by novels—*The Odyssey* and *Candide*, others—and dreams, not necessarily in that order. The brief but productive school years taught by Allen Montcalm at an Indian reservation, forays into small towns via canoe, until the day came to assert his will and act on his dream. A difficult upstream journey interrupted then enhanced by Monica. A pleasant then not so pleasant detour at George's, seeing Allen, visiting another camp before resting at Heather's in Hearst, taking her car to Kapuskasing. Ken telling what Otto had suspected, more he didn't grasp until later. An encounter with that drifter, Randall, while Ken fixed the car. In Driftwood, where Monica was to separate but happily did not. The incident with Randall before the Timmins oasis with James and Roscoe and Desirae. Talking about family Values. Desirae guiding him through the bureaucratic protocols, nagging when necessary, preventing potential disaster with the woman in the pool, who was now watching him in stunned silence while it all came back. Not unlike his own stunned silence upon meeting Esmeralda in her suite, then an awkward dinner with Professor Baxter van Leer, leading to Desirae being whisked off and back to NewSud while Otto toured NewTor in a famdrone with the Doyenne who wasn't physically there, and Grace. Ending the tour alone and curious, venturing on his own, meeting Josh and Lloyd, smiling with wonder at Otto now, who'd taken him to a bar with crude naked woman, only to abandon him after they'd crossed into another zone. Hours frozen until breaking free of his bracelet at the cost of a horrible feeling of his brain emptying of memory. Aimless peregrinations about NewTor, before Rico, and helping him catch a salmon. Meeting Aziz, Aniyah, sweet Patty. A strange encounter with an old man, Pavel, before being ushered away from Rico's, left to fend for himself after Aniyah's betrayal. A temporary haven at the peaceful cemetery. Joining Calvin and his friends, until he asked too many questions and then let instinct guide him to this place, assisted by the craft that likely transported Lloyd and the odd woman from the bus here.

Those memories, and others, came back lucidly, but did not resolve his confusion at seeing Lloyd with this woman. Felicity remained still and it was Lloyd who beckoned him to enter the yard and explained how they got together because Felicity was recruited by Esmeralda to find Otto. How Felicity, with Grace's help, had used his Values token log to find the restaurant where he'd met Lloyd and Josh. The explanation gave Felicity time to compose herself. She and Lloyd left the pool and guided Otto to the basement to wait while they dressed.

A cozy room with old sofas, large chairs, and a massive brick fireplace. The light grey walls were filled with oil paintings and the large screen appeared to be a television. He didn't have long to admire it because they were quick in changing and bringing snacks and a bottle of Riesling.

Otto declined wine to stick to water, but devoured the potato chips and peanuts. Lloyd seemed star-struck just being in the Doyenne's childhood home with her daughter thanks only to an accidental encounter with the grandson. Otto was grateful for his presence; it would have been awfully awkward with just the woman who was his biological mother.

54

Esmeralda was alone in the penthouse, idle, save for lamenting Otto's absence, fretting over Felicity, fearing Baxter. Her efforts to contact her partner, or James, fruitless, each setback piling on top of a stack of frustrations she often took out on Grace, whose indomitable forbearance didn't wilt. If it had, Felicity's request for Esmeralda to hurry to Willowdale might have been delayed, or missed. Part of Esmeralda wished it had. The early evening late summer sky nudged at more wine to help digest her lobster rather than venturing out so far.

The message's vagueness was distinctly vexing. Didn't Felicity understand the effort it took for Esmeralda to leave the suite? If she'd said Otto had shown up—a remote possibility that didn't warrant serious consideration—Esmeralda would already be on her way. Instead, she'd only mentioned an issue at the house requiring Esmeralda's immediate and personal attention. Grace was still smarting from Esmeralda's earlier mood but mollified and surprised to learn the Doyenne had opted to go by herself. Grace understood once told someone was needed at the suite in case a message arrived from Baxter, James, or Otto. She asked Grace to chart a famdrone route to bypass the denser zones and thus avoid as much citizen interaction as possible.

It was cloudy but frequent pockets of sunshine opened up as the famdrone drifted north and west away from the towers, and into older suburban neighbourhoods. Esmeralda recalled taking Otto this way just days ago; it seemed longer. Telling him about Ken and her childhood.

How surreal to know the boy was somewhere below, alone. A notion that didn't frighten her. She sensed he'd cope, that he'd inherited Ken's ability to survive, maybe even his cleverness to escape NewTor. No, that was impossible. But then why hadn't he been located yet? She didn't want to contemplate the other explanation and was grateful for the interruption when a screen lit up saying it was time to disembark. The famdrone hovered while she attached belts for the lowering seat. The door opened, a humid breeze blew, the gusts making her glad she'd put on slacks. The seat fell gently into the roof opening of the waiting limousine, slotting in place, the driverless auto on its way.

Minutes later it pulled into the driveway, a slight bump as the left rear wheel rolled over the old water access pipe that always woke her from long drives with her parents, to tell her she was home. The front door opened and an exuberant Felicity met her with an embrace that heartened Esmeralda.

"So what's the matter?"

"Follow me."

They went through the kitchen, past the living room—untidy, but tidier than expected—through to the patio. Esmeralda saw Lloyd sitting by the pool, gave him a nod to indicate he needn't rise when he started to rise for her. Only he wasn't getting up to greet the Doyenne, merely shifting to let Esmeralda see the man sitting next to him. Otto.

Esmeralda almost tripped rushing to embrace her grandson around the neck. His muscles tensed. She let him go to take the lawn chair Lloyd had vacated to stare. No one spoke at first and no doubt it was the awkwardness that prompted Lloyd to say he'd be going.

That left the three—grandmother, mother, son/grandson—but instead of Lloyd's departure lessening the tension, it increased it. Not a negative tension, though. Esmeralda sensed the others, like herself, rather enjoyed this pure, peaceful impasse. That it could go on indefinitely.

The doorbell ring was faint but Esmeralda still jumped as she used to jump at the arrival of a date. The several sharp knocks that followed no one could miss.

"Maybe Lloyd forgot something."

Felicity rose to check but Esmeralda would have preferred to ignore it. The knocking stopped and her daughter retreated, but it was replaced by footsteps on the stone walkway.

Baxter and Ken, side by side.

Esmeralda nearly fainted at this unthinkable image. Felicity's mouth widened as the men approached. Otto and Ken smiled at each other while Baxter's grin was one Esmeralda could choose to read as satisfied or sardonic. His words chilled her.

"How interesting. A little family reunion."

No one said anything.

"I'm glad you're all here. Ken and I had a long talk and we all need to do the same. So please everyone, let's relax."

Esmeralda found herself nodding. Felicity seemed frozen, in shock until suggested to get refreshments. It took her a moment to respond but she seemed relieved for a chance to get away.

Baxter took a seat beside Esmeralda and motioned for Ken to take the one vacated by Felicity. Other than asking what people wanted, no one spoke. She came back with two beer cans for the men, a carafe of rosé for the women, and for Otto a tall glass of chocolate milk. She took a seat on the grass next to Esmeralda.

The stalemate of silence was broken by an abrupt yet not fully shocking admission by Ken he had killed Felix, and had agreed to surrender, if Baxter let Ken see Otto before his arrest. Which meant Baxter circumventing his precious rules to overlook Ken using his illegal Values token to hasten the entry process.

"We went to the penthouse first, expecting to find you there, but Grace told us you were on your way here."

"What will happen to Ken?"

The challenge in Otto's question nonplussed Baxter at first but then amused him.

"Of course there will be a trial and . . ."

"No. He has to go back north."

"Nonsense, I can't just—"

Now Felicity stood up to face Ken. She was sobbing. His chair almost fell over when she gave him a hug.

"If you did do it, if you really did kill Felix, thank you."

Shocked silence. Esmeralda gently coaxed Felicity to explain. She was hesitant and took a long time to compose herself.

Ken looked away but Esmeralda knew he paid close attention as Felicity told how Ken's stepmother's death had led to Felix anointing himself as his sister's protector, vilifying Ken, vowing to keep their evil father from harming her and them. She trusted her brother who always treated her well. Until the day he began to lust after her. He broke her resistance, saying things like Ken would do worse. Once her innocence was lost, she was sexually tied to him. Her dependence became irreversible when she got pregnant with Otto. Getting rid of the baby changed nothing, it now was a secret Felix held over his sister. Esmeralda noticed Baxter looking concerned in a non-clinical way. Watching him helped temper her own reaction to this horror.

No lights had been turned on. The only indication of a power failure was the sudden silence of the swimming pool's heater. It cast a gloomy eeriness on the group that seemed interminable but only lasted a few minutes before the power returned. Then the swimming pool lights turned on. Seeing these faces around her in that artificial light, Esmeralda couldn't hold back, knew it was the moment for her confession, her honesty.

"I need to share something, something that affects all of you, a thing I'm not proud of, that I'm . . ."

She was stumbling, hesitant and in a hurry to get it out at the same time. Her poise shattered by decades of shame agitated by the anxiety of recent events. She was a wreck. Their silence only made it worse, isolated her. She had no clue how to say it, not in any way that wouldn't lead to her utter self-destruction.

"The night of the party with the send-off for Baxter . . ."

No good. She didn't want to start with that, wanted to keep it as neutral as possible. Keep the emotion out, defer the guilt. But how, trembling as she was inside and out? The longer a secret is kept, the more likely it erupts out of control. For all these years knowing this, couldn't she have rehearsed how to say it?

They continued to watch her, showing no sign of impatience, giving her the space she needed. Baxter was unreadable, as was Ken, while Otto and Felicity didn't hide their confusion. Then a brief flick of the mouth from Baxter, almost a grin. She nodded at him, pleading for him to say something, to help some way, as he so often did before. As if commanded, he stood up. When he did, Esmeralda thought she saw disappointment in Ken as if he was saddened by her, or disgusted—as she was herself—by her turpitude and cowardice.

All this delayed the numbing realization as Baxter spoke with his damn professor's coldness that he'd known all along.

"Heteropaternal super-fecundation is the scientific name for a woman impregnated at the same time by different men, who then delivers fraternal twins, each with a distinct father. Felicity from me, Felix from Ken. That wasn't known to me until I found out Ken had successfully used Felix's bracelet, which could only be possible if they have an exact blood and DNA match. Using Felicity's would have been too painful, possibly lethal. Felix was always independent like Ken too while Felicity, like me, always needed rules and restrictions. Or so I was told."

The numbness wore off as Esmeralda braced for repercussive, berating reactions. She desperately hungered for them. Without them, she'd feel . . . well, she had no idea how she'd feel except it would be a lonely existence. They'd forgive her, eventually, if asked, but such forgiveness would be empty food for a starving soul if unaccompanied by some form of emotional punishment onto which she could latch. It was not to be.

The secret, this source of guilt, fear, horror, loathing, countless other varying emotions she'd carried more than three decades, now no more than an academic oddity greeted by indifference. Except from Felicity, who was upset at discovering Baxter was her true father, not Ken. Baxter did treat her harshly at famSud, but was it enough to counteract the hatred she'd nurtured her entire life towards Ken?

"What am I then?"

Otto's question froze Esmeralda who didn't know how to take it, confused by its matter-of-fact tone. Baxter's grin proved he'd known all along. Or had worked it out. Accessing tests and data acquired at each stage of Otto's journey to NewTor. Esmeralda expected he'd respond; instead it was Ken breaking the silence.

"I think our journey has been a success."

"What do you mean?"

"You found what you were looking to find, didn't you? It's up to you to determine what you are. Nothing wrong if you don't know what that is yet. At least you're on the way."

"But at what cost? Especially to you?"

"Never mind about me."

"You could be convicted of murder."

Their exchange touched Esmeralda but also made her jealous of the life those two had shared.

"I'm curious, young man. What do you intend to do? You can stay at the penthouse with Esmeralda and me. I'll make sure it's easy to visit your grandfather—"

"Do you want me to stay?"

He was asking Esmeralda. She nodded, afraid to say anything to spoil it, but did venture a glance Ken's way. His stoic facade was to be expected but she saw past it. While he might not feel as he did when he wrote the letter, he didn't despise her enough to fight it. He'd let Otto choose. She looked at her grandson.

"Of course we want you to stay. You should stay."

"I will. On one condition: Ken is sent home, tomorrow."

"Impossible. He is . . . allegedly . . . guilty of a serious crime. Not to mention his abuse of a Values token and because he . . .?"

"Professor."

Esmeralda couldn't recall seeing Baxter heed to the command of a voice, let alone a voice so young. Otto eloquently explained that punishing Ken might expose what Baxter might prefer not be exposed: the ease with which an *Indo* adapted a Values token not belonging to him to get to NewTor; or how Otto, as an *Indo*, shed his *Transitory Indo* bracelet; or the troubling nature of the biological relationships just revealed.

Otto had read Baxter well in accurately guessing the integrity of family Values was more important to her partner than any prideful gain avenging Ken. Otto added a commitment to assist in plugging those gaps, fixing those bugs. To Esmeralda it was the unspoken awareness Ken had killed his child, not Baxter's, that clinched it.

"You impress me, young man."

"I have another condition."

"Really."

"You never ask me to wear a Values token."

"I don't know about that."

"Without a Values token, I'll be an ongoing tester to make sure future glitches are identified and addressed."

"I'll consider it, if you agree to get sterilized."

Otto nodded without hesitation.

Esmeralda suppressed a grim grin. If that had worked before, they wouldn't be here. Still, it was proper. Otto was a potential genetic time bomb. He had turned out well and healthy, but his offspring likely would not. Everyone glanced at Ken to see what he might say. He showed nothing, as if not even there.

She momentarily felt herself transported back to another time, to the fragile period between his leaving with the twins and her developing the family Values thesis. The link to that time and to the present felt broken, disconnected. When she tried, she failed in reconciling her confusion about her creation; indeed she even entertained the notion James had been right: she was a fraud, or rather, the Doyenne was a fraud.

A deep sigh from Felicity.

The girl looked ill. The mother rose to take the daughter to her room to put her to bed. The house was silent for a while but then the men began to talk. The mother closed her daughter's bedroom door to tune them out to let Felicity sleep.

A fresh energy swelled inside Esmeralda, one assuring her all these troubles would be resolved over time, her burdens lifted, that she'd be Doyenne again, in a deeper, more powerful sense than ever.

Project Girdwood

Final Report and Recommendation

I am pleased to approve the enclosed final report, including its resolution to commence populating NewBax with five hundred thousand (500,000) residents this August 1, 2055 to augment the approximately 25,000 workers already in place. Considering the various challenges—the details of which, including impacts, comprise the bulk of the report—it is a remarkable achievement.

Legal challenges from our Indigenous partners were the most significant, the most drawn out, but in the end profitable for all. They did have legal grounds to contest our land appropriations, but we achieved consensus via airtight labour agreements that can mutually serve both parties for future Girdwood ventures.

That fortuitously helped address intermittent labour issues in general by providing a stable work force that prevented stalling due to the US civil wars, managing multiple established cities in their family Values stage progressions and, frankly, the general poor quality of hires from family Values cities, emblematic of a universal decline of so-called skilled labour.

The presence (and growth) of family Values resistant entities, such as Timmins and famCoch, proved more a political obstacle than a tangible one, once we adopted an approach to treat them not as adversaries but as outlets for those unsuited to the family Values life. An urban version of the status held by Indigenous peoples. While this is seen by some as a concession, a shrinking of family Values, others, including me, view it as a strategically and realistically sound measure. For the individual spirit is not likely to pass on and will eventually die out. Nature will take its course. This also applies to racial blending, which I see moving faster when not overtly pushed, and when unforced migrations are allowed to balance racial inequalities in family Values cities over time.

I'll conclude by declaring not only my full recommendation to proceed with NewBax, but also my confidence we have refined our processes so well we have, in effect "captured Stage Four in a bottle." Meaning the ability to implement future cities within Ontario, in accordance with the recent changes at the behest of the United States to prioritize the north, to help fortify strategic locations there before trying to establish family Values beyond Ontario.

Lastly, with NewBax, we have also addressed several obscure technical issues between Values tokens and *arbiter* discovered in 2048. I can personally pledge the "fixes" have been exhaustively tested and resolved, and to back this up I am prepared to forego the unique status I've held these past seven years and begin to wear a Values token with the intent to become a *familyar* at the earliest opportunity.

Otto van Leer,
April 1, 2055.

www.ingramcontent.com/pod-product-compliance
Lightning Source LLC
Chambersburg PA
CBHW020904200626
46814CB00001BA/164

* 9 7 8 1 9 9 9 1 8 1 5 3 6 *